NOA

Full Circle

By the same author

Abigail's Secret
No Sin to Love
On Wings of Song
Threads of Silk
Love or Duty

Full Circle

Roberta Grieve

ROBERT HALE · LONDON

© Roberta Grieve 2012
First published in Great Britain 2012

ISBN 978-0-7090-9837-9

Robert Hale Limited
Clerkenwell House
Clerkenwell Green
London EC1R 0HT

www.halebooks.com

2 4 6 8 10 9 7 5 3 1

Typeset in 10/13½ Sabon
Printed in Great Britain by the MPG Books Group,
Bodmin and King's Lynn

CHAPTER ONE

'Well, girl. Have you nothing to say for yourself?' Lady Letitia Davenport's icy voice brought Daisy's chin up and she stared defiantly at her accuser, her dark eyes flashing.

'You called me a thief and I've told you I'm not. What else can I say?' She was proud that her voice remained steady. But behind her back her nails dug into her palms and her knees trembled beneath the long skirt and as soon as the words were out she bit her lip. What had possessed her to speak out to the mistress like that? Now, even if the ring turned up and they realized she hadn't pinched it, she'd lose her job for sure.

She turned to Miss Georgina but the girl avoided her eyes. No help there, Daisy thought, as Lady Davenport began to speak again, the cold words making her tremble.

'So – you add insolence to dishonesty.' She curled her lip. 'You were taken out of the kitchen to become Miss Georgina's personal maid against my wishes. But she asked for you specially. And Mrs Harris gave you an excellent recommendation. If you'd remained a kitchen maid, this would never have happened. Temptation would not have been placed in your way. You have betrayed the trust placed in you and I have no alternative but to let you go – without a reference, of course.'

Daisy gasped. How would she get another job? She opened her mouth to protest but Lady Davenport held up a thin jewelled hand. 'You will be out of this house within the hour.' She went to the fireplace and tugged at the bell pull.

When Mrs Harris answered the summons, she was told to accompany Daisy to her room and oversee her packing.

Resenting the inference that she wasn't to be trusted, Daisy stalked out of the room behind the housekeeper, her head held high, hiding her hurt. She couldn't prove she was innocent. But she had hoped that Miss Georgina would speak up for her.

In her little room at the end of the corridor next to her mistress's room, she pulled off the starched white cap, releasing a cloud of dark curls to tumble around her shoulders. She took off the snowy frilled apron and black dress and changed into a shabby gown of dark green wool, wondering how such a lovely day could have turned so quickly to disaster.

Earlier that afternoon Miss Georgina had come upstairs to change and show off her engagement ring with its half circle of sapphires and diamonds. They'd been expecting the announcement below stairs for days. Henry Thornton was a friend of the family who owned a large brewery in Portsmouth and had many other business interests. He was not only wealthy but completely besotted with the Davenports' only daughter. Everyone agreed it was a good match.

Now the ring was missing and Daisy had racked her brains to try and imagine what had happened to it. She remembered Georgina taking it off before she dressed for dinner. But she'd looked everywhere and there was no sign of it.

As she threw her things into a bag with no attempt to fold them, she began to cry. It wasn't just the accusation of stealing that caused the tears to fall faster, it was the realization that she might never see Master Jack again. A mere glimpse of the handsome lieutenant in his naval uniform could set her heart racing. And a smile or a brief word would ensure her happiness for days afterwards.

She moved to the window and looked out at the darkening sky. After the pleasantly mild March day, a wind had got up and was now whipping the bare branches of the elm trees surrounding the paddock. Dusk was falling and the rooks were making their usual evening racket as they settled onto their twiggy nests for the night. A jackdaw flew across the garden, disappearing into the tangle of ivy and creeper that almost smothered the corner of the old dairy. How she hated the thought of leaving all this. Even without those longed-for encounters with Jack, she would have been happy in this house with its beautiful grounds and the Downs in the distance. It was all so different from her life in the cramped little cottage in Fish Lane down by Kingsbourne Harbour.

Since her promotion to lady's maid, her life had improved immeasurably. But even working in the kitchen hadn't been too bad, despite the attempted assaults by Philip, the Davenports' elder son, and the unwanted attentions of Ernest Jenkins, the groom turned chauffeur. Still, she should have looked for another job ages ago, especially when she first realized she was falling in love with Master Jack. If only she could see him before she left. But surely if he felt the same way as she did, he'd have sought her out?

She brushed a hand across her eyes, consoling herself with the thought that she'd be with her family again. She hadn't missed the damp little harbourside cottage, but she'd missed them, worried about how they were managing. How could she tell them she'd lost her job? Well, at least *they'd* believe she wasn't a thief.

Behind her Mrs Harris coughed. 'Come along, girl. No use moping here,' she said. As Daisy turned away from the window she continued, 'We're all behind you, love. No one below stairs thinks you took it.'

'Then where is it? And why is the mistress so ready to think I stole it?' Daisy said, a sob catching in her throat.

'She wants an excuse to be rid of you,' Mrs Harris said. 'She's noticed the way Master Jack looks at you.'

Daisy's heart leapt but she forced a laugh. 'Don't be silly,' she said, picking up her bag and following Mrs Harris down the back stairs. Word of her disgrace would have reached the kitchen by now in the mysterious way that news in big houses always filtered below stairs without anyone quite knowing how.

She couldn't face them and, instead of going through the servants' quarters, she said a hasty goodbye to the housekeeper, pushed open the door and marched across the wide entrance hall. Servants were forbidden to use the front door but, squaring her shoulders, she thought, at least they can't sack me for it now.

As she reached the door, a voice startled her. 'Daisy, I'm so glad I caught you.' It was Miss Georgina, her eyes red, clutching a sodden handkerchief. Even so, Daisy was struck by her beauty – and her likeness to Jack – her golden hair and startling blue eyes.

'I've been talking to Mama, trying to make her change her mind,' Georgina said.

Daisy swallowed her pride. 'You believe me, don't you? I didn't take your ring.'

'Of course I believe you. But Mama says there's no other explanation. The ring's gone and you were the only one in the room.'

Anger at the injustice of it welled up. 'So you *do* think I took it. Well, where is it now? You searched my room and didn't find it.' Daisy thrust her bag at Georgina. 'Why don't you search this before I go?'

It was Georgina's turn to get angry. 'I said I believe you.'

Daisy turned away and wrestled with the big front door. Without another word, she left the house. As she started down the long drive, she looked back, wishing that she could have seen Master Jack just once more before she left.

It had grown darker. The wind was cold and it started to rain. She shivered, pulling her hat down over her ears. It was a long walk to Kingsbourne Harbour.

As she trudged along, head down against the wind, she refused to give way to the threatening tears. Who cared what the Davenports thought? Still, it hurt that they believed the worst of her after she'd worked blame-lessly for them for six years. But the ring *was* missing. Where could it be?

She remembered the young mistress coming in and showing off the beautiful sapphire and diamond ring.

'Would you like to get married, Daisy?' she'd asked.

Daisy had carried on laying out her mistress's clothes, the lace-edged chemise, the fine silk stockings. 'Haven't thought about it much, miss,' she said.

'I expect you will one day. After all, you don't want to end up like Mrs Harris.' Georgina giggled and tossed her fair curls.

Daisy smiled but didn't reply. Before she could suppress it, the image of Jack Davenport in his naval uniform, fair haired and blue eyed, had filled her mind and she felt her face and neck grow warm. She had busied herself picking up her mistress's discarded clothes and putting them away. No point in dreaming, she told herself firmly.

Daisy tried not to think of the future too much. She didn't want to remain in service all her life. She wanted to better herself, but she wasn't quite sure how. There were so few choices for a girl of her station. Because of her family's troubles she had been unable to fulfil her dream of becoming a teacher. Her father had been crippled in an accident and Daisy had left school to help at home, while her two older brothers tried to earn a living fishing. Nursing Dad had been no hardship but the fishing had been bad for several years running. With little money coming in, Daisy had overcome her family's protests and gone into service.

Contrary to her expectations she'd been happy at Ryfe Hall, especially when she became Miss Georgina's personal maid. It was a step up from kitchen or parlour maid anyway. And her young mistress was easy to work for. A bit spoilt, maybe, but always full of fun and ready to share a joke. Until today, that was.

As she trudged down the long drive, head bent against the wind, she pictured Miss Georgina sitting at the dressing table in her peach satin robe while Daisy brushed her hair. 'Did I tell you we're going to Paris for our honeymoon? Then Venice and Florence.' Her mistress had seemed excited at the prospect.

However, Daisy thought she'd detected a false note in her voice, almost as if she were trying to convince herself. It's none of my business, she thought. But she couldn't help wondering if it had anything to do with Master Jack's friend who'd visited the house several times over the past few months. Like Jack, Lieutenant Tom Lazenby looked dashing in his naval uniform and Daisy felt a pang of sympathy for her young mistress. She knew how easy it was to fall in love with a dream.

She'd finished brushing Georgina's hair, but despite securing it with pins, a few blonde curls still managed to escape.

Georgina shrugged her off impatiently. 'Oh, that'll do, Daisy. Don't fuss.' She had gone over to the window, holding her hand up so that the jewelled ring sparkled in the sunlight. She twisted it round her finger and her pretty mouth drooped in a pout. 'I just hope they sort out all this business in Europe before the wedding,' she said. 'I've never been abroad.'

'Mr Fenton says the Kaiser wants to start a war,' Daisy said, quoting the butler.

'Nonsense. He wouldn't dare. Besides Henry – Mr Thornton – is quite sure that even if he does start something we'll soon sort him out. Anyway I don't want to think about unpleasant things today.' Georgina was gazing out of the window across the parkland, when suddenly she threw open the window and leaned out, waving excitedly.

'It's Jack!' she cried.

Daisy had smiled at the sudden change in the other girl's demeanour. Her heart leapt too at the sound of the little car coming up the drive and she moved casually towards the window. But she couldn't wave as her mistress had.

Now, remembering how happy she'd been just a few hours ago, she began to cry again. It wasn't just the realization that she'd never see Jack again but the injustice of her dismissal. Hot tears mingled with icy needles of rain. But Daisy, wrapped in her misery, was oblivious to the rising storm.

The thud of the heavy front door closing echoed in Georgina's ears. She hesitated, wondering whether she ought to go after Daisy, try to convince her that she, at least, believed in her innocence. But what was the use? Mama had never really liked Daisy and it had taken a lot of persuading to secure her promotion to personal maid.

Tears welled up at the memory of Daisy's angry words although she didn't really blame her. But it was the last straw after the scene with her mother. She ran upstairs and slammed the door of her room behind her.

If only she'd had a chance to talk to Jack before all this happened, she thought, throwing herself down on her bed. He was her only confidante and she knew he'd understand her doubts about her engagement. Although she'd firmly put the thought of Tom Lazenby out of her head and done what was expected of her, she needed reassurance that she'd taken the right decision.

She was fond of Henry, of course, but she didn't love him. Tom had changed her views on love and marriage. But until she'd fallen in love with him she'd been quite willing to comply with her parents' wishes. Only once had she tried to confide in her mother about her feelings.

Mama had pursed her lips and straightened her already ramrod-straight back. 'The notion of romantic love is for servant girls and flibbertigibbets,' she'd declared strongly. 'Henry is a good man, kind, generous. He'll make a good husband. You could do worse.'

Rich too, Georgina thought now, knowing in her heart that was the important thing as far as her parents were concerned. Henry had already taken over the family brewery and there were plans for him to put money into their maltings and hop-growing business. And his links with the family depended on her marrying him. Georgina sighed, comforting herself with the thought that at least that pinched worried look would disappear from Mama's face.

But that afternoon, as she waited for Jack to come home, praying that Tom would be with him, she knew she couldn't just forget him. And feeling as she did, she couldn't possibly marry Henry. With a little exclamation, she'd pulled the ring off and thrown it down on the window seat. It was beautiful, it was expensive, but it wasn't a symbol of love. More a symbol of possession, she thought.

Then Jack had arrived and she'd dashed downstairs to greet him. He'd understand even if the rest of her family didn't. But she didn't have a chance to talk to him alone.

He was with Mama and for once she was smiling. At least someone was happy about her engagement, Georgina thought, dreading the moment when she'd have to confess that she'd changed her mind.

'Show Jack your ring, my dear,' her mother said.

'I've left it upstairs,' she said.

Her mother's smile faded. 'Go and get it at once.'

Upstairs, she hunted frantically. Surely she'd left it on the window seat? She knelt down and ran her fingers over the thick rug, in case it had fallen to the floor.

Daisy was tidying the bathroom and Georgina called to her, thinking she might have put it away.

But Daisy denied seeing it and she'd had to go back downstairs and confess that the ring was missing.

'Why on earth did you take it off in the first place?' her mother stormed. Georgina had never seen Mama so angry and she looked to Jack for support.

He smiled sympathetically and said, 'Don't worry, Georgie. It'll turn up. I'll go and look.'

Jack left the room and Lady Davenport continued to rage. 'What Henry will think of your carelessness I dread to think,' she said. 'You say you've looked everywhere, so there is only one explanation. It must have been stolen.' She rang the bell by the fireplace and told the maid to fetch Daisy.

Georgina was horrified. 'You don't think she stole it? That's ridiculous! Please – wait and see if Jack finds it.'

But when it failed to turn up, Mama became convinced that Daisy was to blame. Miserably Georgina had stood by as her maid was dismissed.

When she'd gone, Georgina burst into tears. 'I'm sure she didn't take it,' she sobbed.

'It's too late now. You should never have taken it off.'

Georgina blew her nose and tried to get her tears under control. She had to tell her mother sooner or later. Why not now? She took a deep breath and blurted out. 'I took it off because I'm not going to marry Henry.'

'Not going to. . . ?' Mama clutched at her throat, her face pale. But she quickly recovered. 'What nonsense you talk, child. Of course you're going to marry him. You've accepted his ring, it's all arranged.'

'I can't, Mama. I've thought it over and it's impossible.' Georgina was proud of her steady voice, although her knees trembled.

She stood silently, head high, while her mother paced the room, alternately raging and cajoling. When she finally ran out of steam and sank into a chair, Georgina said quietly, 'I should never have accepted in the first place.'

'But you must marry. And there's no one else suitable in our circle.'

And no one else as rich, Georgina thought, setting her lips in a mutinous line. 'I won't do it, Mama,' she said. 'My mind's made up.'

'Then you'd better go to your room – and stay there till you come to your senses. Your father will be home soon. Perhaps you'll listen to him.'

They couldn't make her, Georgina thought now as she lay on her bed, twisting her sodden handkerchief between her fingers.

A few minutes later there was a quiet knock. 'Go away. I don't want to talk to anyone.'

The door handle rattled and Jack called, 'Let me in, Georgie.'

She jumped up and unlocked the door, managing a smile for her favourite brother. 'Where have you been?' she asked.

'I thought your ring might have fallen out of the window when you leaned out to wave to me. I've been rummaging in the shrubbery but it's getting too dark to look now.' He threw himself down on the bed.

'Oh, Jack, I've really made a mess of things. I've never seen Mama so cross,' Georgina said and burst into tears.

'Come on, old girl. It's not that bad, surely.'

'It is. They've sent Daisy away and I told them I wouldn't marry Henry.'

Jack patted her back. 'You're not making sense, Georgie. Why would they send Daisy away?' he asked, ignoring her last statement.

Georgina sniffed and blew her nose. 'They think she stole my ring. She's been dismissed.'

'That's nonsense.' Jack's eyes flashed and he jumped up.

'Mama threw her out.'

'You mean she's gone already?' Jack asked.

'She just packed her bag and went. The last I saw she was walking down the drive.'

Jack was at the window and Georgina went to stand beside him. It was almost dark and black rain clouds were scudding in from the sea, borne on the March wind. 'It's a long way to walk in this weather,' he said.

Georgina linked her arm in his. 'Poor Daisy. What a mess I've made of things.'

'It's not your fault, Georgie,' Jack said. He gave her a hug. 'I'd better go and change. The dinner guests will be arriving soon.'

Georgina gave a nervous little laugh. 'I can't imagine what Mother is going to say to them all.' She clenched her fists and squared her shoulders. 'I'm not backing down, you know.'

'Silly girl, it's probably just nerves,' Jack said as he made for the door. 'We'll talk about it later.'

As he left the room Georgina said, hoping her voice sounded casual, 'Didn't Tom come with you this time?'

'No. He's on duty.'

When Jack had gone, Georgina sat on the edge of the bed, her face in her hands. How could she have imagined that Tom might change his mind? He hadn't been to the house since Christmas. It was obvious now that he was avoiding her. She went to the dressing table and began to brush her hair, missing Daisy already. I suppose I'll have to train another maid now, she thought. It was so tiresome. None of them seemed to stay very long. But Daisy had been different. She had more spirit than her predecessors.

12

Georgina knew very well why so many maids left Ryfe Hall, either dismissed or because they'd found another position. She wasn't as naïve as her mother thought and was well aware of what her older brother Philip got up to. He was at their London house most of the time now, but even on his rare visits he hadn't seemed interested in Daisy. Georgina was surprised because he usually admired girls like Daisy, pert and pretty and with a trim figure. She didn't think it was marriage that had changed Philip either.

She had hoped Daisy at least would stay. They'd got on well, almost friends despite their difference in station. She wasn't like those girls of her own class whom Mama would have deemed suitable. They were either do-gooders like Lady Agatha Phillips, or only interested in the season and the eligible bachelors they could snare. Daisy was easy to talk to and she was certain that the girl would respect her confidences.

She'd been shocked when Mama had accused Daisy. She certainly didn't believe that the girl she'd become so fond of was a thief. Anyway, she told herself, the ring was sure to turn up soon. Thoughts of Daisy fled when her mother sent for her and she had to face her family.

Philip was furious, more so than her father. He didn't speak but the look he gave her was pure malice. Why were they all so determined to see her married off to Henry?

Her father was angry too but instead of ranting he spoke in a measured, reasonable voice. 'You are not just letting Henry down, you are letting down the good name of this family,' he said. 'How can we face our friends and neighbours, let them see what a wilful and disobedient daughter we have?' His face was grave, his tone sorrowful.

I'm not wilful, Georgina thought rebelliously. She knew she'd been spoilt as the youngest child and only daughter and she usually got her own way in little things. But she'd always tried to please her parents. Anyway, Father was a fine one to talk about the good name of the family. She had a good idea of what he got up to in town. The thought made her defiant. 'There's been no official announcement. No one need know,' she said.

'But everyone knows it's what we planned for you,' her mother said.

So that was it. They were more concerned about what people would think than how she felt. 'Well, I won't marry him and that's that,' she said.

There was silence in the room, broken only by the sound of logs settling in the grate. Lady Davenport looked at her husband, who gave a sigh and a defeated shrug.

'We only want your happiness, Georgie,' he said. 'And we think Henry is the man for you. He is devoted to you, always has been. Perhaps we should wait a little, till you're older.'

'She is already twenty-one,' his wife broke in.

'Mama, it wouldn't do any good. Even if he agreed to wait forever, I still wouldn't want him. He's so, so – nice and good and, and – boring.'

'Excellent qualities in a husband, my dear,' her mother said with no trace of irony. Philip's timid little wife Jane nodded in agreement.

The conversation was halted by the announcement that Mr Thornton had arrived and was waiting in the library.

Sir John turned to Georgina. 'Well, miss, since your mind's made up, you must tell Henry without delay that you won't marry him. And, should he ask for his ring back, you must admit your carelessness in allowing it to be stolen.'

Georgina turned and left the room, dreading the coming confrontation. She'd known Henry since childhood and had always been fond of him. Until recently she'd never questioned that one day they would be married. Both their families had seen it as a foregone conclusion, a successful merger not only of families but of the two businesses, further cementing the friendship between them.

She'd even been looking forward to it, excited by the thought of being mistress in her own home, a Georgian townhouse facing the common in Southsea. She'd looked forward to travelling with Henry too, taking an interest in his business in a way that her parents would neither expect nor allow.

Then nine months ago Tom Lazenby had accompanied Jack on a weekend leave and Georgina's views on love and marriage had changed overnight. She found herself thinking of him constantly, waiting eagerly for Jack's next leave and hoping that the young lieutenant would be with him. Her head was filled with dreams and fantasies, thoughts that made her flush with embarrassment and tingle with excitement.

Deep down, a small grain of common sense told her that such dreams would never be realized. Tom was friendly enough but he treated her in the same way as Jack, teasing and joking, enjoying her company but never seeking to be alone with her. Tom would soon go away to sea, would be gone for years. He would probably forget Jack even had a sister. She would marry Henry and be a perfect wife and mother.

Perhaps nothing would have changed but for the family party last Christmas. The house had been filled with distant cousins, aunts and uncles and there was dancing and games for the young people. Tom, whose parents lived in Norfolk, was unable to travel home for the holidays because of the bad weather and Jack invited him to stay at Ryfe Hall.

Henry was there too and Georgina couldn't help comparing the two. Fond as she was of Henry, she knew which of them she would rather spend her life with.

One wintry afternoon the large pond in the centre of the village froze and the young people decided to go skating. Henry elected to stay behind and talk business with Sir John and Georgina and Tom found themselves alone.

Georgina, coming downstairs as her brothers and cousins made off down the drive, found Tom lingering behind. They walked together in silence, their footsteps crunching on the frosty grass as they neared the village green.

At last Tom spoke. 'Jack tells me you are soon to become engaged.'

Georgina nodded without speaking.

'If I may say so, you do not seem entirely happy at the prospect,' Tom ventured.

'Well, our families have always been close. It is expected . . .' Her voice tailed off and she felt a rush of colour to her cheeks.

Tom took her hand. 'Georgina, I know I shouldn't speak. I promised myself I wouldn't.' He hesitated and Georgina held her breath, willing him to continue.

'It isn't just that you are promised to Mr Thornton. Your parents would never look upon me favourably – the son of a poor clergyman. Even if I'm promoted, it will be many years before I can support a wife in the manner they would wish.'

Georgina felt a little giddy. The word love hadn't been spoken but nevertheless Tom was saying what she longed to hear. 'I don't care that you're poor,' she whispered. 'I love you.'

Tom took her in his arms, crushing her to him, and she leaned into his embrace with a sigh of content. In the minutes that followed, Georgina tasted passion such as she had never dreamed of. The shouts and laughter of the skaters on the distant pond faded away and there was only Tom and his kisses, his tender caresses.

At last he drew away. 'Forgive me. I shouldn't have let my feelings get the better of me,' he said, a bitter little smile twisting his lips. 'Now I've had a taste of what I'm leaving behind, it's harder to say goodbye.'

'Goodbye? You can't mean that?' Georgina stammered. To her, it seemed so simple. He loved her, she loved him. She would marry Tom, not Henry. Surely her family would understand. But he was moving away from her, his hands falling helplessly to his sides.

'I must do the honourable thing. You must marry Henry as your family wishes. Jack has explained the situation to me. I'll go and pack now. I can't stay.'

A huge sob, like a fire raging in her chest, fought to get out, but there were only ragged hiccups, as Georgina pleaded, 'You can't! You mustn't leave.'

But he had turned and left her staring after him. She dried her eyes, wondering what situation Tom had referred to. She wasn't sure she liked her brother discussing her with his friend. She decided to ask Jack outright and continued on to the pond, where the young people's merry shouts carried to her on the frosty air.

'Where's Tom?' Jack called.

'No skates. He decided not to bother,' Georgina replied, surprised that her voice sounded so normal.

'Chump, I would have lent him some,' Jack said and Georgina even managed a little laugh. While she skated with their friends, pretending she was enjoying herself, the optimist in her kept insisting that if Tom loved her they would find a way to be together.

But she hadn't seen him again. He and Jack had left early next morning and, although Jack had been home since then, Tom hadn't been with him. Georgina was sure that he would at least write. But as the weeks went by and she realized that he wasn't going to get in touch, she found she had no strength to fight the inevitable. Her engagement to Henry became a reality, the wedding later in the year a foregone conclusion.

Then, with the ring on her finger, she had suddenly realized how impossible it was and the unfairness of it all made her weep with impotent fury. Philip was free to pursue any girl who took his fancy, despite his now being married to the insipid Jane. And Jack could follow the career he loved. While she, a mere girl, had to be content to stay at home, her only escape marriage and moving to another man's house where she would be subject to the same restrictions as now.

Well, it wasn't enough. Tom couldn't truly love her, at least not enough to flout convention and her parents' disapproval. And she wouldn't settle for second best. She must be brave and tell Henry so.

Now she mentally straightened her shoulders and entered the library. Henry was standing by the fireplace, gazing into the dead ashes. But he turned quickly, a warm smile lighting his square pleasant face.

'Georgie, what kept you?' The smile faded and his face creased in concern. He came towards her and took her hand, leading her to a chair. 'You're not ill, are you?'

'No, Henry. I'm perfectly all right but I need to talk to you.' She twisted her hands in her lap. 'Henry, I'm sorry, I can't marry you.' The words came out in a rush, bluntly, no softening of the blow. It wasn't how she'd planned to tell him. But what other way was there? Best to get it over with, she thought.

A sudden gust of wind rattled the window and she got up and twitched back the heavy curtain, checking that the latch was secure. Anything to avoid that look of dumb hurt in his eyes, like Philip's spaniel that time in the stable when she'd come upon him beating the animal.

Henry still hadn't spoken and at last Georgina turned to him. 'I'm sorry,' she said and stumbled blindly towards the door.

'Georgie, wait.'

She stopped with her hand on the door handle.

'It's him, isn't it? Jack's friend – Lazenby. I've seen him looking at you.' Henry's strangled voice betrayed his jealousy and hurt. He took hold of her arm, turning her to face him. 'Your parents will never allow it. He has nothing to offer you – no prospects, nothing. Whereas I . . .'

At last Georgina looked at him, eyes blazing. 'I don't care how rich you are – or how poor he is.' She stopped, realizing she'd betrayed herself, and fumbled for the door handle again. 'Anyway, it's got nothing to do with Tom. I just don't want to get married, to anyone – ever.'

CHAPTER TWO

Wrapped in misery, Daisy trudged down the long drive. She wasn't aware of the approaching motor car, the sound of the engine obscured by the wind in the trees and the driving rain, until it stopped alongside her and someone called, 'Pass me your bag and jump in.'

She hesitated, thinking at first that it was Philip Davenport looking for an excuse to force his attentions on her once more. The icy rain was lashing down now and her teeth were chattering but she was determined to refuse the offer of a lift.

'Come on, girl, don't be foolish. You'll get soaked.'

Her heart skipped as she realized it was Jack. He leaned over, holding the door open, and she climbed in, staring ahead, unwilling to meet his eyes. He must have heard of her disgrace, so why was he helping her? But he'd always been kind, not like his spiteful older brother. Despite looking alike, they were totally different in character.

The seeds of Daisy's love had been sown when Jack had rescued her from Philip's attempted rape. It wasn't the first time he'd tried. But there was no one around and this time Daisy was sure he would succeed. Jack had heard her muted cries and thrown open the door, dragging his brother off and allowing her to escape.

Since then, whenever he was at home, Jack had sought her out, reminding her of her promise to let him know if his brother stepped out of line again. He would smile his special smile and sometimes his hand would reach up as if he were about to touch her. At these times she dared to hope that he returned her feelings. But the hand would drop to his side and he would sigh and turn away. Once he'd turned back and said, 'I'm not like my brother, you know.' But before she could reply, his mother had appeared at the end of the corridor and he had hurried away, leaving Daisy confused and unhappy.

Now, pulling her coat collar up against the chill, Daisy stole a look at Jack's profile. His lips were set in a firm line. Only once before, when he'd grabbed his brother by the collar and dragged him off her, had she seen such anger on his face. Perhaps he does think I'm guilty, she thought.

But, seeming to sense her gaze, he turned towards her, and his expression changed instantly to the wide friendly smile she was used to.

He reached out and took her cold hand in his. 'I know you didn't steal the ring. And truly Georgina doesn't believe it either.'

'Your mother does though,' Daisy replied in a small voice.

'Daisy, I shouldn't say this. She is my mother, after all. But I know she's been looking for an excuse to get rid of you.' Jack stopped the car and turned to her, taking her hand and looking into her eyes. 'You were such a thin little waif when you first came to us, just a child. But look at you now.' He reached out and brushed a strand of wet hair away from her face. Daisy held her breath as something seemed to spark between them and she thought that this time he would surely speak of his feelings. But he laughed nervously and started the car again. 'The trouble is, Daisy, my sweet, you're too pretty. Mother could never abide having pretty maids about the place.'

It took a while for his words to sink in. Then Daisy realized what he meant. Lady Davenport knew of her older son's liking for servant girls. The loss of the ring was merely an excuse to dismiss her, as Mrs Harris had hinted. But where could it be? She remembered Miss Georgina taking it off and putting it on the window seat. Then she'd rushed downstairs to greet Jack. Later, when the wind got up, Daisy closed the window and looked for it. But it wasn't there and she assumed Georgina had put it on again.

She sighed and Jack reached for her hand. 'We're nearly there,' he said.

She peered through the darkness and in the distance saw the lights of the fishing boats on the harbour.

'You'll have to direct me to your home,' Jack said as they reached Kingsbourne market square.

'Stop here. I'll walk the rest of the way,' she said.

'In this weather? No, I'll take you right to your door. It's the least I can do.'

Daisy wasn't ashamed of where she lived even if it was a shabby run-down fisherman's cottage. So she was speaking the truth when she said, 'You'll never be able to turn round if we go right to the door.' She pointed to the narrow lane and the row of shabby cottages and net sheds right at the water's edge.

'Are you sure you'll be all right?' Jack asked.

'Of course. I know the way blindfolded.' Daisy smiled at him, pleased at the genuine concern she heard in his voice.

'I meant not having a job. How will you manage?'

'I don't know – without a reference it'll be difficult.'

'I'd like to help, Daisy. And I know my sister would too. Let us know if there's anything we can do.' He got out of the car, leaving the engine running, and lifted her bag down.

The bitter wind whipped her hair across her face and her teeth were chattering as she turned to thank him. He took her hand and pulled her towards him suddenly, murmuring, 'Daisy, my Daisy-bell.' When his mouth sought hers she leaned towards him, opening her lips to his. It was what she had dreamed of for months.

When he released her abruptly, she staggered back in confusion. Before she could protest, he had leapt back into the driving seat.

'Daisy, I'm sorry. It just won't do, you know,' he said, his voice jerky and harsh above the revving engine.

She took a step forward. 'Jack!' she called. But he was gone. Suddenly aware of the bitter cold, she turned and stumbled down the dark lane. Later she knew she would savour the feel of his lips on hers, a memory to treasure in the lonely days ahead.

Struggling to keep her footing in the mud, her nostrils wrinkling against the smell of fish, Daisy's common sense told her that Jack was right. They came from such different worlds. But she was sure now that Jack felt the same way as she. And he had promised to help her find another job. What was the use, though, she thought. He couldn't help her. No one would hire a maid who had been dismissed for theft.

She reached the dilapidated cottage, hesitating before pinning a cheerful smile on her face and opening the door. The smell of poverty, a combination of mould, fish and crumbling plaster, was like a slap in the face.

Effie March looked up from the pot she was stirring over the meagre fire and a smile lit her tired features, revealing something of the pretty girl she'd once been.

'Daisy, what are you doing home? Never mind, we're pleased to see you, aren't we, Dad?' Her eyes went to the man in the narrow bed across the room. His eyes opened and he too managed a smile of welcome.

Daisy dropped her bag by the door and went over to her father. 'How are you, Dad?' she whispered.

''Bout the same, girl. Mustn't grumble,' he said.

Daisy took in the face lined with pain, the thin hand which reached out to take hers. In the weeks since she'd last been home, her father had deteriorated. Now he made no effort to sit up, to pretend he was the man he'd been before his accident.

'Given you time off, have they – up at the big house?' he asked.

Daisy nodded. How could she tell them what had really happened? Her mother was frowning and she knew she must have realized something was wrong.

She called her to the table. 'Let the girl eat, Albert. She's come a long way to visit. And on such a dreadful night too.' She lifted the pot from the stove. 'You didn't walk all that way, I hope, on a night like this too.'

'Master Jack brought me.'

Effie's lips tightened. 'I warned you about the young masters up at the Hall. I hope he wasn't taking liberties.'

Daisy laughed. 'Of course not, Mum. He was just being kind. As you said, it's a dirty night out there. Besides, Master Jack's not like that. It would have been a different matter if it'd been Master Philip. But I'd never get in a car with him, don't you worry.'

'They're all alike,' Effie muttered.

'Don't say that, Mum. Master Jack's different.'

Something in her tone caused Effie to look at her sharply. 'I hope you've not done anything silly, my girl.'

'Of course not, Mum.' Daisy's face grew warm.

Effie turned to get plates down from the dresser and changed the subject. 'The boys will be home soon. They're down at the harbour, making sure the boats are secure. If this storm keeps up, they'll not be able to go out in the morning.'

'They're still at the fishing then?'

'Even young Billy now,' Effie said proudly.

Daisy shivered, remembering the loss of their boat in the accident which had crippled her father and left the family penniless. She hated the thought of her three brothers earning their living in such a dangerous way. The wind rattled the door and windows, echoing that night almost six years ago when they'd brought her father home, barely alive. Daisy recalled the struggles of the family to survive until the two older boys got a place in one of the boat crews.

When she'd started work at Ryfe Hall, things had improved a little. Besides sending money home, she always brought something with her on her days off – a couple of eggs, fresh vegetables from the garden. Mrs Harris had a soft spot for her and never let her come home empty-handed.

Daisy joined her mother at the table. 'I've already eaten,' she lied. The smell of the fish stew was making her feel queasy. She put her hand over her mother's. 'I'm sorry, I haven't managed to bring anything this time,' she said.

'Don't worry about it, Daisy. We're managing. Billy's money helps.' Effie ladled a little of the stew into a bowl and took it over to Albert. He struggled to sit up but the effort left him breathless.

'Let me help.' Daisy was by his side in a moment. She pulled a stool up to the bedside and held the bowl while her father ate. It took him a long time to manage even a few spoonfuls. When he'd finished he lay back on the pillow with a sigh.

Daisy put the bowl in the sink and went to sit by the fire. 'There's something I must tell you,' she began.

Effie looked towards her husband with a little gasp, her hand at her throat.

'I've been dismissed,' Daisy said, then she leaned forward and started to sob, her hands covering her face.

'Oh, Daisy, you're not in trouble, are you?'

Daisy looked up and almost smiled as she realized what her mother was thinking. 'No, Mum – not that kind of trouble anyway,' she said.

'I'm sorry, love, but why else would they get rid of you?'

'It's worse than that, Mum. They think I stole Miss Georgina's ring.' The whole story tumbled out and Daisy began to cry again. She was wiping her nose and eyes when the boys came bursting in, bringing a gust of cold air and the smell of the sea with them. Their wet coats and boots were put by the fire and they were sitting at the table hungrily eyeing the stew pot before they even registered Daisy's presence.

Then she had to go over the whole thing again. Jimmy, always more volatile than the others, was all for going straight up to the Hall and confronting them, but Dick stopped him. 'That won't do any good,' he said, crumbling bread into his stew.

'But they can't get away with it,' Jimmy protested. 'Slander, that's what it is, calling our Daisy a thief. Anyway, what's one diamond ring to them with all their money?'

'That's not the point, Jimmy lad,' Albert said from his bed. 'Besides, who'd take any notice of the likes of us?'

Young Billy tucked into his stew, pausing with the spoon halfway to his mouth. 'I don't care about the Davenports,' he said 'At least we've got our Daisy home.'

Daisy dried her tears and smiled at her younger brother. 'I don't care about them either. All I'm worried about is getting another position. What can I do, Mum?'

'Have a good night's sleep first, love. Things'll look brighter in the morning.'

Daisy wished she shared her mother's optimism as she lay beside her on the lumpy mattress, listening to her father downstairs coughing into the small hours. As she went over the events of the day, she hated the Davenports for their lack of trust – even Miss Georgina, who she felt should have stood up for her. She wanted to hate Jack too, but she couldn't lump him in with the rest of his family. Hadn't he said he would help her? But she wouldn't depend on it. She was quite capable of fending for herself.

When Jack arrived back at Ryfe Hall, he could hear Philip's angry voice and, without taking off his outdoor things, he went into the drawing room to find Georgina crying, her face blotched red with tears of anger and frustration. His mother sat tight-lipped and upright by the fire while his father paced the room, adding his comments to Philip's furious tirade.

'What on earth. . . ?' Jack put his arm round Georgina, rounding on his brother. 'I know you're upset, but shouting at Georgie won't do any good. Anyway, it's none of your business really, is it?'

A disdainful smile curled Philip's mouth. 'Of course it is. You just don't understand, do you, little brother? Our sister's selfishness is going to ruin this family, that's all. But of course, you don't care about that, do you? You've got what you wanted, joining the navy, having a career.' There was a barely concealed sneer in his voice.

'What's my career got to do with it?' Jack asked. Philip had always been jealous of him, but he'd never understood why. After all, as the older brother he was the heir. That's why Jack had wanted a separate career – so that Philip couldn't think he was trying to take anything away from him. But an undercurrent of hostility had always flowed between them – though it had never been more evident than at this moment.

Sir John Davenport stopped his pacing, coming to a halt in front of them. 'Stop it, both of you. Nothing can be gained by this sort of display.' He turned to his younger son. 'Jack, I thought you understood. The business has been doing badly lately. Henry Thornton was to have invested. We were even contemplating a merger, making it one family business. Of course that won't happen now.'

'I knew about that, of course,' Jack said. 'But things aren't as bad as that, surely? I can't believe Henry's investment is conditional on him marrying Georgie.'

Georgina began to cry again. 'Mother, please, make them stop behaving as if my engagement was a business deal,' she sobbed.

'Don't talk nonsense, Georgina,' Lady Davenport snapped.

But it wasn't nonsense. Jack had long been aware of why the family had encouraged the engagement. He'd even hinted as much to Tom when he saw how smitten his friend was. Things must be a lot worse than he'd thought.

Being away from home so much the past few years he hadn't fully realized that money was tight. But now he came to think of it, the signs were all there – the gates and fences that needed repair, the neglected outbuildings. There were fewer servants now, only two gardeners instead of the small army that had once tended the grounds. They still had a butler but no footman since the last one had been dismissed. And now there was only Jenkins to look after the motor cars that were gradually taking over from the horses.

Jack blamed his father for the family's problems and he didn't see why his sister should suffer for it. He glared at Sir John as Georgina gave a final sob and rushed from the room. Philip made to follow her, but Sir John stopped him.

'Leave her alone for a while. She'll soon calm down. I expect it's just nerves,' he said blandly.

'Someone's got to talk sense into her. She's must tell Henry it was all a mistake, that she didn't mean it,' Philip said.

Sir John turned to Jack. 'You talk to her, son. She'll maybe take notice of you.'

He doubted it. Surely his father and Philip must realize that Georgie had a mind of her own. If she refused to marry Henry, then nothing and nobody could make her. He went upstairs slowly, wondering what to say. He certainly wouldn't try to make her change her mind. It was his father's fault the business was failing and sacrificing Georgina wasn't the answer. The trouble was the family had had it too easy for years.

Jack's grandfather Joshua had expanded the family's small brewery, building a thriving business to hand over to his son. He'd also bought up several neighbouring farms and built his own malthouse in Kingsbourne.

As a boy Jack had followed his grandfather around, anxious to learn everything he could about the business. But things had changed when he died and his son had taken over. Young as he was, Jack soon realized that Father had no real conception that money and the business that made it must be managed. Inheriting a ready-made fortune had gone to his head and he'd spent thousands modernizing and furnishing Ryfe Hall in a grand style. He'd also developed a taste for gambling which amounted almost to an obsession. After Joshua's death he'd left the running of the brewery and malthouse to a manager and the land and farms to an agent, preferring to spend time indulging his excesses in the clubs and gambling houses of London. And Philip was just as bad.

At one time Jack had hoped that he'd be allowed some say in the business, but Sir John had made it clear that his older son would take over. The fact that, like his father, Philip was also bent only on pleasure seeking seemed not to matter.

Jack had always been fascinated by ships and the sea and he decided to join the navy, if only to get away from the constant arguments. Now, he realized he'd chosen the right career. Still, if he'd known how bad things would get, he'd have made more of an effort, he thought. Money troubles were probably the reason for his mother's pinched, worried look. She must also be sorely disappointed in her two sons – the one following in his father's dissipated footsteps, the other abandoning them to pursue his own career. He sympathized with her desire to see Georgina settled with a reliable and wealthy man.

Outside his sister's room, Jack knocked before entering. She turned from gazing out at the stormy night and, with a brave attempt at a smile, said, 'Good job you're not at sea on a night like this,' she said.

'I wish I was. Anything to get away from this place.' He sat beside her, putting out his hand to brush a stray tear from her cheek.

'I'm glad you're here. You're my only friend,' she said, taking his hand.

'Don't be silly. You've lots of friends. But I am on your side.'

A little sob escaped her but she smiled back at him. 'I mean it, you know, Jack. I'm not going to marry Henry.' Then her bravado evaporated and she said. 'They can't make me, can they?'

'Of course not. Don't worry, sis. It'll all blow over. In the meantime, what are you going to do? You can't stay locked in your room for ever.'

'What can I do? It's all right for you. You've got your navy career. The only way I'll ever escape is to marry some boring man or join a nunnery.'

Jack laughed. 'I can't see you as a nun somehow. But you're right. I do see the difficulty. It's different for girls, though, isn't it?'

'Why should it be?' Georgina's eyes flashed. 'Oh, I hate being a girl! I want to do something with my life, not sit here waiting for some man to carry me off.'

Jack managed to stop himself laughing. It was plain Georgina was really upset and it wasn't just over Henry, or even Tom. He knew she'd been discontented with her life for a long time and this latest row had brought things to a head. He wanted her to be happy but he realized that he hadn't really thought about it from her point of view.

'I do understand – at least I try to. But you can't say you're not doing

25

anything with your life. You help Mama with her committees and things. And there's your Red Cross work. That's worthwhile, surely?'

'I suppose. But rolling bandages and stuff – it's more a social occasion really, our Red Cross get-togethers.' Then Georgina turned to him, her eyes shining. 'I know . . .'

'What?' Jack smiled at her with tolerant amusement.

'I'll be a nurse. Do proper training.'

Jack laughed. 'That would really please Mother. Don't you think you're already in enough trouble?'

'I'm serious, Jack. I've got to do something. Besides, if we're really short of money, I may have to earn my own living soon.'

'I don't think it will come to that.' Jack tried to keep his voice light. But he couldn't help thinking perhaps she was right.

'You're never here so you probably don't realize,' Georgina said, interrupting his thoughts. 'I heard Father saying that if he got out of this mess he'd never gamble again. Mama just gave that sarcastic laugh of hers. Then he shut himself in his study and got drunk.'

'Georgie, you're exaggerating,' Jack said. But he wasn't really sure. If only he could stay longer and find out just how bad things were. He moved towards the door. 'I have to leave early tomorrow. You'll see me off, won't you?' he asked.

Georgina managed a smile and a nod. As he left the room, she whispered, 'Thanks, Jack. I don't know what I'd do without you.'

CHAPTER THREE

Daisy slept badly, but when she woke the storm had blown itself out. The sun was shining and she was ready to face the uncertain future with her usual optimism.

Her mother was already up and the boys were leaving to go down to the harbour to inspect the damage done by the gale. Daisy went to her father and kissed his cheek.

'Can I do anything for you, Dad?'

Albert tried to sit up but the effort was too much and he sank back on to the pillows, coughing painfully. Daisy raised him in the bed and when her mother brought a bowl of warm water, she gently washed away the sweat which, despite the chill weather, had bathed his pain-wracked body during the night. As she ministered to him, Daisy's mind wandered back to happier days before the tragedy that had wrecked their lives.

Then the little cottage had been warm and comfortable, with roof, doors and windows secure against the gales which lashed the harbour in winter. Albert owned his own fishing boat and the two older boys were all the crew he needed. It was a precarious way to earn a living. Sometimes the fishing was good and the catch was sent by train to the big towns inland: Guildford, Basingstoke and even to London. If it was poor and not worth selling, the family lived on fish and little else. But they were a happy family, secure in their love for each other.

Daisy had always loved her lessons and stayed on at school, helping with the little ones, hoping to become a fully fledged teacher one day. There was no talk of her going into service like other girls of her age.

Then came the big storm of 1908. It had been unseasonably cold for late April but the day began with sunshine and showers. The fleet put to sea but that afternoon, a blizzard blew up, raging for only two hours. But in that short time many boats were lost. The little fishing town of Kingsbourne only remembered its own. Fifteen boats put out to sea that day, but only nine came back.

The Marches' boat had almost made it back when a freak wave lifted it, smashing it against the harbour wall and washing Albert overboard.

Dick had almost managed to pull him up, but the boat crashed against the wall again, trapping his legs. By the time the boys had dragged him free of the wreckage and scrambled up the steps, the boat had disappeared. For weeks Albert had hovered between life and death, nursed devotedly by Effie and his daughter.

But knowing he would never walk again, as well as losing his family's means of livelihood, sent Albert into a deep depression and he never really recovered. It hadn't helped that his wife was helping to keep a roof over their heads by taking in washing and that his beloved daughter would have to forsake her ambitions and go into service.

Even on his worst days, though, Daisy had been able to get a smile from her father. Now it seemed more of an effort and she tried to hide her concern. Since her last visit he had deteriorated and now his chest was sunken and his body heaved with the effort to draw breath. As she finished bathing him and settled him back against the pillows, he took her hand and with a grimace that passed for a smile said, 'You're an angel, girl, like one of them nurses that went with Miss Nightingale to the Crimea.'

Daisy gave him a light kiss. 'I'm no angel, Dad,' she said, managing a laugh.

Later, as she walked down the narrow muddy lane towards the harbour, she remembered her father's joking words and wondered if it were possible. Florence Nightingale had made nursing respectable and there was proper hospital training for girls of good family.

If she tried for a nurse, she'd know what to expect, Daisy thought, remembering the times she'd held the basin while her mother bathed her father's dreadful wounds. Such chores held no terrors for her now and she realized that it was a job she could do – and do well.

But without a reference, how would she get a job anywhere?

She walked on into town, passing her old school. Her former teacher, Miss Cooper, was watching the infants as they ran and skipped in the playground. She looked up and saw Daisy and gave a friendly wave. 'How is your father today?' she called.

Daisy opened the gate and entered the yard. 'He's getting worse, I'm afraid.'

'Is that why you're home?'

'Not really.' Daisy could have let Miss Cooper believe she had come home to help nurse her father, but Kingsbourne was a small town and she was sure to hear of her disgrace some time. 'I've got the sack,' she said.

Before she could explain, Miss Cooper nodded. 'I had heard that things are going badly for the Davenports. You're not the first servant to be dismissed. What will you do?'

'I'd really like to do nursing but I don't know how to go about it.'

'Perhaps I can help,' said Miss Cooper. She went on to explain that to train as a nurse cost money – money Daisy didn't have. She would have to pay for her uniform, books and so on. There would be no wages until she'd qualified, just her food and lodging.

When Daisy protested that she couldn't afford that, Miss Cooper laid a hand on her arm. 'I said I might be able to help. Mr Thornton is a governor on the school board and also a hospital trustee. I will recommend you for a bursary to cover your training.'

Daisy swallowed her disappointment. Surely Georgina would have told Mr Thornton that she was suspected of stealing her ring. She had no chance of getting a bursary – whatever that might be.

As she opened her mouth to protest, the teacher went on to explain. 'The hospital realizes that there are ambitious young women who want a proper career. You are well qualified, having helped to nurse your father. Leave it to me, my dear. I will write to Mr Thornton today.'

Daisy thanked her and ran home to tell her parents. She hardly dared hope she'd be accepted but it was good to know her old teacher had faith in her. She prayed that Mr Thornton had not heard of her disgrace or that the ring had been found after she left.

Back at the cottage her father was sleeping and her mother was in the wash-house pushing sheets through the mangle. As she helped to peg them out in the strong breeze, she told her the news. She explained about the bursary although she didn't think her mother would be happy about accepting anything that seemed like charity.

She was wrong. 'I'm sure you'll get it,' Effie said. 'You deserve it. Look how you've helped me with Dad.'

Daisy let go of the sheet she was pegging up to give her mother a hug. The breeze caught the material and wrapped it round them. As they disentangled themselves, they started to laugh, and Daisy thought how lucky they were that even in the midst of their troubles they could find something to laugh about. She thought of Miss Georgina and the times they'd giggled together, more friends than mistress and maid.

That's all in the past, she told herself. She had something to look forward to now; she wasn't going to look back. But that night, as she settled down to sleep, her thoughts turned to the Davenports – and Jack. She couldn't forget the warm expression in his eyes as he'd driven her home. She hadn't imagined it – that kiss had been real enough. He wasn't like Philip; that's why he'd driven off so quickly. Daisy sighed. He'd made it clear that there was no future in it. And she had to acknowledge that he was right.

Jack had been up early too. Georgina was still upset and he wished he could stay longer but he had to get back to Portsmouth. Jenkins brought his car round to the front of the house and, although it was still chilly after the storm, he asked the man to put the top down.

Georgina came down to see him off at the door with the rest of the family and he gave her a hug. 'Chin up, old girl. Don't let them talk you into anything,' he whispered.

'I won't,' she said, returning his hug.

'Good for you,' he answered. Georgina could be really stubborn at times, but this time he felt she was right and he admired her for making a stand. It was just a pity she'd left it so long before speaking up. Perhaps there wouldn't have been all this fuss if she hadn't accepted Henry's ring in the first place. Mother could be stubborn too. But Georgina was of age. They couldn't force her into anything.

He started the car and, waving to his assembled family, turned the bend in the drive. Away from Ryfe Hall, bowling along the country lanes towards Portsmouth and enjoying the feel of the wind in his hair, he breathed a sigh of relief. In a way he was glad to be going back to his ship, away from the family tensions, although he would have preferred to stay and give Georgina his support.

He recalled the conversation with his sister the previous evening and some of his pleasure in the bright spring morning evaporated as his thoughts returned to his family's troubles. He knew his father and brother enjoyed a gamble – cards, blackjack, roulette. They'd tried to involve him at one time but he couldn't understand the attraction. He wondered just how much of his grandfather's and his mother's fortune had been drunk and gambled away. He supposed he should have realized how bad things were when he'd heard about the sale of the Portsmouth brewery to Henry Thornton.

No wonder they'd been so pleased when Philip married Jane, one of the richest women in the county. But despite the fact that Jane obviously adored him, Philip still carried on as if he were a bachelor, gambling and drinking and chasing servant girls.

Jack's face darkened at the memory of his brother's assault on Daisy. Thank God he'd been there. He knew what would have happened if he hadn't stopped it. Over the years several maids had been dismissed, no one seeming to care what happened to them or their babies once they'd left.

He'd watched over Daisy since then, although it had become harder once he joined the navy. But he was sure his warnings had been effective. Jack's feelings for Daisy had strengthened each time he came home on leave and he dared to hope she felt the same. But he knew what would happen if his mother suspected. Daisy would be dismissed straightaway. As it was, Mother had seized the opportunity to get rid of her. Jack didn't think for one moment she really believed that Daisy was a thief.

How was she coping? Would she be able to get another job? Thinking about her, he was tempted to drive down to the harbour, try to catch a glimpse of her. But, hard as it was to resist the temptation, Jack drove on, remembering the feel of her soft lips parting under his. Even as his head told him their love stood no chance, his heart was telling him that there must be a way.

The letter inviting Daisy for an interview at Kingsbourne Hospital arrived a week later and she tore it open with shaking fingers. As she read, her face paled and the sheet of paper fluttered on to the table.

'Oh, love, have they turned you down?' Effie asked, pausing as she ladled out the breakfast porridge.

Daisy read the letter again before replying. 'I can't believe it – they've accepted me. I have to go and see the matron, sign some papers and get measured for my uniform.' She pushed away the bowl her mother set in front of her. 'I can't eat. I'm too excited.'

'I knew it,' Effie said confidently. 'Hear that, Dad? Daisy's going to be a nurse.'

Daisy went over to her father and kissed his cheek. 'It was your idea, Dad. Thanks.' She turned to her mother. 'I won't be able to send money home, Mum.'

'Don't you worry about that – we'll manage,' said Effie.

'And we've got young Billy's wage coming in now,' Jimmy said.

His brothers nodded agreement and Daisy gave in. She knew it would be hard for them, but when she'd finished her training she'd be able to send money home again.

And best of all, she wouldn't be at the beck and call of people like the Davenports. They aren't worth crying over, she told herself, swallowing a lump in her throat. She'd miss Georgina, of course. Although she'd always been conscious of the difference in their situation, Georgina had never talked down to her or made her feel like a servant. They'd giggled together as Georgina tried on new clothes, or when Daisy tried out different hair-styles on her mistress. Growing up in a family of boys and spending so much time with her father, Daisy had never had the chance to develop friendships with girls of her own age. Georgina was the nearest she'd ever had to a real friend.

And what about Jack? He was probably at sea now. But she wouldn't think about him. With a determined smile, she wiped away a stray tear and said, 'I'd better make myself tidy for my interview.'

Daisy was well into her training at Kingsbourne Cottage Hospital and she was loving the life. This was what she was meant to do, she thought, as she made notes at her first nursing lecture.

She hardly had time to notice what was going on in the outside world, but when the war they'd anticipated for so long finally broke out, her thoughts immediately flew to Jack. She knew it was a hopeless love but she could not forget him. She had thrived on those brief encounters during his visits home, treasuring their few moments together. How could she forget his warm smile and the tender way he would say her name, calling her 'Daisy-bell' and softly humming the tune of the popular song? She had dared to hope that he returned her feelings, while at the same time dreading she'd read too much into it.

When she'd gone into service her mother had warned her that the men of the household might try to force themselves upon her. It had happened to her when she'd worked as a maid before her marriage. Mum had been proved right in the case of Jack's older brother. But Daisy refused to believe that Jack was like Philip. He'd always treated the servants with respect and, as she remembered that last tender touch of his hand, the warmth of his farewell kiss on that dreadful March night, she knew she was right.

Now that war had come she knew her chances of ever seeing him again were slim. She thought of her brothers too, feeling a pang of guilt that her first thought had been for Jack. On her last day off Jimmy and Dick had talked of joining up if war came. Even Billy was eager to follow his brothers, speaking enthusiastically of whipping the Kaiser and teaching the Germans a lesson. Thankfully, he was far too young.

Now her two older brothers were in the army, signing up as soon as war had been declared. The news had made the war seem real and Daisy prayed for the safety of her brothers and the man she loved.

CHAPTER FOUR

As the weeks passed, Daisy had little time to dwell on her family or Jack although she prayed for them every night. The small cottage hospital was always busy but, so far, she'd hardly seen a patient, let alone done any nursing. Most of her time was spent scrubbing bedpans or counting sheets in the linen room. And there were lectures given by Sister Tutor to attend, as well as written work to complete.

It's like everything else, she thought. You had to start at the bottom and work your way up. At least the other girls were friendly enough and Sister Green, although strict, was not quite the ogre she'd expected.

The hospital consisted of four wards – male and female surgical for those recovering from surgery; male and female medical for other illnesses – and there were only six trainee nurses. The small operating theatre dealt with minor operations. More serious cases were sent to Portsmouth.

When Daisy was eventually allowed on to the wards she was accompanied by a probationer nurse who had a little more experience than herself. Sarah Bowman was a tall sandy-haired girl, the daughter of a Portsmouth grocer. They hit it off straightaway and together they made beds and washed the patients, tidied the lockers and watched carefully as Sister and the staff nurse gave out medicines.

Lilac Ward was devoted to elderly women, many recovering from broken bones or long-term illnesses. Daisy was thankful that so far the expected casualties from France had not materialized. Far better to gain a little experience first, she thought.

Not that they'd have to wait long. Despite the meagre information offered by the official bulletins put up outside the post office every Sunday, Daisy knew that the nearby hospitals were overflowing. Some had been taken over by the army and it was only a matter of time before Kingsbourne was as well.

Thinking of the hundreds of casualties, Daisy couldn't help worrying about her brothers and wondering how Mum was coping without them. At least they were able to send money home, lightening the financial burden on her parents.

Thank God it would all be over before Billy was old enough to join up. She dare not think of Jack.

As Daisy sterilized the bedpans, she tried to take her mind off her worries by attempting to memorize some of the facts she'd need for her exam. She was startled when a ward maid came in, saying that Matron wished to see her. She went over the past few days, wondering what she could have done wrong. Matron didn't suffer fools gladly and many a trainee nurse or ward maid had left her office with the telltale signs of tears streaking her face. But Daisy couldn't think of any misdemeanour as she smoothed her hair, straightened her cap and hurried along the corridor. Before knocking on Matron's door, she took a deep breath and entered with a show of confidence.

Matron looked up from her desk and smiled encouragingly. 'Well, March, I expect you're wondering why I've sent for you,' she said. 'It's this wretched war. The casualties are far higher than expected. All the hospitals on the south coast have been warned to prepare for any overflow – and that includes us.'

What did that have to do with her? Daisy wondered.

Matron went on, 'I know of your family's tragedy and how you helped to nurse your father. Although you haven't finished your training, I feel you are already well qualified for this job. We have need of sensible girls, who won't faint at the sight of blood.' She paused and picked up a letter. 'I'm expecting some Red Cross volunteers. Frankly, I don't think they'll be much use – at least to start with.'

'What do you want me to do, Matron?'

'Show them the ropes. Firstly, you'll help Sister Green to prepare for the reception of the wounded. We'll have to move some of the beds and also set up a wing in the annexe for the severest cases. Report to Sister in the morning at seven o'clock.'

Georgina had wheedled and cajoled, sulked and thrown tantrums but her parents refused to give in. As she'd expected, they had ridiculed the idea of her becoming a nurse, but when war was declared she'd hoped she could make them change their minds.

'It's not seemly for a girl of your station,' Lady Davenport repeated, lips primly pursed.

Georgina knew she'd let the family down by refusing to marry the man of their choosing and hated upsetting her mother. But it's *my* life, she thought rebelliously. Her family were only thinking of themselves. They didn't care about her feelings at all. Only Jack was really on her side and he was away at sea.

Up in her room, she raged and sulked yet again. The more she thought about it, the more she wanted to be a nurse. But to become a probationer she would need the permission of her parents. Since the start of the war, everyone was keen to be seen doing their bit but Mama thought rolling bandages and knitting socks was enough. Georgina didn't agree. She was bored; she wanted to do more.

As she dressed for dinner, she told herself that they must come round in time. At least Philip wasn't there to undermine her. To her relief, he'd returned to London, but not before he'd voiced his anger at her treachery. 'You've let the family down,' he said.

'And you haven't?' Georgina could hardly conceal her contempt.

Philip paled but he answered coolly enough, 'I don't know what you mean.'

'I know what you get up to. It's hardly my fault if you and Father have ruined us between you.' She forced herself not to flinch at the look in her brother's eyes. She'd really thought he was going to hit her. Then he'd turned away, his hand falling to his side.

Now, she mentally squared her shoulders and went down to face her parents. Mama would probably sigh and wonder what she'd done to deserve a daughter so lacking in the ladylike graces. But Georgina had always been bored with the social round of balls, tea parties, the season. It was a measure of her discontent that she'd become so involved with the weekly Red Cross meetings and the Voluntary Aid Detachment. Now that war had finally come, it was her chance to do something really useful.

What had at first seemed something that might be fun had now become an obsession. Georgina was determined to win her parents round and was confident that eventually she would get her own way.

As she sat down to dinner she decided that sulks and tantrums had failed, so she would try being sweetly reasonable. She kissed her father's cheek before sitting down and smiled at her mother. 'How did your committee meeting go today, Mama?' she asked.

Lady Davenport looked gratified at this unaccustomed interest and launched into a description of the charity fair she was organizing.

'I'd like to do something more useful as well,' Georgina said.

'Well, we can always use another pair of hands. Why not come down to the village hall with me tomorrow?'

'I was thinking of something else. I know you don't want me to train as a nurse but I really feel—'

'We've been through all this,' her mother interrupted.

'Mama, hear me out, please. I was going to say that I understand your reservations and I promise I won't keep on about it if you'll just agree to me doing a little more work for the Red Cross.' Georgina crossed her fingers under the table. She had no intention of forgetting her ambitions.

'I don't see why not. Lady Phillips is very much involved as well as her daughters, so I think it would be suitable for you,' her mother said.

Georgina breathed a sigh of relief. 'Thank you, Mama. You see, they need more people now. And the VAD organizers are asking for volunteers to help out at Kingsbourne Hospital. Lady Agatha has already signed on.'

'What do you think, dear?' Letitia asked her husband. Sir John appeared to have been concentrating on his food and now looked up with an abstracted air.

'Whatever you say, my dear,' he answered. Georgina smiled to herself. Poor Father had other things on his mind lately – mainly their financial situation. She supposed he was worried about the war too. That's all anybody could talk about these days.

It was a small victory for Georgina – she was now registered as a VAD and had been fitted for her uniform. She felt a warm glow of pride as Lady Phillips addressed the volunteers in the village hall.

'As you know, the military and naval hospitals in this area are struggling to cope. Many of the wounded will be sent to our local hospital and your services are badly needed. You will be required to take on tasks you've never performed before. The work will be hard and the hours long. But you have volunteered and I know you will all do your patriotic duty. I'm very proud that there are so many of you willing to do this work.'

Georgina vowed to be worthy of Lady Phillips' confidence. She'd work hard and make herself indispensable. That would show the parents she wasn't just a spoilt girl wanting to play at nurses. If Lady Agatha could do it, so could she.

Lady Davenport pursed her lips when Georgina got home and explained that she would be required to live in.

'Why can't Ernest take you each day in the trap?' she asked.

'Mama, can't you understand that I want to be treated like the other girls? Why should I have special treatment?' Georgina played her trump card. 'Agatha Phillips will be staying in the VAD hostel too.'

'Oh well, perhaps it will be all right. And if what they say is true, it won't be for long,' her mother said.

Georgina smiled. She knew Mama couldn't bear to be upstaged by Lady Phillips.

*

The hostel was a rambling old house on the outskirts of town, a few minutes' walk from the hospital. The quarters were cramped with two or three girls sharing a room. The kitchen was in the basement and there were only two bathrooms.

It was damp with inadequate heating and Georgina shivered in the November chill of the room she shared with Lady Agatha Phillips, a large girl with freckles and a loud laugh. Georgina felt quite fragile beside her and wondered how she would compare when it came to the real work of nursing. But she was determined to do her best.

Despite their apparent differences they got on well and Agatha, who'd spent most of her life helping her mother with her charitable works, took Georgina under her wing.

'Are you nervous?' Agatha asked as they put the light out and settled into bed.

'A little,' Georgina confessed.

'So am I,' her friend said. 'We'll just have to stick together.'

Georgina was glad that, despite her seeming confidence, Agatha was apprehensive too. Thank God she didn't have to face Matron and the real nurses alone.

Over by Christmas? What a hope, Daisy thought as she left Matron's office. The news from the front was grim; casualties had been far in excess of those expected. Some of them were due to arrive at Kingsbourne the next day. Matron had also added that the VADs had arrived and were ready to start work.

Despite being a little nervous, Daisy was looking forward to the responsibility of supervising the new girls, under Sister's eagle eye, of course. They would be making the beds and seeing that everything was ready before the ambulances arrived.

Since her dismissal from Ryfe Hall, her bitterness at being unfairly accused of theft had abated. Now, she was doing a job she loved and gaining the respect of those she worked with. Only the nagging worry about Jack and her brothers prevented her from feeling completely happy.

As well as extra beds within the main hospital, Langley House, a large villa opposite the hospital had been requisitioned to cope with the overflow. Since October when hundreds of wounded Belgian soldiers had arrived after the retreat from Antwerp, there had been a steady flow of casualties. Now it was British troops who were expected.

Daisy wondered how she'd cope with the ladies as she still thought of them. It wasn't so long ago that the volunteers, all from upper-class homes, had been giving *her* orders. But when she'd expressed her doubts, Matron had smiled encouragingly. 'You'll cope, Nurse. You have a way with people.'

Daisy hoped she was right and, as she entered the room, no one would have guessed that she trembled inwardly as she introduced herself with a smile. 'I'm Nurse March. I'm to show you the ropes. I know it isn't what most of you are used to, but you have volunteered, and rest assured your presence here is valued and needed.'

She wished she felt as confident as she sounded, but her little speech seemed to have gone down all right. 'Now, if you would all tell me your names,' she continued, looking at each girl in turn. Lady Agatha Phillips she recognized immediately; she'd been a frequent visitor to Ryfe Hall with her mother. The other girls were all strangers – or were they? Surely that was Miss Georgina hiding behind Lady Agatha!

Daisy's heart sank. How was she going to cope with giving her former mistress orders? And how would Georgina react? But she managed to smile and greeted her former mistress with equanimity. 'Miss Davenport and I are already acquainted.'

Georgina said nothing and Daisy, considering the circumstances in which she'd left Ryfe Hall, was grateful for her silence. Would Georgina keep her secret? Hadn't she protested Daisy's innocence? Despite parting on such bad terms, she'd always been a fair mistress. But she was a chatterbox and Daisy worried that she might let something slip.

CHAPTER FIVE

Georgina had not forgotten Daisy's dramatic exit from Ryfe Hall all those months ago. When she'd protested that she was on her side, she'd thrown it back in her face. As she tried to absorb the shock of seeing her former maid in charge, she thought, I won't have it. If Daisy March tries telling *me* what to do, she'll soon see what's what. She looked out of the window, scarcely paying attention as Daisy told them what was expected of them. She couldn't be a proper nurse, surely? She hadn't been here long enough. As she fiddled with a stray curl which had escaped the confines of the unfamiliar cap, she gradually became aware that Daisy's words echoed her thoughts.

'In many ways I'm as inexperienced as you are,' she was saying. 'I expect you realize from my cap and apron that I'm not yet fully trained. But many of our older nurses have already gone overseas so we're very short-staffed. I'm very conscious of the trust Matron has placed in me so I'm relying on all of you to help me make sure that trust is not misplaced.'

Daisy smiled at them warmly but Georgina refused to smile back. She still hadn't adjusted to the reversal of their positions. She frowned as Agatha said eagerly, 'We've only done our Red Cross training but we want to do our bit.'

Daisy then showed them round the house. An extra table had been squeezed into the dining room so that now it could seat about twenty people. The former drawing room looked much the same as it must have done when this was a family home and would be somewhere for convalescent patients to relax. The rest of the rooms had been furnished as wards. As many beds as possible had been crammed in with just enough room for the nurses to move between them and for screens to be placed round them when necessary.

A heap of mattresses cluttered the hall and the girls squeezed awkwardly past them. Bundles of sheets and blankets were piled on every available surface.

Daisy paused and said, 'Your first task is to make up all the beds, then every surface must be wet-dusted. I want to see all the lockers and cupboards spotless. Dirt breeds germs as we all know and infection is our greatest enemy.'

'Don't they have maids?' Georgina whispered.

'Doesn't look like it,' Agatha replied.

She couldn't have her former maid overseeing her doing menial tasks. It wasn't right, Georgina thought. As the other girls set to with more enthusiasm than skill she stood watching for a few moments. Then she noticed Daisy looking at her. Just let her try bossing me around, she thought with a sulky pout.

But Daisy didn't say anything directly to her. Instead she clapped her hands. 'Stop. This won't do. We must be more methodical. I suggest you work in pairs.' She beckoned one of the girls. 'I'll show you.'

Within minutes they'd placed the mattress on the bed and made it up with fresh sheets and pillows, the corners neatly boxed, the counterpane ruler-straight.

Daisy stood back and gave the girl a smile of approval. 'Now let me see you do one.'

When the demonstration was completed to Daisy's satisfaction, she set the girls to work, one pair to each side of the room, then nodded to Georgina and Agatha. 'You two can make a start upstairs,' she said. 'I'll come up in a minute and see how you're getting on.' With a sigh and a shrug, Georgina followed Agatha up to the next floor.

As they left the room, Daisy called after them, 'When you've done, make sure each locker has a jug of water and glass.'

'Yes, Nurse,' Georgina said, emphasizing the 'nurse' with a sneer.

Daisy left the room without a word and Georgina and Agatha started to make up the beds. 'Do you two know each other?' Agatha asked.

'She used to be my maid,' Georgina said.

'I thought I knew her from somewhere. How come she's nursing, I wonder?' Agatha pulled the sheet tight, intent on doing it exactly as Daisy had shown them.

'It's a long story. I might tell you about it sometime,' Georgina said.

When Agatha didn't reply she realized that the other girl was too polite to pry. She must be curious though, she thought. I know I would be. She was tempted to tell her about the missing ring. But she really had no quarrel with Daisy and, until now, had felt sympathy for the way she'd been treated by the Davenport family. But this was such a strange situation to be in and she wasn't quite sure how to handle it.

She carried on working in silence and even found she was enjoying herself. There was a sense of satisfaction in doing the job well and she couldn't help feeling pleased when Daisy returned and complimented them. They hadn't finished, though. There was the linen cupboard to be re-stocked, the pantries inventoried and the bathrooms cleaned.

After supper Georgina was too exhausted to do anything except fall into bed. The other girls felt the same. Any ideas they'd entertained of cosy chats round the fire in the evening were quickly squashed. It would be even harder when the patients arrived, Georgina thought as she fell asleep with the smell of polish in her nostrils.

Daisy was tired too. The effort of explaining everything over and over while keeping a rein on her impatience and a smile on her face had been a real strain. But she was pleased with herself too. The new VADs, even Georgina, had responded well to her teaching and seemed willing and enthusiastic. Daisy hadn't missed the resentment on Georgina's face when she had realized who was in charge. Emphasizing her own inexperience had been intended to put her at ease; anything to forestall any awkwardness between them.

Tomorrow they would light fires in all the rooms. The old house had been empty for some time and the high-ceilinged rooms had a dank chill atmosphere. Daisy smiled at the thought of Lady Agatha and Georgina struggling with paper and kindling.

This isn't what I had in mind when I volunteered, Georgina thought, sitting back on her heels and sighing. She was close to tears. The fire just would not light.

'Damn, damn, damn,' she muttered, pulling the charred sticks and pieces of paper out of the grate. She didn't care if Matron did hear. She shouldn't have to do this. It wasn't fair. Why couldn't Daisy do it? She'd have to if she didn't want Matron to know why she was dismissed from Ryfe Hall, Georgina thought childishly. She still hadn't quite come to terms with the fact that Daisy was her superior in this new life.

She wiped her hand across her eyes, leaving a smudge of soot on her forehead, and re-laid the fire, frowning with concentration. She wouldn't let a little thing like this beat her. As she worked, the absurdity of the situation struck her and her usual sense of humour came to the fore. What would Mama say if she could see her now? This was something the servants normally did, something she'd always taken for granted.

Well, she *had* volunteered, so she must make the best of it. She gave a little nod of satisfaction as the wood caught at last. She was carefully placing the last knob of coal onto the now cheerfully blazing fire when the door opened and Daisy came in.

'I thought you might want some help but it seems you can manage without me,' she said, giving Georgina a cheerful smile.

'I wish you'd been here a few minutes ago when I needed you,' Georgina replied with a return of the resentment she'd been feeling a few moments ago.

'I knew you could do it. You just need a little practice, that's all,' Daisy said. She walked down the room, checking that everything was ready, seeming oblivious to Georgina's feelings. The beds were neatly made, a jug and glass of water stood on each bedside locker, and most importantly, the fire was now blazing merrily, giving a welcoming air to the ward.

'Well done, Nurse. You're picking things up nicely,' Daisy said.

Georgina's anger flared. 'You don't have to be so condescending. I'm not stupid.'

'Of course you're not. And I'm sorry if you thought I was talking down to you. It's just that I'm new to this as well and – well, it is rather an awkward situation.'

'I should say so, especially as you told the others you knew me. They keep asking questions. How do you think it would look if they knew I was taking orders from my former maid?'

To Georgina's satisfaction Daisy coloured but she was taken aback when she replied, 'You're just worried how it will look for you. What about my feelings? What if people who I respect and admire find out I was sacked for something I didn't do?'

'I would never tell anyone,' Georgina protested. 'I know you didn't do it. It's just – well, this is all so difficult.'

Already a little ashamed of her childish outburst, Georgina hoped Daisy would understand. Looking at it from someone else's point of view, she realized she was being rather petty. Given that she'd had people rushing to do her bidding ever since she was a child, it was hard for her to take orders. But she hadn't really considered Daisy's feelings.

'It doesn't have to be difficult,' Daisy said. 'I don't mind people knowing I was once your maid, but if it makes you uncomfortable I'll keep quiet.' She sighed. 'We ought to try to get on though, for the sake of the patients if not for our colleagues.'

Georgina remembered how she'd been the one to ask for Daisy's promotion from the kitchen and how fond she'd become of her over the years. With a shamefaced smile she said, 'Can we start again? I know you think I'm just a spoilt rich girl playing at nurses but I'm really keen. You've been so patient with me. I don't deserve it.'

'As I said, you are doing well – and I'm not being condescending,' Daisy replied with a small laugh. 'Now, we'd better get on. Those ambulances will be arriving soon and there's a lot to do.'

'How many are we expecting?' Georgina asked.

'We can't tell until they get here. But the casualties have been very heavy and the military hospitals at Southampton and Portsmouth are full to bursting. That goes for most of the smaller places too. I wouldn't be at all surprised if we have to put up more beds.'

'You can't possibly get any more in here,' Georgina protested.

'We may have to,' Daisy said as they left the ward together. 'I suggest you go and get something to eat. When the ambulances arrive we won't have a minute to spare.'

As Georgina walked back to the hostel she felt a lot better about her relationship with Daisy. Was it possible they could become real friends? They hadn't had a chance before, given their different social positions. Who knew what lay ahead in these changed circumstances brought about by the war?

Langley House was ready for its new tenants and there was a tense air of expectancy as the regular nurses and volunteers waited for their arrival.

Daisy wondered how the young VADs would cope with their first sight of the wounded. She'd had little experience herself since starting her training but she was no stranger to the reality of festering wounds. Nursing Dad had been good experience.

But how could these young ladies, who'd probably never even seen a grazed knee, be expected to deal with all this? Lady Agatha would be all right. Daisy knew that she often visited the sick in the workhouse with her mother. And that doctor's daughter, Millicent Hardy, seemed a sensible girl. She wasn't so sure about some of the others.

It was Georgina she was worried about. She'd led such a sheltered life. Daisy hoped she wouldn't go to pieces when faced with a dying man. So far she'd proved a very apt pupil, Daisy thought, remembering Georgina's stubborn efforts to light the fire.

Now she looked at the girls, lined up in their uniforms, some with eager anticipation on their faces, some looking nervous. Nurse Bowman joined her in the hall, followed by Sister Green.

'The ambulances have just turned up,' she said. 'Brace yourself.'

Daisy tried to control the fluttering in her stomach. It wouldn't do to let the others know how nervous she was. They looked to her for guidance but they probably didn't realize that this was her first time of unloading the ambulances too. The patients she'd encountered so far had been already bathed, pyjamaed and safely tucked under militarily precise blankets. She just hoped she wasn't going to see her father's pain reflected in each one. At all costs she must conceal her feelings.

It wasn't as bad as she'd feared. Most of the wounded had been treated at the casualty clearing stations near the front before the men were shipped back to England.

Daisy took her lead from Sister Green and for the next few hours was so busy organizing and issuing orders that she hardly had time to think of herself.

As she came off duty, she fell into step beside Georgina, noticing the shadows of exhaustion under the blue eyes. 'It wasn't as bad as I thought,' she said. 'But I suppose this is only the beginning.'

'Things are bound to get worse,' Daisy replied. 'There are so many now – most of them are being sent straight back to England before their wounds are assessed. I expect some will come here.' She passed a hand wearily across her forehead.

Georgina touched her arm. 'I don't like to ask – but what about your brothers? Have they joined up?'

'Billy's too young but the other two are in the army.' She didn't want to talk about it and they walked on in silence, until Daisy summoned the courage to ask, 'Your brothers?' She daren't mention Jack by name.

Georgina gave a short laugh. 'Philip's managed to avoid the war so far. He just carries on as usual.' Her eyes clouded. 'It's Jack I'm worried about.'

Daisy's stomach churned. 'He is all right, isn't he?'

'I don't know – that's the worst part. It's ages since I heard from him.'

'I'm sure you'd have heard if . . .' She couldn't go on but Georgina interrupted.

'That's what I tell myself.'

They parted at the hospital entrance and Daisy went to her own quarters. There she sank into bed, so weary she was sure sleep wouldn't be long in coming. But it was almost the start of another exhausting day before she fell into a restless slumber, tormented by thoughts of Jack out there on the ocean, his ship at the mercy of German U-boats.

CHAPTER SIX

Georgina and Agatha were sitting in the garden of the hostel one evening in early autumn 1915. The day had been unseasonably hot and they'd gone outside after supper to make the most of the light breeze which had sprung up as dusk fell.

'I suppose we should go in. Early start again tomorrow,' Agatha said.

'I'm too exhausted to move.' Georgina stretched and her leather writing case slipped from her lap. Bending to retrieve it, she said, 'I'm just going to post this.'

'I'll come with you.' Agatha got up and they walked to the gate. 'Been writing to Jack?'

'Yes, it's really hard. He's not allowed to tell us where he is and I'm so worried. I try to keep my letters cheerful and chatty but there's not much cheer here, is there?'

Agatha nodded sympathetically. 'It's even harder when you don't know exactly where they are,' she said.

'Somewhere in the Mediterranean, he says. Every time I hear about a naval engagement I imagine him involved – and Tom too.' Georgina implied that he was a casual family friend. She didn't think Agatha was fooled though.

Despite her dedication to her nursing and worry over her family, Georgina hadn't forgotten Tom and included him in her nightly prayers. Although she'd asked Jack to pass on her regards, he hadn't contacted her since that dreadful winter evening so long ago. Surely he must know about her broken engagement, she thought. Had she misunderstood? Didn't he love her at all? But the memory of that kiss still burned.

'Hard to imagine the war still going on after more than a year, isn't it?' Agatha said, interrupting her thoughts. 'Especially on an evening like this.'

After posting the letter they walked back to the hostel in silence. Exhaustion or no, Georgina was looking forward to her next shift. She had discovered a surprising aptitude for nursing, even the grimmer aspects of the job.

It was when she'd helped Sister to change a dressing on a particularly nasty wound. Terrified she might faint, she'd bitten fiercely on the inside of her lip, and managed to smile and talk to the young man without a glimmer of her feelings showing.

She supposed it was because he'd looked like Jack. And he was so brave. She couldn't let him see how she felt. The memory of Jack, egging her on in his boyhood escapades, his ridicule if she failed to live up to his expectations, brought a smile. Having older brothers had certainly been a help when it came to dealing with the patients. Some of the raw young volunteers had never even seen a young man close up before.

Now, as she approached each bedside, Georgina imagined Jack there, grinning at her, daring her to be as plucky as he was. She still wasn't very good at lighting fires though. And the everlasting washing up, scrubbing and mopping still irked her.

It had taken months to lose her resentment at being treated like a skivvy, but now she saw it as part of the job. She still didn't like making tea for the senior nurses, though, especially Daisy. Despite their improved relationship it still didn't seem right somehow. Proper nursing jobs were different. She accepted Daisy telling her what to do. After all, it was for the benefit of those poor wounded lads and she had to learn to do it right.

The other girls grumbled, but in a light-hearted casual way. 'That's what we're here for,' Millie Hardy said when Georgina was indulging in a bout of self-pity.

'Thank goodness we're under Sister Green and Nurse March. At least they treat us like human beings,' Agatha said. 'Some of the senior nurses are so superior. I heard one of them telling Sister Green that they had to keep the VADs in their place.'

Georgina had giggled. 'I put in my letter to Jack how they hate it when any of the patients call us Sister,' she said.

Agatha laughed. 'I suppose you can't blame them really. Some of them have done years of training to get where they are.'

Now, as they reached the entrance to the hostel, Agatha paused. 'I've put in for a transfer,' she said suddenly.

'I knew you were thinking about it. But it won't be the same if you go,' Georgina said.

'They need more of us at the front and I feel it's where I should be. Why don't you apply?' Agatha said. 'We'd still be together then.'

Georgina was tempted. It would be quite an adventure. Some of the other girls had already gone, inspired by the example of Nurse Cavell, who had been arrested by the Germans in Belgium for helping allied soldiers to escape. There had been no news of her fate yet and Georgina shivered at the thought of what might happen to that brave woman.

I couldn't do anything like that, she thought. Why not stay here where she could still tell herself she was doing her bit? Besides, over in France, she'd be cut off from any news. What if Tom were wounded? How could she nurse him back to health? She shook her head. That was just a silly romantic dream, her common sense told her.

To Agatha she said, 'Even if I was accepted, Mama would never give permission. It was hard enough becoming a VAD.'

But now that her friend had planted the idea in her head, Georgina found herself thinking about it and she made up her mind to apply, although it could be months before a transfer came through and she might not be sent to the same place as Agatha.

Daisy and Nurse Bowman were busy decorating the wards for Christmas when Sister Green called her into the office and told her that Nurse Davenport was being transferred.

'I'll be sorry when they go. Nurse Phillips is off to France next week and Nurse Davenport leaves for Malta in the new year,' she said.

Daisy was surprised that Georgina hadn't told her but they had been rushed off their feet lately and there had been no time to chat.

'I'll miss her,' she told Sister. It was the truth – they worked very well together now that Georgina had got over her resentment at being supervised by her former maid.

'I'll miss her too,' Sister Green said. 'She has the makings of a good nurse. Like you, she can be relied on not to faint at the sight of blood or worse. We could do with more like the two of you.'

Daisy blushed at the compliment and thanked the older woman. She had thought of applying for overseas herself but now wasn't the time to mention it. Besides, she couldn't leave her mother to cope with Dad with Dick and Jimmy away.

She left Sister's office and went in search of Georgina to congratulate her.

She found her in the sluice, scrubbing bedpans, and she turned to face Daisy with a grin. 'My favourite job,' she said, laughing.

Daisy returned her smile. 'I hear you're leaving us.'

To her surprise the other girl threw her arms around her and Daisy found herself returning the hug. 'It's so exciting, isn't it? And Malta – it's a navy base, you know. Perhaps I'll run into Jack out there – and Tom.'

Daisy's stomach flipped. Jack – would she ever be allowed to forget him? But then, she didn't want to. She felt a momentary envy that if his ship put into Malta, Georgina might see him. A more sobering thought came. If he were wounded, a meeting might be under far worse circumstances. Would Georgina be able to cope with that?

She kept her thoughts to herself, however, although she knew it must have crossed Georgina's mind too. Her eyes had clouded momentarily but she soon brightened and said, 'Why don't you apply too, Daisy?'

'I'd like to but my dad's getting worse and Mum's finding it harder now.'

'I understand – but I'll miss you, Daisy – sorry, Nurse March.' She giggled. 'I mean it. I know I was a bit prickly and difficult when I first came but I've enjoyed working with you.'

'Me too,' Daisy said. 'And I'm sorry you're going.'

'I'm sorry too – about the way my family treated you.'

Daisy realized that the young carefree girl she'd known at Ryfe Hall had long gone and in her place was a mature young woman. I suppose I've changed too, she thought. 'Oh, it's long forgotten,' she lied. She'd never forget, nor would she forgive Lady Davenport, but she'd always known that Georgina had nothing to do with it. 'I just wish the ring had turned up. It's hard to live with people thinking you're a thief.'

'Well, I never thought you were.'

'I know, Georgina. Don't let's talk about it.'

'I'd like to think we're friends, Daisy. Maybe we'll work together again. I've made up my mind I'm going to train as a proper nurse after the war – just like you.'

'But you won't need to work, surely? And you'll probably get married.'

'Oh no – not me.' A fleeting sadness crossed her face and Daisy guessed she was thinking about Tom Lazenby.

However, she pretended not to notice and laughed instead. 'Me neither,' she said.

When Georgina had gone she realized how much she'd miss the other girl's bright presence on the wards. She would miss Agatha too. The combination of her dependable common sense and Georgina's cheerfulness had made them a good team. Now I'll have to start training new girls, Daisy thought despondently. It was accepted that the more experienced nurses were needed overseas and a new batch of trainees was due soon.

A day off was a rare treat and exhaustion a way of life but everyone perked up as Christmas drew near. The wards were decorated and, despite food shortages, the kitchen staff managed to come up with a celebratory dinner for the patients. The nurses toured the wards carrying lanterns and singing carols. The old familiar songs brought a lump to Daisy's throat as she thought of Christmases at home with her brothers. What sort of Christmas were they having and what about Jack, probably somewhere at sea? She was pleased she had Boxing Day off and was free to go into town to see her parents.

'We saved Christmas dinner for you, Daisy love,' her mother said, giving her a hug.

Billy was home and he hugged her, releasing her quickly to go and kiss her father. His face was drawn and grey, but he struggled to sit up and give her a welcoming smile.

The absence of Dick and Jimmy cast a shadow over the day but Daisy was glad she'd gone home. Effie had managed to provide a good meal of roast chicken and potatoes with a small pudding to follow. They exchanged small gifts and for a few hours the cottage was filled with laughter – sometimes tinged with sadness. Daisy stayed longer than she'd intended, helping her mother to bath and change the sheets for Dad before declaring that she really ought to get back to the hospital.

It was starting to get dark and fog was rolling in from the sea as she left the cottage and hurried through the town. At the top of the hill there was no pavement and she hugged the grass verge, feeling her way through the thickening fog.

She didn't hear the motorcar until it was almost upon her, the lamps clamped to its bonnet ghostly in the gloom. She scrambled onto the verge, shaking as she realized she could have been knocked down. The car pulled up some way ahead and she caught her breath as she recognized Jack's open-topped Hispano-Suiza. Was he home on leave? A dark-coated figure leaned across to open the passenger door and she ran forward, her heart leaping with joy. But the voice that called to her wasn't Jack's and she felt a little foolish. Hadn't Georgina told her that Jack was in the Mediterranean? To her dismay she realized it was Ernest Jenkins offering to give her a lift.

'No, thank you, Ernest. I'm nearly there now,' she said. The truth was, she'd never felt comfortable with him, especially since he'd made a pass at her when she was working at Ryfe Hall. She'd rather walk the rest of the way than endure his company.

Ernest laughed. 'Come on, Daisy. Jump in, do. It's a fair step to the hospital.'

As she hesitated he grasped her hand and she tried to pull back, suddenly nervous. But he tightened his grip and pulled her up into the seat beside him.

'Why walk when you can ride?' he said with another of his irritating laughs.

'How did you know I was going to the hospital?' she asked. 'And what are you doing with Master Jack's car?'

'There's no secrets in Kingsbourne, is there? Besides, I made it my business to find out where you'd gone after you left Ryfe Hall. As for me driving this car, I do have permission, you know.' He sniggered. 'I suppose you thought it was the young master offering you a ride? Sorry to disappoint you.'

Daisy didn't reply, her face burning at the insinuation in his voice.

He started up and inched forward into the blanket of fog. For a few minutes there was silence as he concentrated on keeping to the road. Daisy leaned as far away from him as possible. If only she'd realized who was driving. It seemed an age before they drew up at the hospital gates. She couldn't get away quickly enough.

As she reached for the door, Ernest's hand clamped over her wrist. 'Don't go yet, Daisy. I want to talk to you.'

'I must go in. I'm late already and Matron will be on my back,' she protested, fighting the urge to struggle. It wouldn't do to let him see how scared she was.

'Daisy, love, you've got time to chat to an old friend, surely. I stood up for you, you know. I never believed you stole that ring. It was just an excuse to get rid of you.'

'What do you mean?' But she knew the answer. Jack had told her already. She didn't really want to hear – especially from Ernest.

'Her ladyship knew Master Phil was sniffing round and she didn't want trouble. I told you once before if you'd walk out with me I'd look after you. The offer still stands.'

Her fear turned to anger at his presumption. He still grasped her wrist and she tried to free herself but with his other arm he pulled her towards him. When he let go of her wrist, she scrabbled for the door. But he twined his fingers in her hair, jerking her closer. 'Come on. Give us a kiss and forget about them Davenports,' he whispered.

Ignoring her struggles, he fastened his lips on hers and she pushed at his chest, gagging at the smell of alcohol on his breath. She was really frightened now.

'What's wrong, Daisy? You used to be friendly enough when you were a kitchen maid.'

Silently she struggled, afraid to scream, cursing her stupidity for getting in the car. Fear lent her strength and she kicked out, determined that he would not have his way.

He twisted his hand in her hair again and she cried out with the pain. He gave a contemptuous laugh. 'You should have walked out with me when I asked you,' he said. 'I would've treated you right. But you've got above yourself, think you're too good for the likes of me.' He fastened his wet mouth over hers again.

In desperation she jabbed her knee into his stomach and he grunted in surprise. But he didn't let go. Tightening his grip, he pulled her down across the seats. 'So, I'm not good enough for you,' he sneered. 'I suppose you get what you want from Master Jack. We all know he fancies you too. Well, I can give as good as what he can.' He pushed her cloak aside and tore at the front of her dress. His hand was on her breast, while the other fumbled with her skirt, trying to push her legs apart.

Daisy whimpered. But she wouldn't give in. As she scrabbled frantically to gain purchase on anything that would help to fight him off, her fingers closed over the pin which fastened her cloak. She brought her hand up, stabbing him in the face. With a howl of rage he released her, raising a disbelieving hand to his cheek.

She seized the opportunity to scramble out of the car, but instead of running towards the nurses' home, she turned to Ernest and said coldly, 'I'm not afraid of you, Ernest Jenkins. In case you weren't already aware of it, I have three brothers – hulking great fishermen who would make mincemeat of anyone who dared to treat their sister badly. I wouldn't like to be in your shoes if they ever get to hear of what happened tonight.'

Gathering her torn dress across her body, she turned, head high, and walked without haste across the courtyard towards the porter's lodge.

CHAPTER SEVEN

The next day, as Daisy did her rounds, she tried to put Ernest Jenkins out of her mind. She'd managed to get back to the nurses' home unobserved and, after taking off her torn dress, she'd soaked for hours in a hot bath, trying to wash away all traces of him.

By morning she'd persuaded herself that it was only a matter of time before he was called up. Conscription was now in force. He was young and fit; he'd soon be gone.

Anyway, she wouldn't spend the rest of her life looking over her shoulder, she thought, as she finished swabbing a wound. Carefully replacing the soiled dressing with a fresh one, she forced herself to smile at the young man propped up against the pillows.

'It's bad, isn't it, Nurse?' he said, bravely attempting to return her smile.

She could have offered him a comforting platitude. But nursing these painfully young men, many hardly out of their teens, she'd learned that they preferred the truth.

She met the soldier's gaze and said quietly, 'Yes, it is bad. But not as bad as we thought. Provided we can keep the infection out it should heal all right.'

'But I will be scarred, won't I?' The voice was matter-of-fact but Daisy saw a flicker of panic in the blue eyes. Not trusting herself to speak, she finished the dressing and adjusted the pillows behind his head. As she smoothed the sheet across the thin body she said, 'You'll have to speak to the doctor. He'll be able to tell you more.'

She turned away and moved on to the next bed. The wounds were different but the conversation was almost the same. They all demanded to know the worst and then wanted reassurance. How hard it was to meet their eyes, knowing that most of them would carry scars, mental or physical, for the rest of their lives.

Keeping the smile firmly in place, she made her way down the ward, swabbing wounds, changing dressings, trying to bring a little comfort. It's getting easier, she thought, the sight of those ugly festering wounds, the overwhelming smell that no amount of disinfectant could disguise. She could cope with the practical side. Years of helping with her father had inured her to the physical side of her work, unlike many of the nurses.

Yes, she could cope with the work, not to mention the constant tiredness, aching legs, sore feet. But would she ever be able to harden her heart to the suffering in these lads' eyes, the sobs and screams each night as they fought their way out of their nightmares? Any one of them could be Jack, or Jimmy or Dick.

Daisy passed on to the last bed, concentrating on the patient instead of her own feelings. She wasn't the only one whose stomach fluttered apprehensively as each new flood of casualties was brought in. One day, she knew, a stretcher would arrive and she would see one of her brothers. She sighed. It was something they all had to live with.

Now, she thought again about applying for overseas service – not to France, though. Perhaps she could ask to be sent to Malta. It wasn't just the idea of being nearer to Jack. She just didn't think she could cope if she had to nurse one of her brothers. It would be like Dad all over again.

By the time she came off duty that evening Daisy had convinced herself she would have no more trouble from Ernest Jenkins. Surely the threat of her brothers would deter him? He couldn't know that they were away fighting. And, with any luck, he'd soon be gone.

But as she and Sarah crossed the road to the nurses' home after supper, someone loomed through the dusk and accosted her. 'Good evening, Nurse. Nice to see you again.' The words were innocent enough, but Ernest's voice held a hint of menace. Why couldn't he leave her alone? Daisy felt a little tremor of fear although she told herself she wasn't afraid. She'd proved that last night. But he could ruin her career if he chose.

She squared her shoulders. She wouldn't let a little runt like Ernest Jenkins get the better of her. Just ignore him, she thought, taking Sarah's arm and hurrying up the steps to the front door. But she shuddered as his voice followed her. 'Well, Nurse March, too high and mighty to talk to me, are you?' His voice slurred and she turned to see him walk away, mumbling to himself.

'Who on earth was that?' Sarah asked.

'Someone I used to work with.' Daisy couldn't bring herself to tell Sarah the full story. 'Take no notice of him. He's obviously been drinking.'

He was there every day after that and although Daisy made sure that she never left the hospital alone on these dark winter evenings, the strain of avoiding Ernest began to tell. Only once had she spoken to him, first making sure one of the hospital porters was within earshot. She had tried to speak reasonably, telling him that if he continued to make a nuisance of himself she would be forced to make a formal complaint.

He had laughed derisively. 'Do you think anyone would take notice of you – a servant dismissed for theft?' The threat in his voice was unmistakable and Daisy trembled at the thought of Matron, not to mention Sarah and her other friends, finding out about her past. Surely he'd be called up soon and she would be rid of him.

Things came to a head when Matron called Daisy into her office. One look at her expression told her that she was in trouble and she swallowed nervously.

'There's been a complaint – a young man's been hanging around the hospital and the nurses' home,' she said. 'Apparently he is a friend of yours, Nurse March. When challenged he admitted he was waiting for you.'

'He's not a friend, Matron, I assure you.' Daisy looked her in the eye.

'He says you quarrelled and he wants to make it up before he's sent away to the front.' Matron's voice softened. 'As you know, there are strict rules about having followers. But as the young man is off to fight, I could let you say goodbye to him.'

Daisy sighed. Ernest could turn on the charm when he wanted to. Hadn't she herself thought he was quite nice until she got to know him? She stood firm.

'Matron, I don't want to see him at all. And as he's not even in uniform, I don't believe he's off soon. He's just trying to get sympathy.' She took a deep breath. 'The truth is, he treated me badly and can't accept that I don't want anything to do with him.'

Matron smiled sympathetically. 'Very well then. I'll have the porters move him on if he shows up here again.'

Daisy sighed with relief and thanked her. But as she left the office she wondered if it would be that easy. Ernest seemed determined to repay her rejection of him, not once but twice. She dare not contemplate the havoc he could cause if he made good his threats.

She couldn't put off visiting her parents any longer and on her next day off she decided to risk bumping into Ernest. She would have asked Sarah to go with her but she was on duty. Besides, she still hadn't told her about Ernest's assault. To her relief, there was no sign of him but he could be lurking along the road.

Effie was looking much happier when she reached the cottage. Excitedly she said that there'd been a letter from Dick and a postcard from

Jimmy. Although they'd taken ages to arrive, she took comfort from the fact that, up to the time they were posted at least, the boys were together, and seemingly fit and well. Billy today was out with the fishing fleet. And Dad seemed brighter too. He wasn't coughing so much, although his face was still drawn with pain.

Daisy didn't want to burden her parents with her own troubles, but she should have known her mother wasn't easily fooled. When Albert had drifted off to sleep, she asked in a low voice what was wrong.

'Nothing, Mum. I'm just tired, that's all.'

'I didn't say anything before because I didn't want to worry your dad, but I know something's up. You've not got involved with some lad, have you?'

'No, Mum. I haven't got time for that sort of thing.' Daisy managed a laugh.

Effie looked sceptical. 'You don't have to tell me if you don't want to. But if you're in trouble I'd help, you know that.'

Her sympathy was Daisy's undoing and she found herself spilling out the tale of Ernest's treachery. 'He says if I'm not nice to him, he'll tell everyone about Georgina's ring and how I lost my job at Ryfe Hall.'

'Better not let your dad know,' Effie said. 'It would kill him, knowing he can't do anything about it – and your brothers not here either.'

Daisy managed to laugh and told her mother how she'd threatened Ernest with the boys.

'And if they *were* here they'd soon sort him out,' Effie said, standing up and stirring the stew. She added dumplings, while Daisy set the table.

Later as they sat down to eat, Effie looked at Daisy thoughtfully. 'There is one way to solve this problem, you know.'

'I can't think what. He's determined to carry on making a nuisance of himself, despite Matron getting the porters to speak to him. It's getting really embarrassing.' Daisy sighed and glanced across at her father. To her relief he was still asleep.

'If he won't leave you alone, you'll have to leave instead,' her mother said.

'What do you mean? I can't leave here. Besides, he'd find out where I was,' she said, putting her fork down and pushing the plate away. 'Oh, I wish he'd get called up. I can't think why he's not in the army already.'

Effie screwed up her face. 'He strikes me as the type who'd wangle his way out of it somehow. That's why I say you must get away from him. You should apply for a posting abroad, like your friends have.'

'I can't leave you and Dad now,' Daisy protested, although she knew that, if it weren't for her father's illness, she would have gone before now.

'We'll be all right. Besides, I know you really want to go. I could tell you were envious when Miss Georgina was accepted.'

Despite protesting, Daisy knew her mother was right. Hadn't she often dreamt of being sent to the Mediterranean where she might catch a glimpse of Jack? Just daydreams, she told herself. Her duty was to her parents and her patients here in Kingsbourne.

Eventually she had to agree that it might be for the best. Her mind was finally made up when Effie said, 'You want to continue nursing as a career after the war, don't you? If Jenkins lets on that you were suspected of thieving it could mean the end of all that. Your dad and I won't be here for ever; you've got to make your own way in life.'

Daisy nodded miserably. 'I don't like thinking of you coping with Dad on your own. I know I don't get home that often but I'm not too far away if you need me. Suppose something happened when I was overseas?' The thought was too painful and she was relieved when her father stirred and started to wake up.

Effie put her hand on Daisy's arm. 'We've still got Billy, thank God. Think about it, love.' She rose and went to help Albert sit up, while Daisy fetched a bowl of the nourishing stew from the pot on the range.

For the rest of her visit she sat with her father, pleased when she brought a smile to his face with her tales of hospital life. She left early, anxious to get back before dark. As she walked back through the town, keeping a wary eye out for Ernest, she wondered if she could bear to leave her parents, knowing how ill her father was. But maybe her mother was right, even if it did seem a bit like running away.

Daisy lost no time in applying to go to Malta with the next lot of nurses. She hoped her transfer order would come through in time for her to go with her friends. Sarah Bowman had applied as well as Georgina. Lady Agatha had already left for France.

She'd just come off duty and was looking forward to a hot bath when Georgina rushed over to the nurses' home. 'There's a letter from Jack,' she said, waving it under Daisy's nose. 'His ship's due back in Portsmouth for a refit. Oh, I do hope he gets here before we sail.'

Daisy's heart started to pound and she felt her cheeks growing hot. Would he try to see her?

Before she could speak, Georgina went on, 'He mentions you, says he'd like to see you again. He's teasing me about taking orders from my maid. Silly old Jack,' she said fondly, smiling and putting a hand on Daisy's arm.

'You know I don't think of you like that now.' She turned the page and a blush flooded her cheeks. 'He says a certain lieutenant – he means Tom, of course – is anxious to renew his acquaintance now that our circumstances have changed.' She frowned. 'I suppose he means now I'm not engaged.'

Daisy was scarcely listening. Jack was coming home and he wanted to see her. 'I hope things go right for you and Lieutenant Lazenby now,' she said mechanically.

'And for you and Jack,' Georgina said.

Daisy smiled but didn't reply. Thrilled as she might be at the prospect of seeing Jack again, she knew in her heart that nothing had changed for them. She was still a poor fisherman's daughter and he was still the son of the local squire.

Later, though, as she soaked away the tensions of the day in a hot bath, she couldn't stop the pictures forming in her head – Jack meeting her at the hospital gates, taking her hand, walking with her up on the Downs or along the harbour wall.

When she went in to supper she was still daydreaming until Sarah's voice jolted her back to reality.

'March, wake up. What were you dreaming about? If I didn't know better I'd say you were in love,' Sarah teased.

Daisy turned a blushing face to her colleague and laughed unconvincingly. 'I haven't got time for that sort of nonsense.'

'Well, I wouldn't blame you. That good-looking lieutenant in bed three has his eye on you. He lights up when you come on the ward.'

'Really? I hadn't noticed,' Daisy said, stifling the urge to confide in her but she didn't want her friend to tell her she was being foolish. Georgina might entertain silly romantic dreams but Sarah was more down to earth. Still, she couldn't stop her heart leaping at the thought of seeing Jack again. It was almost two years since she'd left Ryfe Hall, but in all that time she'd never forgotten the feel of her hand in his, the look in his eyes as they'd said goodbye. But could he ever forget that she'd been just a lowly lady's maid, especially one who'd been dismissed for theft?

Daisy stood up, pushed her dreams firmly to the back of her mind and went back into the ward to settle her patients for the night.

When Daisy's letter of transfer arrived and she learned she would be leaving for Malta on the same ship as the other girls, excitement and anticipation warred with the fear that they would sail before Jack's ship arrived in port.

She also felt a little guilty that thoughts of Jack were uppermost when she should have been worrying about her parents, not to mention Dick and Jimmy. The news from the front was not good. There had been heavy casualties in the area of the River Somme where another huge battle had been raging for weeks. Perhaps I should have applied to go to France after all, she thought guiltily. As she knocked on Matron's door to let her know that her orders had come, she wondered once again if she'd done the right thing.

Despite yet another influx of new wounded, Matron allowed Daisy a couple of hours off to go and break the news of her imminent departure to her family. Her steps slowed as she reached the cottage and again she was attacked by a pang of guilt. How could she go and leave Mum and Dad like this, especially when they were so worried about the boys as well? She knew her mother understood, but it was hard just the same.

Albert was sleeping as usual, but her mother hugged her as warmly as ever when Daisy told her how little time she had left in England. 'We'll miss you and worry, of course,' she said. 'But it's the right thing to do.'

Daisy glanced towards the bed where her father's frail form scarcely made a dent in the covers. 'How is he?' she whispered.

'About the same, love. Look, when he wakes up don't tell him you're going so soon. Let him enjoy your visit. I'll break it to him later. You'll be able to come and say goodbye before you go, won't you?'

'I hope so,' Daisy replied and her eyes filled with tears as it suddenly occurred to her that this might be the last time she would see her father. Every time she came home, Mum said 'about the same' but she could see for herself how much he had deteriorated.

Effie put a hand on her arm. 'Don't feel sad. I think he's ready to go now. He's held on for so long. But these last months it's been such a struggle for him, trying to catch his breath. I lie awake each night, wishing I could breathe for him.'

Daisy turned to the bed as her father stirred and opened his eyes. 'That you, gel?' he said, his voice a mere breath on the air. 'Come and give your dad a kiss then.'

She hugged the frail body, feeling his shoulder blades through his pyjamas. 'It's lovely to see you, Dad. I'm afraid I can't stay long – as usual.' She sat on the edge of the bed and took his hand in hers.

'Tell us what you've been up to then, girl. Fallen in love with any of them handsome soldiers yet?' His laugh turned into a wheezing cough and Daisy was able to bring her blushes under control as she held a mug of water to his lips.

'I'm too busy for romance, Dad,' she said when the coughing fit was over and her father sank back on the pillows.

'Bet they fall for you though, gel,' he said. 'Best nurse in Sussex you are.' He sighed and closed his eyes but the pressure on Daisy's hand did not lessen. She sat there for a long time, stroking his hand and occasionally brushing the hair back from his forehead. His breathing became erratic and noisy as he slipped into a doze and Daisy turned to her mother in concern. 'How long has he been like this?' she asked.

'It gets a little worse each day,' Effie said. 'But he does have the odd good day in between. Still, like I said, he seems to have given up since the boys went.'

'I wish I hadn't put in for overseas duty now,' Daisy said, getting up and crossing the room to the table. 'I didn't realize he was so bad. How can I leave you to cope with this, Mum?'

'Stop it, Daisy. You're going and that's that. When this horrible war is over you'll have finished your training and you'll be able to get a job anywhere. You'll never have to worry about money and keeping a roof over your head.' Effie poured a cup of tea and pushed it across the table.

Daisy stirred it slowly, but before she could say anything, her mother spoke. 'I know you're convinced you have to do your bit like the boys, not to mention getting away from that nasty Jenkins.' She sighed. 'I'm thinking about the future, love – after the war. I know you'll probably get married but there could still come a day when you need to earn a living and at least you won't be reduced to taking in washing like I was.'

'It's true I needed a job, but Mum, I really like nursing. Besides I don't think it's likely I'll ever marry.'

Effie laughed. 'We all say that till a good-looking chap with a twinkle in his eye comes along.'

Daisy glanced at the frail figure in the corner bed. Yes, her dad had been like that once. She could remember the boat coming into harbour, Albert leaping onto the quay, sweeping Effie into his arms and laughing, always laughing. There'd been precious little laughter in this house since the accident. But Albert's good nature and joy in life had kept him going far longer than they had expected – that and the love and support of his family.

Daisy swallowed the lump in her throat, drank her tea and tried to act normally, telling her that Georgina was also going to Malta.

Effie sniffed. 'I'd have thought you'd had enough of the Davenports after the way they treated you,' she said.

'Georgina's not like the rest of them. She's turned out to be a very good nurse and we've even become friends.'

'People like us can't be friends with the likes of them,' Effie said.

Daisy didn't reply, not wanting to upset her. But she gasped when her mother said, 'That's what I told that young man when he came knocking. No good you coming round now saying you're worried about how my Daisy's managing since you threw her out. We don't want anything to do with you or your family. That's what I told him.' Effie set her cup down firmly, slopping some tea in the saucer.

'Jack came here? When – when was he here?' Daisy's hand shook as she grabbed her mother's arm.

'This morning.'

Daisy felt the blood drain from her face. Jack was back in England already and he'd come looking for her. Why hadn't he come to the hospital? 'You sent him away?' she almost screamed. 'Oh, Mum, how could you?'

Effie face set in a stubborn grimace. 'Yes, I sent him away. I saw which way the wind was blowing when you were up there at the Hall. Master Jack this and Master Jack that. You'd have been in trouble soon enough. Maybe it's a good thing they sacked you.'

'Mum, how can you say that? I would never . . .' Daisy was near to tears.

Effie put her arm round her. 'I know you wouldn't do anything wrong, love. But people like that, they take advantage. That's why I sent him away.' Effie dropped her arms and sighed. 'He'll never marry you, Daisy love. You must know that.'

Daisy nodded slowly. Her mother had put into words her own fears and in the process dashed her hopes to the ground. Her common sense told her Mum was right. Davenports didn't marry the daughters of poor fishermen. Despite her conviction that Jack returned her feelings, she knew deep down it had been a foolish dream. Maybe it was just as well that her mother had turned him away. She had to face up to reality. She returned the hug and changed the subject. It was getting late and she had to get back.

Albert was still sleeping and she bent to kiss his cheek. 'Goodbye, dear Dad. I'll try to come again soon,' she promised.

CHAPTER EIGHT

Daisy managed to choke back her sobs until she was away from the cottage and turned towards the harbour wall, trying to get herself under control before attempting the walk back up the hill. The sun reflecting off the water combined with her tears to blind her and she reeled in alarm as a figure loomed beside her. She side-stepped, ready to give Ernest Jenkins a piece of her mind.

But the man who took hold of her arm spoke before she had a chance to pull away. 'Don't you know me, Daisy? I know it's been a long time but I hope you haven't forgotten me.'

Daisy gave a nervous laugh. 'Master Jack? Is it really you?'

Only a few minutes ago she'd been telling herself it was for the best if she didn't see Jack again. But now, his warm smile, the blue eyes gazing into hers, turned her knees to jelly. She was sure she'd have fallen if he hadn't held on to her arm. The warmth of his hand through her sleeve travelled through her whole body. Was he really here?

He was laughing down at her. 'Not Master Jack – just plain Jack, if you please. Or you can call me Lieutenant Davenport and I'll call you Nurse March, if you insist on the formalities.' He cupped her chin in his hand. 'Tears – again. Last time I saw you, you were crying. I hope my family aren't to blame this time.' His finger brushed the moisture away from her cheeks.

Daisy shook her head and tried to speak but the tears still flowed. Only now, she wasn't crying for her father. It was true then, she thought. It was possible to cry from happiness too.

Jack pulled her towards him, guiding her into the shelter of a doorway. There he held her head against his shoulder, stroking her hair until her tears dried. 'I went to the hospital first with Tom. He's taken Georgina out to tea – she told me it was your day off. I had to see you before we sail again. And Georgina tells me you're both leaving for Malta soon.'

'I want to go but I feel awful leaving Dad like this,' she said, telling him how ill her father was now.

'I'm sure he understands. He wouldn't want you to feel guilty,' Jack replied.

He was silent for a moment and Daisy wondered what he was thinking. His hand still stroked her hair, while his other arm held her close to him. She savoured the moment. Now, at last, he would say the words she longed to hear. Why else had he sought her out, if not to let her know that he felt the same way as she did?

She had to say something. 'My mother told me she'd sent you away. I thought I'd never see you again.'

'We Davenports don't give up so easily,' he said. 'Daisy, you remember the last time we met? I've thought of you constantly since then.'

How could she forget? 'I've thought of you too, Jack,' she murmured, waiting breathlessly. Now he would say it, she thought.

But instead of words of love, he spoke abruptly. 'This damned war. When will it be over?' Then he drew her to him again. 'Daisy, my love, I can't make promises. It wouldn't be fair, the way things are. But when it's all over . . .'

She gazed into his eyes, her own full of hope. Instead of speaking he pulled her to him and kissed her. It was nothing like the brief hard kiss of their last parting. This was sweet and sensuous, stirring feelings she had only imagined before. She could have stayed there forever, oblivious to the curious stares of any passers-by.

When he let her go at last, he gave a shaky laugh. 'I don't want to let you go but I must. I'm on duty this evening.'

'So am I,' she replied.

'I hope it won't be too long before we see each other again. You never know, our ship might put in to Malta.' He grasped her shoulders. 'You will write to me, won't you?'

'Of course,' Daisy said. 'But I wish you didn't have to leave so soon.' Tears threatened again.

Jack held her away from him and looked into her eyes. 'Don't cry, Daisy-bell. You don't know how much I've been looking forward to seeing your lovely smile – not floods of tears.'

He pulled her towards him and kissed her again. 'Darling Daisy-bell, you must know how I feel about you.'

He still hadn't said he loved her – not in so many words – but Daisy was sure now. 'Oh, Jack,' she whispered.

Then she heard the mocking laugh from behind her. 'So, my saintly brother's not above seducing maids after all. All that talk about the family honour indeed.'

Daisy gasped as over Jack's shoulder she saw Philip's sneering face.

Jack whirled to face his brother. 'What are you doing here?'

'Maybe I came to see the delightful Daisy,' he mocked. 'Well, it's a good job I'm keeping an eye on you. What would Mama say if she knew you'd been tumbling one of her former maids right here in town? At least I'm discreet.'

'It's not like that at all, Philip.'

'I can see exactly what it's like,' Philip drawled, his insolent gaze raking Daisy's body. She felt herself grow hot with shame. Please, tell him you love me, that we're going to be married, she begged silently.

But Jack appeared to have forgotten her presence as he stepped up to his brother with clenched fists.

Philip laughed again. 'Now I know why you lost your temper that time. You wanted her for yourself. Well, don't be a dog in the manger, old man. Didn't Mama bring us up to share our goodies?'

Daisy didn't wait to hear more. She turned and ran down the narrow street, her sobs deafening her to Jack's pleas for her to stop and let him explain. Coming so soon after her conversation with her mother and the revived memories of Philip's attempted rape, she didn't want to hear any explanation he might have.

Jack hadn't actually mentioned love or marriage, although for a moment she'd been so sure. She suppressed the thought that perhaps he was just better at seducing maids than his brother was, using soft words instead of brute strength. Could her mother have been right? She leaned against a low wall, breathing heavily. As her breathing slowed, she realized she'd overreacted. Deep down she knew Jack had been sincere. She looked back towards the harbour. But there was no sign of Jack – or his brother.

She was almost late and, in the confusion of changing over shifts, she pushed her personal concerns to one side. They were frantically busy and when she fell into bed long after her shift should have ended, she couldn't sleep. Instead, she relived those tender moments with Jack before Philip had turned up and spoiled everything. If only Jack had said 'I love you', asked her to marry him. Surely he knew she wasn't the sort of girl to settle for less. Perhaps she should write to him, explain why she'd reacted so hastily?

'Things always look better in the morning,' her mother was fond of saying. But Daisy couldn't agree when Sarah woke her with an urgent shake and the message that Albert had taken a turn for the worse and Matron had given permission for her to go home.

'I hope you're in time,' Sarah said, watching anxiously as Daisy threw on her uniform and hastily pinned up her hair.

The lump in her throat stopped her from replying. As she hurried through the quiet streets towards the cottage, her thoughts were only for her father. It wasn't until she neared her home that an image of Jack intruded. Was it only yesterday? She'd been so happy for those brief moments. But only Dad mattered now.

She entered the cottage at a run. Effie was at the bedside, her face drawn with grief. Daisy pulled up a chair beside her and they sat silently, each holding a hand as Albert's ragged breathing became fainter and gradually ceased.

The day after the funeral, seeing Daisy onto the train for Southampton, Effie was silent, holding tightly to Billy's arm. How could she leave her family now? she asked herself. But she had no choice but to follow orders. She kissed her mother's cheek, holding back the tears with difficulty. Turning to Billy she hugged him fiercely, saying, 'Look after Mum, won't you?' This time he didn't try to squirm away as he usually did.

The train pulled out and Daisy sat down opposite an excited Georgina and Sarah but she couldn't share their excitement. As they neared Southampton she glimpsed the grey outlines of the ships in the harbour and inevitably her thoughts turned to Jack. Georgina followed her gaze. She'd recounted every minute of her romantic meeting with Tom but Daisy had been unable to reciprocate.

She had told Georgina she'd quarrelled with Jack, letting her friend assume that her reservations about their different stations in life had caused it. She couldn't bring herself to mention Philip. Georgina, predictably, had told her not to be so silly.

She had gone over every moment of their meeting and realized she'd acted too hastily. Philip had been trying to cause trouble. If only she'd stayed to listen. In her heart, she didn't believe he was like his brother. Was it too late now? She'd written saying she was due to sail and hoped there'd be a reply awaiting her when they docked. Somehow, she doubted it. But she prayed for his safety and that their paths would cross one day. Deep inside, scarcely acknowledged, was the hope that she might get a second chance.

CHAPTER NINE

Daisy's first sight of Malta wasn't at all how she'd pictured it. Instead of the baked terraces of brown and beige rising out of the vivid blue sea of her imagination, the island was almost hidden behind a curtain of squally rain. The ship surged and swayed beneath her feet and she clutched at the rail, her knuckles white with cold.

'I wish I'd brought gloves. I thought it would be warm out here,' she said, shivering.

Sarah Bowman nodded agreement. 'One of the sailors told me it's the start of the rainy season. I didn't even realize they had one.'

Daisy's reply was lost as a violent clap of thunder and lightning streaked across the purple sky, briefly illuminating the tops of the waves. At least we're in sight of land, she thought. It couldn't be long now.

Unlike most of the nurses, Daisy hadn't been seasick, but she still longed for the moment when the ground under her feet stayed still and her eyes no longer had to adjust to a moving skyline. I'm the daughter of a fisherman, she told herself, the sea is in my blood. To think she used to envy the boys when they went out in the boat with Dad.

Sarah pulled at her arm. 'Let's go below. I'm freezing.'

'I think I'll stay up here. We'll be landing soon.'

At the harbour entrance Daisy watched the sailors manoeuvring the huge ship, skilfully avoiding the small boats which had been kept in harbour by the storm. In the gathering dusk Daisy noticed how different they were from the fleet at home with their brightly painted hulls and pointed prows. Still, the sight gave her a pang of homesickness, which was quickly dispelled as Sarah and Georgina came back carrying their bags.

'Thanks. I couldn't bear to go back down there. The heat and the smell were really getting unbearable.'

'No worse than what we'll have to put up with when we get to the hospital, I expect,' Sarah said.

Georgina shuddered, then grinned. 'Think of it as an adventure,' she said.

Daisy couldn't help smiling but she still felt apprehensive as they crowded towards the gang plank and finally set foot on dry land.

They were greeted on the quayside by an orderly with a clipboard who ushered them into a truck. For those who'd been suffering from seasickness, the drive to the hospital along twisting roads, bumping over pot-holes, was the last straw and the air was filled with groans and sobs.

Now that they were here, Daisy felt a return of her earlier optimism. After all, nursing here couldn't be much different from at home. And here she was, abroad at last. Who'd have thought she'd ever travel like this? She remembered her envy when Georgina was planning to honeymoon in Paris. What a turn both their lives had taken.

The truck bumped to a stop in front of a long low building. 'Here we are, ladies,' the orderly said as they jumped down and stood in a confused huddle. 'This is the new hospital where you'll be based. Follow me and I'll show you to your quarters.'

By now too tired to take in her surroundings, Daisy followed her friends into a hut to leave their bags. Then they trailed along behind the orderly to the mess hut where most of them could only manage a little of the supper they were served. Daisy hoped it was only her tiredness that made the food seem so unappetizing. She smiled, remembering her mother's saying that things always looked better in the morning, as she followed her friends back to their quarters where she fell into an exhausted sleep.

Daisy woke next morning to bright sunshine falling across her bed. She got up and looked out of the window, where far below sunlight sparkled on a turquoise sea reflecting the blue of the sky. Last night's storm might have been a dream, she thought, as she hastily washed and dressed. This was more how she'd imagined Malta.

By the time she'd combed her hair, bundling her thick waves under the starched cap and securing it with pins, Sarah was already up. She tied the strings of her apron, straightening the bib and smoothing the skirt and she and Sarah walked across a small courtyard to the other hut where the VADs were quartered. Georgina came out with a group of girls, laughing and chattering, her seasickness already forgotten.

After breakfast they assembled to be given their orders. Daisy was disappointed when both Sarah and Georgina were sent to different wards. She found herself under the supervision of Sister Hatton, a nurse with sharp eyes and rigid bearing, who informed Daisy that she was the only qualified nurse assigned to this wing.

'We have half a dozen VADs to do the routine work,' Sister said, 'so I shall be relying on you heavily.'

Daisy nodded, hoping Sister wouldn't realize that, despite her two years' experience, she wasn't yet fully qualified.

'Oh, and please bear in mind that there is to be no fraternizing with the patients. They will persist in falling in love with the nurses and the silly girls encourage them.' Sister's lips tightened. 'I will not have my nurses falling in love, Nurse March.'

Daisy nodded. 'I'm not likely to do that, Sister,' she stammered.

'I hope not,' Sister snapped.

Daisy nodded. It was true. But what if Jack was brought in as a patient? She couldn't bear the thought and forcibly turned her attention back to Sister Hatton.

'Well, to work,' Sister said briskly. She introduced her to the two VADs who were on duty and then led her on a round of the ward.

To her surprise very few of the men had physical wounds, although they looked sick. 'What's wrong with them?' she asked, back in Sister Hatton's office.

'Dysentery mostly. They were lying in the open while waiting for evacuation from the peninsular with no water, no sanitation, then crowded onto the ships like cattle. No wonder infection spread so rapidly. Many of them died before they reached port.'

'Shouldn't they be sent home?' Daisy asked. 'They look very weak.'

'The worst cases will be. The rest will go back to their units when – if – they recover sufficiently.'

'Poor lads,' Daisy whispered and couldn't help thinking of her brothers in France.

'They're safer here,' Sister assured her with a momentary softening of her stern features. 'You know yourself how much danger there still is from the German U-boats. There aren't enough hospital ships to take them home and even those aren't safe from attack.'

Daisy nodded, remembering the *Britannic*, which had been torpedoed earlier in the year while carrying nurses and orderlies. She'd tried not to think about it on the voyage.

And there was no time to think of it now as she was plunged into the hectic routine of the ward. With so few staff and inadequate supplies it was a wonder the men survived, let alone recovered, Daisy thought as she moved briskly from one bed to another.

The hospital consisted of a series of long two-storeyed buildings with verandas along each side. The nurses were housed in huts behind the hospital. Convalescing patients were wheeled out on to the verandas where those facing the sparkling water of St George's Bay could enjoy the early morning sun before it got too hot.

Daisy soon found that she was too exhausted to think about her family back home, or even to worry about Jack. The hours were long and the work arduous and she wondered with an amused grin how any of the staff had the energy, let alone the time, for dallying with the patients.

'It's ridiculous the way Sister prowls around, looking for trouble,' she said to Sarah as they prepared for bed after a long demanding shift.

'I agree. I found one poor little VAD sobbing her heart out in the sluice the other day. Sister Dragon had given her a ticking off simply because one of the men grabbed her hand and kissed it. The poor lad was half delirious and thought she was his sweetheart.'

Daisy giggled at the nickname. 'Your Sister Drummond is far worse than my dragon. Hatton's very strict but I know she turns a blind eye sometimes. She only steps in when things look like getting out of hand.'

'Wish ours was like that.' Sarah finished brushing her teeth and jumped into bed. 'Let's hope we get a quiet night. I'm exhausted.'

Daisy agreed but, despite her tiredness, she couldn't sleep. Her conversation with Sarah had made her think of Jack. Suppose he turned up at the hospital. Would she get the chance to speak to him? But he must have got her letter and if he'd forgiven her for doubting him, surely he'd have replied by now.

They had been in Malta for several weeks and Georgina confided in Daisy that she'd had no word from her brother. He hadn't replied to her letter either. Daisy was beginning to worry.

Georgina was looking tired and had lost her sparkle in recent weeks. Daisy was worried about her too. Life at the hospital was hectic and the hours of duty long and arduous. In addition to the sheer numbers of patients, the nurses were hampered by the constant battle to maintain hygiene. It could just be that her friend was suffering from exhaustion but Daisy was sure there was something on her mind. Was it just the worry about Jack and Tom?

Daisy was exhausted too. She'd spent the morning washing towels as there were no clean ones available. There was only a cold water tap and all the washing, including dressing bowls and bandages, had to be done in one sink. Supplies of everything were low and although more were expected on the next ship they were never sure if they'd even reach the island.

'I really didn't believe how bad it was going to be,' Daisy said to Sarah as they managed to meet up for a brief lunch break.

'How they expect these poor lads to get well in these conditions, I don't know,' Sarah agreed. 'You'd think we'd at least have proper sheets instead of those rough old army blankets.'

'Thank goodness the rain's stopped for a bit,' Daisy consoled her. 'Maybe the towels will have dried by the time I get back.'

Sarah picked at her food, glancing at her watch. 'I suppose we'd better go. Besides, I can't eat any more of this.'

'You must eat, Sarah. I'm worried enough about Georgina without you getting sick.'

'I'm just so fed up with all this tinned and dried stuff. When I went down to the town yesterday on an errand for Sister, they had all this lovely fresh fruit in the market. It made my mouth water but one of the other girls said not to touch it unless I wanted to be laid low with an upset stomach.'

'I know, it's so frustrating. The men could do with fresh stuff as well. What with the water and the local milk being unsafe as well, it's a wonder we manage to get them fit at all,' Daisy agreed.

'I couldn't understand why we didn't use goat's milk. You'd think it would be nourishing enough. But I asked Sister Drummond and she said it carries some disease – Malta Fever they call it, although it's got some proper medical name.'

Daisy sighed and stood up to go back to work. The supplies of food and dried milk from England were the least of her worries at the moment. For the past couple of weeks her life had been dominated by the fact that there was no news from home and now that there was, it had only brought more worry. Her mother had written that Sir John Davenport had gambled away the family's home, leaving them penniless. Now she knew what had been troubling Georgina.

'Was that a letter from your mother?' Sarah asked, echoing her thoughts.

'Yes. Nothing from the boys though. Maybe I'll get several letters at once when the next ship arrives.'

'Is everything all right?'

'Yes,' Daisy answered shortly as they parted at the entrance to the ward. She knew Sarah was genuinely concerned, but she also knew that the other girl loved a gossip, so she was reluctant to talk about Georgina's family. It was none of her business, after all.

Instead of joining Sarah in the mess as usual at the end of her shift, Daisy went in search of Georgina, calling a greeting as she saw her crossing the compound.

The other girl turned and Daisy recoiled in shock at the expression on her face. 'Come to gloat, have you? I suppose you think we're equal now that my family's in the gutter too.' Her face was white and the blue eyes glittered. 'I suppose it's you that's been telling everyone what's happened.'

Daisy put out a placating hand. 'How could you think that? I wanted to tell you how sorry I was. I know there's nothing I can do but I thought it might help to talk. . . .'

'I don't think I want to talk to you, Nurse March,' Georgina said, straightening her shoulders and holding back tears with a visible effort.

'Georgina, please – I thought we were friends.' What had got into her?

'After the way you treated my brother, I don't think so,' Georgina said.

Daisy's heart sank. Jack must have written to his sister, telling her why she'd rejected him. The injustice of it welled up and she spoke without thinking.

'What about the way he treated me – the way both your brothers treated me? You weren't there.' Her voice broke. 'I was right to get angry. Just because I was a servant doesn't mean I don't have feelings too.'

'But you didn't give Jack a chance to explain. He was heartbroken.'

Despite Daisy's efforts to tell her side of the story, Georgina wouldn't listen. 'If you'll excuse me, I have to go on duty,' she said with dignity. She walked towards the ward entrance but Daisy followed her.

'Can't we meet after your shift and talk this over?' she asked.

'No. And it's no use you writing to Jack. You wouldn't stand a chance with him.'

Before Daisy could reply, the door to the ward swung open to reveal Sister, eyes blazing angrily.

'What on earth is going on here? I will not have raised voices in my ward. Whatever your quarrel is, please remember the patients. I will not have them disturbed by such unladylike behaviour.' She turned to Georgina. 'Nurse Davenport, you were due on duty five minutes ago. And Nurse March, I'm sure you have business elsewhere.'

Georgina, her face scarlet, muttered a hasty 'Sorry, Sister,' and scuttled into the ward.

Daisy walked away, her thoughts in turmoil. After working together for so long, she thought they'd really become friends. For her part she had long since shed her prejudices about empty-headed society girls playing at nurses. She'd always been fond of Georgina but since the war had thrown them together she'd come to respect the other girl's dedication and hard work. Perhaps Mum was right, Daisy thought. They might be able to work together but real friendship with someone of a different class just wasn't possible. And what about love? she asked herself. Would it have worked? Probably not.

But she couldn't help a little lift of the heart. Could it be true that Jack had been as heartbroken as Georgina had said? Had his feelings been genuine after all? If only she'd given him the benefit of the doubt. She made up her mind. She didn't care what Georgina had said. She *would* write to him again – she just prayed he'd understand.

When she went in to supper, she was dismayed to hear Sarah and the other girls discussing the scandal about Georgina's family. She didn't join in and she wished there was something she could do to help her friend. She didn't blame Georgina for suspecting her of spreading gossip but she was determined to put things right between them. For one thing, another scene like the one Sister had witnessed would do nothing for her professional standing in the hospital. Besides, their differences seemed petty when she realized how unhappy Georgina must be about what had happened to her family.

Later, when she sat down to write to Jack, she didn't mention what had happened. Instead she wrote from the heart, holding back none of her feelings. She hoped that he'd understand and forgive her quick-tempered reaction to the confrontation with Philip. She didn't say that she'd written before – he might not have got the letter anyway.

Once she'd sealed it, she felt a lot happier. It was up to Jack now, she thought.

Despite her intention to make things right between them, there was no chance to see Georgina during the next few days. A sudden increase in patients from a new offensive in the Dardanelles meant more pressures of work for all the nurses.

Daisy was washing bandages and dressing bowls in the little sluice room off the ward when Sarah came in, her eyes alight.

'I know that look. What is it now?' Daisy asked with a laugh.

Looking round carefully to make sure no one was in earshot she whispered, 'It's all round the hospital. You know about the Davenports losing all their money? Now they're saying Sir John not only gambled everything away, he stole to pay his debts.'

Daisy sighed. 'It's hardly Georgina's fault, is it?' She was surprised that the normally good-natured Sarah seemed to be enjoying the other girl's misfortune. 'Anyway, I thought you liked her.'

'She's not so bad, I suppose,' Sarah said. 'But it's not just her – it's all these snobby upper-class girls thinking they're better than us.'

'Sarah, that's not fair. I felt the same way as you at first. But they've more than proved themselves – especially Georgina.' Daisy finished rinsing the bowls and stacked them on the trolley. She was annoyed but she knew it was a common prejudice.

Sarah followed her from the room, clearly intent on carrying on the conversation, but Daisy stopped her. 'I hope you're not going to repeat this. After all, we don't know if it's true, do we? And how do you think Georgina feels?'

Daisy sighed, picturing the furtive looks, the sudden hush of conversation as she entered the room. It was time to make up their squabble.

CHAPTER TEN

Georgina was convinced that Daisy had spread the story of her family's disgrace. Who else would have known? It must have been her. And to think she'd tried to be friends, she thought as she sat in her room, trying to write a letter home. She chewed the end of her pen and gazed out at the sparkling waters of the bay. A cool breeze brought the scent of the spring flowers and herbs which now clothed the dusty hillside through the window. But she closed her mind to the beauty of the scene.

She hadn't written to her parents since hearing the news. What did you say to someone who had brought scandal and disgrace to them all? She felt thoroughly miserable, but anger had the upper hand.

I'll never forgive him, never, she thought fiercely, snatching up a fresh sheet of paper. She wrote furiously, covering several sheets of paper in her large scrawling writing. That would show him, she told herself with satisfaction as she blotted the pages and sealed the envelope. She would write to Mama later.

She hurried down the corridor to put the letter with the outgoing post. If she hesitated, she wouldn't send it and she wanted her father to know just how she felt. It wasn't the loss of her home that had upset her, although she loved Ryfe Hall and was sad that now she would never return. It was the way her mother had been treated that hurt. Mama had put up with a lot from the man she'd married, turned a blind eye to his infidelities, watched as her fortune trickled away through his mismanagement and pleasure-seeking. She didn't deserve this. And neither do I, Georgina thought, as the tears started again.

She spotted Daisy crossing the compound and on impulse ran after her. 'I hope you're having a good laugh behind my back,' she called, her voice loud and harsh.

Daisy spun round. 'But I didn't—'

Giving her no chance to speak, Georgina pushed her against the wall. 'It must have been you; no one else here knows my family. You don't know what it's like, having everyone sniggering behind my back.' She punctuated each phrase with another push.

Daisy put her hands up to fend her off. 'Look, Georgina, I know you're upset. But it won't help matters if Sister catches us arguing again. We'll get sent up before Matron and that won't do either of us any good.'

'You needn't worry. You've wormed your way into Matron's good books. I dare say you hope to end up as a sister yourself before much longer. But you wouldn't stand much chance if they knew what I know.'

'What do you mean?' Daisy said, wriggling away from Georgina's flailing hands.

'Suppose they knew you'd been dismissed from Ryfe Hall for stealing?' Georgina knew she was behaving childishly but the words were out before she could stop them.

'You know I never took it,' Daisy said. She looked as if she were about to cry. 'I thought that was all ancient history now.'

Suddenly Georgina wished she hadn't uttered those hasty words. Her shoulders slumped. 'Don't worry, I won't tell anyone,' she said. 'But I won't forgive you either.'

Before Daisy could reply she turned and walked quickly away.

It was hard to ignore the covert looks of her colleagues but Georgina determined to get on with her job and not let it worry her. There were more important things to concern her, like the survivors of a torpedoed cruiser who'd been sent up from the naval hospital. She could only thank God that it wasn't Tom's ship.

When she'd calmed down, she regretted quarrelling with Daisy. On reflection, she couldn't really believe she was to blame for the gossip. Perhaps she'd got it all out of proportion. It was so easy to lash out at the nearest person when you were hurt and angry.

Georgina was right about other sources of gossip taking over from the speculation about her family's misfortunes but she was quite dismayed on going in to breakfast a few days later to find that this time the object of the whispers was Daisy herself.

It was Nurse Bowman who confronted her. 'Is it true?' she asked.

Georgina nodded.

'But how did she manage to get into nursing with no references?'

'I don't know. I do know she wasn't guilty though,' Georgina said.

'I know you've quarrelled but it's a bit spiteful to spread stories like that especially as you say she didn't do it.'

'You must believe me,' Georgina said. 'I'm not that vindictive.'

'But no one else knew. Who else could it have been?' Sarah looked at her accusingly and Georgina knew that she wasn't convinced.

'Well, it wasn't me – please believe me, Sarah. And if you hear anyone gossiping about it you must tell them she didn't steal my ring. It was all a misunderstanding.' She pushed her plate away, unable to finish her breakfast. How she wished she could take back those hasty words of a few days ago. She stood up, scraping her chair on the stone floor. She must see Daisy and, if necessary, she would brave Sister's wrath and confront her on the ward.

But she didn't get the chance. Daisy was on the night shift and was asleep in her hut on the far side of the compound. She'd be late on duty if she confronted her now.

When she reached the ward, Sister Drummond was consulting a list and looking harassed. 'Ah, Nurse Davenport, you're to escort these men on the ferry to Sicily.' She held out the list. 'They're being sent home but they need a nurse in attendance. Someone else will take over when you reach port.'

Georgina was pleased to be given the responsibility, as well as welcoming the chance of a break from routine. If only she'd had time to talk to Daisy before she left, though. She had soon realized it was too much of a coincidence for both of them to become the subject of gossip in the past few days. But who could possibly be to blame?

Daisy was well aware of the whispers circulating about her but she refused to believe that Georgina had carried out her threat. She might be hot-headed and impetuous sometimes, but she'd never been spiteful. It must be the same person who'd spread the story about Georgina's family – but who?

Sarah insisted it must have been Georgina. 'She thought you were gossiping about her and she's getting her own back,' she said in her forth-right way.

'I won't believe it till I've heard it from her,' Daisy declared. 'In the meantime, I hope I can rely on you to stick up for me.'

Sarah put her arm round Daisy. 'Don't worry, your friends don't believe it.'

If only Georgina would get back from her trip to Sicily so that they could thrash things out, Daisy thought. Surely, once everyone saw that they were friends again, they'd realize that there was nothing in the rumours.

It was a very uncomfortable few days for her, but as usual she took refuge in her work. Many of their original patients had been sent home to convalesce, or back to their units when they were declared fit, but there were always plenty more to take their place.

*

A few days later, lost in thought, Daisy smiled absently as she hurried along the corridor, passing a soldier on crutches. But when he called her name, she shivered as she recognized the hated voice. She would have ignored him and continued on her way but the clatter of one of his crutches falling to the ground halted her.

Reluctantly, she turned back as he whined, 'Come on, Daisy, I need a hand here. You wouldn't leave a poor wounded soldier to struggle by himself, would you?' Despite the lines of pain, the old smirk still twisted Ernest Jenkins' face.

She retrieved the crutch, sure that he'd dropped it on purpose. Inwardly trembling, trying to maintain her professional demeanour, she handed it to him, flinching as he grabbed her arm. Was he merely trying to steady himself? The memory of the last time he'd laid hands on her almost overwhelmed her. But he couldn't hurt her now, could he?

She took a deep breath, resolving to treat him as she would any other patient. 'Perhaps you should get back to the ward, Jenkins,' she said, surprised at how steady her voice sounded. 'You shouldn't be wandering around on your own. You could have had a nasty fall.'

'Well, Daisy, I heard you was working here and I couldn't pass up the chance of seeing you again. I made it my business to find out where you were.'

Daisy's face burned. The cheek of the man. She was about to make an angry retort when he glared at her, his eyes glittering with hatred. 'You made trouble for me back in Kingsbourne. Don't be surprised if I make trouble for you.'

Now everything made sense. He had spread those stories. But she spoke calmly. 'You made trouble for yourself, Jenkins – hanging around the hospital and making a nuisance of yourself.' She held the ward door open. 'By the way, it's Nurse March – not Daisy.'

She hurried away but she sensed he was still there, his eyes boring into her. She only hoped he'd be shipped home before he could make more trouble.

When she got back to her ward, she was still trembling. Later, when Doctor Holloway made his rounds, she asked him about Ernest's wounds. If the doctor was surprised by her interest in his patient, he didn't show it. Daisy told him that she knew him from home. 'We used to work together,' she explained briefly.

He nodded thoughtfully. 'Corporal Jenkins wasn't too badly wounded,' he said. 'Luckily, he escaped infection, unlike some of his fellows.

However, there's no chance of him returning to the front. It will be a long time before he's able to walk without crutches, and I'm afraid he'll always have a limp.'

'So, he'll be sent home soon?' Daisy said, unable to hide her gasp of relief when Doctor Holloway nodded.

He smiled kindly, perhaps mistaking her reaction for sympathy that at least one of their patients would be spared the horrors of returning to battle. If only he knew, Daisy thought. How she wished that he was going back to the Salonika front. She didn't suffer one pang of guilt for her wicked thought.

When Georgina returned to Valletta she was impatient to see Daisy and apologize for her hasty words. She could understand why Daisy had blamed her for spreading the story of the lost ring. It was clear that someone wanted to hurt both of them. But who?

As she stepped off the ferry she was met by an orderly, who told her that, instead of returning to the hospital, she was to escort another group of patients to Sicily. Her apology would have to wait. Frustrated, she joined the waiting group, most sporting bandages, walking sticks or crutches. As she helped them up the gangplank on to the ferry, one of them addressed her by name.

'You don't know me, Miss Georgina, do you?' he said

She looked closely, recognizing her father's former chauffeur. 'Jenkins. I didn't realize you were here.'

'It's a small world, miss, so they say.' He swung his crutches with practised ease and boarded the boat. 'It's Corporal Jenkins now, miss. Who'd have thought we'd see such changes in such a short time, eh?'

Georgina had never really liked him, and she winced at his words. He must be referring to what had happened back home. She ignored his insinuation and asked how long he'd been in the hospital.

'I was wounded on the first day here. But I'm on the mend now, miss, and off to dear old Blighty.' He coughed and lowered his eyes. 'Sorry to hear about your troubles. Must have come as quite a shock to you – being out here away from your family.'

Georgina bit back the angry retort, fighting the feeling of revulsion. His words were sympathetic but something in his eyes told her he was revelling in her discomfort.

She forced a smile and said briskly, 'I must go and see to the rest of the men.'

But he wasn't ready to let her go. He indicated his crutches and plastered leg, saying mournfully, 'I'm going home but I don't know when I'll work again – not that I've got a job to go back to.'

Georgina coloured. It wasn't her fault. 'I'm sorry, there's nothing I can do about that.' She turned away and helped one of the other soldiers to a seat by the boat's rail.

She hoped to be able to avoid Ernest during the short journey across the strait but a little later he appeared at her side.

'I saw that Daisy March in the hospital – her what stole your ring. You want to watch her, miss,' he said. 'Getting above herself if you ask me.' He turned away, but not before Georgina had seen the malicious smile on his thin face.

What a nasty little man, she thought, beginning to shake as his meaning dawned on her. He knew about her family's troubles; he knew Daisy was here in Malta. His twisted smirk told her that it was he who'd been telling tales. Should she confront him? Perhaps not. He was on his way home and couldn't do any further mischief.

Now she was determined that when she returned she would talk to Daisy and clear the air once and for all. And from now on she would let nothing spoil their friendship.

Two days later she was back in Valletta and she waited impatiently for the ferry to dock. She must get back to the hospital and hope to find Daisy off duty. She was prepared for a rebuff but if necessary she would lock her in the sluice until she listened.

She was rehearsing what to say when she heard her name called. There was Daisy on the quay. Now's your chance, she told herself as she hurried down the gangway. But before she could speak, Daisy threw her arms round her. 'Oh, Georgina, I'm so sorry. How could I have let that horrid little man come between us like this?'

Georgina gently pushed her away, smiling at her friend. 'We are talking about the same horrid little man, I take it?'

'How did you know?'

'He was on the ferry,' she said. 'He didn't admit it in so many words, but it must have been him. You should have seen the look in his eyes – pure malice. I can understand him having it in for me and my family – losing his job and all.'

'But he would have been called up eventually anyway. It's not your fault, Georgina – none of it is.'

'But why pick on you?'

Daisy took a deep breath and finally told Georgina what had happened back in Kingsbourne. Georgina gasped. 'Why didn't you tell me before this?'

'I didn't tell anyone – it was too dreadful.' She gave a little laugh. 'Anyway, I managed to fight him off so no harm done. But he didn't take it too well and started hanging around the hospital. He wouldn't leave me alone,' she said. 'That's why I applied to come here.'

'You should have confided in me before now. I would have made sure he was sacked,' Georgina said. 'Well, he can't hurt us now. Come on, I need a nice cup of tea.'

Daisy laughed shakily. There was nothing like a 'nice' cup of tea in Malta since they'd been forbidden to use local milk and supplies of the dried variety were almost non-existent.

Once their colleagues saw that Daisy and Georgina were friends again, the gossip died a natural death. There was too much else going on, not least the increasing naval casualties.

Georgina hadn't heard from either Jack or Tom recently and each time a new intake of patients arrived she steeled herself to ask for the name of the ship. The constant fear that they would be brought in, combined with long shifts and lack of sleep, had etched lines of tension on her face. She was no longer the carefree girl she'd once been.

There was little leisure time in the early summer months of 1916. The nurses no longer stuck to their strict rotas, staying on duty as long as they were needed and crawling into bed exhausted.

Usually, Georgina was too tired to write letters but tonight she found the energy to scribble a brief note to Tom. She'd been writing since the start of the war, cheerful friendly epistles such as she might send to her brother. And he'd replied in the same vein. She treasured the letters, re-reading them in the limited privacy of her quarters until they were tattered and almost illegible. It was hard to sound cheerful, to keep the note of anxiety from intruding, but after much scratching out she finished and got into bed.

Next morning she put the letter with the outgoing mail, hoping there might be one for her, if not from Tom, then from her parents. After posting that impulsive letter to her father, she wished she could retract her angry words. But it was too late. She'd written to her mother, hoping she'd understand. So far, there'd been no reply.

As she approached the row of boxes nailed to the wall near the front entrance, she could see an envelope sticking out. She snatched it up. It was from Tom – and this one was different. It started off '*My Dearest*

Georgie' and she read on avidly, her heart pounding.

Her family's misfortune seemed to have paved the way for a declaration of his true feelings. *'I realize that your parents would not have looked favourably on me in former times. But the change in your circumstances gives me hope. I can offer you so little in the material things your parents would deem necessary. But the little I have, is yours, together with my heart and my everlasting love,'* he wrote.

Georgina sighed and clutched the sheets of paper to her breast. That was all she'd ever wanted – his love. He went on to remind her of that Christmas before the war when he had so nearly declared his feelings. *'I could not speak out then. But later, when your brother told me you had broken your engagement, I dared to hope that it might be because you loved me.'* He finished by begging her to reply *'and make me the happiest man in His Majesty's navy'*. Georgina kissed the place where he had signed his name. She would keep this one for ever, she thought, folding the letter carefully and putting it into her apron pocket.

When she came down from her cloud of euphoria, she wondered why the post had brought nothing from Jack. He and Tom were on the same ship, after all. Thoughts of Jack inevitably made her think of Daisy and she hoped that her friend would find the same happiness as she had with Tom. She was glad they were friends again.

Meantime, there was work to do. As she went about her work with a dreamy smile, she found herself going over his loving words again and again, as she contemplated their rosy future – after the war.

CHAPTER ELEVEN

The high point of all the nurses' lives was getting mail from home. But by late 1917 supplies had become even more sporadic and that included the post. Daisy had long since given up expecting to hear from Jack although Georgina had received two more letters from Tom. Either he hadn't received her letter, or he wasn't going to reply.

It was no good fretting about it – easy to say during the busy hours of ward duty, not so easy when she was lying sleepless through the long nights. And there was the added worry of her family. The sharp grief for her father had given way to a dull ache, but her mother would be feeling the loss far more now that she was alone in the little cottage. Her brothers were still at the front and Billy had given up fishing to join the merchant navy – one more person to worry about, Daisy thought.

She smiled though, thinking of young Billy's pride in contributing to the family income. She always thought of her brothers as she did her rounds of the ward, seeing in the soldiers she nursed an echo of their fresh young faces.

She was trying to coax one of her patients to take a drink of water when one of the newer VADs came into the ward. 'Mail's come,' she announced with a wide smile.

Daisy nodded and felt a flicker of anticipation. Would there be one from Jack this time? She steeled herself against disappointment but she couldn't stop herself from hurrying to the main hall to check her pigeon-hole the minute her shift ended.

But there was only a package from Effie with a note from Billy and a long letter in her mother's neat round handwriting. Daisy quickly skimmed the first page, knowing that any bad news would be there. With a sigh of relief she folded the pages, putting them in her pocket to be read and digested later.

As she walked away, Georgina came towards her. 'Anything for me?' she called.

Daisy looked in the box and pulled out an envelope. 'Here you are.'

Georgina grabbed it, grimacing as she saw it wasn't what she'd hoped for. 'It's from home,' she said.

'I'll leave you to read in peace,' Daisy said and turned away, stopping abruptly as she heard a sound somewhere between a sigh and a groan. She looked back to see Georgina leaning against the wall, a sheet of paper drifting from her hand to the floor.

Jack, she thought immediately, taking in the white shocked face. 'What is it? Tell me.'

'It's my father,' Georgina said, a tear creeping down her cheek. 'He's dead.'

Thank God it wasn't Jack. Daisy knew it was callous of her, but she couldn't feel any sorrow for Sir John. She made soothing noises and led Georgina into a storeroom down the hall. She pushed her down onto a wooden crate and held her in her arms.

'Oh, Daisy, I feel as if it's all my fault,' Georgina sobbed.

'What nonsense. Of course it's not.'

'I was so horrid to him. I wish I hadn't said all those beastly things.'

'But that didn't cause his death. You must understand that,' Daisy said. 'What happened?'

'He's had a heart attack. Died instantly, my mother says.'

'And why should you be blamed for that?'

'When I heard what he'd done I was so angry, I wrote and told him how ashamed and disgusted I was. I said that as far as I was concerned he wasn't my father any more.'

Georgina burst into fresh sobs and Daisy murmured sympathetically, 'But that was months ago.'

'There's nothing left except the London house – Philip and Jane are living there. And my mother's staying with my uncle in Kent,' Georgina told her.

Daisy already knew that Ryfe Hall had been sold and the servants dismissed without their pay. That had been the source of Ernest's vindictiveness towards the family. But Georgina's tears were for her father and the fact that now she would be unable to make amends. Daisy tried to comfort her, but she was still grieving for her own father. At least she had no regrets about their relationship, and she'd been with him at the end.

The sobs diminished and Daisy handed her friend a clean handkerchief. 'Would you like me to speak to Matron – arrange for compassionate leave?' she asked.

'There's not much point really. The funeral's already been held and besides – I haven't got a home now,' Georgina said bitterly.

'You could stay with Philip in London, couldn't you?'

'No, thanks. We've never been close and although Jane's not bad, I think we'd get on each other's nerves after a bit. Philip will be all right though. He's got Jane's money,' Georgina said with a twisted smile. 'And Mama's decided to stay down in Kent so she'll be fine. If only I could see Jack but God knows where he is at the moment.' She almost started to cry again but she choked back the sob and tried to smile. 'I should have married Henry, then none of this would have happened,' she said.

'Marrying him might have been the answer for your family but it would have been wrong for you. Besides, you're not responsible for them and certainly not for your father's heart attack. I expect it was brought on by all the worry.'

Daisy, who had so often had to comfort the relatives of the bereaved, felt she should be able to offer more than platitudes to comfort her friend. But Georgina nodded.

'You're probably right.' she said, standing up and pacing the small cupboard-like room. 'I wish I knew where Jack was.'

So did Daisy. But this was no time to think of her own feelings.

'He knows about the family troubles – Tom mentioned it in his letter,' Georgina continued.

Daisy nodded sympathetically. 'Jack's sure to get in touch soon,' she said reassuringly. But who knew what might have happened since Tom had last written?

'Thanks for being so kind to me. I don't deserve it after the way I behaved.'

'Nonsense. It was just a misunderstanding.'

'We are friends again – aren't we?' Georgina asked, sniffing back a stray tear.

Daisy answered with a hug. 'Now, we should be getting back to work,' she said.

'You haven't heard from Jack either, have you?' Georgina asked, as they hurried back to their wards.

'I don't think he's forgiven me for being so nasty to him last time we met,' Daisy replied.

'I think you're wrong.'

'What makes you say that?'

'Well, you do realize he's in love with you don't you?'

Daisy sighed. 'Love doesn't always mean marriage, Georgie. And I'm not the sort of girl who would settle for less.' But would she, if she had another chance?

'He was very hurt about what happened when he saw you at home that time.' They had reached the entrance to Daisy's ward and she was about to go in when Georgina said, 'I know Jack wouldn't hurt you. Give him a chance, Daisy.'

Daisy smiled and nodded. But she couldn't help wondering why, if what Georgina said was true, Jack hadn't answered her letter. Georgina had heard from Tom, so letters from his ship couldn't have gone astray. Surely he'd have written if he really loved her?

But she wouldn't give up hope, she thought, as she plunged into the round of bedpans and medicines. She was glad that she and Georgina had made up their differences. She'd missed her friend's sunny smile. Not that the poor girl had much to smile about now.

'Christmas Eve! Doesn't seem much like it, does it?' Georgina said with a sigh.

'The third one of the war, let's hope it's the last,' Daisy said. They were in Sister's office, filling stockings to hang at the foot of each patient's bed. Sweets, nuts and cigarettes had been supplied by the Red Cross Comforts Fund and there were small gifts donated by the hospital staff.

'We must do our best to make it special – for the patients' sake,' Georgina said, picking up and sniffing a tablet of soap. 'Who'd have thought this would ever be considered a luxury, especially in a hospital.'

'And razor blades too,' Daisy agreed.

They carried on selecting from the pencils, notebooks and other gifts. Earlier in the day they'd laughed together over their efforts to decorate the ward with makeshift paper chains and greenery. Instead of a Christmas tree, a nativity scene carved by one of the convalescent men stood on a small table surrounded by candles in odd containers. Daisy thought it summed up the spirit of Christmas far better than a gaudy tree.

After supper they turned down the lamps, leaving the ward bathed in soft candlelight, and the nurses gathered to sing carols. Despite the sheen of tears in the eyes of staff and patients, the whole wing of the hospital soon resounded to 'Noel' and 'Adeste Fideles'. As they finished, one young soldier started to sing 'Silent Night', the German carol which transcended all national barriers with its poignant message.

Daisy wasn't the only one crying as the last notes died away. She even noticed a suspicious glint in Doctor Holloway's eye. She turned away when he glanced in her direction and hastily wiped her own eyes as Sister turned up the lamps and the nurses settled the men for the night. The stockings were placed at the foot of the beds and Daisy and Georgina were able to go off duty.

Christmas Day could have been an anticlimax but the nurses outdid themselves in keeping the men's spirits up and the ward often rang with laughter. The cooks surpassed themselves in creating a meal from their limited supplies. There was even plum pudding sent out by the Red Cross.

A few days later the festivities seemed just a dream. The new year brought bright cold weather. Not as cold as it would be in England though, Daisy thought. Back in England it was the coldest winter for years with coal in short supply and very expensive. She wondered how her mother was managing and worried about her brothers. The last she'd heard, Dick and Jimmy were still together in the trenches and Billy was now sailing regularly across the Atlantic where the danger from German U-boats was as great as it was here in the Mediterranean.

Apart from the constant worry, Daisy's life was a little easier at the moment. Most of the men she'd been nursing when she first arrived were now convalescent, so her duties were lighter and there was more time for training the VADs so they were becoming more useful, lightening the load of the regular nursing staff. Georgina had been attending lectures in her free time and was proud of her progress although she no longer spoke of doing professional training after the war. Daisy was sure that if Tom came through unscathed, Georgina would defy convention and marry the penniless lieutenant.

Daisy wondered how she herself would adapt to life back home after the war. The shabby little harbour cottage and life as a maid at Ryfe Hall now seemed like a dream. It was all so different out here, she thought, as she walked across the compound in the cool sunshine. Later in the year it would become unbearably hot, the land parched and dry. Then she knew she would long for the cool green Sussex hills.

She and Georgina often talked of home, but never about what they'd do when they returned. It would be tempting fate, Georgina had said with an attempt at a lighthearted laugh. So Jack and Tom were seldom spoken of, although Georgina's brother was never far from Daisy's thoughts. He had never answered the impassioned letter she'd written several months ago and she'd tried hard to put him out of her mind.

It was easier said than done though, she thought, trying to convince herself it was for the best, when yet again there was no mail for her. Georgina always seemed to have plenty of letters. She was reading one from her mother now.

'I'm pleased she's making a new life for herself,' Georgina said after reading the latest. 'I know I was a disappointment to her. But she seems to have accepted that the war has changed things. I wonder if Ryfe has been sold yet.'

'Maybe it's been requisitioned by the army or something,' Daisy said. 'They wouldn't just let it stand empty. I wonder what happened to Mrs Harris and Mr Fenton and all the other servants.'

'Don't remind me,' Georgina said. 'I feel dreadful thinking of them laid off without their wages, with nowhere to go.'

'Well, we know what happened to Ernest.' Daisy shuddered at the recollection of how he'd almost wrecked her friendship with Georgina.

'I can understand his bitterness though,' Georgina said. 'Still, I'm glad he's been shipped home. He can't cause any more trouble now.'

Daisy wasn't convinced she'd heard the last of him; she suspected he would always bear a grudge. Returning to the subject of Ryfe Hall, she said, 'Perhaps whoever buys it will re-employ the servants.'

Georgina sighed. 'There's nothing I can do about it anyway.' She put her mother's letter aside and picked up another envelope, turning it over in her hands with a little smile, savouring the moment before opening it.

'I can guess who that's from,' Daisy said with a laugh. Georgina blushed and turned away, hunching her shoulder to give herself the illusion of privacy. She could have taken the letter to her room but Daisy guessed she couldn't wait to see what Tom had written.

Through their correspondence, their relationship had grown warmer, especially since John Davenport's death. Tom had apparently taken heart from the family's change of circumstances. Now, Daisy thought, there was nothing to stand in the way of their romance – apart from Lady Davenport's certain disapproval. But Georgina could cope with that, Daisy thought.

She smiled as she watched her friend devouring the closely written pages, but there was a pang of envy too. Why hadn't Jack written to her? He knew where she was, and if he was as sincere about his feelings as Georgina had implied, why hadn't he written? Her pride wouldn't allow her to write to him again. She'd poured her heart out once. Now it was up to him.

Despite her own heartache, Daisy was pleased that her friend was happy. In fact, everyone seemed in a more carefree frame of mind these days. Despite Sister's vigilance, all the nurses seemed to be falling in love, including Sarah. Already badly wounded in the assault on Suvla Bay, Sergeant Chris Robbins had suffered severe frostbite as he waited in the freezing wind to be evacuated to a hospital ship. After months hovering between life and death he'd begun to recover. Now convalescent, he was the life and soul of the ward. Everyone knew where Sergeant Robbins was by the sound of his hearty laughter. Sarah's romance had started innocently enough when he'd produced some gramophone records.

'Some music would cheer us up, if only there was something to play them on,' he said.

Sarah spent her off-duty time scouting around for a gramophone. She'd even raided the barracks on the outskirts of Valletta. When Doctor Holloway heard of her quest, he offered to lend them his.

When she walked into the ward with it, Sergeant Robbins had grabbed her in an impromptu dance to the amusement of the other patients and Sister Drummond's outrage.

Despite the fact that relationships between staff and patients were forbidden, Sarah managed to wangle quite a bit of time with Chris, thanks to Daisy and Georgina, who often covered for her.

Even the doctor seemed to be on their side.

'Maybe it's because he's in love too,' Sarah teased.

Daisy blushed. 'I don't know what you mean.'

'Anyone can see he's smitten,' Sarah said with a laugh. 'You could do worse.'

Daisy liked Peter Holloway and respected his skills as a doctor, but anything else was unthinkable. She couldn't blame the nurses for talking. He'd made his interest obvious, undeterred by Sister Hatton's frowns of disapproval. Their friendship had started on night duty when she'd called him out to a dying patient. Although he could do nothing for the man, Peter had stayed with him to the end, helping Daisy with the little rituals that inevitably accompanied a death.

Afterwards she'd gone into the kitchen to make him a cup of tea. 'How did you take up nursing?' he asked, perching himself on the edge of the table.

'You mean because I'm uneducated, lower class?' Daisy asked indignantly. She was still sensitive about her past.

'I didn't mean that at all,' Peter protested. 'Don't be so hard on yourself. You're beautiful, intelligent, a very good nurse. You've lots of common sense too, that's worth more than education. So why nursing in particular?'

'I needed a job. And I knew what to expect after helping to nurse my father.' Daisy's voice faltered. She still found it hard to believe that Dad would no longer be there when she returned home.

Peter was sympathetic and easy to talk to and she enjoyed their midnight chats, when he would often stop by for a cup of tea. But Daisy knew Sarah was right. He would like to take the friendship further.

If he knew I was in love with someone else, maybe he'd back off, she thought. But she had never talked about Jack to anyone except Georgina. Even Sarah didn't know the whole story.

CHAPTER TWELVE

By the spring of 1917 the island of Malta had become the centre of intense U-boat activity. Every day brought moments of drama and disaster. But, for the nurses, it was nothing like those first dreadful months after the disastrous Gallipolli campaign more than a year ago. For the men who were convalescent and awaiting their return to England, this was a time of rest and relaxation – and a blossoming of romance, despite the ban on fraternization between staff and patients.

As Sister Hatton said, 'I try to be sympathetic but I'm responsible for these girls. However, if they're sensible I try to turn a blind eye.'

Sister Drummond didn't agree. 'We must keep some form of discipline,' she said. 'The rules are meant to be obeyed.'

Daisy paused by the open door and knocked loudly. She hoped the sisters didn't realize they had been overheard as she was seeking permission to take some of the patients for a picnic in the hills. If they refuse Sarah will be so disappointed, we all will, she thought. They'd been looking forward to the expedition but she might have known Drummond would stick to the rules.

Doctor Holloway was there too and he joined in the discussion. 'I don't see that there would be any harm in it,' he said. 'In fact medically speaking it could do a great deal of good.' He turned to Daisy. 'Who were you thinking of taking?'

'Sergeant Robbins, Corporal Smith and Privates Holmes, Douglas and Stewart. They're all reasonably fit now and of course a couple of nurses would go along too, to make sure they didn't overdo it.'

'Very sensible,' said Doctor Holloway, turning back to the sisters. 'As you are aware, people confined to bed for long periods become quite weak. The muscles become soft through lack of use. If these young men are to be sent back to fight, we must try to build up strength in those muscles. Exercise, that's the thing,' he said heartily.

'So can we go, Sister?' Daisy asked eagerly. 'Nurse Bowman and I are both free tomorrow as well as a couple of the VADs.'

Sister Hatton smiled and nodded but Drummond still frowned with pursed lips. Eventually she relaxed and said, 'If Doctor Holloway thinks it will be beneficial to the patients, then I must give way. But it is against my better judgment.'

'Thank you, Sister.' Daisy turned to leave the room, anxious to relay the good news to Sarah.

Sister Drummond's voice followed her. 'I am making you responsible, Nurse March and I trust you will all behave with propriety.'

Doctor Holloway held the door open for Daisy and she smiled her thanks. As he followed her out he said, 'Would you mind if I came too? That way I can make sure there's no impropriety.'

Daisy was sure he had a twinkle in his eye as he strode away down the corridor. At least he's on our side, she thought. But why shouldn't they, as well as the patients, have a little fun?

Sarah flushed with excitement when she heard. A whole day with Chris was to be cherished. They sought out Georgina to make their plans for the next day. When Daisy told them Doctor Holloway was coming too, Georgina smiled knowingly.

'Oh, don't you start,' Daisy said crossly as her friends exchanged grins.

When she woke next morning, Daisy's first thought was for Jack and she murmured her usual prayer for his safety and that of her brothers. Then she leapt out of bed and strode to the window. The sun was sparkling on the waters of the bay and she hoped it wouldn't be too hot for their expedition. She opened the window and a cool breeze on her arms reassured her.

She turned to Sarah, who was yawning and stretching.

'Come on, lazybones. I thought you'd be first up today. Aren't you excited?'

'Why didn't you wake me?' Sarah cried. 'I can't believe the old dragon gave in. Just think, a whole day away from the hospital.'

She didn't mention Chris Robbins but Daisy knew it was his company she was looking forward to. 'It'll be good to get out in the fresh air,' she agreed.

The men were waiting with the VADs by the time Daisy and Sarah joined them at the hospital entrance. Chris Robbins and two of the men still leaned on walking sticks but despite Sarah's anxious fussing they declared they could well manage the planned walk.

'Where's Doctor Holloway?' Daisy asked.

'I thought you weren't interested in him,' Sarah laughed.

'I'm not, but I want to get an early start before the sun gets too high – and before Sister Drummond changes her mind.'

'It's all right. He's here,' Sarah said.

They turned, laughing as Doctor Holloway approached the gates leading a very reluctant mule. It was pulling a cart, which contained rugs and an ornate ladies' parasol which Peter had found in one of the store cupboards.

He patted the animal's nose and it showed large yellow teeth. 'I don't think it likes me,' he said, laughing.

They loaded the picnic baskets and set off, the mule picking his way delicately over the ruts and stones on the unmade road. There was a carefree atmosphere as they left the strict regime of the hospital behind. Even those relying on walking sticks on the rough track seemed to be enjoying themselves but Daisy kept a watchful eye on them.

After an hour's steady walking they stopped, leaning on a dry stone wall and looking back at the town, the golden stone of its buildings glowing in the sun. Beyond, the waters of the bay were a brilliant turquoise. On the horizon the silhouettes of battleships marred the peaceful scene. Daisy shivered at the thought of the U-boats lurking beneath the calm water and turned away. I won't think about Jack today, she told herself. But it was easier said than done.

As they made to move on and Daisy helped Private Stewart to his feet, she noticed he was limping. A large blister had formed on his heel. Thank goodness she'd brought a first aid kit.

'Should we turn back?' she asked, glancing up the track. Sarah and Chris were well ahead, obviously enjoying each other's company and the freedom from hospital rules. It would be a shame to spoil the outing for them.

'Perhaps Private Stewart could ride in the cart,' Doctor Holloway suggested.

'I'm fine, Doc. Don't let me be a wet blanket,' Private Stewart said. But he climbed up on the cart with obvious relief.

A little further on they reached a natural hollow surrounded by tumbled rocks. Georgina helped Private Stewart down from the cart and he sat with his back against a smooth rock. The other patients threw themselves down on the short springy turf, still green from the winter rains. The doctor braved the mule's bared teeth and unhitched the cart. The animal wandered a few yards away and began to crop the grass and wild flowers at the edge of the track.

By the time the men were settled the nurses had unpacked the food – plain fare, mostly bully beef sandwiches, but the men ate heartily, appetites sharpened by exercise and fresh air.

Daisy noticed with a smile that Sarah and Chris had moved away from the group. But where was the harm? In these uncertain times people deserved to snatch what happiness they could. She glanced at Doctor Holloway who was also looking at the couple with a thoughtful expression.

'You won't say anything to Sister Drummond, will you – about Sergeant Robbins and Nurse Bowman being so friendly, I mean?' she asked anxiously.

He turned to her with a smile. 'There's no harm in an innocent friendship,' he said. 'I was just thinking what a handsome couple they make.'

'I think the rules are silly. They just make people sneak around. It's much better to be open about these things, Doctor,' Daisy said impulsively.

'Please – call me Peter. I'm only Doctor when I'm on duty,' he said. 'And I couldn't agree more. The rules are made with the best of intentions but they only foster deceit. It applies to us doctors too. If I asked you to attend a concert in town, or to go for a walk, I'd be breaking the rules too.' He leaned closer and continued, 'I would very much like to break the rules with you, Nurse March. I know we're friends but I'd like to be more than that. Would you consider spending time with me when we're off duty?'

Daisy flushed and she began to fuss with the picnic things, unsure how to reply.

'I'm sorry, Daisy. I didn't mean to embarrass you. Please forget I spoke,' he said.

'It's all right. It's just that . . .'

'I know I shouldn't have said anything. But out here, away from the hospital, it seemed the right time.'

'I'm sorry, Peter. I couldn't possibly. You see . . .' She wanted to tell him about Jack but she couldn't go on.

'There's someone else,' he said in a flat expressionless voice.

She nodded wordlessly.

'Then I'll say no more,' he said, leaning across to take another sandwich. After a few moments' silence he spoke again. 'I don't know if Nurse Bowman realizes it but the sergeant will be leaving us soon.'

'He seems much fitter but I hardly think he's ready for combat yet.'

'I agree. We send these young men back far too soon. But we have to bow to higher powers I'm afraid.' Peter sighed. 'Sergeant Robbins is one of the lucky ones. He'll need further treatment when he gets back to England – more specialized than we can give him here. By the time he's fit to fight again, let's hope this damned war is over.'

Daisy nodded agreement, pleased that Peter had dropped the subject of his feelings for her and was keeping their conversation on a more professional footing. 'The war seems so far away up here, doesn't it?' she said, leaning back and gazing up at the tranquil blue sky. 'But I can't forget that it's all still waiting for us down there.' She gestured towards the distant town.

'Things have been quiet for a while though. We should make the most of it while we can. These poor lads will be back in the thick of it soon enough.'

'What about Corporal Smith? Will he be shipped out with Chris?'

'I'd like to keep him here longer but he's physically fit now. I can't in all honesty say he's fit for duty though. But again, I'm powerless to do anything.'

Although the corporal's wounds had healed quickly, he still hardly ate anything and the slightest noise set him trembling. Daisy had often sat with him through the long nights as he thrashed around, mumbling and occasionally shouting out in his tortured nightmares. One night he'd sat bolt upright, eyes staring, for once so lucid that Daisy thought he was awake. 'It's all right, Jim. Hold on. You'll be all right, mate.'

Next day she'd asked him who Jim was. 'My mate – joined up together we did.' They'd both been wounded but he'd lost sight of him when they were taken off the beach. 'He'll be OK, won't he, nurse?'

She'd tried to reassure him. But the nightmares went on, crying out an endless stream of names. Daisy knew the casualties had been high in Suvla Bay but how many of his mates had the poor boy lost, she wondered. She looked at him now, face turned up to the sun, and a sob caught in her throat. He was so young – they were all so young.

She glanced across at Georgina, who was leaning on the wall that protected the olive grove from the ever-present wind, gazing towards the sea. The ships they'd seen earlier were now little more than smudges on the horizon. Daisy guessed she was thinking of Tom and her brother but she wouldn't let herself follow her friend's train of thought. You just had to get on with it and take each day as it came, she told herself.

The men had finished eating and, tired after their long walk, settled back on the mossy turf, closing their eyes against the midday heat. Sarah and Chris had wandered off hand in hand.

Quietly, so as not to disturb her companions, Daisy and the doctor began gathering up the remnants of their picnic and re-packing the baskets. 'We ought to be getting back soon,' Peter said. Reluctantly, Daisy agreed and handed the baskets to him to go in the cart.

93

The mule had wandered away from the group and was still quietly munching. As Peter reached for the bridle, the animal shied away, scrambling across the track in a clatter of stones. The noise woke the men and Daisy noted sadly how each of them reacted to the sudden disturbance. Corporal Smith ducked his head and appeared to be praying and two of the privates were trembling and ashen-faced. The doctor was right. None of them was fit to go back to the front. What horrors had they endured to make grown men react like that?

The brief respite enjoyed by both staff and patients didn't last long. There were no more expeditions into the hills as a fresh onslaught of sick and wounded began. Now, the casualties were survivors of the torpedoed and mined ships, giving both Daisy and Georgina more anxious moments as each ambulance arrived at the hospital gates.

Tending to the men's dreadful burns and wounds, Daisy wondered how they'd managed to survive at all, let alone after hours and sometimes days in the water.

The danger from submarine attack was now so great that no civilians were allowed to leave the island, although the convalescent patients were still sent home whenever there was a boat available to take them to Sicily and on to mainland Italy.

A week or so after their picnic in the hills, Sarah came to Daisy in tears. 'Chris is leaving,' she said. 'I know I should be pleased that he's well enough, but they'll send him out to France or Belgium and God knows what will happen to him there.'

'The others are going too. Don't worry, Sarah, Chris is nowhere near fit enough for duty yet. Let's hope, by the time he is, it will all be over.' Daisy tried to instill a note of confidence into her voice but her words had a hollow ring. She knew all too well that if a man could walk and hold a rifle he was considered fit to fight.

Until recently, despite the anxiety about her brothers, she hadn't understood how bad things were at the front. It was brought home to her when Dick was wounded. They couldn't remove all the shrapnel in his leg and now he might always walk with a limp.

'I am just thankful that it wasn't worse, and that at least my boy is home now,' her mother had written.

The news was already out of date as she discovered when a letter arrived from Dick. While she'd been thanking God that at least one of her brothers was safe at home, he'd been recalled to his unit, passed fit for active service and was now somewhere on the western front. Of Billy and

Jimmy there had been no recent news at all.

So Daisy's words of comfort rang hollow. Sarah must know in her heart that there was little chance she'd ever see Chris again.

With the departure of the convalescent patients, the earlier discipline, which lately had become very slack, was reinforced. The gramophone disappeared from the ward, together with the sounds of 'Long Long Trail A-winding' and 'If You Were The Only Girl In The World', and the 'no fraternization' rule was reinstated once more.

Casualties continued to pour in, most of them merchant seamen or troops on their way to the east whose ships had been struck by mines or torpedoed. Despite the royal navy patrols, there were massive losses.

Working alongside Georgina, Daisy realized how confident and efficient her friend had become in the time they'd worked together. She watched her friend replacing a dressing, reassuring her patient with a sweet smile and tender touch, and thought she's a better nurse than I'll ever be. No one would guess her real feelings as she dealt with the dreadful suppurating wound. Some of the girls had never really adapted as she had.

The orderly had come in with the supper trolley when Sister Drummond strode purposefully down the ward. Sweeping past Daisy, she advanced on Georgina. 'Nurse Davenport, you know the rules. But apparently your brother does not.'

Daisy gave a little gasp and Georgina looked up from her work, a broad smile lighting her face. 'My brother?'

'Lieutenant Davenport is in my office. I have given permission for him to speak to you only because he has news from home. Ten minutes – that's all.' Sister Drummond turned to Daisy. 'Nurse March, you will go with her.'

CHAPTER THIRTEEN

Daisy's heart raced. Was Jack really here? Even as she tried to keep her expression neutral, she noticed with surprise that Sister's usual grim expression had softened somewhat.

'Wait outside while Nurse Davenport speaks to her brother,' she said. 'It may be bad news.'

Georgina had already taken off her apron and was flying up the ward while Daisy stood for a moment, her heart thumping, her legs weak. Would there be a chance to make amends for her hasty reaction the last time she and Jack had been together?

'Well, run along, Nurse.'

Daisy followed Georgina along the corridor to Sister's office, hesitating at the open door as she saw her friend being swept into a bear-like hug. As she broke away, laughing and crying at the same time, Daisy's euphoria vanished. It wasn't Jack.

Her disappointment was a sour taste in her mouth. She didn't blame Tom for the deception though and she gave a wry smile. Sister would be furious if she ever found out.

I'll let them have their ten minutes, she thought, backing away from the open door. But as she turned away a voice said, 'Aren't you going to say hello, Daisy?'

Jack, who'd been hidden by the open door, came towards her, handsomer than ever in his naval uniform. 'Why didn't you write?' he asked.

Daisy had been about to ask the same question. Instead she said, 'You didn't get my letter then?'

Jack frowned and she realized they'd spoken at the same time. He closed the door and moved closer. 'I wrote apologizing for my bad behaviour when we last met,' he said.

'I did too,' she whispered.

It took only a few moments for them to realize that, as so often happened in wartime, their letters had never reached their destination. Each of them had spent more than a year thinking that the other did not care.

Jack glanced across at Georgina, still locked in Tom's arms, oblivious to both of them. 'Sister's only given us ten minutes. We'd better not waste it, had we?' he said.

Daisy went willingly into his arms and the kiss that followed was everything she'd ever dreamed of and more. 'I love you, Daisy-bell. I really mean it. When the war's over I want to marry you.'

'I love you too, Jack. I've dreamed of this moment for so long,' Daisy murmured. At last he'd said the words she'd longed to hear. Why had she wasted so much time in doubting him?

'I couldn't believe it when I saw you standing there. When we docked at Valletta I was determined to see you. I guessed they'd let me see my sister and I was going to get her to arrange a meeting. I wrote a letter in case we didn't manage to meet.' He took an envelope from his pocket and Daisy snatched at it. 'We haven't got long so read it later – it says everything I've longed to say in person.'

Daisy put it in her pocket and reached up to kiss him again. He held her closely as if he couldn't bear to let go but she gently pulled away.

'I'm afraid our ten minutes is up and if we don't report to Sister, she'll come looking.' She smiled and glanced across at Georgina. 'You wouldn't want your sister to get into trouble, would you?'

Tom and Georgina had moved nearer the window and now stood hand in hand gazing down at the bay, their words inaudible to the other couple.

Jack tapped his sister's shoulder. 'We're supposed to be discussing family affairs, don't forget. Wipe that silly grin off your face or she'll guess something's up.'

Georgina sighed. 'I suppose you must go.' She let go of Tom's hand and turned to her brother, giving him a quick hug. 'Oh Jack, I've hardly had a chance to speak to you. Will we see you again before you sail?'

If only it were possible, Daisy thought. She couldn't bear the thought of not seeing Jack again and she knew Georgina felt the same way about Tom. Surely it wouldn't hurt to break the rules just once? She looked at Georgina and grinned.

'Do you think we could persuade Sarah to cover for us if we slip out later?'

Georgina bit her lip and squeezed Tom's hand. 'We'll try – it's worth the risk.'

After arranging to meet that evening if they could manage it, Daisy opened the door just as Sister came in sight. By the time she entered the room, Tom was standing by the window twirling his cap in a bored fashion. Georgina and Jack were seated on either side of Sister's desk while Daisy stood at the open door.

Sister Drummond looked at them suspiciously, pursing her lips. 'You'll be going back to your ship now, Lieutenant Davenport?' she asked.

'Yes, we only put in for some minor repairs. We'll be off tomorrow morning.'

'I trust your family business was settled satisfactorily?' Still the suspicious glint in her eye.

'Oh yes, thank you, Sister. Most satisfactory.' Jack gave his most charming smile and shook her hand. He turned to Georgina. 'Cheerio then, sis. You can stop fretting now. Mama's perfectly all right and all the legal stuff's been sorted out now.'

He and Tom donned their caps and strode smartly down the corridor. Daisy and Georgina watched them go, hugging to themselves the thought of tonight's meeting.

'Well, nurses, there's work to be done. Don't just stand there.'

The girls hastily made their way back to the ward where one very new VAD was struggling to manage the suppers on her own.

'I suppose it was good of her to let us see them,' Georgina said, 'even if it was only for a few minutes.'

'Only because Jack's your brother. Can you imagine her face if she'd realized?' Daisy giggled happily.

'What a stroke of luck, Sister letting you come with me.'

'I was sure she guessed – she did look a bit suspicious when she came back.'

'Only because she's got a nasty mind.' Georgina laughed.

That evening more than one patient remarked how nice it was to see Nurse Davenport looking so much happier now she'd had news from home. It was a wonder any work got done at all, Daisy thought, as she washed the dressing bowls and put them to be sterilized, her body warm as she relived those few moments in Jack's arms. But her heart sank when she contemplated the possibility that Sarah might refuse to help them leave the hospital later that evening.

When their shift ended they hurried to the mess hut where Sarah, who was now working on the dysentery ward, joined them for supper.

'You two look like the cat that's pinched the cream,' she said.

'My brother came to see me. His ship's in the harbour,' Georgina said excitedly. 'And he had a friend with him.' She paused dramatically.

'Not your lieutenant? Oh, Georgie, you lucky thing. You mean you were actually allowed to see each other?'

'In a way – yes.' Georgina lost no time in telling Sarah the whole story and had them all laughing with her mimicry of Sister's suspicious looks.

When they stopped laughing, Sarah looked solemn. 'I'm so glad you managed to sort out your misunderstanding with Georgina's brother,' she told Daisy.

Daisy nodded thoughtfully. 'They're sailing in the morning. If only we could see them before they go.'

Sarah took a mouthful of her shepherd's pie and said, 'You'll have to sneak out.'

'We've already thought of that,' Daisy replied. She was worried about getting Sarah into trouble but they needed her help.

Georgina had no such qualms and asked Sarah if she would cover for them.

When she readily agreed, they made loud remarks about getting an early night and went to their respective dormitories.

Half an hour later, with Sarah keeping watch, they crept out and waited in the shadow of the hospital gates. After a few minutes they heard scuffling and a torch beam found them. They shrank back from the light, convinced their escapade had been discovered until Tom's deep voice reassured them.

'Over here,' Georgina whispered and the light was extinguished.

Moments later, Daisy found herself crushed in Jack's arms. He released her after a breathless moment. 'I was dreading you wouldn't make it,' he said. 'We can't stay long. We're on watch at midnight and the ship sails at dawn.'

'Where are we going?' Daisy asked as he took her arm and led her towards a bend in the road. She could hear Georgina and Tom stumbling behind them in the darkness.

Around the corner two horse-drawn carriages waited, their sleepy drivers instantly awake as they climbed in. After arranging to meet Tom back there in two hours, Jack spoke quietly to the driver, leaned back in the padded seat and took Daisy in his arms.

Afterwards, she had no recollection of where they went, but she would always remember the hypnotic clip-clop of the horse's hoofs, the drooping head of the sleepy driver and the diamond stars in a velvet sky beyond the folded-down hood of the carriage.

At first they spoke in whispers, eagerly catching up with what had happened to each of them since their parting in Kingsbourne. They hardly dared to mention the future. Gradually they stopped talking and the kisses became more passionate. Daisy glanced at the impassive back of the driver, embarrassed to have a witness to their lovemaking. But he never once turned round and she wondered whether he was indeed asleep, the horse left to find its own way through the darkened streets of Sliema.

As Jack's caresses became more insistent, Daisy found herself responding with equal ardour, and she forgot the driver, the occupants of the other carriage and everything else. A small part of her said that what they were doing was wrong. But her love for Jack overcame everything else. He was going away tomorrow; she might never see him again. Her love was a gift, she thought. Besides, by now she wanted it as much as he did.

Sensations such as she had never dreamed of flooded her body as with hands and lips they eagerly explored each other. Daisy gave herself up to the moment, wanting it never to end. But at last, with a gasp and a sigh they were still, and she lay content in Jack's arms, gazing at the stars, until the carriage swayed to a stop.

Jack leaned across and stroked her tumbled curls. 'My beautiful Daisy-bell. If only I didn't have to leave you,' he murmured.

She paused in buttoning her bodice and clutched at him with a stifled sob.

'What's the matter, Daisy? I didn't hurt you, did I?' He held her away from him, frowning, but she shook her head wordlessly.

'What is it then?' He frowned. 'You're thinking I'm just like my brother. But it's not like that, Daisy-bell. I love you.' He turned away in frustration. 'I should have waited, taken things more slowly.'

'No, Jack, no. It's not that. It's just that I can't bear the thought of you going away.' She started to cry in earnest.

He kissed her wet cheek, holding her close. 'You know I have to go. But I promise, I'll come back as soon as ever I can, my love. Wait for me.'

'I will – for ever,' she said, summoning up a watery smile.

He climbed down from the carriage and helped her down, enfolding her in a last quick embrace.

The other carriage drew up behind them and she and Georgina stood silently, watching until they'd disappeared round the bend. The gate was locked and they helped each other over the wall.

As Daisy climbed over the window sill into her room, Sarah sat up and whispered, 'All clear. No one suspected a thing.' She swung her legs out of bed, her face alight with curiosity. 'I gather they turned up. Did you have a good time?'

Daisy was in no mood to give a detailed account of her evening but Sarah was the sort of girl who told all and expected her friends to do likewise. 'I'm tired, Sarah. Let's go to sleep. I'll tell you about it in the morning.' Well, not all of it, she amended in her thoughts. She would just tell Sarah about the carriage ride and that Jack had asked her to marry him.

Sleep would not come and eventually she got out of bed and sat by the window, gazing out towards the invisible harbour. She was still there as the first light of dawn tinted the sky and she turned away. Jack's ship would be weighing anchor now.

She managed to sleep for a couple of hours and woke late. Scrambling into her uniform, she discovered the letter that Jack had given her the previous day. She sat on the edge of the bed and devoured his loving words before folding it carefully and putting it in her writing case. She hurried down to breakfast where her friends were just finishing, pleased that she managed to evade Sarah's eager questions. What had happened between her and Jack was too precious to share.

Georgina too had found sleep almost impossible, waking from a fitful doze with dark shadows under her eyes. She should have been feeling on top of the world. After all, she'd had two hours in her lover's arms, which was more than most people managed these days, she thought. But she couldn't suppress the image of Tom's ship at the mercy of mines and torpedoes. She'd seen so many survivors lately, many with terrible burns and injuries. And she also knew that the proportion of those lost when a ship sank was far greater than the number rescued. She knew she might never see Tom again.

Even the patients commented on the change in her since yesterday, as she mechanically went about her duties. 'Have you had bad news?' one of them asked, his tone solicitous.

'She's worried about her brother,' Daisy said quickly and Georgina gave her a grateful smile.

'He'll be all right, Nurse,' another patient, a stoker in a merchant ship, who'd suffered gruesome burns, said cheerfully.

How could they be so optimistic after what they'd been through? Georgina managed to summon a smile and move on to the next bed. If they could put on a brave face then so could she. For the rest of her shift she worked harder than ever, smiling and joking with the men as if she hadn't a care in the world. It helped to push her anxiety about Tom to the back of her mind. Only that night, as she listened to the regular breathing of her companions, did the nagging worry return to keep her from sleep.

There would be no letters to bring her comfort either. She and Daisy had written care of the base at Gibraltar where the ship was due next. But it could be weeks before they reached there. Neither he nor Jack knew where their next tour of duty would take them.

CHAPTER FOURTEEN

During the next few weeks Georgina's mood swung from euphoria to despair. She and Daisy both rushed for the post eagerly, only to groan with disappointment when they saw the empty pigeonholes. Then they would try to comfort each other with reminders of those magic moments under the stars – moments they would treasure whatever happened in the future.

Before long, they had no time to dwell on the past – or the future. With the onset of the summer heat a bout of sickness swept the hospital. Chronic fatigue from the long hours of duty, combined with bad conditions and poor diet, lowered resistance to infection and many of the nurses fell ill.

When Georgina began to feel unwell, she told herself that she'd succumbed to the fever too. But the illness that had laid low so many of the staff and patients had only lasted a few days. Most of the nurses, including Daisy, had been back on duty within twenty-four hours.

Georgina's sickness continued daily for several weeks, and eventually she was forced to face up to the fact that this was not 'just a tummy upset'. She'd seen other girls in the same predicament and in the past had almost despised them for getting themselves into trouble. Now she was in trouble herself and she didn't know where to turn. She couldn't even bring herself to confide in Daisy, dreading the condemnation she was sure she would see in her friend's eyes.

She was leaning over the sink in the sluice room when Daisy came in. 'Are you all right? You look very pale,' she said.

Georgina wiped her mouth with a cloth and bent to splash her face with cold water, avoiding her friend's eyes. 'Just something I ate,' she mumbled. 'Give me a minute and I'll be back on the ward.'

'No you won't,' Daisy said firmly. 'Go over to the hut and lie down. I'll tell Sister you're ill. Go on. I'll come over and see how you are later on.'

Georgina felt too wretched to argue and went back to her quarters, relieved to find the room empty. She kicked off her shoes, unpinned her apron and lay down on the bed, facing the wall. If anyone came in she didn't want them to see the tears which now coursed freely down her pale cheeks.

The sickness and giddiness subsided and she knew she ought to go back to work. But she couldn't bear to face anyone yet. Gradually she fell into a restless doze, dreaming of Tom and Jack adrift in a dark sea, with images of her father, Philip, her mother, all mixed up together. She woke with a start as someone came into the hut, then closed her eyes again. I can't talk to anyone, she thought.

'How are you feeling now, Georgie?' Daisy asked, sitting on the edge of the bed and touching her arm gently.

She mumbled as if she was still asleep and hunched her shoulder away. Daisy shook her. 'We have to talk,' she said firmly. 'Is there anything you want to tell me?'

Georgina sat up and burst into tears. 'I think I'm going to have a baby,' she sobbed.

'Are you sure it's not something else? We've all been sick lately.'

'It's not that – I just know,' Georgina said, searching her friend's face for the expected condemnation. Reassured when she saw only genuine concern, she sobbed out her feelings and fears for the future.

'Have you written to Tom? Does he know?' Daisy asked.

'Yes, but who knows if he'll ever get the letter.' Georgina started to cry again.

Daisy put an arm round her shoulders. 'It'll be all right. He'll get special leave and you can get married.'

'It'll be too late. By the time he's managed to get leave everyone will know. I'll get thrown out of the VADs – and where will I go?'

Georgina could see no way out. They loved each other and Tom had said they'd get married when the war was over. It had never occurred to her that their one fumbled attempt at lovemaking would result in this mess, as she thought of it. She wanted children, of course, but in the safe, conventional environment of a home and marriage. She couldn't envisage this problem – the sickness, the tenderness of her breasts, the imperceptible thickening of her waistline – resulting in a living breathing human being.

'I just want it to be over,' she sobbed as Daisy patted her shoulder and stroked her hair. 'I can't believe this is happening to me.'

Daisy gave a short laugh. 'Do you think you're the only one this has happened to? At least you have a man who loves you and wants to marry you.'

'But what am I going to do? I'll have to go back to England, I suppose,' she said. 'But where will I go? I couldn't face my mother even if my uncle would allow me to stay with them. And I certainly can't go to Philip in London.'

Georgina was almost ready to cry again but Daisy reassured her. 'First of all we must see about getting you released from your VAD contract. That should be easy enough. Everyone knows you've been unwell so you should be able to get a medical discharge.'

'Oh no, Daisy, I can't do that. You have to have a medical exam and a doctor's certificate. Everyone would know.'

'That won't matter. Once you've gone they'll soon find someone else to gossip about. Besides, your real friends will stand by you.'

Georgina wasn't so sure. 'Sarah's been giving me some peculiar looks lately. I'm sure she suspects,' she said.

Daisy brushed her concerns aside. 'Don't worry about the medical. I'll have a word with Doctor Holloway. I'm sure he'll be sympathetic.'

Georgina almost managed to smile. 'We all know the doctor will do anything for you.'

'Never mind about that. It's you we're talking about.'

'But where will I go?' Georgina wailed.

'You must go home. I'm sure your mother will understand.' Daisy didn't really believe it but she had to reassure her friend. And where else could she go?

Daisy had just come off duty and gone over to the VAD quarters to check on Georgina, who was still waiting for transport to the mainland. Her contract had been ended on medical grounds, but she wasn't looking forward to returning to England. She'd fallen into a deep depression made worse by the fact that she hadn't heard from Tom.

'I'm dreading facing my mother,' Georgina was saying, when the door burst open.

'March, you're wanted on the wards. New patients,' the fresh young VAD gasped.

'They might have let you have supper first,' Georgina protested.

But Daisy was already replacing her cap and cuffs, smoothing her apron before dashing out of the door.

Nurses from the other huts joined her as she hurried towards the main entrance and the sight of the familiar naval uniforms brought a feeling of dread. As she directed the stretcher bearers to the wards, someone mentioned the name of the ship that had gone down. Her heart began to thump and, frantically, she searched the badly burned faces, praying Jack was not among them.

When the last of the survivors was unloaded from the ambulances and either rushed to surgery or made comfortable on the wards, Daisy stopped one of the drivers. 'Is this the lot?' she asked.

'Last load just arriving,' he said.

Daisy waited while the stretchers were lifted down, looking for Jack. She shook her head. 'What about the other survivors?' she asked, clutching the driver's arm.

'Those that didn't need hospital treatment are bedded down in the old port,' he said.

'But there must be more. Those ships carry hundreds of men,' Daisy protested.

'Drowned most likely. There were a lot of bodies in the water.'

Not Jack, Daisy told herself. He must be safe. He was with the other survivors down in the town. She walked slowly towards the hospital entrance, quickening her steps as Sister Hatton called to her.

'Wake up, March, there's work to be done.' The familiar phrase snapped her to attention and she hurried to the wards.

Another new dawn was breaking when Sister finally ordered her to take a break. As she stepped out into the cool air and breathed in the scent of the wild thyme blowing in from the surrounding countryside, she realized she'd been on duty for more than eighteen hours. Her body craved sleep, but she should go and tell Georgina that Tom and Jack's ship had gone down. She hesitated. Perhaps she should go down to the town first and make sure they weren't there.

Before she could make up her mind, Peter Holloway called to her. 'Nurse March, someone's asking for you,' he said.

She hurried towards him. 'Is it Jack?' she asked, hope flaring.

'You mean Nurse Davenport's brother? No. It's a Lieutenant Lazenby,' the doctor said.

Ignoring the question in his voice, Daisy followed him down the corridor, pausing at the ward where the most hopeless cases were left. No wonder I didn't recognize him when he came in, she thought, going towards the bed. His arms and legs were both splinted and a bandage covered the upper part of his head. But even her years of dealing with the most ghastly wounds had not prepared her for the sight of his face, raw and bleeding and puffed up to twice its size from the severe burns.

'Poor chap, he must have been right in the path of the explosion,' Peter said. 'You'll have to lean closer. It's hard to make out what he's saying but I'm sure it was you he was asking for.'

Daisy pulled a chair up to the bedside and sat down, gently taking one of Tom's hands, waiting for him to gather strength to speak. His eyes were deep pools of pain sunken into the swollen flesh. She wasn't even sure he could see her. But she smiled just in case.

'Do you want me to fetch Georgina?' she asked.

His grip on her hand tightened. 'Don't want – don't want her – to see me like this,' he gasped.

'She'll have to know you're here.'

He tried to shake his head and his breath came in short gasps.

'If that's what you really want, all right, Tom. Don't distress yourself. Just concentrate on getting better.'

He appeared to relax a little and she got up to leave. But as she took her hand away he tried to speak again. 'Jack got off OK,' he croaked.

'Thank God,' Daisy murmured.

Tom's eyes closed and Daisy went to fetch Doctor Holloway. 'He's not going to make it, is he, Peter?' she asked, forgetting formality in her distress.

He shook his head. 'He'll be lucky to last the night.'

Daisy gave a little sob. 'Poor Georgina,' she said.

Peter had been frowning but his face cleared at once. 'You mean he's Nurse Davenport's young man? Why did he ask for you then?'

'He doesn't want her to see him in such a state. I can understand that. He still thinks of her as the gently reared girl he knew back in Sussex. He doesn't realize how much she's changed.'

'How do you think she'll feel if she isn't told? I think you should fetch her,' Peter said decisively.

'But he got very agitated when I suggested it. I wouldn't want to do any more harm.'

'He's going to die anyway,' Peter said brutally. 'It might even help if he has a loved one with him. Go and get her.' When she still hesitated, he said, 'Go on. I'll persuade him it's for the best.'

A few minutes later a subdued Georgina entered the ward. She'd been overjoyed to hear that Tom was among the survivors and when Daisy explained how bad things were she refused to believe her. But by the time she reached the ward she was prepared for the worst.

Doctor Holloway met them at the door. 'You can go in. He's agreed to see you now.'

The months of schooling herself not to show her feelings in the presence of patients stood Georgina in good stead and she smiled brightly as she entered the room.

She leaned over to kiss Tom, her lips skimming the bandage round his forehead. Then she took both his hands and kissed them too, her blue eyes brimming with unshed tears.

'Oh, Tom, it's wonderful to see you again,' she whispered.

'Not for long, I'm afraid.' Georgina had to lean closer to hear what he said and she shook her head in denial.

'You can't die, Tom. I need you. We're going to have a baby.' She hadn't intended to tell him so bluntly but the words were out now.

The puffy lips couldn't smile but a light of joy flared in the pain-filled eyes, then quickly died. 'Oh, Georgie, my sweet. I should be here for you. To take care of you.' The words were a tortured croak as he forced them past the swollen tissues of his throat.

Georgina's tears spilled over again and she laid her head down on the counterpane and sobbed. The bandaged hand found her hair and tried to stroke it. 'Listen to me, Georgie – please.'

She rubbed her hand across her wet cheeks and looked up at him. He was struggling to speak and at first she couldn't make out the words. 'You must go to my family – they'll look after you.'

'Don't worry about me, Tom. Just concentrate on getting better.' Foolish words, Georgina knew, but hope refused to die. She forced a smile and bent to kiss him again.

For a few moments he was silent. Then he struggled to speak. 'Chaplain – marry,' he gasped.

'Oh Tom, are you saying what I think you are? You want us to get married now?'

He nodded, then leaned back and closed his eyes. His breathing had become more rapid in the past few minutes and automatically Georgina's fingers felt for his pulse.

'Doctor, Daisy, come quickly,' she called.

They came at once, the doctor pushing her out of the way as he checked Tom's pulse. He turned to Georgina. 'He's very weak.'

She nodded and let Daisy lead her out of the room while the doctor and one of the VADs did what they could to make Tom comfortable.

'Have you told him about the baby?' Daisy asked.

'I know you said I shouldn't because it might upset him. But I'm glad I did.' Georgina hesitated. 'I know he's going to die. I've learned to read the signs. Daisy, could you go and get the chaplain, please?'

'Of course, I know his father's a vicar. We must do the right thing.'

'It's not that. He wants us to get married.'

Georgina managed a small smile at the expression on her friend's face. 'Well, go on then – hurry.' The smile faded as Doctor Holloway came out of the room, his face sombre. 'How is he?' she asked.

'He's barely conscious. He might rally, Nurse. But I have to be honest. The signs aren't good. He may not have long.' He put his hand on Georgina's arm and smiled. 'Go along in. Talk to him but try not to upset him.'

Georgina knew what he meant. 'I've already told him about the baby, Doctor. He wants us to get married. Daisy – Nurse March – has gone to get the chaplain.'

Peter Holloway sighed. 'Let's hope he hurries then. But, Nurse – I don't think this is a good idea. Besides, he may not even regain consciousness.'

'Doctor – please. If it's going to make his last moments easier, knowing he's done the right thing, surely there's no harm.' As the doctor nodded she continued, 'He wants me to go to his parents. His father's the vicar of a small parish just outside Norwich. I could hardly go to them like this if we weren't married, could I?' She gestured towards her stomach and to her relief he smiled.

'I'll be your witness,' he said as Daisy came hurrying down the corridor with the chaplain in tow.

It wasn't how she'd pictured her wedding but Georgina smiled radiantly as she and Tom were pronounced man and wife. As she bent to kiss him her throat closed on a sob. But there would be time for tears later. Now, she smiled into his pain-filled eyes and murmured sweet words of comfort. The chaplain had kept the ceremony short but Tom had visibly weakened as he struggled to make his responses. He rallied to return Georgina's kiss, then sighed contentedly, lay back on the pillows and closed his eyes again.

Georgina held both his hands and only when the slight pressure on her fingers slackened did she realize the end had come. At first she thought he'd fallen asleep, then she looked up in alarm and realized that his eyes were still open. As she leaned over to kiss him and close his eyes, she thought, at least he's not in pain any more. Thank God.

CHAPTER FIFTEEN

Over the next few weeks, Daisy clung to the belief that Jack was still alive, comforting herself with Tom's words: 'Jack got off all right.' But, if he had been picked up, surely there should have been some news by now.

Since Georgina had returned to England, she had no one to share her fears with. Sarah, who might have understood, had her own worries. Her sergeant had been passed fit and sent to the front. Now he was facing the German big guns across the scarred fields of Flanders. Sarah was beside herself with anger at those in charge. 'Doctor Holloway promised he wouldn't be sent back to the front. He's nowhere near fit enough,' she cried.

Sarah had become withdrawn, going about her duties silently and refusing to talk about her lover. To talk about him, to contemplate a future with him, was to tempt fate.

Daisy felt differently. Talking about Jack would have helped to keep him alive in her mind. But soon after Georgina had left for England, she received confirmation that Jack had not been among the survivors arriving at Gibraltar. Daisy knew that an official letter, reporting Jack 'missing believed killed' would have gone to his mother. She sat down to write to Georgina, who was now staying with the Lazenbys in Norfolk. After the impromptu marriage ceremony, she had gone straight to them and had been welcomed as their son's wife and the future mother of their grandchild.

In her letter, Daisy repeated what one of Jack's fellow officers had written to her of the ship's final moments.

'He was very brave – one of the last off the ship according to Sub Lieutenant Winters,' she wrote. *'He stayed to make sure the men under his command were all safely off, then jumped into the water as the ship started to go down.'*

Daisy's vivid imagination pictured the scene, the smoke, the noise and confusion and Jack calmly helping his fellow crewmen. Her eyes filled with tears, which spilled on to the page in front of her, but she carried on writing.

'Mr Winters saw Jack swimming towards the boats but when the smoke and debris cleared, there was no sign of him. They carried on searching till they were picked up. He may have been rescued by another boat but after so long it's very unlikely.'

By now Daisy was crying so much she could hardly see to write. When she felt calm enough to dry her eyes and finish her letter, there wasn't much else to say, except to hope that Georgina was keeping well.

The baby was due early in the new year and Georgina's condition would be starting to show by now. Daisy was glad that her friend had a wedding ring on her finger to shield her from society's hostile stares. She hoped the Lazenbys were treating her well and that she would find happiness in her new life.

In the meantime she had to learn to live with her own emotions. Grief and depression vied with unreasoning hope. Surely she would know if Jack were dead, she told herself. But these flashes of certainty were becoming fewer as time went on.

Work was the panacea which helped her through those first dark months. She drove herself hard, volunteering for extra duties when casualties were high and nurses in short supply.

Many of the girls who'd come out to Malta before her had returned home for long leave. Daisy could have applied for leave herself. She'd been in Malta for almost two years. But the illogical thought persisted that if she stayed here, she'd be more likely to hear news of Jack. Most of the casualties coming in now were naval personnel, the wounded soldiers from the Middle Eastern conflicts going to Salonika or Alexandria.

One evening she was sterilizing the dressing bowls after a particularly harrowing ward round. As she lifted the last enamel bowl out of the sterilizer with the wooden tongs, a wave of dizziness swept over her and the bowl crashed to the floor. The clang as it hit the tiled floor seemed to echo for minutes afterwards and Daisy put her hands over her ears. At last it stopped and she bent to pick the bowl up, thinking, that one will have to go back in the sterilizer. But as her fingers closed over it, blackness descended again.

She came to in Sister's office with no recollection of how she got there. Peter Holloway was bending over her, his face creased in concern. As her eyes opened, he took hold of her wrist, glancing at his watch as he took her pulse.

'I think you've been overdoing it, Nurse. I admire your devotion to duty but there comes a point when we all need to rest,' he said. He looked at Sister Hatton who hovered in the background. 'Sister, I think you'll agree that Nurse March needs a few days off.'

Before Sister could reply, Daisy tried to stand, although her legs still felt as if they were made of cotton wool. 'I'm all right now, thank you, Doctor. It was just a dizzy spell. I bent down too quickly.'

Ignoring her protests, Peter pushed her gently back in the chair. 'You'll stay right there,' he said firmly.

Sister Hatton agreed. 'I can't have my nurses falling down in front of the patients. It's bad for morale. Wait there and I'll get one of the VADs to take you to your quarters.'

As she left the room Daisy looked up at Peter apologetically. 'I'm all right really. I'll go back in a minute. There's so much to do.'

'And someone else will have to do it, Daisy,' he replied, abandoning formality and taking her hand. 'You are on sick leave as from now.'

When she would have protested he said, 'Daisy, listen to me. Nurse Bowman told me about your young man. But you can't keep punishing yourself. Please, do as I say.'

Daisy didn't think she could bear resting in her room with nothing to take her mind off the images of Jack, floundering in the water, struggling to reach one of the boats. With each day that passed hope died a little. Work was the only thing keeping her sane. But as she stood up, her legs almost gave way and she was grateful for Peter's protective arm around her shoulders.

'You're right,' she said. 'I'll lie down for a while. I'll just need a rest.'

One of the new VADs appeared in the doorway. 'Sister said I was to take you to your quarters,' she said nervously.

Daisy realized the girl was apprehensive about ministering to a senior nurse and she smiled to put the girl at ease. 'I just felt a little dizzy. Walk across with me, just in case I feel faint again.' She turned to Peter. 'Thank you, Doctor. I'll take your advice. But I'm sure I'll be fit for duty again tomorrow.'

But she wasn't. When she eventually woke from a delirious dream in which Jack was calling for help, sunshine was streaming across the foot of the bed. When she turned towards the window, the bright light hurt her eyes and she blinked in confusion. Someone had moved her bed; the window was in the wrong place.

She turned her head again and saw that she was at the end of a row of five hospital cots, all occupied by women, none of whom she recognized. Was she dreaming still? Confused, she closed her eyes again.

When she woke again some time later, she realized that she was in one of the hospital wards. She must be really ill. But she felt calm and untroubled. She was even able to think about Jack, remembering their last meeting and accepting that, even if he were gone for ever, she would still have had those happy moments.

The door opened and Sister Drummond came in, smiling. She must still be dreaming. Sister Drummond never smiled.

'Ah, Nurse, you're awake. You gave us all quite a fright. But I think we can safely say you're over the worst.' She laid a cool hand on Daisy's forehead, and took her wrist. 'Yes, much better,' she said, tucking the bedcovers in tightly with an expert hand.

'What happened?' Daisy asked. 'How did I get here?'

'You went down with a fever – together with about half the other nurses in the hospital.' She gestured to the other beds in the ward.

'Are they all right? What about Sarah – Nurse Bowman?'

'She escaped the infection, though it's a miracle she did. She sat with you all through the worst of your illness, when she was off duty, that is.' Nurse Drummond smiled again and Daisy couldn't help smiling back.

She struggled to sit up, hampered by the tightly tucked-in blankets. The headache and the pains in her joints had disappeared. And that awful dizziness had gone too. She wanted to get up and get back to work, especially as they would be short-staffed now.

But Sister restrained her with a firm hand. 'No getting out of bed yet,' she said. 'You're still very weak and it'll be a long time before you're fit again.' She turned to a VAD who was checking a temperature chart at the end of the next bed. 'Fetch Nurse March a drink, please.' She patted Daisy's hand. 'Rest, my dear, that's the prescription for you.' She walked briskly out of the room, leaving Daisy to gaze after her and reflect on how different Sister Dragon was when seen from the perspective of a patient.

When the VAD returned with a cup of very weak tea with no milk, Daisy gulped it down gratefully. Handing the cup back to the girl she said, 'How long have I been here?'

'Just over a week. You were the first to get ill. After that they started going down one after the other.'

A week? Daisy thought it might have been a couple of days but it seemed impossible that a whole week had gone by. She wanted to know more but she suddenly felt tired again. Maybe Sister was right. She needed to build her strength up before going back on the wards.

She lay back and closed her eyes, enjoying the warmth of the sun on her face. As she drifted off she wondered if there'd been any news of Jack. This time there was no feeling of despair, just a calm acceptance that if it was meant to be, they would meet again, even if it wasn't in this life. She would never again feel the black despair that had tortured her thoughts during her delirium.

Two weeks later Daisy was ready to go back to work. She was bored with lying in bed and longed to be outside in the fresh air. But the rainy season had arrived and Sister Drummond wouldn't hear of it.

She was sitting in a chair by the window, a blanket over her knees, waiting for Doctor Holloway and hoping he would pronounce her fit. But her heart sank when she saw his expression.

'I'm sorry, Nurse,' he said. 'I'm sending you home. You're still very weak and it will be some time before you're fit enough to work.'

'But I feel so much better,' she protested.

'Daisy, you know how much I'll miss you but it's for your own good,' he said, taking her hand.

Although Daisy had tried to maintain a formal relationship with him since his declaration of love at the picnic, she knew his feelings hadn't changed. She would never return those feelings but she valued his friendship and, since her illness, had looked forward to his visits.

She snatched her hand away. 'You can't do that! I want to go back to work. I need to work, it's all I've got now,' she cried.

A tiny spasm twitched at the corner of Peter's mouth and she knew she'd hurt him. But it was true. Without Jack, her nursing career was all she had left to cling to.

'I'm sorry, Daisy. It's out of my hands.' He stood up and walked towards the door. 'You're not the only one. We can't keep all of you here convalescent. There isn't the room, and it's tying up staff who should be nursing the really sick.'

Daisy nodded. It made sense, of course, but she wasn't happy about it. What would she do with herself back in England? The war showed no signs of coming to an end, either here or in northern Europe. Then, the thought of going home – seeing her mother and maybe even her brothers – brought a lift of her depression and she gave a small smile.

Peter nodded encouragingly. 'Go home, Daisy. Get yourself really well again. After the war, there'll still be a job for you. Now, I must get off on my rounds. I'll see you before you go, but just in case, I'll wish you good luck.' He walked away quickly.

Daisy had hardly taken in the fact that she was really leaving Malta before it was time to go. An ambulance was to take her and four other nurses down to the harbour at Valletta.

Sarah hugged her, tears in her eyes. 'I'll miss you,' she said.

'Maybe it won't be for long. You'll come and see me when you get back to Portsmouth, won't you,' Daisy said.

There was no time for protracted farewells. 'Walking wounded, all aboard,' the driver called, raising smiles through the tears.

Sister Drummond unbent sufficiently to shake hands and wish Daisy good luck before she joined the others. As the driver pulled away in a cloud of dust, she peered through the rear window. The crowd that had gathered to say goodbye had dispersed, except for Peter Holloway who stood by the door, his hand half raised in farewell.

She was sad that they'd probably never meet again. He'd been a good friend and such friends were hard to come by. But she knew she'd never grow to love him. And it wouldn't be fair to let him keep hoping by staying in contact.

CHAPTER SIXTEEN

Daisy gazed out of the train window and the familiar place names brought a lump to her throat: Fratton, Havant, Emsworth and at last Kingsbourne Halt. She watched the smoke from the steam engine disappearing as the train rounded the bend on its way to Chichester, before picking up her valise and walking through the booking hall. There was none of the usual bustle of station life such as she remembered on market days when she was a child – not even a ticket collector on duty.

She hadn't expected to be met. She wasn't even sure if her mother knew she was coming. It seemed strange to find herself completely alone for the first time in months. She'd become so used to being with other people, to sharing a room, having demands on her time, duties to perform.

She stood for a few moments, savouring the silence and the sooty smell of the station, strangely reluctant to start the walk down through the town to the harbour. She would meet people she knew and they would want to stop and talk. All she wanted was to get home, have a cup of tea, and then go to bed and sleep forever.

As she crossed the station yard she paused to let a car pull out in front of her. It stopped and a man leaned out. 'Going far?' he asked.

Daisy almost ignored him, remembering the last time she'd accepted a lift in a motor car. But as he opened the passenger door she recognized Henry Thornton.

'You don't want to carry that heavy case. Jump in,' he urged.

'Mr Thornton, thank you, sir. You're very kind.' Daisy found herself stammering. After all, last time she'd seen him she'd been a lowly maid in the Davenport household. But he hadn't recognized her, as his next words showed.

'When I saw your uniform I thought you might be making for the hospital. I'm on my way there now.'

'Actually I'm going home. I've been working abroad. Perhaps you'd be kind enough to drop me off in the market square.'

'I'll take you to your door. It's the least I can do for someone who's been serving overseas. Have you been at the front, Nurse—?'

115

'March – Daisy March. I was in Malta.'

Henry looked at her with interest. 'Nurse March – Daisy. I thought I recognized you but I couldn't place you. Didn't you work at Ryfe Hall some years ago?'

Who'd have thought he'd remember her after all this time? He was sure to recall the reason for her dismissal. Perhaps he still thought she was a thief. But if he did remember, he said nothing, merely asking if she was on leave and when she'd be returning overseas.

'I'm on convalescent leave,' she said as they reached the quayside. 'Stop here. The lane where I live is too narrow for you to turn round. I'll walk the rest of the way.'

'If you're sure,' he said, jumping down from the high seat and going to the back of the car where he'd strapped her valise. Daisy jumped down too and held out her hand for the bag. But he held on to it.

'I'll carry it for you. If you've been ill, you must be careful not to overdo things,' he said. 'These foreign fevers really weaken the constitution.'

Daisy agreed with a little laugh. 'I'd never been ill in my life until then. I didn't realize what was happening until I collapsed. But I'm fine now. I wanted to go back to work but they insisted I return home to convalesce.'

'Will you go back when you're fit?' Henry asked.

'I don't think so. They say the war will be over soon anyway. I'd like to carry on nursing though. Maybe I'll try to get back to Kingsbourne Hospital.'

'I remember now – you had a bursary to do your training. I'm sure they'll take you back,' Henry said with a warm smile.

At the end of the lane she stopped and held out her hand for the valise. 'Thank you, Mr Thornton. You've been very kind,' she said.

'Not at all.' He raised his hat in farewell, but as she reached for the latch on the cottage door, he spoke hesitantly. 'Before you go, Nurse March – do you know what happened to Miss Davenport? I expect you know that Sir John died and the family left the Hall, but I've lost touch with them since. I know she joined the VADs and went abroad.'

She looked up at him, noting the sadness in his eyes. He's still in love with her, she thought. She wasn't sure how much to say but his eyes lit up when she told him she'd been nursing with her in Malta.

'Is she still there?' he asked eagerly, then coughed to hide his embarrassment. 'I mean, I'd like to write – to offer my condolences on the death of her father.'

'I'm afraid she left Malta some time before I did.'

'Do you know where she went? Is she with her mother in Kent?'

'She got married – out in Malta. They sent her home as she was expecting a baby.' Daisy watched his face pale and felt sorry for the blunt way she'd told him. She was about to tell him that Tom had died when he turned away and stumbled up the lane to his car. Daisy watched him go, wondering if she ought to go after him. He was clearly upset. But what good would it do? Georgina was settled in Norfolk, looking forward to the birth of her baby. She wouldn't wish to be reminded of Henry Thornton.

She shrugged and reached for the latch once more and, as she entered the cottage, the realization that her father would not be there to greet her was like a physical blow. All the time she'd been away, whenever she pictured her home, it was as it had been before the war, her mother at the kitchen range, Dad lying on his bed in the corner, and the boys filling the little room with their teasing and laughter.

She fought down the threatening tears, forcing her lips to curve in a smile and crying out cheerfully, 'Mum, it's me. I'm home.'

But there was no answering smile. Her mother looked up from where she sat at the kitchen table and the dull pain in her eyes made Daisy rush over to kneel beside her, putting her arms around her.

'What's happened, Mum?' It must be one of the boys. 'Please, tell me,' she begged. But Effie couldn't speak. Her thin body heaved with harsh rasping sobs and Daisy could only hold her, rocking her in her arms until the storm passed. The tears stopped at last and Daisy released her. She poked the fire into life and pushed the kettle over the coals, needing to do something while she gave her mother time to collect herself.

Between sniffs and hiccups her mother said in a shaky voice, 'What a welcome. I'm sorry, love. It was just – I looked up and saw you standing there and it all just came over me.'

'It's one of the boys, isn't it?'

Her mother started to cry again and Daisy's heart was heavy as she made tea from the meagre store in the cupboard. She pushed a cup across the table, then sat down opposite and poured her own. She couldn't stand not knowing any longer. 'Now, Mum, tell me what's happened,' she demanded.

Her mother got up and went to the mantelpiece, taking the telegram from behind the clock and handing it to Daisy.

Daisy read the brief message, a sob rising in her throat. Private James March – Jimmy – had been killed in action at Cambrai. Daisy remembered hearing the news in Paris on her way home. It was the first time that tanks had been used – the amazing new weapon that was supposed to turn the tide of war against the Germans. But the expected victory turned to disaster, with many casualties. Daisy hadn't realized that Jimmy had been there, although as usual she'd said a prayer for her brothers wherever they might be.

In the dark hours of endless nights on duty, Daisy had wept silent tears over her patients, she had cried for Tom and then for Jack, despite her never-wavering conviction that he must have survived. She had thought there were no tears left. But the realization that her big brother was gone brought angry wrenching sobs.

In more than three years of war, few of her friends and acquaintances had escaped the loss of someone dear to them. She'd almost resigned herself to never seeing her older brothers again, especially when Dick was sent back to the front so soon. Now that the fear had become reality, she realized you could never really prepare yourself. Her only consolation was being home now, here to help her mother through the dark days ahead.

Now it was Effie's turn to comfort her daughter. 'I sat here for hours trying to write to you. But I couldn't find the words.' She was composed now, her tears drying on her cheeks, only the shadows beneath her eyes, the set of her lips, showing her inner suffering.

'What about Dick – and Billy?' Daisy asked.

'Billy was home a few days ago. You just missed him. He went back to his ship in Southampton,' Effie said. 'I haven't heard from Dick. I wrote to him about Jimmy. They weren't together any more after he went back.'

'Didn't he go back to his old regiment then?'

'No, he was upset about that, wanted to be with his brother.' Effie fell silent, then she gave a little shudder, looking down at the telegram lying on the table. She picked it up and put it back behind the clock.

'They rang the bells, you know,' she said suddenly.

Daisy was alarmed. What was her mother talking about?

'The church bells. They started ringing and people went out into the street. We thought the war was over. They said we'd won a great victory against the Germans. But we were celebrating a battle not the whole war. How can it be a victory when my boy's dead?' Effie's tears flowed again.

That small victory had brought a wave of optimism and when Daisy went to the shops for her mother the next day, the people she met seemed to think the end of the war might be in sight. It wasn't and she soon realized that things were just as bad as they'd been before she went abroad.

She missed nursing and, as she began to feel stronger, she knew she had to get back to work. But didn't want to leave her mother. Effie was a shadow of her former self, lacking in energy and sitting at the kitchen table drinking endless cups of tea, while uselessly speculating on where

Dick or Billy were. Every time there was a knock on the door she jumped, her trembling hand going to her mouth.

It was almost a relief when one day she suddenly announced that she was going to start taking in washing again.

'Mum, you don't have to. We don't need the money now,' Daisy protested.

'Well, I can't just sit around waiting for the boys to come home,' she said. 'Besides, I do need the money. I want new curtains and a rug – just look at that moth-eaten old thing. My boys will want a nice comfortable home to come back to.'

Daisy had some money saved and was about to offer to pay for the new things when she realized that wouldn't help. Like herself, Mum needed to be busy, to have something to aim for. And now that it seemed she was getting back to normal, Daisy could go back to work with a clear conscience.

The next day, braving the icy wind, she wrapped up warmly in her nurse's cloak and began the long walk up to the hospital on the hill.

As she approached the hospital, she was thinking of Georgina and her baby. Little Jack had been born a week after Christmas and in her last letter, Georgina had given rapturous descriptions of his progress. She hadn't said much about her in-laws this time and, reading between the lines, Daisy thought perhaps living at the rectory wasn't working out so well since the baby came. When she'd first arrived, the Lazenbys had welcomed her like the prodigal daughter and clearly expected her to make her home with them permanently. If only she could have come back to Sussex, Daisy thought, missing her friend and the camaraderie of the hospital wards.

Matron agreed to see her but Daisy was disappointed when she said, 'You may be feeling better, but you still haven't regained your strength. You look as if a puff of wind would blow you over. Nursing is a tough job. You need to be up to scratch.'

'But I'm fully recovered,' Daisy protested. 'I even walked up the hill from the town without getting puffed.'

'I understand, Nurse. But trust me. You wouldn't be able to keep it up and if you fell ill again, I'd blame myself. Give it a bit longer, then we'll see.'

Daisy went away bitterly disappointed. At the hospital gates she stopped and looked towards the Solent where she could make out the shadowy outlines of a Royal Navy ship, a destroyer, she thought. It wasn't the bitter easterly wind which made her shiver. She turned away, trying to think of other things, like the letter which had come that morning from her brother Dick. After weeks of no news it was almost a relief to learn that he was now a prisoner. At least he was out of the fighting, she thought.

As she crossed the hospital forecourt a car pulled up beside her and someone called her name.

'Miss March, are you working again now?'

'No, Matron feels I need more time to get fit.'

She was about to walk on when Henry spoke again. 'Matron speaks very well of you – one of her best nurses, she told me.'

Daisy felt herself blushing but she also felt a glow of pride. She *was* a good nurse so why couldn't she have the chance to prove it? She began to walk away but Henry stopped her. 'How would you feel about private nursing?' he asked.

'I don't know. It depends on the patient.' She imagined he might need someone to look after an elderly relative, someone querulous and demanding. It wasn't what she thought of as real nursing but it would be a job.

'Why don't you come and meet him – then you can decide.'

'Is it here in Kingsbourne?'

Henry shook his head. 'Southsea,' he said.

'I'm not sure. I want to be close to home so that I can keep an eye on my mother.'

'You'd have plenty of time off, I promise.' He smiled but still she hesitated.

'Please, Nurse March. I'm at my wits' end. We could go now. I could have you back here by dinner time.'

'I'd have to go home first and tell my mother.'

'Splendid. Jump in then.' He indicated the car which was parked across the road.

Back at the cottage she found her mother in the yard hanging out washing. 'It'll soon dry in this wind,' Effie said. 'So, did you get the job?'

'No, but I've been offered another – private nursing. I have to go now but I'll explain when I get back.' She planted a hasty kiss on her mother's cheek.

Mr Thornton was waiting in the open-topped Lanchester, the engine running. Ignoring the curious stares of the neighbours, Daisy climbed up beside him. As she settled herself comfortably in the deep leather passenger seat, she reflected that this was the second time recently that the posh car had parked at the end of Fish Lane and Daisy thought with a wry smile that they'd certainly have something to gossip about now.

As they drove through the town, Henry explained what would be expected of her if she accepted the job. 'It's my cousin, Roger. He was in the army, wounded at Cambrai. His physical wounds have healed sufficiently for him to be discharged from the military hospital. Unfortunately, he is still far from well.'

He hesitated and Daisy asked if there was no other family to care for him. She knew that since the death of his mother Henry had lived alone in a cavernous Victorian villa on the edge of Southsea Common. It seemed a strange choice for a convalescent.

Henry coughed and looked embarrassed. 'His parents feel that they are unable to give him the sort of care he needs.'

'Couldn't he go to a convalescent home? He'd get excellent nursing care then.'

'There are such homes for those who've lost limbs or been blinded. But Roger's needs are somewhat different,' Henry said.

He was silent for a moment, appearing to be concentrating on the road, and Daisy started when he pounded his fist on the steering wheel. 'I do not want my cousin sent to an asylum,' he said forcefully.

'An asylum?' Daisy began to feel a little apprehensive. What was really wrong with Henry's cousin? She recalled Corporal Smith on that picnic party up in the hills of Malta. Just the sound of the mule clattering on the stony track had reduced him to a trembling wreck. And the problem was far worse among those who'd been in the trenches in France. In one of his letters Dick had mentioned a friend in a similar state.

So many people – including the powers that be – refused to view these cases with the same sympathy afforded to amputated limbs, blindness and the terrible ravages of gas attacks. Even some doctors were lacking in understanding when they could see no physical cause of suffering – unlike Peter Holloway, who'd shown equal compassion for all those in his care. But was an asylum the only solution?

As she listened to Henry's stumbling explanation of his cousin's problems, she felt a surge of compassion for the unknown Roger and for Henry too. It was kind of him to take on the responsibility for his relative – especially as, reading between the lines, she realized that no one else seemed to want him.

'Now you know. Do you still think you'll give it a try?' Henry asked diffidently.

'Let's wait till I've met your cousin, shall we?' Daisy said with a smile. 'I do know about shell-shock. We had a couple of cases out in Malta.'

As they drove towards Southsea Common, Henry turned to her. 'I know you must feel a little apprehensive and I'll quite understand if you say no, but once you've met Roger I think you'll realize he just needs

121

someone to watch over him. I'm so busy with my business these days and I don't like to leave him alone.'

Daisy nodded and looked away, wondering for a brief moment if she was doing the right thing. Despite having nursed such cases, her experience of shell-shock was very limited. What had she let herself in for? Well, she hadn't decided to take the job yet.

The car pulled up in front of a large red-brick house facing the common and, reminding herself that this was only a preliminary meeting and that she could still change her mind, she stepped down from the Lanchester and went up the front steps to Victory House, a determined smile fixed firmly in place.

When Daisy got home she was smiling. 'I've got the job,' she said.

'It doesn't sound like proper nursing,' Effie said.

Daisy explained about Henry's cousin. 'It's no different to nursing soldiers in hospital,' she said.

Effie didn't seem happy about it but Daisy reassured her that she'd only agreed to a trial period. Later she sat down to write to Georgina, wondering what her friend would think about her working for Mr Thornton.

'Georgina will be surprised,' she said as she sealed the envelope.

Effie sniffed. She'd never become reconciled to Daisy's friendship with the girl from the 'big house', as she still called it. 'I don't know why you bother with her,' she said. 'I expect she's making new friends now – Mrs Tom Lazenby, living at the vicarage. She won't have time for the likes of you.'

Daisy sighed. It was an old argument. 'Georgina's not like that,' she said. 'Besides, it was different when we were all working together – we were all equal.'

'Ah but you wouldn't invite her home here for tea, would you?' Effie said.

'I might,' Daisy said defiantly. Perhaps her mother might be right though. It had been different when they were working as part of a team. The class differences had seemed unimportant to most of the nurses although of course there had been a few exceptions.

Daisy refused to take any notice of her mother. Georgina was her friend, not to mention a fragile link with Jack. Deep down, she still hadn't given up hope that he'd been rescued and was a prisoner somewhere.

CHAPTER SEVENTEEN

Georgina should have been content – as content as anyone coping with widowhood could be, that is. When she'd arrived at Thorpe Rectory, Tom's parents had made her more than welcome, immediately accepting her as one of the family. She had expected some reservations, especially in view of her hasty marriage and the obvious fact of her pregnancy. But they had taken the frightened, grieving girl to their hearts.

The vicar, whom she'd most dreaded meeting, didn't seem worried by the fact that they'd done things in the wrong order. 'These things happen in wartime,' he'd said with a tolerant smile. They'd been blessed with the opportunity to put things right and must now look forward to doing their best for the forthcoming little one.

Strangely enough, these platitudes had a ring of sincerity and Georgina found herself warming to the thin stooped man with his gentle eyes and wistful smile. She liked Muriel Lazenby too, although she was quite different from her husband, a bundle of energy, forthright and independent – a little bossy too.

In the last days of her pregnancy, when she'd felt so tired and depressed, the thought of facing the future alone had been too daunting. It was true she sometimes had moments of looking forward to the birth of her baby, which in other circumstances would have amounted to joy. But these came rarely. The months of strenuous work under appalling conditions, the trauma of Tom's death and the arduous journey home across Europe had all taken their toll.

It was easier to let Muriel mother her, to eat what Muriel told her to, to rest when she said. Easier to bow her head in prayer and make the responses the Reverend Lazenby expected even though her heart told her that if there was a God he would not have taken Tom away from her.

Georgina floated through the last few months of her pregnancy on a tide of lethargy, buoyed up by the affectionate concern of Tom's parents. She had become very fond of both of them but now their affection and concern for her and the baby's welfare were beginning to smother her and since the birth of little Jack she was beginning to feel trapped.

It was clear that the Lazenbys expected her to make her home with them permanently, but Georgina had started to have reservations and as each day passed it became harder to tell them that she wanted a home of her own. She had a little money, left in trust by her grandmother – enough to buy a small cottage and provide a modest income. She certainly had no intention of being dependent on Tom's family.

The first stirrings of resentment came when Muriel first held her grandson. 'Hello, little Tom,' she cooed.

'No, I don't want to call him Thomas,' Georgina said. 'He's Jack – after my brother. You don't mind, do you?'

Muriel pursed her lips, then shook her head. 'Of course not. It's your decision, my dear. Though I did hope . . .' She paused at the door. 'I'll go and tell the vicar he has a grandson. He'll be so delighted.'

A gentle tap on the door heralded Tom's father. He pushed his glasses up on to his forehead and peered at the wrapped bundle, touching the baby's cheek gently. 'Well, little man, are you going to be a sailor like your daddy, or a clergyman like Grandfather?' Turning to Georgina, he said, 'I'm so pleased it's a boy. We must put his name down for Tom's old school. I'm sure that's what he would have wanted.'

For a brief moment Georgina wished she'd never come to Thorpe Magna. She was sure the Lazenbys only wanted what was best for their grandchild but it seemed as if she was to have no say in anything to do with him. She closed her eyes against the angry retort which rose to her lips. They mean well, she told herself firmly, and she was an ungrateful wretch to feel this way. At least she'd made her wishes known about the baby's name. If she hadn't spoken up, she was sure they'd have started calling him Tom without even consulting her.

And that's what happened. Despite her protests, they referred to him as 'little Tommy', even after his christening when Georgina had insisted that Thomas would be his second name.

Then there was all the advice on how to feed him, what he should wear. It wasn't as if she was a naïve young girl. If she could bandage an amputated stump and endure ghastlier sights than most people encountered in a lifetime, she was sure the needs of a small baby were not beyond her.

But Muriel would interfere. Every time he cried, she would appear, saying, 'Everything all right, dear? I thought I heard him crying.'

Although Georgina knew it was with the best intentions, it was beginning to get on her nerves.

The last straw came one morning towards the end of March when she woke to sunshine streaming through the window after weeks of rain. She jumped out of bed and went to the cradle where little Jackie still slept, his lips moving in a sucking movement, his fair curls damp against the plump neck.

The bright spring day beckoned and after breakfast Georgina put Jackie in his pram, well wrapped up in his woollies – despite the brightness of the day, the wind was still keen, the sun occasionally obscured by racing clouds. As she walked down the drive, noticing the signs of spring appearing at last after the long hard winter, she met the postman bringing the second delivery.

There was a letter from Daisy and she tore the envelope open at once. Engrossed in the letter, she didn't notice her mother-in-law until she spoke.

'What are you doing outside with little Tommy in this freezing wind?' Muriel said sharply.

Georgina looked up, frowning. 'It's Jack,' she said sharply, 'not Tommy.'

Her mother-in-law's lips thinned. 'You'd better take him inside at once.'

Instead of meekly complying as she usually did, Georgina rounded on the older woman and said, 'I think I can make decisions about my own baby.' She hadn't meant to snap, but she'd had enough of Muriel's interference. It was time she started standing up for herself.

'Well, of course, dear.' Muriel seemed taken aback by her response. 'I'm sure you didn't realize quite how cold it was. After all, you haven't been out much lately.'

Georgina decided to let it go for now, knowing that what she saw as Muriel's interference was only natural concern for the wellbeing of her grandson.

They entered the house and Georgina lifted Jackie out of the pram. She wanted to escape to her room. But Muriel hadn't finished with her yet.

'Georgina, dear, I don't want to interfere – but you haven't been very strong since baby came and I worry about both of you. Perhaps you should stay indoors while this cold wind persists. It may be spring on the calendar but here in Norfolk it can be very unpredictable.'

'You know I wouldn't do anything to hurt little Jack,' Georgina protested. 'I thought a bit of fresh air would be good for both of us.'

'Of course, dear.'

Georgina would not be mollified. 'Well, Jack is my baby and as I said earlier, I'm the one who decides what's best for him.' She could hardly get the words out but her raised voice woke Jack and he started to wail.

'There, now you've set him off,' Muriel declared, reaching out to take him.

'I'll see to him,' Georgina snapped and almost ran up the stairs, slamming the door to her room and plonking herself on the bed, where she sat and rocked Jack into silence.

Later, when she was calmer, she thought perhaps she'd been a little harsh. Muriel was still grieving for her son and it was quite natural that she would dote on her grandchild, perhaps seeing the baby as a substitute for the child she had lost.

'I'll say sorry later,' she told little Jack, bending and kissing his head. 'It's only because she loves you. I know that really.'

Yes, she would apologize. And she'd try to be more careful of Muriel's feelings in future. But at the same time she'd be firm. She recalled her earlier resolve not to become dependent on Tom's family. Perhaps it was time to think about making a life of her own.

As she changed to go down to dinner, she remembered Daisy's letter. After her first astonishment that her friend was working for Henry Thornton, her feelings changed to envy. She couldn't help comparing Daisy's new life with her own which, despite her love for baby Jack, had become rather boring. She still thought fondly of Henry, knowing that if she'd never met Tom she would have been content to marry him. Not that she would want to do the job that Daisy was doing, she thought.

Reading the letter again, she began to question her own life. Yes, it was definitely time to move on. She put the letter down on her dressing table and went to look at Jack, now settled peacefully in his cradle.

'It's time for a change, my lad,' she murmured. 'Your grandparents aren't going to dictate your upbringing. I want you all to myself.' She bent and brushed her lips across the downy cheek, smiling.

She went back to the table and got out her writing case. '*Your letter has made me realize how homesick I am for Sussex,*' she wrote to Daisy. '*I have decided to come back. I'll have to wait till the warmer weather before travelling with the baby. But I can't wait to see you.*'

As she sealed the letter she felt as if a weight had been lifted from her. Despite her earlier resolution not to upset Muriel, she knew it would only be a matter of time before her mother-in-law did something else to annoy her. She truly didn't want to hurt her. Going back to Sussex would solve the problem. She would take a small cottage by the sea for the summer and then decide what she would do with the rest of her life.

She went downstairs and put the envelope on the hall table. Then with a lift of her chin, she went in to face the Lazenbys. She would apologize to Muriel for her angry outburst but it really was time she started making decisions for herself. And the first decision was to tell her in-laws that she wanted her own home. She would promise to bring Jackie back for frequent visits. She couldn't wait to get back to Sussex and see Daisy again.

Daisy sat in the corner of the room sewing. She appeared to be totally absorbed in her work but she never took her attention off Roger for a moment. In the weeks since she'd started caring for Henry Thornton's cousin, she'd learned that it didn't do to lower her guard. Not that Roger Thornton was dangerous – only to himself.

She recalled her first sight of the young man. Emaciated, hollow-eyed and trembling. His physical wounds had healed some time ago, but mentally he was a wreck. The slightest sound or movement could set him trembling, eyes darting round the room in terror. Henry had prepared her for Roger's condition, telling her that he spent hours curled up on his bed, his fingers flexing and unflexing ceaselessly.

When he'd been introduced to her, she spoke to him gently but she could feel his apprehension at meeting a stranger. Tentatively, Daisy had suggested he might be better off in a hospital. 'The doctors can do so much these days,' she said.

'No doctors,' Henry said sharply. He leaned forward and touched her hand. 'Please, Daisy. All he needs is someone to care for him, to talk to him and treat him like a human being. I have to be out such a lot, taking care of the business, and there's no one else.'

'What did the doctors at the hospital recommend?'

'They agreed with his parents – that he should be put in an asylum. His father . . .' Henry broke off and his lips tightened.

'Mr Thornton, I need to know everything if I'm going to take this job on.' Daisy bit her lip. The poor man looked so distressed. She realized that any hint of mental illness was a matter for shame to most people but Henry seemed only to want what was best for his cousin.

Henry had sighed, clenching his fists. 'My uncle, Roger's father, is a colonel. He views soldiers with conditions like this as what he calls "lacking in moral fibre". He called Roger a milksop and said that if I could make a man of him I was welcome to try.'

'So you brought him here rather than have him locked away in an institution?'

'I really don't know if it's the right thing for him, but I must try,' Henry said. 'You will help me, won't you, Miss March?'

Against her better judgment, Daisy had agreed and now, months later, she could see the improvement in her patient. From needing to be washed and dressed and fed like a toddler, he now looked after himself. He no longer jumped and ducked at the slightest noise. She had even persuaded him to sit by the open window on sunny days. And at last she was making some headway in persuading him to talk to her.

Her main worry now was that his earlier apathy had been replaced by displays of anger and she wasn't sure how to handle those. She wasn't frightened for herself. Roger had never tried to harm her, even during the worst of his rages.

His anger was directed towards himself, for surviving when so many of his friends had not. He would repeatedly bang his head against the wall or punch his arms and legs until they were purple with bruises, all the time muttering, 'Why me, why me?'

Henry, fearful that his cousin would be locked away, still refused to consult a doctor about his cousin's condition and Daisy didn't know what to do. When she told her mother of her concern, Effie had said vehemently that she should give it up and come home. But Daisy was determined to do what she could for the young man.

When she'd written to Georgina of her frustration, her friend had suggested contacting Doctor Holloway for his advice. Why hadn't she thought of it herself? Daisy wondered. She immediately wrote care of the hospital in Malta, careful to keep the letter businesslike and impersonal so that he couldn't read anything into her contacting him.

If only he'd write back, she thought now, as she looked up from her needlework to see Roger staring fixedly at the wall. She studied him covertly, looking for the signs of an imminent attack of angry self-abuse.

The sun streamed through the open window, highlighting Roger's golden hair, which had been allowed to grow out of its regimental cut. When he turned to her and smiled, Daisy caught her breath. For a brief moment he'd reminded her of Jack.

The moment passed when he said in a rather childlike voice, 'I'm getting better, aren't I, Nurse?'

'Yes, Master Roger, you are.'

'I'll never be the man I was before though, will I?' He lapsed into silence again.

A slight breeze ruffled the curtains and Daisy wrinkled her nose as a tang of the sea wafted in. She was reminded of her brothers coming home from work, their salt-stiffened clothes bringing that same smell as they burst noisily through the cottage door.

Roger's words echoed in her head. None of us will be the same again, she thought, choking back a sob. At least she'd survived and it was up to her to make the best of the life she'd been given. She couldn't do anything for Jimmy, for Jack and Tom and all the others who'd gone, but she could help those who were still here.

Roger didn't seem to expect a reply. He gazed at the wall, rocking slightly to and fro. Today was one of his better days but she could never predict when another outburst might happen. If only Peter would answer her letter.

She went back to her sewing. Despite her concern for Roger, she was happy here. Mr Thornton paid her generously, as well as allowing her ample free time to visit her mother. She had a pleasant room overlooking the common and beyond it, the sea. And, in the evenings, if her employer wasn't away on business, he would invite her to dine with him. If Roger was well enough, as he was more often now, he would join them.

I should be content, she told herself. But after being responsible for a ward of forty badly injured or sick men, looking after just one person hardly seemed like work at all. Not only that, she had far too much time in which to dream about Jack, to persuade herself that he would return. She'd never really convinced herself that he was dead, reliving Tom's words – 'Jack got off all right'. But after so long, surely she should have accepted that he wasn't coming back?

Until now she'd always been able to submerge herself in hard physical work whenever these thoughts threatened to get the upper hand. Living in Victory House, with servants to wait on her and a patient who sometimes hardly realized she was there, there wasn't enough to do. But she couldn't let Mr Thornton down, or Roger either, she thought, getting up restlessly and crossing to the window.

Below on the common, two children were trying to get a kite aloft. Their high laughter floated into the room on the breeze and Daisy smiled, envying their childish exuberance. She wished she were out in the fresh air with them. But so far she hadn't been able to persuade Roger to leave the house. The slightest suggestion of going out brought on an attack of terror. Even the sound of the children playing outside sometimes made him flinch and sink into his chair.

Daisy contemplated closing the window to shut out the noise. But it was a warm day and the fresh air would do him good, she thought, withdrawing her hand from the latch. She couldn't shield him from the sounds of normal life for ever.

'Time for tea, Master Roger,' she said, in as cheerful a tone as she could. At first he'd taken all his meals in his room, unable to leave the safety represented by these four walls. But gradually Daisy had persuaded him to move across the landing to the little sitting room which Henry had given her. From there, it had been a short step to getting him downstairs to the dining room.

Tea, however, was still taken upstairs and now Daisy opened the door, waiting until Roger got up and joined her. At first she'd helped him out of his chair, cajoling him like a child if he was reluctant to move, then holding his arm as he took hesitant steps out on to the landing.

One day it had struck her that, instead of treating him like a baby and ministering to his every need, she should look on him as a child who was gradually growing up. Instead of doing things for him, she showed him what she wanted done, then left him to try for himself. After initial tantrums of frustration, he took a stubborn pleasure in performing small tasks, turning to her for approval when he was successful.

Like a child, he basked in her smiles of encouragement and every day saw some small step forward. If it were not for the outbursts of self-destructive anger, she would have said he was well on the way to being cured, a vindication of Henry's insistence that he should not be shut up in an institution.

While they were having tea, Henry joined them. He looked tired, having just driven up from Southampton, where he was having some trouble at his other brewery. He sat down with a sigh and accepted the cup of tea which Daisy handed to him.

'It's not just the staffing problems, although we could do with more men, especially as we've had such a good barley harvest. If we do as well with the hops in a couple of weeks' time, we should be on target for record production,' he said.

'That's good, isn't it?' Daisy said tentatively. His remarks had been addressed to his cousin, but Roger ignored him and she only spoke to give a semblance of normality.

'It is good,' Henry said. 'But where are we going to store the stuff? There's a shortage of barrels and there are no coopers to make more. And then there's the question of transport. There's little petrol available. And we can't go back to using the drays because the war has taken all the horses.'

Daisy thought of her mother's remarks about the likes of Henry Thornton, rich men making more money out of the war. Now she realized how hard he worked. And how much he cared for the people in his employ. She listened sympathetically as he unburdened himself, seeming more concerned that if his business failed he wouldn't be able to offer jobs to those fortunate enough to return from the war.

Lost in thought, she took a moment to absorb his next words. 'I think I made a mistake in buying Ryfe Hall,' he said. 'I needed the land but the house is in such a state. Besides, it's not worth doing it up if I don't intend to live there.'

'Can't you sell it – just keep the land?' Daisy asked, shocked to hear that he now owned Georgina's old home, bringing as it did memories of her years there as a servant.

'I don't think anyone would buy it in its present state,' he said.

As Daisy moved to pour him more tea, he stopped her and stood up. 'I'm sorry. It's not fair to unload all my troubles on you. You're too good a listener.'

Roger, who had remained silent during tea, spoke up. 'She's a good talker too. She tells me stories about when she was a little girl.'

Henry smiled and ruffled the young man's hair. 'What would we do without her, eh, old chap?' He paused at the door. 'You're due a day off, aren't you, Daisy?'

'Yes, but it doesn't matter, Mr Thornton.'

'No. You must visit your mother. We shall manage quite well for a day or two. Go tomorrow and stay overnight. You can come back on Thursday afternoon.'

When Daisy tried to protest, Henry insisted. 'You see, it might be a while before you get another chance. I can stay with Roger for a couple of days but I'll have to go down to Southampton again. It may take a while to sort out these problems at the brewery. I'll feel happier if you're here while I'm away.'

He left the room and Daisy rang for the maid to clear away the tea things. When she turned to speak to Roger, she saw that he'd started his rocking again and she realized he'd been disturbed by her mention of going away. For a moment she was tempted to insist on staying. But she wanted to see her mother. Besides, she told herself, Roger was becoming far too dependent on her. It couldn't be good for him.

Once again she wished Peter would write. Although she felt she was handling her patient correctly, it would be reassuring to have his professional opinion. Had he even received her letter?

CHAPTER EIGHTEEN

When Daisy arrived home she was pleased that Effie was looking far less tired. Giving her a warm hug, she noted that she even seemed to have put on a little weight.

The bright smile and clear eyes were soon explained when her mother reached for the letter on the mantelpiece. 'It's from Dick. They're sending him home,' she said.

'But he's still a prisoner. I thought he'd be kept there till the end of the war,' Daisy said.

She read the letter with a growing feeling of unease. Dick was to be repatriated under the terms of the Geneva Convention, he wrote, explaining that his old wound had been giving him trouble. But Daisy was uneasy. She knew something far worse must be wrong for him to be considered for repatriation.

'Isn't it wonderful? Our Dick's coming home,' Effie said. 'Not yet, though, it says he'll have to stay in hospital for a while.'

'He's probably back now. But we don't know which hospital, do we? I do hope he's all right.'

Some of the light went out of Effie's eyes. 'Nothing else could have happened, could it? Perhaps he's written and the letter's gone astray?'

'Yes, that's probably it,' Daisy said, attempting a smile. 'We need to know where he is so that we can visit him. I'll speak to Mr Thornton about it.'

'What can he do?'

'He's a trustee on the hospital board. He'll be able to find out where Dick is and if he's a long way away, he might be able to arrange a transfer nearer home. Anyway, Mum, don't worry about it till we know more.'

Daisy spent the rest of the day helping with the washing, turning the heavy handle of the mangle while Effie fed the sheets through in a never-ending stream. Then they hung the linen on the line in the back yard and at last Daisy was able to persuade her mother to sit down and enjoy a well-earned rest. 'I thought you were going to ease off on the work, Mum,' she said. 'You don't need the money, surely.'

'It takes my mind off things,' she replied.

Daisy couldn't argue with that. She knew that tonight, at least, physical weariness would ensure a good night's sleep, free from tormenting memories and worry about Roger Thornton. Henry had been right to insist she stay the night here and have the following day free as well. She'd take a walk down to the harbour tomorrow, she thought, as she said goodnight to her mother later that evening.

It was another bright sunny day but with a crisp autumn tang in the air. Daisy went downstairs, relishing the thought of a few hours to herself. She'd tried to persuade her mother to join her but she was already hard at work. The washing, which had been brought in yesterday evening and hung on clothes-horses in front of the range, was now neatly folded on a chair in the corner and the flat irons were heating on the kitchen range.

Daisy knew better than to offer to help. It was a job her mother took great pride in, but which she herself had never mastered to the degree of perfection Effie required.

She finished her breakfast and, after washing the dishes, said, 'I won't be long, Mum. I need some fresh air. I don't get out very much at Mr Thornton's.'

Effie nodded understandingly. Daisy had explained Roger's problems to her. 'You enjoy your day off, love,' she said, picking up one of the irons and spitting on it to test the heat.

As Daisy stepped out into the narrow lane, the post boy on his bicycle almost knocked her over. He skidded to a stop and jumped off, holding the bicycle steady with one hand whilst fumbling in his sack. 'One for Mrs March,' he said, jumping back on his bicycle and pedalling away, whistling as he went.

Effie looked up from her ironing as Daisy came back into the kitchen. 'You didn't stay out long. Too cold, was it?' she said. Then her face blanched as she took in the official-looking letter in her daughter's hand.

She put the iron down with a trembling hand and felt blindly for a chair. Daisy held the envelope out to her but she pushed it away. 'You read it, Daisy,' she said, putting her hands over her face. 'Oh God, I don't think I can take any more.'

'It's all right, Mum,' Daisy said, quickly scanning the single sheet of paper. 'It's from the hospital where Dick is.' Her eyes skimmed down the page and she was glad her mother hadn't read it first. As she'd suspected, Dick's old leg wound wasn't why he was being kept in hospital. Reading between the lines, Daisy realized that her brother's symptoms were almost identical to Roger Thornton's. Her heart sank when she read the address at the top of the letter. This was no military hospital.

'Does it say when they're sending him home?' Effie asked, her eyes full of hope.

'Not for a while, Mum. He's still quite ill, you know,' Daisy said gently.

'But we can go and see him, can't we?'

Daisy hesitated. Not for anything would she have her mother subjected to such an ordeal. From what Mr Thornton had told her, she knew what to expect – high brick walls, long echoing corridors, small rooms with high ceilings and tiny windows. The thought of her laughing carefree brother in such a place brought unbearable pain.

'It's a long way, Mum,' she said hurriedly, hoping her hesitation hadn't been too obvious. 'And he may not have to stay long. Let's wait and see, shall we? No point in rushing off across the country when Dick could be on his way home.'

Effie agreed, if a bit reluctantly. She squared her shoulders. 'Well, at least he's out of that prison camp and back in dear old Blighty,' she said with a little laugh, picking up the iron and attacking the linen with renewed vigour.

Daisy put the letter back behind the clock, pausing for a moment to look at the photograph which stood in its cardboard mount on the mantelpiece. There was her father, her two elder brothers either side, leaning again the hull of the boat, Billy squatting in front of them. They were dressed identically in their dark Guernsey jumpers, trousers tucked into their boots. It was a sharp reminder of happier days and Daisy wondered how her mother could bear to leave it where she would see it every time she stoked the fire or checked the time.

When it was time to return to Southsea, Daisy kissed her mother and begged her not to worry about Dick. 'He's in the best place, Mum,' she said. 'I'll find out what's happening – they'll take notice of a nurse – and let you know as soon as I hear.'

As the train drew into the station, Daisy thought about the letter from the Kent hospital. Dick must be in a really bad way to have been sent there. Roger had been in the military hospital and his relatives consulted before any decision was made. Of course, Roger was an officer – not that that should make any difference.

Whatever happened, she must do her best to make sure Dick wasn't shut away for good. Having seen what strides Roger had made in recent months, she was sure her brother would respond in the same way, given the chance.

The thought brought a quick decision. She would bring him home and look after him herself, she thought – even if it meant leaving the Thorntons.

She walked up the drive to Victory House to find the place in uproar. One of the maids had threatened to leave and the housekeeper was in a rebellious mood. Daisy had established quite a good relationship with Mrs Johnson so it was a shock to be greeted with such a tirade.

'Thank goodness you're back, Nurse,' she said, hardly giving Daisy time to get indoors. 'I can't be doing with all this upset. Master Roger's been that difficult. No one could calm him. It's like having a young child in the house – a badly behaved child at that. I was at my wits' end, just about ready to hand in my notice too. It's not part of my job to look after him. He needs to be in a hospital or somewhere.'

'Where's Mr Thornton?' Daisy interrupted.

'He had to go out,' she muttered, adding that he should have waited for the nurse's return before leaving the servants with such responsibility.

'What happened?'

'He knocked the teacup out of Carrie's hand. Smashed china, tea splashed all over the place, just because you weren't back.' Mrs Johnson's ample bosom quivered. 'Then when poor Carrie burst into tears, he starts a-crying and a-wailing too,' she went on. 'Hitting himself in the face, he was, and rocking, rocking all the time.'

'Is he all right now?' Daisy asked, her hand on the banister. She knew she should have come back yesterday.

'*He's* all right. But what about poor Carrie? Not to mention my nerves shredded to pieces.' Mrs Johnson's fat cheeks shook with indignation.

'I'm sorry, Mrs Johnson. He's been so much better lately. Besides, I thought Mr Thornton was here.'

She ran upstairs, going straight to Roger's room, dreading what she'd find. He was sleeping, one hand tucked beneath his cheek, the other flung out above his head. Like this he seemed like a child. But his sleep wasn't peaceful. As she gazed down at him, he muttered restlessly and the fingers of his outflung hand clenched spasmodically.

Daisy's heart was torn with pity for him. If this was what happened after leaving him for only two days, what would happen when he discovered she was going away for ever? She shouldn't have let him rely on her so much, but she hadn't realized how dependent he'd already become.

She sighed. Telling Mr Thornton she was leaving to look after her brother was going to be harder than she thought. She leaned over and tucked in a fold of the sheet. 'I know you need me,' she whispered. 'But Dick needs me more.'

She crept out, closing the door softly behind her, and went to hang up her coat before going downstairs for supper. During the meal she made an effort to smooth things over with Mrs Johnson and Carrie. Knowing how hard it was to get domestic help these days, she felt sure that Henry would be willing to take on another nurse to cover for when she wasn't there, so she took it upon herself to assure them both that they would never again be required to take the responsibility for Master Roger.

Mrs Johnson seemed satisfied. She'd worked for Henry for a long time and knew him as a fair and considerate employer. It was harder to convince Carrie.

'Well, I'm not going in that room again and that's that,' she said, with a defiant look at Daisy. 'And you can't make me.'

'I promise, I'll be there all the time. You won't have to be alone with him,' Daisy said. 'Besides, he wouldn't hurt you. He's only a danger to himself.'

Carrie seemed unconvinced and Daisy let the matter drop. She found herself sympathizing with the girl. After all, it was only her training that enabled her to deal with her patient so confidently. How could she expect a young girl, scarcely out of school, to understand?

As she turned to leave the room, Mrs Johnson said, 'Oh, I almost forgot. A letter came for you. It's on the hall table.'

Daisy thanked her and took the envelope upstairs. It was probably from Georgina saying she'd finally found a house to rent in Kingsbourne. It would be so good to see her.

After glancing in at Roger, Daisy went into her sitting room, leaving the door ajar so that she'd hear when Henry returned. Before opening her letter, she glanced at the postmark. It wasn't from Georgina after all. Curious as to who could be writing to her from Southampton, she tore open the envelope. To her surprise and pleasure it was from Peter Holloway, apologizing for taking so long to reply. He reassured her about her handling of her patient and had several suggestions to make.

Responding to her concerns about Roger's self-destructive bouts of anger he said, *'It's important that the patient has an outlet for his anger and frustration. If he bottles it up it will fester and cause more problems later on. I'm a great believer in keeping the patient occupied – writing, painting or drawing could be beneficial.'*

It made sense to Daisy and she put the letter away after making a note of Peter's address at a hospital in Southampton. He'd been posted there after leaving Malta for a brief spell in France. No wonder it had taken so long for her letter to reach him.

She was relieved that, according to Peter, she was treating her patient correctly and wondered why she hadn't thought herself of giving him something to occupy his time. Sitting by the window brooding day after day couldn't be good for him. She'd give it a try, she thought. If it worked and his condition improved even more, she wouldn't feel so bad about leaving.

She'd become very fond of her young patient, besides which she hated letting Henry down. But she couldn't let her brother down either. She must put Dick first.

Henry still hadn't returned when Daisy took a last look at Roger before going to bed. He didn't seem quite so restless now but she left the door ajar so that she would hear if he called out.

As she drifted off to sleep she thought how lucky Roger Thornton was. What would have happened to him if Henry hadn't come to the rescue? He'd probably have been locked away from those who could not or would not understand. But Dick wouldn't be hidden away, she decided. She'd bring him home and care for him as she'd cared for Roger.

If only there was somewhere for people like Roger and Dick, she thought. Not a hospital or asylum, but a proper home where they could learn to live normal lives again and gradually become accepted back into society. Even those who couldn't be cured shouldn't be shut off from contact with others. She was sure that Peter Holloway would agree with her.

If she were rich she'd buy a house in the country and start her own home, she thought sleepily. She wouldn't care whether they were officers or ordinary soldiers – all would be welcome. What a foolish thought, picturing her mother saying 'It's not for the likes of us'. But everyone said that things would be different after the war; the old ways would be swept away, including the class differences that made her mother feel so inadequate. In fact, Daisy felt sure that *nothing* would be the same after the war.

She woke next morning still thinking about it. Perhaps it wasn't so foolish after all – there were plenty of rich people who might be receptive to the idea. She would talk to Henry. She had nothing to lose by asking. If she waited till this evening she'd lose her nerve.

He was in the dining room, serving himself from the dishes on the sideboard. He turned as Daisy came in and she was pleased to see that the lines of strain had disappeared from his face. He must have sorted out the problems at the brewery then. He certainly seemed in a much happier frame of mind than when they'd last talked, despite the problems caused by her taking two days off.

'Good morning, Daisy. I'm so sorry you had to come back to all that fuss last night. I'm sure things weren't as bad as Mrs Johnson made out.'

'I couldn't really say, Mr Thornton. Master Roger was asleep when I got in and he's still sleeping.'

'I don't know what to do. He seemed so much better and you deserved a break. But he always gets upset when you're not here.' Henry sat down at the table and motioned her to join him. 'How was your mother?' he continued.

There would never be a better time to broach the subject, Daisy thought, taking a deep breath. 'She was looking much better, mainly because we had news of my brother.'

She went on to tell him of Dick's repatriation. 'I couldn't tell my mother he was in an asylum,' she said. 'She's had a hard enough time coping with the death of my older brother, as well as worrying about Billy at sea. I let her think he was in an ordinary hospital. But she'll have to know sometime. It was all I could do to stop her jumping on a train right away to go and see him.'

Henry swallowed a mouthful of toast and pushed his plate away. 'I think I know what you're going to say, Daisy. It's natural you'll want to look after your brother when he comes home. But we need you here – Roger needs you.'

Daisy fidgeted with the cutlery in front of her; she had to put this in just the right way.

'Well, are you going to give in your notice?' Henry prompted.

'Actually, Mr Thornton, I wasn't – not right away. But it may not be necessary. You see, I've had an idea.'

He sat back in his chair, giving her all his attention, and after a brief hesitation she plunged on. 'First, I have to ask you if you have any plans for Ryfe Hall.'

'I haven't decided yet. As I told you, I wanted the land. The house and surrounding buildings are no use to me. If things had been different I might have thought about restoring it and living there myself.' He gave an embarrassed cough and sipped his tea.

Daisy suspected he was thinking of Georgina but she carried on with her breakfast and waited for him to continue.

'Actually, I'm surprised the authorities haven't been on to me about it,' he said. 'So many big houses have been requisitioned. But it is rather dilapidated and, of course, the war must be over soon.'

'But you don't plan on renting it out, or anything like that, do you?'

'No, it hadn't occurred to me. But what has this to do with your brother – or with your continued employment here?'

138

Daisy smiled and said, 'I'd like to rent Ryfe Hall from you.'

'You? But that's absurd. What would you want with a great rambling house like that? And what about the repairs it needs?'

Daisy swallowed her sharp retort and said, 'I don't think it's absurd at all. I have some money saved and I think Ryfe would be just the place to start up a nursing home for people returning from the war. People like Roger and my brother, I mean – not those with physical disabilities.' Her words fell over themselves as she struggled to voice her idea.

'You mean you want to run a nursing home by yourself? Have you thought of all the implications?' Henry asked.

'Yes, I have. Of course, it would take time to get the house ready for occupation again. It's been empty for a long time and it will need doing up. But I'm sure I could do some of it, painting and decorating.' Henry leaned forward, nodding. At least he seemed to be taking her seriously now.

'It's a lot of work and would cost a lot of money. Of course, I wouldn't think of charging a high rent for such a good cause, but I don't think you could possibly afford to do all that,' he said gently.

Daisy straightened her shoulders and took a deep breath. 'That's where you come in, Mr Thornton. I've thought of a way and, if you'll help, I know it could be done.'

Henry nodded thoughtfully and Daisy thought she saw a suggestion of a smile. 'Go on,' he said.

'You must remember – I know Ryfe Hall. I know how many rooms, bathrooms and so on there are. We wouldn't need to fit it out like a hospital. It will be somewhere the residents can be cared for, a home where they'll feel safe and secure. There must be lots of young men like Master Roger – with no-one to care what happens to them.'

Henry started to say something but Daisy ignored him and plunged on recklessly. 'I don't mean your cousin. I know you care. But supposing you hadn't been willing to take him on? There are plenty of nursing homes for the physically wounded but who cares about the others? They don't deserve to be shut away in lunatic asylums.'

'Well, it sounds like a very worthwhile project. But where do I fit into all this – apart from letting my house to you, that is?'

'I'm not sure how to put this really. You might think it an awful cheek. But you're a successful businessman, well known in the town. I thought you could advise me how to set up a charitable trust, similar to Kingsbourne Hospital Board.'

'That sounds reasonable. The war's almost over and there'll be many young men needing help when they come home. But you can't do it alone.'

Daisy hesitated, not sure how Henry would react if she mentioned Georgina. He often asked for news of her and she was sure he still cared deeply for her. He was waiting for her reply and she plunged on, 'There's a nurse I used to work with – Nurse Bowman – she's due home from Malta soon and then there's Georgina. Did you know she's coming back to Sussex?'

'But she has a baby to care for.'

'She could still help. It would be wonderful for her to return to her old home. She loved Ryfe and was very upset when it had to be sold.'

'Don't you think she'd be more upset, coming back to live there under these circumstances?' Henry asked.

'Maybe. But I won't know till I ask her, will I?' Daisy relaxed a little, confident that she now had Henry's interest. Although the idea of taking over the hall had only occurred to her that morning, it seemed fully formed in her mind. The letter from Doctor Holloway had given her the confidence to share it.

She spoke breathlessly, anxious to outline her plans while Henry seemed interested, telling him about Doctor Holloway's views on the treatment of shell-shock.

'I'm sure he'd be willing to help,' she said. 'Of course, we couldn't afford to take on a full-time doctor. But he may be willing to act as a sort of consultant. He's already been a great help with Roger.'

Henry leaned back in his chair and smiled. 'Do you mean to tell me that this idea simply came to you as a result of needing to care for your brother?'

'Partly. I can't leave him where he is. You, of all people, must understand that. And I don't want to let you or Roger down. Besides, I've been thinking for a while now that I don't really have enough to do here. I need to be busy. This way I could make sure both my brother and your cousin are being looked after in the best possible way, as well as helping others.'

'I'll have to look into the practical aspects as well as the financial.'

Pleased she had piqued his interest, Daisy got up from the table. At least he hadn't dismissed the idea out of hand. Now, she would just have to wait for his decision. But while she was waiting she would make plans.

CHAPTER NINETEEN

Now that Henry had engaged a part-time nurse to cover for Daisy's days off, she felt happier. If she did decide to leave to look after Dick, Roger would be well cared for. Susan Taylor, a former VAD who'd been widowed and left with a child, lived on the other side of the common and her mother would care for the little girl while she worked.

Although Henry had seemed keen to start up a convalescent home, it had been some weeks since he'd mentioned it and she didn't like to badger him when he was so busy. If he decided against it, she would have to go home and look after Dick.

On a drizzly day in October, she set off to visit her mother, no longer worried about Roger now that Susan was there. She got off the train at Kingsbourne Halt, holding on to her hat as a keen wind blew up from the harbour. Thank goodness Mum hadn't taken in any washing today, she thought as she entered the cottage. The fire glowed in the range and without the lines of damp washing strewn around, the little room seemed homely and cheerful.

'I haven't heard from Dick lately,' Effie said, bustling round to make Daisy a cup of tea. 'Do you think he's all right?'

'You mustn't worry, Mum. He's being well looked after, and we'll get him home soon,' Daisy promised. She didn't say that it might be a long time. She'd written to the hospital, stressing her nursing experience and asking for details of her brother's condition. The reply had not been reassuring.

If only Henry would make up his mind about Ryfe Hall, she thought. She was sure she could look after Roger and her brother there without letting any of them down. She hadn't mentioned her plan to her mother and, pushing it to one side, she asked if there'd been any word from Billy. Effie's eyes lit up. 'Didn't I tell you? He came home,' she said. 'He only stayed one night 'cos he had to get back to his ship.'

'I wish I'd known. I'd have asked Mr Thornton for time off.'

'I didn't know myself. You could've knocked me down with a feather when he came through the door.' She smiled proudly. 'He looked so grown up in his uniform.'

When Daisy left, she was pleased that her mother was in a happier frame of mind. The end of the war was in sight and soon she would have two of her boys home.

Daisy was still waiting for Henry's decision when a letter arrived from Peter Holloway, who was now based at the Naval Hospital in Gosport. He asked whether she'd had any success with her patient and Daisy wrote back straight away. Roger had taken up painting with enthusiasm, although so far he'd only produced dark slashes of paint on the canvas. *'Nothing I recognize as art,'* she wrote, *'but he seems to be getting the "dark thoughts" out of his system.'*

She then outlined her hopes for Ryfe Hall, tentatively suggesting that if it came to anything, he might become involved. She hoped she hadn't been too forward. Despite their friendship, she knew nothing of his background or his plans after the war. Perhaps he would return to his old life, taking up general practice in his home town in Surrey.

To her surprise he wrote back immediately, offering wholehearted support. She couldn't wait for Henry to get home, certain that Peter's enthusiasm would help him to make up his mind. But perhaps he already had, she thought. After all, why should he be concerned about Dick or those other shell-shocked soldiers while his own cousin was being so well cared for?

Daisy looked down at Roger, asleep now but restlessly mumbling and twitching. She straightened the sheet and turned away; she didn't want to let him or her employer down. But her brother came first. She couldn't leave him in that place where he'd just get worse. She'd definitely give in her notice if Henry decided not to go ahead with the project. After all, he had Susan to look after Roger now.

But she had underestimated Henry. He knocked on the door and opened it. 'Can you leave Roger for a moment? I need to talk to you.'

She nodded and took him to her sitting room, switching on lamps and drawing the curtains against the chill autumn night. She sat down, biting her lip. She thought she knew what he was going to say. But to her surprise he was smiling.

'Don't look so worried. I'll set your mind at rest straightaway. I've decided to help you with your scheme.' He held up a hand in protest as Daisy gasped her thanks. 'Don't thank me yet. Wait till you've heard what I have to say.'

Since that first conversation he'd had several meetings with the board of Kingsbourne Hospital and local businessmen. 'They've agreed to set up a trust to finance the renovation of Ryfe Hall and staffing for the first year,' he said. 'They all felt that such a home is a solution for those whose families can't care for them. And, once it's done up, Ryfe Hall will be ideal.'

'I can't believe it's really going to happen, Mr Thornton,' Daisy said. 'I was beginning to think it was just a silly dream.'

'Well, there's a lot of work to be done before your dream becomes a reality.'

'I can't wait to get started,' Daisy said, getting up and pacing the room. 'We could convert the stables and outbuildings into workshops. Doctor Holloway says that keeping the patients occupied would be a vital part of their treatment.'

'An excellent idea,' Henry said. 'I'll put it to the trustees.'

Daisy was a little disconcerted. She had hoped that she would be able to make decisions herself. Henry reassured her. 'The house itself will, of course, become the property of the new trust. But they've agreed to appoint you as matron, so you will decide how the home is run.' He smiled. 'That is a condition I insisted upon.'

Daisy rushed across the room and kissed his cheek. 'Mr Thornton, you're an angel.'

Henry blushed and rubbed his cheek. 'I'm doing this for purely selfish reasons,' he said. 'You were planning to leave to look after your brother. This way I can ensure my cousin will receive the best possible care too.'

Daisy was silent for a few moments, but she couldn't stay still for long. She opened a drawer and brought out a large notebook. 'I've been jotting down ideas,' she said. 'We could grow our own vegetables and keep chickens.'

Henry read in silence, then handed the book back to her. 'You've certainly thought it through,' he said. 'I like your ideas.'

'I can't thank you enough for backing me up and believing in me,' Daisy said.

'We need to take a look at the house – we'll go tomorrow. Susan will look after Roger.' He paused in the doorway, gesturing towards her notebook. 'And bring that with you. We'll need to make notes of what wants doing.'

As they came up to the drive, the sun came out, reflecting off the windows. From here, Ryfe Hall looked just the same as it had on that dreadful day when Daisy had been turned out in the rain and cold. It was hard to believe it had been empty for so long, but as they drew nearer the signs of neglect were obvious. The paintwork was flaked and blistered and the steps up to the front door were slippery with moss. It was sad to see the weeds in the drive, the rusting iron gates, but today she was full of optimism. The beautiful old house would soon be restored to its former glory – and not as a home for the idle rich but a haven for those who'd sacrificed their lives just as those who died had.

If only Georgina were with her. Daisy had hoped her friend would have returned to Sussex by now. But little Jackie had been unwell and the Lazenbys wouldn't hear of her leaving just yet.

She got out of the car and, while Henry struggled with the rusty lock, she thought that in many ways nothing had changed. The untidy rooks' nests, empty now, were visible through the remains of the leaves on the stand of elms beyond the house. The ivy-covered stables, where the jackdaws nested in spring, were more dilapidated than ever.

Henry pushed the door open and Daisy wrinkled her nose at the musty smell. She looked round the wide hall, remembering again the last time she was here, the humiliation of being dismissed for something she hadn't done.

'I'm surprised that you want to come back here after what happened,' Henry said.

'I've put it all behind me. I know the truth and that's all that matters,' Daisy retorted.

'Of course – and Georgina believed in you. She tried to get you reinstated.'

'We put that behind us when we worked together. We're friends now.'

Henry smiled rather wistfully and Daisy knew that he still loved Georgina. Perhaps it wasn't such a good idea for her to come back after all. Changing the subject, she said, 'It's so sad to see this lovely house empty and neglected like this.'

They went into the former drawing room. The cream and gold striped wallpaper that she remembered was now speckled with mould and hung in damp strips. 'Just wait till we've finished with it,' Henry said, looking round at the damage. 'You won't recognize the place.'

Daisy followed his gaze, suddenly realizing how much work there was to do. Were they taking on too much? But Henry said confidently, 'I had it surveyed when I bought it so I know it's structurally sound. Jot down what needs to be done – your own ideas too.'

'It's going to take a lot of work to put this right,' Daisy said.

'A lot of money too but I'm not worried about that. The trust has agreed to finance it. Call it our contribution to the war effort.'

Henry's enthusiasm was infectious and, as they went from room to room discussing the alterations and repairs, Daisy filled the notebook, jotting down Henry's suggestions and occasionally making notes of her own. She was absorbed in writing, hardly taking any notice when he said, 'I almost volunteered when war broke out. I was so wretched when Georgina broke off our engagement I just wanted to get away.'

She smiled but he didn't seem to expect a reply. 'I'd have gone too, but for the business,' he went on. 'My manager and many of the workers joined up. I felt I should try to keep things going so they'd have jobs to come back to after the war. You can imagine how I felt when I realized my businesses were making more money than ever. It was almost as if I were profiting from the war – from other people's misfortunes.'

'I'm sure no one seriously thought that,' Daisy protested.

'You're very kind, Daisy. But there were murmurs among those I thought were my friends, especially those who'd lost someone at the front.'

'That's only natural, I suppose. But it's ridiculous to think that everyone should join up. Some had to stay behind and keep things going.'

They reached the top of the house and the attics, which ran the length of the main house under the eaves. Daisy's heart lurched as memories bombarded her.

She looked out of the little dormer window, recalling how often she'd gazed out across the parkland, hoping for a glimpse of Jack returning from an evening ride. And later, when he'd joined the navy, the sight of him bowling up the drive in his open-topped Hispano Suiza.

The image of the car made her shudder, recalling Ernest's rape attempt. He must have been driving the car without permission that day, she thought. She wondered what had happened to it – sold, along with all the family's possessions, to pay off Sir John's creditors, she supposed. The reminder of her former employer brought a stab of anger, replacing her sadness at the ruin of the lovely old house. Georgina should be living here with young Jack, not miles away from friends in a gloomy old vicarage.

'These rooms will still be the staff quarters,' Henry said, interrupting her thoughts. 'But I think we could turn one of the small rooms into a bathroom. What do you think?'

'I should have thought of that,' she said, recalling how often she'd climbed the narrow stairs with her jug of water, only to find it had frozen overnight. 'It will be important after the war to provide good conditions for staff, otherwise no one will want to live in. Those girls who'd have gone into service have been enjoying the extra money and freedom they get from doing war work. They won't want to go back to how things were.'

'I agree. And why should they?' Henry said as they went downstairs to inspect the bedrooms. 'Should we knock down walls and make dormitories?' he asked.

'I think individual rooms would be better,' Daisy said. 'I want our patients to think of Ryfe Hall as a home. After all, some of them could be here for a long time.' She told him about the young man who'd kept the others awake with his shouting and screaming. 'Doctor Holloway explained that it was part of his illness but of course it upset the men. It would be better if they each had their own room,' she said.

Henry nodded agreement and they descended to the kitchens and pantries in the basement. Daisy rushed about, opening cupboards, making suggestions, scribbling in the little notebook, while he stood in the doorway, smiling. 'You really are keen to get started, aren't you?' he said.

Daisy turned to him, pink with pleasure. 'I can't tell you how much it means to me, having something worthwhile to do.' Her smile faded. 'I was doing a good job out in Malta. But when I got ill, they wouldn't let me stay. It's wonderful to think I can do some good again.'

'You've been doing very well with Roger,' Henry said.

'But it's not enough. Do you understand?'

Henry nodded. 'There's only one problem. Suppose you meet some young man and decide to get married, what will happen then?'

'I won't marry,' she said, her eyes clouding. 'You see, there was someone but . . .'

She couldn't go on and Henry shuffled his feet, coughing with embarrassment. 'I didn't mean to pry. Please forgive me. This damned war has a lot to answer for.'

'You weren't to know. But I'd rather not discuss it.'

A moment ago she'd been happy, making plans, but now it was as if the sun had gone behind a cloud. These moments always came when she thought of Jack and what might have been. Would the pain ease as time went on? But if she came back to Ryfe Hall she'd find reminders of Jack in every corner. Was she doing the right thing?

Since returning to England she'd begun to persuade herself that their passionate but all-too-brief interlude in Malta couldn't have been true love. Could such intense feeling last, or at least mellow into the warm intimate affection her parents had enjoyed? Easy to believe so when she'd been in his arms, to believe that their different stations didn't matter. But after the war and a return to a normal life, it might be a different story.

Daisy sighed. That scarcely mattered now. For all her clinging to the hope that somehow he'd survived, common sense told her that if he'd been rescued, perhaps taken prisoner, his family would have been informed. And Georgina would have told her.

Henry coughed again and Daisy smiled as he apologized once more. 'It doesn't matter. I can't spend the rest of my life moping.' She opened her notebook and began to write. 'There's so much to do,' she said with a determined smile.

Dusk was falling as they left but Daisy hadn't noticed the fading light. Ryfe Hall had always been rather gloomy, being too far from the town to have gas lighting installed. Remembering the dirty and time-consuming chore of filling and trimming the oil lamps, Daisy hesitantly suggested that they could put in electric lighting. But Henry had already arranged for a generator to be installed in one of the outhouses. It seemed he'd thought of everything. Daisy wondered if he was doing it for Roger or himself – perhaps to make up for not having seen active service.

When they reached Kingsbourne it was completely dark and Daisy knew Susan would be anxious to get home to her little girl, but Henry insisted she pop in to see her mother. 'I'll wait for you,' he said.

Her mother looked up with a worried frown. 'I was beginning to wonder what had happened to you. I was sure you were coming today,' she said.

Daisy gave her a quick hug and explained where she'd been. 'Ryfe Hall's going to be converted into a nursing home – I'm going to work there,' she said. Effie was impressed until she learned that Dick would be one of the first patients.

'But you said he was getting better,' she protested. 'Why can't he come home?'

Daisy then told her the real reason why Dick was still in hospital. Although she knew of Roger Thornton's problems, it was hard for her to grasp that Dick was in the same state. 'Why didn't you tell me?' she asked through a haze of tears. 'I would have gone to see him. He must think nobody cares.'

'Mum, he hasn't been fit enough for visitors. It would only upset him, and you as well. When the hall's ready I'll fetch him and you can visit as often as you like.'

Effie nodded and wiped her eyes. 'I just feel so helpless.' A little sob escaped her. 'Oh, my poor boy,' she whispered.

Daisy comforted her mother, but she didn't want to keep Henry waiting. 'I'm sorry, Mum. I must go. Mr Thornton's waiting.'

As Effie kissed her, she said, 'It's good to see you looking happy again, love.'

Not exactly happy, Daisy thought, as she got into the car and turned to wave. She didn't think she'd ever be really happy again but she was content, and now she had something to aim for, a goal in life. That was enough, she decided. It had to be.

CHAPTER TWENTY

When Daisy had told Georgina of her plans, her friend had written back, eager to be involved in the project. *'At first I couldn't bear the thought of seeing my old home so changed. But it's better than it standing empty and going to rack and ruin. Besides, I must get away from here. You can't imagine the frustration of living with Tom's parents. I know they mean well, and they want the best for little Jack, but it's so stifling.'*

There was more in this vein – the boredom of doing the church flowers, afternoon tea with the church ladies discussing the goings-on in the parish. But whenever a move back to Sussex was mentioned, Muriel managed to find a reason for her to stay 'just a little longer'. The latest 'crisis' was Jackie's bad cold which still lingered on. Georgina was eager to get away from her in-laws and airily dismissed Daisy's concern that she might be embarrassed by seeing Henry again. *'We won't see much of him, once the home's open,'* she wrote. *'I'll come straight away. I want to be involved right from the start.'*

Daisy hadn't expected this and hadn't thought about where Georgina and Jackie would stay. They couldn't move into Ryfe Hall while it was still being renovated. 'Could she and the baby stay here?' she asked her mother, looking round the tiny kitchen of the cottage. 'They could have my room while I'm still at the Thorntons.'

Effie gave her customary sniff. 'She won't want to stay here with the likes of us,' she said.

'Mum, how many times have I said that Georgina's not like that? Besides, she can only say no,' Daisy said, wishing that her mother could rid herself of these feelings of inferiority, although she did understand.

Georgina and little Jack arrived at the beginning of November, settling happily into the cottage. 'This is better than the dorm in Malta,' she said, bouncing on the bed.

Effie looked sceptical but she soon mellowed. It was little Jack's blue eyes and gummy smile that won her heart. And once she'd overcome her initial reservations, she admitted that Georgina was 'a nice enough girl'.

With the addition of the baby to the household, Daisy had the perfect excuse to stop her mother from taking in washing. The autumn days continued with a pervading dampness which carried on into an early winter. Fog curled through the narrow lanes, creeping up from the harbour, and it was impossible to dry the washing. Effie had to agree that the damp air wasn't good for the baby. Not that she needed persuading. She'd enough to do looking after Jack. The girls spent every available moment at the hall overseeing the work and helping with the cleaning and decorating, and Georgina was happy to leave him in her care. Susan stayed with Roger and it seemed as if everything was working out. And if Daisy wasn't exactly happy, at least she was content.

Georgina sat back on her heels and surveyed the shining wet floor with satisfaction. The uneven flagstones had been ingrained with dirt and there'd even been a few weeds growing between the cracks. The house had been empty for so long, it no longer seemed like the home she'd lived in for most of her life.

Surprisingly, she was beginning to enjoy this new phase of her life. These days she seldom thought of Tom. The love she'd felt for him had now been transferred to baby Jack. She hated leaving him, although he seemed quite content in Effie's company. Funny how she didn't mind Daisy's mother looking after him, yet she'd been so resentful when Muriel had tried to take over. Perhaps it was because she hadn't been allowed to make any decisions for herself. Now, she was doing something because it was what *she* wanted.

She was enjoying Daisy's company too. Working together was almost like being back in Malta but with a more carefree atmosphere. The empty rooms rang with laughter as they stripped damp ribbons of wallpaper and scrubbed the mould from the paintwork.

Daisy confided that she was enjoying herself too, glad to be free of the responsibility of caring for Roger for a while as Susan had agreed to work longer hours.

'It's only until the home opens,' she said.

'Will Susan want to carry on working then?' Georgina wondered. 'It's a long way for her to travel each day from Southsea.'

'I'd like to have her. She's a good nurse. But we'll have to see if there's enough room for live-in staff. Don't forget she's got a baby to look after as well.'

'So have I,' Georgina said. 'I don't need to work, not for the money anyway. But maybe she does. We must try and help her if we can.'

Because of the shortage of workmen, they had decided to do the decorating themselves. The outside work, as well as the painting of the hallway and the high ceilings in the drawing and dining rooms, had been completed by professionals.

Henry joined them whenever he could spare the time. With his tie loosened and his sleeves rolled up, he seemed a different person to the man Georgina remembered.

But then, we've all changed, she thought, as she wielded her brush. Who'd have thought she'd be down on her knees scrubbing, and in her old home at that? She stifled a giggle as she pictured the horrified expression on her mother's face.

The door opened and Daisy came in, stepping carefully on the wet floor. 'I've just heard Henry's car,' she said.

Georgina stood up and smoothed down her apron, ruefully examining her reddened hands. She pushed back the strand of hair which had escaped the neat bun at the back of her head, colouring as she caught Daisy's smile.

'Old habits die hard, Daisy,' she said. 'I was thinking of what Mama would say if she could see me now.'

Daisy laughed and pursed her lips. 'My dear, you must remember you are a lady and it is not seemly . . .' she said in a passable imitation of Lady Davenport's prissy voice. They were both laughing so much they didn't notice that Henry had come in. His face was flushed and he was flourishing the early evening newspaper.

'Ladies, ladies, didn't you hear me?' he said.

At the word 'ladies' they collapsed in giggles again, but quickly got themselves under control when they took in Henry's words.

The war was over. 'They signed the armistice at eleven o'clock this morning,' he said.

Georgina looked at Daisy and realized they were thinking the same thing. They should have been jumping for joy but all they felt was a dull numbness. Victory had come too late for them. They had lost too many loved ones in the past four years. Wordlessly they hugged each other, unshed tears gleaming in the dimness of the large old kitchen.

Henry coughed and said, 'I think the work can wait for a while, don't you? Let's go and tell your mother, Daisy. She may not have heard yet.'

They climbed into the Lanchester and drove through the misty November morning towards Kingsbourne. Although they'd been expecting the announcement of the armistice for some days, the reality had still to penetrate their dazed minds.

As they drove through the village they saw that flags were already draped over the front of the King's Arms and some of the cottages. Knots of people had gathered in the street, smiling and waving at the car. The church door was open and, as they passed, a peal of bells rang out.

Near Kingsbourne, the crowds increased, and the sound of church bells filled the air from all directions. It was impossible to drive the car through the throng which choked Market Square, so Henry pulled up in a side street and they walked down towards the harbour.

As they approached the quayside, Effie came towards them, little Jack bundled into a shawl and balanced on her hip. Over the noise of the crowds and the pealing church bells, the horns and sirens of ships in the Solent added to the cacophony.

Little Jack started to cry, bewildered by the noise, and Georgina took him from Effie. Holding him close, she murmured soothing words, but still he cried. His distress released the emotions she'd held in for so long, and she began to cry too. Huge wrenching sobs such as she hadn't been able to release since Tom's death shook her body. She hardly noticed when Daisy took Jack from her, leaving Henry to draw her to the edge of the crowd, holding her against his broad chest and patting her back until her sobs died away.

She took the handkerchief he silently handed her and wiped her eyes, blowing her nose vigorously. She managed to smile and thank him, then turned away. 'Let's join the others, shall we?' she said. 'We should be celebrating, not crying.'

She pushed through the throng to where Daisy and her mother leaned on the harbour wall, holding Jackie up to look at the boats, now decorated with flags and coloured streamers that seemed to have appeared from nowhere. The little boy was laughing now and Daisy was smiling with him. Georgina noticed that despite the smile, her face also showed a suspicion of tears, as did Effie's. Everyone in this laughing, singing crowd had probably lost someone, and there were still those who didn't know if their loved ones would ever return.

Suddenly, the noisy celebrations seemed too much, and she longed for the haven of the Marches' little cottage. Daisy looked up and she knew her friend felt the same. They pushed their way through the press of bodies and into the comparative quiet of Fish Lane.

Indoors, Effie rattled the poker between the bars of the range until the embers glowed and swung the heavy kettle over the fire. Henry took the coal scuttle and went outside. When he returned, the girls were laughing as Jackie tried to pull himself up by holding onto the arm of a chair. Henry made up the fire and sat down in front of it. He picked the little boy up, bouncing him on his knee and chanting nursery rhymes.

Georgina watched, a faint smile curving her lips. How could she have thought him stuffy and pompous? Of course he was older than she was, older than her brothers even. He'd seemed more of her father's generation in those years before the war. But I've had to grow up a lot these past four years, she thought. Since her return to Sussex, she'd begun to see her former fiancé in a new light. He'd make a wonderful father, she thought, and a faint flush crept over her cheeks as she caught Daisy's glance. She would never regret her relationship with Tom, and she knew that a part of him would always hold a place in her heart. But she couldn't help wondering how things might have turned out if she'd married Henry.

After months of hard work, Ryfe Hall was transformed into the luxurious home of Daisy's imagination and now, in the spring of 1919, they were ready to receive their first patients. Officials from both the Red Cross and the military had inspected the alterations and, to Daisy's relief, they had passed the test.

Henry advertised in the medical journals for a doctor with experience of mental problems, but some still refused to accept the definition of shell-shock as a real illness and they were having difficulty finding the right person.

'Why not write to your doctor friend? He might be interested,' Henry asked.

'I think it would be better if you wrote – more businesslike,' Daisy said. She was wary of becoming too involved. Friendship was all she wanted at present.

Peter wrote back straightaway, saying that he was still under navy regulations. However, he was willing to act as a consultant during his free time and once he was discharged from the service. He could easily come over from Gosport once a week and they could telephone him if they had any problems.

The authorities agreed. 'They say that with a small number of patients and such experienced nursing staff, we won't need a doctor on the premises full-time,' Henry said, showing the official letter to Daisy.

Today as she, Georgina and Henry awaited their first patients, Daisy felt proud of their achievement. She couldn't believe that from now on she'd be living here – and not as a servant but as the matron in charge. The east wing had been converted into two self-contained apartments, so that Daisy and Georgina could live in and Daisy hoped that her mother would move in with her. 'I don't like her living in that damp cottage,' she said.

Henry agreed. 'With Mrs March on the premises, things will be easier for Georgina. That is, if your mother agrees to carry on looking after young Jack.'

'Just try to stop her,' Daisy laughed. 'It's been good for her, having him to care for. It's helped to take her mind off what happened to my brothers.'

But Effie refused to give up the cottage. 'It's my home,' she said. 'Besides, have you forgotten Billy – he'll be home when this voyage is over.'

'Billy's going to stay in the merchant navy, Mum,' she'd protested. 'He'll be away most of the time.'

'But he'll be coming home on leave. And what about Dick? How will he feel, coming back to find his home gone? No, I'll look after Jack while you and Mrs Lazenby are working. But here I stay, in my own home.'

Effie had persuaded herself that once Dick was home he'd be able to go back to the fishing. She'd even spoken to a friend of her husband's asking if any of the fleet needed crew members. But Daisy knew it would be a long time before Dick was fit enough to work and had tried to prepare her mother for the reality of his condition. Effie stood firm and Daisy let the matter drop. Once Dick was here, she hoped her mother would change her mind.

Now, as they waited for the first patients, Daisy tingled with anticipation. Henry's faith in her had given her confidence. She'd achieved a lot in the past few years. At last she really felt she'd proved herself, that she was as good as anybody else.

She glanced at Henry, whose eyes were on Georgina, and wondered if she was aware of the way he looked at her. Anyone could see he was still in love with her. And, although Georgina's only interests nowadays seemed to be her little boy and the transformation of her old home, Daisy wouldn't be surprised if she was beginning to return Henry's feelings. She had noticed that Tom was seldom mentioned now.

The ambulance pulled up at the door, interrupting her thoughts, and she helped the men up the steps into their new home. There were only four of them at present, as well as Roger Thornton, who had come over earlier with Henry.

After supper Henry left and Daisy and Georgina settled the men for the night. They took their coffee into the office which had once been Sir John's study. There were no reminders now of Georgina's father. The dark panelling had been ripped out, the walls painted pale blue with darker curtains and carpet. A large desk stood in front of the windows. Here, Daisy would keep the accounts and oversee the running of the home.

She'd been unsure about handling the business and had admitted as much to Henry, but although he was happy to give advice, he'd said, 'I've got my businesses to run and it's the profits from those that will help to pay for all this. Don't worry, Daisy, if I didn't think you could do it, I wouldn't have supported you.' Despite her nervousness she'd flushed with pleasure at Henry's confidence in her.

'Well, this is it; we're on our own,' she said now, settling into an armchair beside the fire. 'I couldn't have managed without you, Georgina.'

'And your mother too – she's been marvellous, caring for Jackie the way she has.'

'We've been lucky with staff too, especially getting Mrs Harris out of retirement.' Daisy gave a sigh of satisfaction. They also had two live-in maids, Ruby and Millie, and a daily woman from the village. They could take on more staff as it became necessary.

'In some ways it's as if nothing has changed,' Georgina said, lapsing into silence.

Daisy wondered if she was feeling sad because this was no longer her family home. 'I wasn't sure you'd approve of all the alterations,' she said.

'It's for a good cause – besides, I'm not sentimental,' Georgina replied, looking at the clock. 'I hope Jackie's all right. It's the first time I've missed kissing him good night.'

'It's only for one night. Henry will pick them up in the morning.' Daisy sighed. 'It would be so much easier if Mum moved up here. It's a long trek from the village.'

'Perhaps she'll change her mind when your brother gets here.'

After their busy day they were ready to turn in and, after making a round of the patients to make sure everyone had settled, they went to their own rooms.

The next day Daisy woke early. Her sleep had been disturbed several times when she thought she'd heard someone cry out. But the men were all sleeping soundly. It was her own anxiety keeping her awake. Had she taken on too much? It was a big responsibility. But Georgina was here and she could always telephone Peter if she was worried.

She went down to the kitchen where Mrs Harris had already started on the breakfasts. 'Like old times, isn't it?' she said.

'Not quite, Daisy. Or perhaps I should call you Matron now,' she said.

'Daisy will do.' She felt a bit uncomfortable and hoped she'd be able to cope with the reversal of their positions. 'Mrs Harris, are you sure this isn't going to be difficult for you? I don't want to appear bossy or anything.'

'Don't worry, Daisy. I wouldn't have taken the job if it was going to be a problem. Besides, your mother told me you were in charge of a ward in Malta so I'm sure you'll do well.' She began to stir the porridge and check the toast under the grill.

Daisy looked at the clock. 'The maids will be here soon. I'll show them their rooms and then send them down for their orders. Meanwhile we'd better serve breakfast.'

When she knocked on Georgina's door, she was already up and tying on her apron. 'All ready,' she said. 'I can't wait to get started.'

Their patients, used to army discipline and hospital routine, dressed and came down to the dining room, although they ate mechanically with no conversation. Daisy had tried to cajole Roger into leaving his room too, but although he'd been prepared for the move to Ryfe Hall, he'd slipped back into his childlike behaviour and she was worried about him.

Georgina reassured her. 'Wait until Susan gets here – she knows how to handle him. He can stay in his room for the time being.'

The morning passed quickly and it was almost noon before the friends paused for a break. As they went through the hall on their way to the kitchen, Georgina broke into a smile. 'I can hear a car. Perhaps it's Henry,' she said.

Daisy smiled. She was right about her friend's growing fondness for him.

They opened the front door just as Henry and Effie got out of the Lanchester. Henry lifted little Jackie down, holding his hand as he took steps towards his mother.

Georgina swept him up in her arms. 'My baby's walking!' she cried.

Effie smiled proudly. 'I knew he were ready,' she said. 'Kept pulling himself up on the furniture.'

It was a lovely moment and they could have stayed there in the spring sunshine marvelling at Jackie's progress but for Susan saying it was time for the medicine round.

Henry left soon afterwards, saying that he'd call again in a few days, and Georgina took Effie and Jackie to her apartment.

After dispensing the midday medicines, Daisy left Susan to keep an eye on things and went to the kitchen. She was pleased that Millie and Ruby, the two new maids, were working hard under Mrs Harris's direction and that lunch was well under way. Then it was time to try to persuade Roger to come down to the dining room for his meal.

Everything seemed to be going smoothly so far but as she went upstairs she couldn't help thinking of her past life in this house. Then she wouldn't have dared to walk up the main staircase. It was the back stairs for her. Despite all her achievements over the last five years, Daisy still sometimes felt like Daisy the lady's maid, unfairly accused and humiliated by the former owners of Ryfe Hall.

CHAPTER TWENTY-ONE

After a few minor hitches, the home soon settled into a routine, but when Henry said he'd arranged a visit from the trustees, all Daisy's old feelings of insecurity and inferiority returned, especially when she heard that among them was Agatha's mother, Lady Phillips, together with a retired Royal Navy commander and some local businessmen.

Daisy's knees trembled as she and Georgina showed them round but to her relief they seemed impressed. Roger and Sergeant Bill Smythe still kept to their rooms but the other three were in the day room. Mick Collins and Joe Bolton were playing chess and Lieutenant David Rawlins, the only other officer, was reading a magazine.

Lady Phillips stopped to speak to the chess players and Daisy, standing in the doorway, strained to hear what they were saying. She needn't have worried. When the group withdrew to Daisy's sitting room for tea, the trustees all declared themselves satisfied that their money had been well invested.

Daisy's confidence was greatly boosted when the naval commander turned to her and said, 'You and Mrs Lazenby are doing a grand job, Nurse March.'

Behind his back, Georgina winked and Daisy hid a smile.

After they'd gone, Henry stayed to have tea with Georgina and Jackie in the nursery in the east wing, while Daisy excused herself to deal with some paperwork in her office.

She was adding a column of figures when there was a knock on the door and Millie came in. 'Excuse me, Matron. There's a gentleman to see you – Doctor Holloway.'

'Show him in, Millie,' Daisy said calmly. She rose from her desk, surprising herself at the flush of pleasure she felt. Although they spoke often on the telephone this was the first time they'd met since leaving Malta. She hardly recognized him. He was thinner and seemed a lot older now.

'Doctor Holloway, we weren't expecting you so soon,' she said, afraid to greet him too warmly in case he misinterpreted her feelings.

'Peter, please,' he said with a laugh. 'I don't remember us being this formal back in Malta.' With the laugh, the lines of strain disappeared and he seemed more like the old Peter. Perhaps he too had felt nervous about meeting again after so long.

Within minutes they were chatting as easily as they did on the telephone, but Daisy was aware of the admiration in the doctor's eyes and, although she was pleased that they'd be working together again, she resolved to keep their relationship formal.

Peter apologized for arriving unannounced. 'I'm returning to Gosport from visiting my family and as it wasn't too far out of the way, I thought I'd pop in. I hope it's not inconvenient but I need to discuss how I can fit your patients in with my other work.'

'It's not at all inconvenient,' Daisy said. 'I've been meaning to get in touch – it's about time you saw what we're doing. I'll show you round.' They finished their tour outside the dining room where the men were having tea.

'By the way, we don't refer to them as patients any more,' Daisy said quietly, pausing at the door. 'We like them to think of this as their home so we call them residents. After what they've been through we feel the fewer reminders of hospital the better. That's why my staff, as well as Georgina and I, don't wear uniforms.'

'Excellent,' Peter agreed. 'The only way they can return to what we call normal is for them to have as ordinary a life as possible, but without the stresses and strains.'

Daisy opened the door and said brightly, 'I've brought my friend Doctor Holloway to visit.'

Roger Thornton looked up and Daisy introduced him. Peter shook hands and started to chat is if this were a purely social occasion. The others seemed oblivious to them. But Peter, appearing not to notice their lack of reaction, went round the room, greeting them with his warm smile and firm handshake.

To Daisy's surprise he got a response from each of them and she began to feel that maybe there was some hope for even the most traumatized among them. She knew that caring for them wasn't simply a matter of providing a safe home and she resolved to learn all she could about their treatment. She couldn't do it alone though, and watching Peter as he spoke to her patients, she felt a surge of gratitude that he was willing to give his time so freely.

Back in the office, the conversation became more personal when Peter enquired if there had been any news of Jack. He'd guessed from Daisy's distress that Georgina's brother was the man she loved, although she'd never openly told him so.

'Did I tell you Georgina named the baby after him? He's being looked after by my mother at the moment,' she said.

He nodded. 'She seems happy now. It must have been a great help to her, having something to fill her time. It seems as if everything's working out for you both.'

'We have Henry to thank for all this,' Daisy said.

'A good man,' Peter said. 'How did you meet him?'

'I thought you knew. He and Georgina were engaged at one time, but she fell in love with Tom. I think Henry still loves her, and she seems fond of him. But that's not why he's done all this. He really believes in it.'

'It could have been awkward for her – Thornton being so closely involved.'

'I know, but as it happens they've managed to put the past behind them. Now they're good friends,' Daisy said with a direct look.

He smiled and reached for her hand. 'Like you and me?' he said.

'And that's all we can be, Peter. I'm sorry,' she said, moving away.

'Daisy . . .' Peter stopped abruptly as the door opened and Georgina came in.

'Still catching up on old times? I thought you were giving Peter the grand tour,' she said. If she'd noticed the tension in the room, she gave no sign of it.

Daisy laughed, grateful for the interruption. 'We've just finished. I think I can say without conceit that he was favourably impressed.'

Peter agreed and stood up, pausing at the door. 'You mentioned your brother in your last letter. Is there any more news?' he asked.

Daisy told him that the hospital superintendent felt Dick was better off in his care. 'But I can't bear to think of him there. I've heard they're dreadful places.'

Peter tried to comfort her. 'They're not all bad. He may be well cared for. It could be the best thing for him – and you,' he said.

'Mum wants him home, but I don't think she really understands his condition,' she said, choking back a sob. 'She's been through so much lately, I don't think she'd cope.'

'She nursed your father, too, didn't she?' Peter said.

'Poor Mum. She's had such a hard life. I hoped she'd have an easier time now.' Daisy sighed. 'Anyway, I won't know if Dick's fit to travel until I've seen him. And I won't tell Mum I'm going. She'd want to come too and I don't think that's a good idea.'

'How will you get there?'

'I was planning to go on the train.'

'Let me take you. It's too long a journey – you'd have to go up to London first.'

Daisy protested but he insisted. As he ran down the steps and jumped into his car, he called, 'I'll let you know when I'm free.'

Although she still said a nightly prayer for Jack, wherever he might be, Daisy had accepted that she would never see him again. Life was good for her now – the home was running smoothly, their staff were hard-working and loyal and the residents were making progress. But being Daisy, she always had someone to worry about and now it was her mother, who insisted on staying in Kingsbourne. She came in each day on the new village bus to look after little Jack, who was now toddling round on sturdy legs and constantly getting into mischief.

She was still convinced that Dick would soon be coming home and, when she wasn't at the Hall, she spent her free time turning out cupboards and black-leading the kitchen range until it shone like a mirror. Then she whitewashed the outside privy and wash-house.

'Mum, you shouldn't wear yourself out like this,' Daisy protested when she went home on a rare afternoon off.

'I've got to have it nice for when Dick comes home,' she replied.

Daisy couldn't think what to say. She'd tried to impress on her mother that Dick would need nursing and that he'd have to stay at the Hall, but she clung to the belief that once back home, a mother's loving care was all the nursing he'd need.

With a sigh, Daisy managed to hold her tongue. She was concerned that Effie was even thinner than she'd been when they first heard about Dick and she didn't want to upset her even more. For a while, looking after Jackie had seemed to help, but now she was jumpy and irritable one minute, saying that Dick should have been home by now, then bubbling with excitement at the thought of seeing her boy again.

When Daisy returned to the Hall after making her promise to rest, she confided in Georgina. 'If only Peter would get in touch. He promised to take me down to Canterbury on his next day off. He's busy, I know, but if I don't hear by the end of the week, I'll go on the train as I originally planned,' she said.

'It's hard for your mother – and you,' Georgina agreed. 'She thinks once he's home, everything will be just as it was before the war.' She sighed. 'Silly, really. How can it be the same?' She'd just put Jackie to bed and she stood looking down at him, her face sombre. Then she turned to Daisy with a smile. 'At least something good came out of it,' she said, indicating the sleeping child.

Daisy leaned over the cot, brushing her fingers over the fair curls. Jackie opened his eyes and smiled at her, then closed them again. Once more Daisy wished that she'd had a child – sometimes it was hard not to feel a little envious. But Georgina had suffered too, she reminded herself, not only losing Tom but being left to bring up their son alone.

Their companionable silence was broken by a voice at the foot of the stairs. It was Ruby, one of the nursing assistants. 'Can you come quickly, Matron? It's Lieutenant Rawlins. He's started screaming and carrying on and we can't get him calmed down.'

Daisy ran downstairs, pausing to reassure the wide-eyed girl. 'It's nothing to worry about, Ruby. He has these turns sometimes,' she said.

'I'm not bothered. My old gran used to carry on like that sometimes, when she was poorly and couldn't remember where she was. But Millie's shut herself in the scullery crying cos she thinks it's all her fault.'

'What happened?'

'She dropped a tray and the noise set him off,' she explained.

Daisy called out to Georgina, 'Go and find her – tell her she's not to blame,' then opened the door to the drawing room.

David Rawlins was huddled into a corner behind one of the armchairs, his hands over his ears, his mouth open in a silent scream. When Daisy touched his arm, he flinched away in terror.

'Ruby, clear this up as quickly as you can and bring more coffee,' she said in a low voice. She turned to the men who stood helplessly, staring. 'Just go back to what you were doing. I'll take care of it,' she told them.

Mick Collins and Joe Bolton sat down at the low table where they'd been playing chess. Roger hadn't left his chair but he'd started rocking back and forth, a habit Daisy thought he'd abandoned. Bill Smythe, the most withdrawn of them, stood at the window pleating folds of the curtain in his fingers. Daisy glanced at him worriedly, then turned to Rawlins, her chief concern at the moment. She crouched on the floor beside him and began talking in a low voice. Afterwards, she never knew what she said, but the soothing words had their effect. Gradually the trembling ceased, the man's face muscles relaxed and he slumped back against the wall.

When some of his colour had returned, Daisy took him up to his room where she helped him undress and get into bed. Then she went to the locked cupboard on the landing for a dose of the sedative he'd been prescribed. Within minutes he was asleep.

Downstairs Daisy glanced into the drawing room where Mick and Joe were drinking their after-dinner coffee. Bill Smythe was still standing by the window but his nervous fumblings with the curtain had stopped. Roger still sat in the corner, but she noted with relief that he was now still.

In the kitchen she found Georgina with her arms round a weeping Millie, while Mrs Harris, the housekeeper, looked on impatiently.

'I couldn't help it, Matron,' she sobbed. 'I know you said to be careful not to make any sudden noises, but I was nervous and that made me clumsy.'

'Just try to be more careful in future,' Georgina said and Millie's sobs started afresh.

'Perhaps it would be better if she stayed in the kitchen. There's plenty to do here,' Mrs Harris suggested. 'Let Ruby serve the drinks.'

Daisy agreed, wondering if they shouldn't have opened until they were fully staffed. But with only five patients they should be able to cope. If only Sarah was here as well as Susan, she thought, not for the first time. But Sarah was now married to Chris and expecting her first child. And Susan only worked part-time because of her daughter.

Daisy had hoped to recruit one of the trained nurses from the local hospital but because so many prisoners were still returning and needing hospital care, there were no staff available. For the time being they had to manage with untrained girls, who were little more than housemaids. She counted herself lucky that they had Susan.

When Daisy had finally calmed Mrs Harris and Millie down, she and Georgina went back to the office after first checking that young Jack was still asleep.

'Poor Rawlins – he was coming along well until this evening,' Georgina said.

'He'll never be able to go home though. His family don't want anything to do with him. His father practically called him a coward – only visited once at the hospital. He'd have had him committed if the doctor at Netley hadn't refused to sign the papers.'

'Just like poor Roger,' Georgina said.

Rawlins was sleeping soundly when Daisy peeped in a little later and she closed the door softly. Next door Smythe was pacing up and down. The incident in the drawing-room earlier had clearly unsettled him and he'd need a sedative too, she decided.

She couldn't help thinking about Dick. Was her brother like these men – or worse? She remembered how strong he'd been. It had been his quick thinking that had saved her father from being dragged down with the crippled boat. She had hero-worshipped him, looking up to him as the oldest, admiring the way he'd taken on the responsibility for his family after the accident which had crippled their father.

The residents of Ryfe Hall were getting better, there were minute improvements daily, and she had to believe that her brother's case would prove the same. If only Peter would telephone. She was becoming increasingly anxious about Dick.

She voiced her concerns to Georgina, who sympathized, but couldn't help teasing her about wanting to see Peter again. 'I always said he was keen on you,' she said.

Daisy was on the point of telling her not to be so silly, but she decided it was best to be frank. 'He asked me to marry him,' she said.

Georgina's face was a study. 'Why didn't you tell me?'

'It was after you left Malta.'

'Did you tell him about Jack?'

'He guessed. I still thought Jack might be alive then.'

Georgina put out a sympathetic hand. 'Oh, Daisy. I know how you feel, but you must accept it now. It's been too long.'

'I know, but the pain's still there.'

'You can't grieve for ever,' Georgina said with a sigh and Daisy knew she was thinking of herself as well.

She was silent, wondering what to do about Peter. Friendship was all very well but she dreaded him reading more into it than she was prepared to give.

Georgina echoed her thoughts. 'You could do worse, you know. He's a very attractive man.'

'I know. But I'm not ready yet – if I ever will be.' She shrugged and gave a little laugh. 'This won't do. I'm a working woman and there's plenty to do, so let's get on.'

As they started on their evening routine of supper, medicines and settling the men for the night, she reflected sadly that if she'd never met Jack she probably could have loved Peter. He was a kind, compassionate man with a warm sense of humour, who would make any girl a good husband.

But he's not Jack, she thought. And the pain knifed through her again. The war might be over but life would never be the same again. Daisy knew that the only way she could begin to cope was to throw herself into her work and make sure that at least some of those lives ruined by the events of the past few years were given the chance to mend.

CHAPTER TWENTY-TWO

A few days later Peter telephoned to say he could take Daisy to Canterbury the following day. She quelled the butterflies in her stomach and said she'd be ready first thing. She was dreading it, anticipating her feelings when she saw Dick. But the reality couldn't be any worse than her imaginings, she told herself firmly and she was determined to bring him home.

She thought the hospital authorities might be against releasing him so she decided to wear her uniform. The blue dress with its white starched apron and red-lined navy cloak, would lend her an authority that merely being the patient's relative might lack.

'Why are you all dressed up?' her mother asked.

'Doctor Holloway's coming. I thought I ought to look the part,' Daisy said, feeling slightly guilty that her mother didn't realize where she was going. She'd only insist on coming too. But Daisy still wasn't sure what to expect and it would be cruel to raise her mother's hopes. She asked Georgina to break it to her after she'd left.

Georgina agreed, then hurried off to supervise the staff and to do the morning rounds.

When Peter's little black Austin car stopped outside, she noticed his frown and said, 'You don't think this is a good idea, do you?'

'I think a short visit would have been better in the first instance. You've raised his hopes about going home now, so we must go through with it. I don't want you to be disappointed, Daisy.' As they set off he glanced at her, taking in the crisp nurse's uniform. 'You look very smart and efficient anyway. I'm sure the hospital superintendent will be most impressed.'

Although the words were accompanied by a smile, Daisy sensed the underlying disapproval. He might be right, she thought. Maybe she'd find Dick was worse than she'd anticipated. But looking after the men at Ryfe had given her confidence.

When they reached the asylum – you couldn't call it a hospital – she tried to hide her dismay. The red-brick fortress a few miles outside Canterbury was huge, set in an area of wooded parkland. How many tortured souls were locked away here, away from the uncaring eyes of the world? she thought. But when they entered the reception area, she was slightly reassured by the soft carpeting, comfortable chairs and colourful flower arrangements on low tables. She hoped the rest of the hospital was like this but, through an open door, she caught a glimpse of a long gloomy corridor echoing into the distance and her heart sank.

She took a deep breath when a thin little man with spectacles perched on the end of his nose, came in and introduced himself as the superintendent. He shook hands with Peter and inclined his head towards Daisy.

She bristled with indignation as he addressed his remarks solely to Peter, his conversation spattered with 'I'm sure you understand, Doctor,' and 'Cases like these, as I'm sure you are aware, Doctor.'

When he referred to 'the young lady's brother' almost as if she were not in the room, her anger boiled over. 'Excuse me. The "young lady" is a qualified nurse, the matron of a convalescent home, and as such, has ample experience of "cases like these". If you don't mind, perhaps I could see Corporal March. Doctor Holloway will decide if he's fit to be moved.'

After a moment's shocked silence, the superintendent blustered, 'My dear young lady, I'm sorry if I offended you. But these poor young men are my responsibility, as are all the patients here. I have to be sure that . . .'

'I can assure you, Corporal March will have every care at Ryfe Hall,' Daisy interrupted. 'The home is staffed by nurses who've served in the war. Doctor Holloway is our consultant. He has also made a special study of the effects of shell-shock.'

'I'll have Corporal March brought in then,' the man said, summoning a maid.

Daisy dared not look at Peter, who had so far said not a word. She was afraid she'd gone too far, but the pompous little man had infuriated her. At least the rush of anger had covered her nervousness. Now, as she watched the door for the first sight of Dick, her trepidation returned.

When he appeared, resting heavily on the arm of a male nurse, she had to stifle a gasp. If she'd passed him on the street, she'd have walked by without another glance. Dick was tall, and had once been a big man. His years of work on the fishing boats had broadened his already muscular frame. Now, the giant that Daisy remembered was pale and gaunt. He shuffled into the room, his gaze on the carpet, and she saw that his once thick dark hair was now patchy and thin and showing threads of grey.

He looked up at her stifled sob and a flicker of recognition showed in the dark eyes, to be replaced by clouded uncertainty. 'Mum?' he whispered.

To Daisy's surprise, the superintendent touched Dick's arm gently. 'This is your sister, March. She's come to take you home,' he said, no pomposity in his voice now. He indicated Peter. 'This is Doctor Holloway. They've come to take you home.'

Dick shuffled forward a few steps. 'Home? Daisy?' he said. 'Is it really you?'

It was too much. Daisy threw her arms round him and burst into tears. Clasping his thin body to her, she felt the sobs which shook him too. For a few moments they cried together, then she gently pushed him away, and guided him into a chair. Taking his hand, she said, 'Dick, do you want to come home? Do you feel well enough to travel?'

He glanced at Peter as if asking him for the answer. 'You don't have to go if you don't feel up to it,' he said. 'But your mother wants to see you.'

Dick's eyes clouded and tears welled up. 'I don't want to see her. I can't face her. It was my fault, you see.' He squeezed Daisy's hand so hard her knuckles cracked.

'Dick – she doesn't blame you for Jimmy joining up. He'd have gone anyway.'

He shook his head vehemently. 'I promised I'd look out for him. And I did. We were together until I was wounded. But they sent me back to a different unit. I couldn't look out for him then, could I? If I'd been there perhaps it wouldn't have happened.'

Daisy looked at Peter helplessly. 'You weren't to blame, old chap. Blame the powers that be who posted you,' he said.

'I should've been more careful. If I'd not got wounded, he would've been all right.' He hung his head, still clutching at Daisy's hand. She returned his grip, trying to convey her support. Her insides were churning. She'd never imagined seeing her strong dependable brother in such a state. Although she'd grown used to dealing with similar conditions, this was too close to home.

After a brief silence, Peter said, 'You don't have to see your mother until you're ready. But you can still leave here. Daisy has prepared a room for you at Ryfe Hall.'

She managed to smile, determined to put on a brave face – she must if she were going to help him.

Dick's eyes clouded again. 'But you said I was going home.'

'Ryfe Hall will be your home. I live there now,' Daisy told him.

'But you left there – went to work at the hospital.'

'A lot has happened since then,' Daisy said with a smile. 'Ryfe Hall doesn't belong to the Davenports any more.'

'You said Mum wants to see me but I can't face her, Daisy. I don't want to hurt her but I really can't.'

He was becoming agitated and Daisy said softly, 'Why not stay at Ryfe Hall with me for a while then, just until you feel better.'

Once he realized he didn't have to go home and face his mother, Dick agreed and after Daisy had signed the necessary papers, she settled him in the back seat and got in beside him. The long journey was uneventful. Dick leaned against her, appearing to doze but still tightly clutching her hand. To begin with she tried to make conversation but, daunted by his monosyllabic replies, she lapsed into silence. As they neared home, she asked herself if she'd done the right thing. This wasn't one of her patients. This was Dick, her big brother. She sighed. She'd have to think of him that way. Maybe then she'd be able to cope.

It was almost dark when they got there and Daisy leaned across to say to Peter. 'I hope Mum's not here. I dread telling her that Dick doesn't want to see her.'

Peter pulled on the handbrake. 'I expect Georgina will have persuaded her to go back to the cottage but if she hasn't I'll put on my doctor's voice and say he must rest.'

Daisy smiled gratefully. Exhausted by the emotional day, she couldn't cope with any further upset.

Dick got out of the car and, leaning heavily on her arm, stumbled up the steps to the front door. There was no one about and they took him straight to his room, where he quietly submitted to being prepared for bed. As he lay down, Daisy kissed his pale cheek. 'I'll get you some cocoa – help you sleep,' she whispered.

Dick nodded gratefully and closed his eyes. Peter followed Daisy downstairs. 'I won't stay,' he said in response to her invitation to have some supper.

When she'd thanked him and seen him out, she went into the kitchen where Mrs Harris sat in front of the range toasting her feet. She made to get up but Daisy told her to stay put. 'I'm going to make some cocoa for my brother. Do you want some?' she asked.

Mrs Harris shook her head. 'So you brought him home then? Your mum's been in such a twitter about seeing him.'

'She's not around, is she?' Daisy turned from the stove in alarm, turning back just in time to snatch the saucepan before the milk boiled over.

'Don't fret. Miss Georgina persuaded her to go home. Said you were probably staying overnight. But she'll be up here with the lark, I bet.'

'Where's everybody else?'

'Miss Georgina's seeing to Master Jack, the maids are in bed and the residents are settled for the night. I saved some supper for you and you should then go to bed too.'

'I couldn't eat, Mrs Harris. I'll just take this up to Dick and then I'll turn in.' She stirred the milk into the cocoa powder, added sugar and put the cup and saucer on a tray.

Upstairs Dick was already asleep. She tucked his hand under the blankets, smoothing his hair and wondering how to tell her mother that he didn't want to see her.

The next morning Daisy rose earlier than usual, anxious to see Dick before her mother arrived and make sure he had recovered from yesterday's journey.

He was sitting by the window gazing out at the misty Downs and rolling countryside. He turned to her and she saw tears rolling silently down his face. His smile was more of a grimace as he recognized her. 'Daisy, is it really you? I thought I was dreaming.'

'It's no dream, Dick. You're home now and I'm going to take care of you.'

He seemed bewildered. 'But what am I doing here – this is Ryfe Hall, isn't it?'

Daisy once more explained that the hall no longer belonged to the Davenports and that it was now a sort of hospital. 'I work here,' she said.

He looked relieved. 'When you said home, I thought you were taking me to Fish Lane. I don't want to see Mum.' He became agitated and Daisy soothed him. But despite her reassurance that he wasn't to blame for Jimmy's death, he couldn't stop feeling guilty for not protecting his younger brother. 'I can't face her,' he sobbed.

She urged him to rest and hurried out, stifling her own sobs. Had she done the right thing? Would Mum understand when she told her it would be better for her not to see Dick just yet?

She reached the kitchen just as Effie burst through the back door, throwing off her coat. 'Where is he? Is he here? I want to see my boy.'

Daisy put her hands on Effie's shoulders. 'Wait a minute, Mum. We need to talk first. Sit down and have a cup of tea.'

'I don't want tea. I want to see my boy.' Her face crumpled and she sank into a chair at the kitchen table. 'He *is* all right, isn't he?'

'His wounds have healed but there's a long way to go yet,' Daisy said, taking her mother's hands. 'It's his mind that's wounded, Mum.' As gently as possible she explained that Dick was like the other young men at Ryfe. He needed peace and quiet to heal. It was harder to tell her that Dick didn't want to see her.

'I don't believe you. Why wouldn't he want to see his own mother?'

'Mum, I think it's best if we leave him alone for now. He needs time.'

'What makes you think you know what's best for *my* son?'

'It's what he wants, Mum,' Daisy replied gently, and went on, 'He's gone through so much, I think he needs time to come to terms with things.'

'You think? Oh, Daisy, my girl, running this place has really gone to your head, hasn't it? You think you know what's best for everyone.' Effie burst into tears. 'I knew no good would come of you mixing with these people.'

For once, Daisy allowed her anger to surface. 'These people as you call them are doing their best for Dick. If it weren't for Georgina and Henry and Doctor Holloway, my poor brother would still be in that dreadful hospital.' Then she too burst into tears.

Effie's anger melted away and she put her arms round her daughter. As they grieved together, Daisy realized that it had been a long time since she'd given way like this. She'd become used to masking her feelings when dealing with the residents. Perhaps Mum was right and she did always think she knew best.

'I'm sorry,' she said. 'I was so busy thinking about Dick's feelings that I didn't consider yours.'

Her mother managed to smile. 'I'm sorry too, love,' she said. 'But it's hard, you know, having to accept that your own son doesn't want to see you.'

'I realize that, Mum. But he'll come round. Perhaps we should ask Doctor Holloway's advice. Would you abide by his decision?'

Effie nodded and Daisy telephoned him straightaway. With some reluctance, she took the receiver from Daisy and listened to what the doctor had to say. She nodded and handed the telephone back to her daughter.

'Well, Mum?' she asked, putting the phone down.

'It'll be hard but I'll stay away. Your doctor friend agrees with you.'

From then on she spent more time at the Hall, only going home to sleep. But when Daisy once more urged her to move in she refused, clinging to the hope that one day Dick would be able to return to his old home and take up fishing again.

Although she had plenty to do looking after Jackie, she took over the running of the laundry with the help of one of the maids. Daisy protested that it wasn't necessary for her to work so hard but she gave her usual sniff, saying, 'You know I like to keep busy.'

Dick still hardly left his room and Daisy could only shake her head when Mum asked how he was getting on. She was really worried about him. Her success with Roger and the other residents had led her to believe somewhat optimistically that her brother would respond in the same way. But he continued to show no improvement. If anything, he was worse now than when she'd first seen him at the hospital. On bad days, she wondered if he might have been better off there, but she couldn't have left him.

Dick had retreated into his own private world, silent for the most part. But occasionally the staff reported that when he was alone, he could be heard muttering to himself. Once, she heard him herself and realized he was apologizing to his dead brother. Nothing would convince him that he wasn't to blame for Jimmy's death. More worrying still was that on bad days, he'd have to be washed and dressed, sometimes even fed, by one of the nurses.

'Peter says he'll come out of it in his own time. We just have to be patient,' Daisy told her anxious mother. 'Roger was like that at first and look at him now.'

One day Effie was sorting linen away in the big cupboard at the end of the corridor when she heard Dick's voice raised in a petulant cry. 'Don't want it, you can't make me.'

She dropped the pile of towels and ran to his room. Dick was sitting by the window, with Ruby facing him. The girl was holding a dish of something and trying to tempt him to eat. He pouted and pushed her away, looking very like a six-year-old.

All Effie's motherly instincts rose to the fore and she marched in, snatching the bowl from the startled Ruby. How dare she upset her boy like that? But as she prepared to give the girl a piece of her mind, she saw that Dick was cowering in the chair. Instantly she realized he wasn't a little boy, he was a grown man. Perhaps they'd been approaching him in the wrong way. These doctors don't know everything, she thought grimly.

Treating him as she'd have done when he was in fact six years old, Effie said sharply. 'Come on, lad, eat up. Can't hang around all day when there's work to be done.'

Dick raised his eyes. 'Yes, Mum, sorry,' he said and obediently took the next mouthful that Ruby offered him.

Effie stood by the door, watching until the bowl was empty. 'Good boy,' she said. 'If you keep that up you'll soon be able to sit up at the table and manage by yourself.'

Dick managed a weak smile, then his face crumpled. 'Mum, I'm sorry. I couldn't help it.'

She knew he wasn't talking about refusing his food and with a little cry she went and knelt by the chair, holding him in her arms while they both sobbed. As when he was a child, there were times to be tough and times to be soft, she thought, as she rubbed a hand across her eyes. The other hand was clasped in Dick's surprisingly strong grip. She knelt there for a long time until the ache in her knees became unbearable and she knew she'd have to move. She shifted awkwardly, but despite the pain, she didn't get up. She would stay as long as he needed her.

When Ruby sought Daisy in her office and said that Mrs March was with Dick, she hurried upstairs. Dick had been adamant that he didn't want to see his mother, had reacted violently whenever it was suggested, and she was afraid of what she would find.

She stopped short in the doorway, a lump rising to her throat as she took in the scene. Dick was sobbing against his mother's shoulder, while she knelt awkwardly beside him, rubbing his back and stroking his hair as she murmured comforting words.

Daisy wanted to speak but she was reluctant to intrude on this precious moment. As she hesitated, her mother looked up. 'It's all right, Daisy. We're going to be all right,' she said, getting painfully to her feet.

Daisy smiled, although she was still anxious. This might prove to be the turning point they'd been waiting for, but she knew it might still be a long time before Dick was once more the man he had been. Would he ever be fit enough to go home to Kingsbourne and rejoin the fishing fleet as her mother so desperately hoped?

But from then, Dick gradually began to come out of his shell. Effie spent part of every day cajoling and encouraging – sometimes even bullying – him, so that soon he dressed and fed himself. He even came down to the drawing room occasionally, although he didn't join in the recreational activities. He still wouldn't venture outside either but Daisy felt more optimistic about his progress as the months passed.

CHAPTER TWENTY-THREE

The home now had ten residents, all of whom were making good progress under Daisy and Georgina's care. There had only been one failure, although Peter assured them it wasn't. Rawlins had been unable to adjust to the home's routine, with its emphasis on normal activities. He continued to become distressed at the slightest sound and, after another painful incident, it was agreed that he should return to the hospital.

They had now settled into a domestic routine and Daisy was pleased when Mick Collins and Joe Bolton approached her one day asking if they could work in the garden. It had long been her dream to become as self-sufficient as possible. The charitable trust which Henry and his friends had set up almost paid its way, with contributions from the families of those who could afford it, but Daisy hoped to grow their own food and produce eggs, butter, and milk to cut down on their running expenses.

So far, the difficulty of obtaining outside help had meant postponing the fulfilment of her dream. There was only one gardener, an elderly uncle of Mrs Harris, who came whenever his rheumatism allowed and kept things tidy. And, although Peter had agreed that physical activity could be good therapy for the men, Daisy and Georgina worried that it might be too much for them.

Mick and Joe were keen, however, and immediately began clearing the old walled vegetable garden. Within the crumbling flint and brick walls a riot of weeds covered the rotting frames of the greenhouses. Broken pots and seed trays were scattered among shards of algae-stained glass. It was a daunting task, but whenever the weather allowed, Mick and Joe worked at clearing the debris. They wanted to be ready for next spring's planting and Daisy looked forward to their first crop of fruit and vegetables.

Watching them hard at work, she felt a glow of satisfaction. The men were hardly recognizable from the gaunt shadows that had arrived here such a short time ago. Although there were still days when one or the other of them stayed in his room enduring an attack of the shakes, as the months passed these occasions were becoming fewer.

*

Effie's increasing involvement in her son's care meant that she had less time to spend with Jack, especially as she still insisted on doing her share in the laundry. Daisy was concerned that she was becoming worn out with all the rushing about. 'If only she'd give up the cottage and move in,' she said to Georgina, it seemed for the hundredth time. 'But she won't take any notice of me.'

'Perhaps Peter could have a word,' Georgina suggested.

'She wouldn't take any notice of him either. She thinks she knows best.'

But Daisy determined to have one more try and she went upstairs where Effie was standing beside Dick's chair at the window. It was a bright sunny day, with a wind off the sea chasing the clouds along the top of the Downs.

'It's nearly spring,' Dick said, turning round and smiling. 'Look, the rooks are building their nests. And the daffodils will be out soon.'

Daisy, pleased that he seemed to be taking an interest in the outside world, put her hand on his shoulder, looking out at the familiar scene. For a moment she watched Mick and Joe working industriously in the kitchen garden.

'You ought to get out in the fresh air too, Dick,' she said. 'It's not good to be cooped up in this room all the time.'

An apprehensive frown crossed his face. 'Do I have to?' he asked in the childish voice that Daisy had come to dread. She looked at her mother, who was in Dick's room.

'Daisy's right, love. It's a lovely day. Why don't you just step outside for a bit?'

'I'm not up to digging though,' he said, indicating the two men below.

'You won't have to,' said Daisy smiling.

'I'd like to when I get a bit stronger. I'd like some chickens too.'

Daisy and her mother exchanged a puzzled glance. 'I never realized you liked chickens, Dick,' Effie said.

'Well, you can't keep chickens in a fisherman's cottage, can you? And being away at sea all the time . . .' His voice trailed away and he plucked at his trousers. It was the first time he'd referred to his life before the war and Daisy looked on it as a positive move forward.

Encouragingly she said, 'We could get a few hens. The eggs will be useful. Would you like that, Dick?'

He smiled eagerly. 'Would I? I've always wanted to grow my own vegetables and keep hens. A smallholding, like.' For the first time, he sounded really animated.

Effie looked a little put out. 'Why did you never say anything before about this hankering for the country life?' she asked.

'Well, what was the point? It was always assumed I'd join Dad at the fishing. Then he had the accident and I couldn't say anything then. How could I with him the way he was?' The light in his eyes died and he resumed picking at his clothes.

Daisy looked at her mother in dismay. Why had they never realized how he felt? There was a lightening of the heart – surely now her mother would see that it was pointless keeping on the cottage. Dick would never go back to the old life. But here he could have the sort of life he'd always wanted.

She smiled and said, 'You'll have your chickens, Dick. But first you must get well. Chickens need looking after and you'd be responsible for them.'

'I'm feeling better already,' he replied as she and Effie left the room.

'Now, Mum, you really must see that moving in with us is for the best – there's plenty of room,' she said, as soon as the door closed. 'I know you want Dick at home, but it'll be ages before he's well enough. And you heard him. He doesn't want to go back to the fishing anyway.'

'I'm not giving up the cottage,' Effie said, once she'd finally agreed that Daisy was right. 'I'll come and stay here for the time being but that house is Billy's home too.'

'But he could stay here when he's home,' Daisy said.

'Suppose he decides to get married – he'll need a house then.'

'You're right, Mum. I hadn't thought of that.' They could sort out the details later, she thought, pleased that she had finally persuaded her mother to stay at the Hall. It would be so much less tiring for her.

After speaking to her brother, Daisy wondered where they could build a henhouse and run. Apart from the walled garden which was now flourishing under Joe and Mick's hard work, the rest of the grounds were still badly neglected. She went outside and through a gate into what had once been an orchard. The trees were in need of pruning and the grass below was a tangle of weeds. She could picture the hens running around, pecking at the ground.

She hurried indoors to speak to Georgina about it. Her friend liked the idea but she said, doubtfully, 'You can't expect Dick to do it all – he hasn't been outside the house since he arrived.'

'But he's thinking about it. I want to have everything in place so that when he feels ready, he can make a start.'

'Perhaps we could take on an odd-job man,' Georgina suggested.

'A good idea – maybe someone to live in. There's such a lot of outside work, not just the chicken run. There's the maintenance on the electric generator and I'd like to get some of those outbuildings repaired. It could work out cheaper than paying someone from the village every time we need something done.'

'But where would he stay? Have we got room?'

Daisy laughed. 'Anyone would think you'd forgotten you were brought up here. Your family employed three times as many staff as we do, and they all lived in. Don't worry, I'll think of something.'

She'd noticed the cloud that passed over her friend's face at the reminder of her earlier life and was sorry she'd spoken so thoughtlessly. It had been insensitive of her, but she couldn't forget she'd once shared not only a room but a bed with another maid, cuddling up together for warmth, while icy draughts swirled round the unheated attics.

It hadn't been Georgina's fault, of course. That was the way things were then. But with the end of the Great War, many of the old conventions were being swept away. It might not happen overnight, but Daisy was determined that here their employees would be treated with dignity and respect.

She'd achieved it too – Millie and Ruby had a bed-sitting room each and shared a bathroom with constant hot water. They would never have to break the ice on their water jugs before being able to wash. Of course, this meant that with ten residents as well as herself, her mother and Georgina, there was less room for live-in staff. Mrs Harris had her own little annexe of bedroom, sitting room and bathroom, transformed from the original housekeeper's room and butler's pantry. The other staff lived locally and didn't need accommodation. Georgina was right though. If they employed a man, he'd need accommodation, but the former estate cottages had been sold off as the Davenports' fortunes declined. All that remained was the dilapidated dairy and the stable block.

She thought for a moment, then stood up. 'I've just had an idea,' she said. 'Come outside with me.'

They hurried across the yard to the stable block, shivering in the chill April wind.

At one end a section had been partitioned off and now housed the electric generator. But the rest of the building was in a terrible state.

She linked arms with Georgina. 'What do you think?' she asked, indicating the gaping windows, the doors hanging off their hinges, the smothering ivy. 'Could it be restored?' She pulled away a swathe of ivy and prodded the brickwork. To her untrained eye, it didn't look too bad.

'It would need a lot of work,' she replied cautiously. 'More than a handyman could cope with, I think.'

'Let's have a look inside.'

Georgina peered through a window. 'I'm not sure it's safe.'

In the old days, the head groom, stable boys and gardeners had all slept in rooms above the stable block – Ernest Jenkins too, Daisy remembered with a shiver. She pushed aside the unpleasant memory.

As she stepped inside, a cloud of dust rose and set her coughing but, after it had settled, she beckoned to Georgina, who followed hesitantly, wrinkling her nose at the dusty smell.

A shaft of sunlight streamed through the doorway and they saw that the stairs were still intact. The low brick walls dividing the stalls remained but the fittings had long gone, even the hay racks which had once been bolted to the walls. Daisy was relieved to note that it didn't smell damp. And it was just a building, after all. There was no Ernest now, to creep up behind and whisper his insinuations in her unwilling ear.

She put her foot on the stairs, testing it carefully before putting her weight on it. Georgina waited at the bottom until she indicated that it was safe to come up.

'The floor seems all right,' she said, bouncing up and down a little to test it.

'Don't!' Georgina gasped. 'You'll fall.'

Daisy laughed. 'No, it's all right, really. I'm surprised. I thought it would be much worse.'

Up here it was lighter, the sun filtering through the ivy-covered windows and settling in patches across the open space. As before, all the fittings had been removed, even the wooden partitions dividing the area into cubicles for the stable boys. But it was dry and seemed weatherproof.

'What do you think, Georgie? Can it be done? A little flat for someone to live in?' she asked.

'We'd have to get a proper builder to do the structural work, but perhaps the men could help with decorating and fittings.'

'But do you agree we get it done up and then take on a man?'

'I agree – but what about the trustees?'

'Will there be enough money, do you think?' Daisy's face fell. She'd been so enthusiastic about the plan but she hadn't really thought about the cost.

Georgina gave a wicked little smile. 'Don't worry – I'll talk to Henry,' she said, running lightly down the stairs.

They passed the old dairy and she realized it was in a worse state than the stables. An elder tree had seeded itself in the guttering, weeds sprouted from cracks in the walls and the roof was almost covered in ivy. 'If we can't get that repaired, we ought to have it pulled down,' she said. 'It's probably dangerous.'

They went back indoors and Georgina said that she'd telephone Henry straight away. Daisy smiled. Georgie could twist him round her finger and he had a lot of influence with the trustees. It wouldn't be long before the work was done and a new man was installed. Dick would have his hens.

CHAPTER TWENTY-FOUR

Georgina walked across the grass, holding tightly to Jackie's hand. The little boy chattered away, pointing and chuckling at the chickens scratching in their run. After a long cold spring, summer had arrived at last and Georgina had decided to take advantage of the weather and take Jackie for a walk. She took a deep breath of the sweet country air and thought with a little jolt of surprise, I'm happy, really happy.

She looked down at the child toddling along beside her and realized why she felt like this. Only a year ago it had been quite different. Then, stifled by the smothering affection of her in-laws, not to mention the depressing effects of living in the gloomy old vicarage, she'd been unable to take joy in her child.

The strangeness of returning here had soon worn off. Now she felt only pleasure that her former home was being put to such good use. As she passed the old stables she saw that the building had been stripped of the encroaching ivy. New doors and windows had been fitted and on the upper floor dividing walls had been built to create a small two-roomed apartment.

It was all ready for the new handyman. So far they hadn't found anyone suitable but Henry had phoned to say he'd interviewed an ex-army man who'd been wounded at Gallipoli. He was still partly crippled but fit for work.

Georgina walked over to inspect the ongoing restoration of the rest of the building. Several of the residents had taken up various hobbies and the drawing room, the only space available, was becoming cluttered with easels and craft materials. The former stables would be used as studios and workshops.

She smiled as she recalled the cleaner's outraged expression when she had yet again to sweep up the shavings left from Joe Bolton's wood carving. And Roger, who was becoming a talented artist, sometimes applied his paint with such enthusiasm that there was more on the surrounding walls than on the canvas. At least now the weather's fine he can take it outside, she thought with a smile. Roger now often roamed the

179

grounds with his sketchpad and paints and had recently produced land-scapes worthy of exhibition.

How she blessed her friend's good sense in encouraging these artistic abilities. It would never have occurred to me, she thought, remembering the tortured daubs that Roger used to paint. Now he painted the beauty around him, rather than those dark images from the war.

It was all thanks to Daisy, Georgina thought, marvelling at the way her life had changed in the past year. Was her friend happy too? She never mentioned Jack; neither of them spoke about the past much at all. The present was too full, their lives too busy to allow for introspection. She knew that Peter Holloway's frequent visits – more frequent than necessary these days, she felt – were due mainly to his feelings for Daisy. But she doubted if, now so confident in her role as matron, she'd ever want to give it all up to become the doctor's wife.

As she strolled through the grounds, only half listening to Jackie's chatter, her musings eventually turned to the subject she'd been trying to avoid. Henry. He'd telephoned earlier to say that he'd call in after lunch and, she thought in sudden panic, she knew what he was going to say. Since returning to Sussex she'd inevitably seen a lot of him and her initial embarrassment had soon worn off. Gradually they'd resumed their friend-ship. He'd made it clear that he still loved her, despite her rejection.

He'd begun to make remarks about the healing passage of time, the fact that Ryfe Hall's residents would not need such intense nursing care for ever and asking about her plans for the future. Until recently she'd given no thought to what might lie ahead. If anything, she'd envisaged staying here and bringing up her son, living much the same sort of life as she had before the war. Common sense told her this could not be so. But was marrying Henry the answer? She'd just have to put him off until she was really sure, she thought, but she couldn't keep him hanging on indefi-nitely. Daisy had said as much quite bluntly only the other evening. And she agreed. It just wasn't fair to him.

Her chaotic thoughts were distracted as Jackie pulled on her hand to gain her attention.

'I'm sorry, darling. What's the matter?' she asked, bending down. His little face puckered in a frown as he struggled to make himself under-stood. His gabbled baby words were sometimes unintelligible, even to his adoring mother. But when he sat down on the grass and refused to move she realized guiltily that he was tired. She'd been so wrapped up in her thoughts that she hadn't realized how far they'd walked.

Scooping him up in her arms, she kissed his frown away and started back. As she cut across the paddock to the front of the house, Henry's car rounded a bend in the drive. Until that moment she still hadn't been really sure. But as he drew nearer, she felt a little lift of the heart and realized how pleased she was to see him. It had crept up on her so gradually that she'd hardly been aware of it. She had only known that the days when Henry didn't put in an appearance were lacking in something. How often lately had she thought, I must tell Henry, and been deeply disappointed when he hadn't turned up.

If he asks me today, I'll say yes, she thought. The old impetuous Georgina would have run towards him and blurted it out before she had time to think. Now, she hesitated a little, feeling suddenly shy, as the car halted and he got out. She put Jackie down and the little boy toddled towards him, gurgling with laughter at the man who always had time to play with him.

She followed more slowly, smiling a welcome. But the smile died on her face as she realized he was not alone.

What was *he* doing here? she thought.

Before she could speak, Henry picked Jackie up and lifted him above his head, laughing. The little boy giggled as he was swung round and deposited back on the ground.

Henry gestured to his companion. 'You remember Jenkins, don't you?'

'Yes, I remember him,' she replied, her expression carefully neutral.

'This is the man I told you about. He assures me he can turn his hand to anything – learned about generators in the army.'

Before she could reply, Ernest took his cap off and said, 'Well, Miss Georgina, quite like old times, isn't it? I never thought to see the old place again. It's changed since the last time I was here.'

Georgina tightened her lips, biting back an angry retort. The cheek of him, being so familiar. And did he really think she'd forgotten the trouble he caused for her and Daisy? 'It's Mrs Lazenby now, Ernest,' she said, hoping to put him in his place.

'I'm sorry, I didn't know. And this is the son and heir, is it?' he said, bending down and ruffling Jackie's hair. He was smiling but Georgina sensed the evil behind it.

She was about to protest, to say they couldn't employ him, but Henry said, 'Jenkins was injured in the war as you know. He was finding it hard to get work and came to me for help – you know I'm all in favour of employing ex-servicemen. I thought of him straightaway when you said you were looking for a handyman.'

As Henry spoke, Ernest straightened painfully and hobbled towards her. 'If you'll just give me a chance to be useful, I'd be ever so grateful, Miss – sorry – Mrs Lazenby.'

She didn't know what to say. If only Henry had mentioned his name before bringing him here. She couldn't reveal what Daisy had told her in confidence and Henry couldn't know what he'd done in Malta.

To give herself time to think, she said, 'Go round to the kitchen and see Mrs Harris. She'll give you a cup of tea.' It would give her time to talk to Daisy. She was sure her friend would refuse to take him on, no matter what Henry said.

When he'd gone, Georgina said, 'I do wish you'd consulted Daisy or me before agreeing to give him a job,' she said.

'But you had no complaints when he worked here before, did you? The only reason he didn't have a job to come back to after the war was because your father . . .' Henry stopped abruptly. 'I'm sorry, Georgina. I shouldn't have brought that up.'

She shook her head. 'It doesn't matter. But Henry – I don't like him. We don't have to take him on, do we?'

'The trustees have agreed to give him a three-month trial – I don't see how we can go back on that.'

'Not much we can do about that then. I don't know how Daisy will feel though.'

'Why should Daisy mind?

'You couldn't have known, of course, but he caused trouble between us. He spread stories about us at the hospital. I don't think Daisy ever forgave him.' She hesitated. Could she tell him about the assault on her friend? No, it was up to Daisy.

'It was a long time ago, Georgie. He probably felt bitter about losing his place here, along with all the other servants. The thing is, he's been promised the job.'

'Well, we could give him a trial I suppose but if he makes trouble again, he'll have to go.'

'Who'll have to go?' Daisy said, coming into the room and sitting down at her desk.

Henry explained that he'd brought the new handyman but before he could say more Georgina interrupted. 'You'll never guess who it is, Daisy – Ernest Jenkins, our old groom.'

Daisy's chin came up. 'Jenkins – no. It's out of the question.'

'I've already told Henry what happened in Malta. But he says the trustees are committed to giving him a trial.'

Henry spoke up. 'Sir John gave him an excellent reference when he left here and, besides, the poor man desperately needs a job and you need a handyman.'

'Poor man?' Daisy stood up and paced to the window, then whirled and faced him. 'That *poor man* was the bane of my life when I worked here and . . .' She couldn't go on.

Georgina went over and put her arm round Daisy's shoulder while Henry walked over to the window and looked out. 'I think you should tell him,' she whispered. 'They wouldn't let him work here if they knew what he'd done.'

Daisy shook her head fiercely. 'No – I couldn't bear it – everyone knowing. Besides, raking everything up wouldn't do the Hall's reputation any good.'

'You're probably right but I don't like it.'

'Me neither.' She took a deep breath and addressed Henry. 'It's only for a short while. But I'll be keeping a close eye on him. The first sign of trouble and he's out – wounded soldier or not. By the way, did you tell him who's the matron? If not, Mr Jenkins is in for a shock.'

Georgina and Henry looked at each other in dismay. 'I don't think either of us mentioned your name,' Henry said.

The minute Daisy walked into the kitchen and saw Ernest sprawled in the chair beside the range, she knew from his spiteful smile that he hadn't changed.

'Well, Daisy, fancy you being back here in the old place too,' he said. 'Or should I call you Nurse now?'

'You can call me Matron,' she snapped.

The leer was immediately replaced by an oily obsequiousness which she found nauseating. He twisted his cap in his hands and began to grovel, thanking her for giving him the chance to make amends for his bad behaviour two years ago. 'I wasn't meself, you see, Miss. I was in pain, and I was still angry, like. Because of losing my position here.' He turned to Georgina with a twisted smile. 'You understand, don't you, Miss Georgina?' he said.

Georgina didn't reply but she managed a smile. Daisy glared at him – she wasn't fooled one bit by his Uriah Heep act. She admitted to a moment of satisfaction when she saw his reaction to discovering that she was the matron, but could that ever compensate for those months of humiliation as a young inexperienced girl and his later assault on her, not to mention slandering her and her friend. She'd be keeping a close eye on him and God help him if he stepped out of line.

*

Ernest settled into his quarters in the stables and, to Daisy's surprise, proved to be a good worker, able to turn his hand to almost anything. Some weeks after his arrival, on her daily tour of inspection, she looked out of the landing window, watching as he chopped wood for the fires that would soon be needed.

So far, he had kept out of her way, and she hadn't been able to find fault with him or his work. She was still annoyed that she'd been forced to take him and thought Henry should have consulted her first. But, as chairman of the trustees, he had every right to make such decisions. Besides, if it weren't for him she wouldn't be here at all.

Perhaps he would have understood and Georgina had tried to persuade her to reveal why she hated Jenkins so much. But she'd tried hard to put the incident out of her mind. Why rake it all up again?

Being in a position of authority now, she doubted that Ernest would try anything. Still, she wasn't happy having him around the place and she kept her ear to the ground. The slightest hint of trouble and he'd be sent packing. She'd have to come up with a very sound reason, for both Henry and Georgina seemed delighted with him.

So far, he hadn't put a foot wrong. Despite his handicap, he worked as hard as many a much fitter man. And on the rare occasions she came in to contact with him he was always respectful, on the surface at least. He kept the generator running smoothly. And she had to admit he'd made a good job of finishing off the stables, which now comprised a studio for arts and crafts, and several smaller workshops.

Aside from Ernest's nagging presence, Daisy was well satisfied with life nowadays. The gardens were flourishing and they were becoming self-sufficient in fruit and vegetables. Dick now had his chickens as well as ducks, a goat and a couple of pigs.

As she completed her daily round of the house and went outside to inspect gardens and workshops, she reflected that everything was going just as she and Georgina had planned. Ryfe Hall was a real home, where their residents had time and space to heal their mental wounds, and to nurture their own interests. And there were some surprising talents among them, she thought, spotting Roger down by the pond, where he had set up his easel.

Henry had been impressed with Roger's paintings and the wood carvings produced by Joe Bolton. He was now trying to arrange an exhibition in Portsmouth. Mick had also taken up painting, although he didn't feel confident enough to exhibit yet. And Bill Smythe, who'd been so withdrawn on his arrival at Ryfe Hall, had written some beautiful poetry which was now in the hands of a London publisher.

She entered the workshops, glancing round in case Ernest was around. He should be fixing the boundary fencing, but he would sometimes appear unexpectedly, a smirk on his face, which told her how much he enjoyed the momentary fright he'd given her.

There was no sign of him and she relaxed.

Joe was engrossed in another wood sculpture. It was only in the preliminary stages, but already Daisy could see the shape of a hovering kestrel emerging from beneath his talented fingers.

'That's beautiful, Joe,' she said and he looked up with his quick shy smile.

'That's because it's a beautiful piece of wood,' he said, caressing the grain. 'See, the shape's already there. I feel as if I'm just releasing it, if you see what I mean.'

He gave an embarrassed grin and ducked his head, concentrating on his work.

Daisy smiled and left him to get on, deciding to walk down to the kitchen garden before going back to the house. As she left the stables, she heard a smothered giggle and recognized Millie's voice. 'I must go. Mrs Harris will be sending out a search party.'

The girl appeared round a bend in the path, her hair tousled and her face flushed, carrying a basket of vegetables on her arm. She looked embarrassed when they came face to face but Daisy just smiled and asked, 'Are those for lunch?'

Millie nodded and hurried up the path in the direction of the house. Daisy continued towards the garden, guessing that the girl had lingered there with Mick Collins.

Her smile disappeared as she spotted a furtive figure disappearing round the side of the tool shed. Surely Millie wasn't getting involved with *him*, she thought. She must warn her what Ernest was really like.

She hurried after him, determined to have a sharp word with him about interfering with the maids' work. But as he reappeared, pushing a wheelbarrow full of wire and tools, she thought better of it. The expression in his eyes held veiled insolence as he stopped and greeted her.

'Morning, Matron. Lovely day, isn't it? You must feel like one of the gentry overseeing your estate.' He gave a short laugh.

'It's not *my* estate, as you well know, Ernest,' she replied. 'And I'm an employee of the trust just as you are. Now, I'll leave you to your work, and perhaps you'll leave me to mine.'

As she walked away she felt his eyes on her and heard him start to whistle. When she recognized the tune, her chin went up and she strode away, determined not to let him see how it affected her. Round the corner, in the shelter of the laurel hedge, she began to shake and the tears welled up. Ernest couldn't know that 'Daisy-bell' was Jack's pet name for her and that she'd always regarded the popular song as 'their tune'. But he had hit the mark.

She managed to regain control of herself and continue her walk but the day was spoilt for her. As she spoke to Roger and the others, her mind was not on them, but on how she could get rid of Ernest Jenkins.

CHAPTER TWENTY-FIVE

The faces of those gathered round the big dining table turned expectantly towards Henry as he stood up and coughed loudly. In the ensuing silence, a spatter of rain rattled the windows and a draught stirred the curtains. Daisy shivered, but no one else seemed to notice. All eyes were on Henry and Georgina as they waited for the announcement that had been whispered about for weeks.

She looks lovely tonight, Daisy thought, remembering the girl whose wayward ringlets she'd tried to tame so often in the past. She recalled the excitement as she'd prepared her mistress for evenings such as this, the giggles, the saucy remarks about her parents' guests. That girl was long gone, replaced by a woman of mature beauty. Tonight, though, Daisy was pleased when her friend caught her eye, a remnant of that girlish sense of fun still sparkling in her blue eyes.

When Henry held up his glass and made the toast 'To my future wife', Georgina blushed and lowered her eyes, then looked up at him with a smile which told the assembled guests that this time there was no doubt in her mind.

Henry fumbled in his waistcoat pocket and, taking out a small box, he slipped the simple solitaire diamond on to her finger. Above the smiles and applause, Daisy heard him whisper, 'This time you mustn't lose it. I can't afford to keep buying diamonds.'

Georgina kissed him in reply, winking at Daisy over his shoulder.

She smiled back but a chill had settled in her stomach. Outside, the rising wind threw rain against the window, just as it had on that other evening long ago. So much had happened since then and she'd thought the past was well and truly behind her. But there was always something to remind her of that dreadful night.

But good had come out of it eventually. Georgina was now a true friend. And then there was Jack. The memory of her love for him brought the familiar stab of pain.

When Joe spoke to her, she smiled and answered automatically, giving herself a mental shake as she looked round at the smiling faces. She *was* happy now, she told herself. Who'd have thought when she was scurrying round the kitchens and sculleries at everyone's beck and call that one day she'd be sitting here at the head of the table?

With a determined effort she returned to the present and made up her mind to enjoy the evening. A superb meal had been prepared and served by Effie and Mrs Harris, with the help of Millie. And for once, all their residents, including Dick, had been well enough to join them at the dining table. Her brother was almost his old self now, his face and arms tanned by working outdoors. And to her mother's joy, Billy was home on leave and had joined them for dinner. At the other end of the table, they were laughing and teasing each other just as they had when they were boys.

It was a real family party, Daisy thought, for everyone here was family now. Joe and Mick were like brothers too, although no one could ever take Jimmy's place. Even Bill Smythe, withdrawn and morose most of the time, was making an effort to join in.

There was a sudden silence as Henry stood up again. 'I'd like to propose another toast,' he said, looking at Daisy. 'If it weren't for Daisy, I might never have met Georgina again and been given a second chance of happiness. Besides that I owe her another debt of gratitude. As you know, I didn't serve in the war – through no fault of my own, I might add. But I always felt a little guilty. If Daisy hadn't come to work for me, infected me with her enthusiasm for the Ryfe Hall Convalescent Home, I would always have felt I should have done more. But it is Daisy's dedication and hard work that made it a success. So raise your glasses please – to Daisy March, Matron of Ryfe Hall.'

After the emotional turmoil of the evening, Daisy was glad to escape to her room. But first she made her rounds of the residents' rooms, making sure they'd all settled down after the excitement of the dinner party. None of them appeared to have suffered any ill effects from the unaccustomed wine and the late night – except for Bill, who was sitting at his little table in the alcove, frantically scribbling in an exercise book. She closed the door quietly, anxious not to disturb him. She knew that sedatives were no good. When Bill couldn't sleep, he wrote, sometimes long into the night. Recently his poetry had become almost lyrical, exploring the beauty of words. But occasionally his work was dark, haunting, a means of exorcising the ghosts which still sometimes plagued him.

As she walked softly down the corridor, Daisy hoped that tonight his thoughts were more cheerful. She'd seen the way he looked at Ruby and wondered if perhaps this poem was about the healing effects of love. Ruby had proved to have a knack for dealing with the patients and had gradually taken over some nursing duties. She and Bill now spent a lot of time together and Daisy hoped that they might soon be celebrating another engagement.

In her room, she kicked off her shoes and sat before the dying fire thinking about Ruby and wondering what would happen if she and Bill did marry. She didn't want to lose her. There must be a way of making sure that Ruby continued working here.

Romance seemed to be in the air. Even Ernest appeared to be serious in his courtship of Millie, spending a lot of time hanging round the kitchen. Daisy had recently seen him laughing and joking with the maid and Mrs Harris. Was it too much to hope that he had changed? She was glad that she hadn't interfered when she realized what was going on. Perhaps he'd stop taunting her now that he had someone who cared for him.

He'd better treat her right, that's all, she thought.

Outside, the wind still howled and she tried to ignore it, grateful for the haven of her little sitting room, where she could relax and be herself. I seem to be able to sort out everyone else's lives, but what about my own? she thought. Her face ached with the effort of smiling all evening. Sometimes it was hard seeing other people so happy.

As she lay back in the chair and closed her eyes she could almost hear her mother saying, 'Count your blessings girl. There's many worse off you know.' Her eyes snapped open, as if she thought Effie was actually in the room. With a nervous laugh she closed her eyes again, gradually drifting into a doze as the warmth of the fire stole over her.

A door slamming and footsteps in the hall outside brought her wide awake. She jumped up, heart thumping, as she thrust her feet into her shoes and stumbled towards the door. A man's voice echoed down the corridor as doors opened and shut noisily. 'Where is everybody? Ma, I'm home.'

Daisy's heartbeat quickened and her hand trembled as she reached for the door handle. I know that voice, she thought. She'd heard it in her dreams often enough. And she was dreaming now. She must be.

As in dreams, it was impossible to move. Her feet were glued to the floor, while her hand still groped blindly for the door and her heart thundered in her ears.

The door bursting open broke the spell and Ruby was there, her dressing gown untied, her feet bare. 'Matron, what's going on? What's all the noise about? I thought it was one of the boys having a go. But I looked and they're all tucked up in bed.'

Daisy put a hand on Ruby's arm to steady herself. 'It's all right, Ruby. We'll find out,' she said, forcing herself to remain calm.

She hurried towards the main staircase, where the intruder could be heard rampaging along the upper corridor. Ruby stayed close behind. As they reached the bottom stair, the door to the kitchen regions opened and Mrs Harris appeared, Effie close behind. They both looked at Daisy with frightened eyes. 'Do you think I should fetch Ernest?' Mrs Harris asked.

'Not at the moment. I'll try to deal with it. Ruby will come with me. If necessary I'll get you to telephone Mr Thornton.' As she spoke, the door to Georgina's quarters opened and, to Daisy's surprise, Henry appeared, Georgina close behind him. She thought he'd gone home ages ago.

Henry immediately took charge, firmly telling the ladies to stay downstairs while he investigated the cause of the disturbance. But Daisy insisted on following him.

'I think I know who it is,' she said, although her head was telling her it couldn't possibly be Jack. But who else would march boldly into the house at this time of night expecting a servant to come running, to take his bag and prepare his room?

Once more Daisy had a vision of Ryfe Hall in the old days, when she'd been newly promoted as Georgina's maid. They would sit at the window waiting for Jack. Then his car would appear in the drive, swinging round the circular path to stop in a flourish of gravel. He would burst into the house, throwing his bag and cap down, shouting, 'I'm home, Ma.' Just as he had tonight, Daisy thought. The hope that he'd survived the sinking of his ship had never quite been extinguished. But now, instead of a surge of joy, a cold finger of fear touched her heart. Something wasn't right.

She followed Henry into Mick Collins' room – the room that had once been Jack's – and stopped short. Mick cowered in the corner, a high-pitched keening coming from his open mouth. A man stood over him threateningly, while Henry tried to pull him away. Was it really Jack?

'Do you want to wake the whole household?' Daisy's sharp voice had the desired effect as the three turned towards her.

When the intruder released the unfortunate Mick, Henry bent and helped him to his feet, assisting him on to his bed where he curled up with his hands over his face.

Until the moment his eyes met hers, Daisy hadn't really believed that Jack had returned from the dead. But there was no doubt. The resemblance to Georgina was uncanny, the fair wavy hair, the sapphire eyes. But where Georgina had softened and rounded with the passing years, Jack was gaunt, almost skeletal, his clothes hanging off his scarecrow body.

Worst of all was the lack of recognition in the eyes which blazed angrily out of sunken dark hollows. Daisy drew a sharp breath as he shouted, 'Who the devil are you – and what is this fellow doing in my room?'

He sank down on the end of the bed, running a hand through his hair and sighing heavily, all the fight suddenly gone out of him. 'Will you please tell me what the blazes is going on, Henry, old chap?' he asked.

It was clear that Jack was as confused as everyone else. Hiding the hurt she felt that he hadn't recognized her, Daisy spoke gently but firmly.

'I'm sorry that no one seems to have informed you that this is no longer your home, Master Jack,' she said. 'It's now a nursing home. However, if you'd let us know you were coming, we would have made sure a bed was ready for you. If you'd like to come downstairs, I'll get you some refreshments and we can let Mr Collins go back to sleep.'

Mick looked up fearfully. 'You won't turn me out, will you, Matron?' he whispered.

'This is your room. No one is going to turn you out,' she replied firmly.

Jack turned to her with a bewildered expression. 'A nursing home? But where's my mother? My sister? And who are you?'

'I'm the Matron of this home, and your sister is right here.' Daisy said, stepping aside as Georgina rushed in and threw her arms round him.

'You're home. Thank God. Whatever happened? Why didn't you let us know?' The questions tumbled out as she hugged him, stroking his hair and crying into his shoulder.

'I wanted to surprise you,' he said, a trace of his old boyish smile twitching his lips. 'You don't know how good it is to be home. But why did you give my room away? How could you do that, Georgie?' His voice was plaintive and Daisy, listening, realized that instead of a returning lover, she now had another patient.

But he was back, he was safe. Nothing else mattered. Gently, she persuaded Jack and Georgie, still clinging to each other, to come downstairs, leaving Ruby to settle Mick back into bed.

In her sitting room, Henry made up the fire and drew chairs up to the blaze. Daisy watched as Georgina helped Jack into a chair and sat down close beside him, never letting go of his hand.

How she longed to be the one hovering over him so solicitously. But she knew it wouldn't do, not while he was still so confused. Instead, as usual, she covered her feelings with activity, going to the kitchens to help Mrs Harris prepare hot drinks and a snack supper.

As she bustled around setting a tray, the housekeeper avidly questioned her. 'Is it really Master Jack, who we thought to have drowned these past three years? Fancy,' she exclaimed. 'Where's he been? What happened to him?'

Daisy answered wearily, 'I don't think he's in a fit state to tell us. He's tired and confused. He doesn't look at all well. Perhaps he was a prisoner somewhere. It will all come out eventually. But I think for tonight, we'd best let him rest.' She took the tray and said, 'In fact, I think we all need some rest. Maybe things will be clearer in the morning.'

When she got back, Georgina was still holding Jack's hand, while Henry stood with his back to the fire. She set the tray down and poured cocoa from the big jug. But Henry made no move to take his. 'I think it best if I leave you to it now, Georgie,' he said. 'I'll come back in the morning. Are you sure you'll be all right now?'

Georgina got up and went to him, kissing him on the lips. 'I'm sorry our celebration day had to end like this,' she said quietly. 'It's not how I planned it at all.' A ghost of her usual mischievous smile appeared, and Henry coughed and looked embarrassed. She took his hand and led him outside, leaving Daisy and Jack alone.

'Well, Matron, I expect you realize all this has come as a shock to me. I had no idea what had been going on while I was away. I think my mother or one of the family might have written to let me know,' Jack said, leaning forward.

'I'm sure they would have – if they'd known where you were,' Daisy said.

A shadow crossed Jack's face, then he brightened. 'I was in hospital. Surely someone informed my family?'

'How long were you there?' Daisy hesitated, not sure how to address him – he wasn't 'Master Jack' any more and Lieutenant Davenport seemed absurd after what they'd been to each other. But he didn't seem to know her. What effect would it have on his state of mind if she threw herself at him, sobbing, 'Jack, darling'?

After a long hesitation, he said, 'I was there a couple of weeks I think.' The puzzled frown crossed his face again. 'It might have been longer. I get these headaches you know. Makes it hard to remember. Got a bit of a knock on the head.'

'Did your sister tell you anything while I was out of the room?' Daisy asked.

'Only that she was nursing here and that the mater was staying down in Kent with Uncle George. Imagine my little sister – a nurse.' A trace of the old Jack, the smile that had always had the power to melt her heart, appeared fleetingly, then was gone. He looked down at his hands. 'Seems funny though, coming back and finding a strange chap sleeping in my bed. Gave me quite a shock, I can tell you.'

'Gave him a shock too,' Daisy said before she could stop herself, and was rewarded with the ghost of a smile.

'I'll apologize to the fellow in the morning,' he said. Then he leaned over and picked up a sandwich. 'God, I'm starving.'

'You always used to say that when you got home on leave,' Georgina said, coming into the room. 'Don't they feed you in the navy?'

The uncertain look showed again. 'Navy?' he said and a shutter dropped down over his face.

'He's been in hospital,' Daisy said quickly, before Georgina could speak again.

'Left there this morning. Took me all day to get here,' Jack said, wolfing down the sandwiches and draining his mug of cocoa.

'You must be tired then,' Georgina said. 'I've organized a bed for him, Daisy. Why don't you go to bed yourself? I'll see to Jack. We can talk in the morning.'

They left the room and Daisy gathered up the supper things and took the tray down to the kitchen. Mrs Harris had gone to bed and the house was quiet. Daisy turned off the lights and stood at the foot of the stairs listening. It would hardly be surprising if some of the patients suffered a disturbed night after the noisy finale to what had already been an exciting evening. But all was quiet and with a sigh Daisy returned to her own room.

She was bone weary but she knew she wouldn't sleep. She undressed and brushed her teeth anyway. Then she uncoiled and brushed her long dark hair, something she never failed to do, however tired she was. As she wielded the brush she looked at herself in the mirror, noting the lines that had appeared under her eyes and round her mouth, the paleness of her cheeks. She was too thin also, never having regained the weight she'd lost during her illness in Malta. No wonder he didn't recognize me, she thought. I look like an old woman. With a choked sob she threw the brush down on the dressing table and gave way to tears of relief that Jack was safe and home at last

But mingled with the relief was the fear that although he had returned in body, her Jack – the real Jack – was lost to her for ever.

CHAPTER TWENTY-SIX

When Daisy went down to the kitchen very early next morning, Mrs Harris and Millie were already up and had made a start on breakfast. A pot of tea stood to one side of the range, and as Daisy poured herself a cup, her mother came in, rubbing her eyes.

'What a night,' she muttered. 'I didn't sleep a wink.'

'I don't think any of us did,' Daisy replied, taking a sip of her tea. Her hopes of a few quiet moments before the start of what promised to be a very trying day were fading. She didn't feel like talking, having hardly slept at all. After tossing and turning for an hour after going to bed, she'd given up the struggle and got up, to spend most of the night at her desk. Going over the accounts had served to keep the turmoil of thoughts at bay and at last her eyelids had started to droop. She'd fallen exhausted into bed, but an hour later she was up again. Jerked out of that fitful pre-dawn doze by a jumble of dreams, she sat up with a gasp. But it hadn't been a dream. Jack really was here.

As she went to the window and pulled back the curtains, she realized that the storm of the night before had abated. The trees were no longer tossing their branches in the wind and a pale misty sun peeped over the horizon. The promise of a fine day seemed to Daisy to be a good omen and at last she allowed the first hesitant stirrings of happiness to intrude. Although her reunion with Jack hadn't quite lived up to her imaginings during those months of hope and anguish, she took heart from the fact that at least he was alive. He hadn't recognized her last night. But then, he seemed to have forgotten much else besides. He was sick and confused. What dreadful trauma had he suffered to still be in this state after all this time, she wondered.

Her first impulse was to rush upstairs to reassure herself that she hadn't dreamt the events of the previous evening. But she acknowledged that Georgina was the best person to talk to him first. He had recognized her as his sister. To him, Daisy was only the matron of the nursing home.

So she had dressed and gone down to the kitchen. Listening to the others chatting as they started their preparations for the day, Daisy realized that she was not the only one to have suffered a shock. Mrs Harris was all of a twitter because the 'young master' had returned. 'It's sure to mean changes now he's back,' she said, seeming to forget that he was no longer entitled to call Ryfe Hall home.

Effie agreed. All her old distrust of the gentry, and the Davenports in particular, rose up again and she was sure that at the very least she would be turned out of her comfortable room to make way for 'Master Jack'.

'You're quite wrong,' Daisy protested. 'Have you forgotten that the house is owned by the trust now? He can't do anything about that.'

'He'll probably find a way,' Mrs Harris said, banging a pan down on the table.

'I'll be all right, I suppose,' Effie said. 'Dick and I can always go back to Kingsbourne. Thank God I kept the cottage.'

'For goodness' sake, Mum. Listen to me for a minute.' Daisy's temper was rising and she took a deep breath before continuing. 'The fact that Jack has come home will make no difference here. His father lost his money and sold the house long before Jack went missing. Henry – Mr Thornton – bought it and made it over to the trust. Don't start getting all het up for no reason.'

Daisy put her arm round her mother and Effie sniffed. 'Well, you can't blame us for being concerned. It's all been a bit of a shock. Not to mention that hullabaloo last night, rampaging up and down stairs. What got into the lad?'

'He's sick, Mum. Like Dick and all the others.' Daisy swallowed the sob that threatened to rise in her throat and looked at her watch. 'Now, I'm going to telephone Doctor Holloway to see if he can come over. And in the meantime, the residents will be wanting their breakfast,' she said with a semblance of her usual briskness.

She handed the dish of scrambled eggs to Millie to take up to the dining room and followed with a tray of tea and coffee. As she left the room she said, 'Mum, why don't you go and see if young Jackie's awake? I expect Georgina's too taken up with her brother to see to him this morning.'

Effie nodded, following Daisy up the short flight of steps to the main hall and continuing upstairs.

Daisy crossed to the dining room, jumping as the front door opened and Susan came in. 'Oh Susan, I'd forgotten you'd be here early today. I'm pleased to see you though. We had a bit of an upset last night and I'm afraid Georgina and I will be rather busy this morning. I'll have to leave you and Ruby to sort out the breakfasts. Then I think you'd better get everyone over to the workshops, try and keep them occupied.'

'What's happened? Is it one of the residents?' Susan looked worried. It had been ages since any of the patients had been upset – they'd been making such good progress.

Daisy decided not to go into details, knowing that Ruby would put her in the picture. 'We've got a new patient. He arrived last night – a bit upset,' was all she said, quickly dismissing her and going into the dining room. She placed the tray she was carrying on the sideboard and asked Millie to carry on.

In her office, she sat down, took a deep breath, and picked up the telephone. It wasn't going to be easy telling Peter about Jack. She must stick to the facts and try not to get too emotional.

To her relief the doctor remained professionally detached, making no comment on the effect Jack's return might have on their personal lives, merely asking for a brief summary of what had happened the previous evening. Daisy told him quickly, adding her fears for Jack's physical as well as his mental condition.

'It sounds as if he's been suffering from amnesia. That would account for the length of time he's been missing and why the family wasn't informed,' Peter said. 'Don't worry, Daisy, these problems usually resolve themselves eventually. I think the fact that he managed to get home is an indication that his memory is returning. I'll come over as soon as I can. Can you try to find out where he was?' He rang off.

How could she help worrying, she thought, as she put the phone down and went to find Georgina. As she mounted the wide staircase, she passed the residents on their way down to breakfast, none of them seeming any the worse for their disturbed night.

Mick Collins wasn't with them though, she noticed, and she put her head round the door of his room to make sure he was all right. He was still in bed, his face turned to the wall, while Ruby tried to coax him to get up.

'Leave him, Ruby,' Daisy said, beckoning the girl over to the door. 'He had a bad time last night,' she whispered. 'If he wants any breakfast you can bring him a tray.'

Poor Mick, Daisy thought, as she continued along the corridor. He'd always felt insecure about his place here, constantly worrying that they would turn him out when he was fit again. What a pity they'd given him Jack's old room. Last night's episode could have set him back weeks in his recovery.

Daisy sighed, slowing down as she neared the room they'd found for Jack. Through the open door she saw him standing with Georgina by the window, his arm round his sister's shoulder.

'You don't know how good it is to be home, Georgie,' she heard him say.

They turned as Daisy entered the room, and she caught her breath. He still looked so ill, she thought, resisting with difficulty the urge to enfold him in her arms. But his eyes still showed no sign of recognition. Had he truly forgotten her, the result of the blow to his head as Peter had suggested? Or was it that those precious hours they'd spent together in Valletta had meant so little to him?

By the time Peter arrived, things had almost settled down into their normal routine. Mrs Harris and the girl from the village were clearing up after breakfast and preparing lunch, while Millie and the daily cleaning woman did the bedrooms.

Mick was still in his room and the other residents, supervised by Susan and Ruby, were in the workshops, except for Joe, who was sweeping up the debris from last night's storm.

While they waited for Peter, Daisy and Georgina gently questioned Jack. He still looked gaunt and ill, but last night's rest seemed to have done him good. His eyes were clearer and he sat easily in the armchair in front of the fire, with none of the restless movements of the previous night.

But as his story emerged it was obvious that he was still confused about the sequence of events. He seemed to think that he'd been rescued and taken to hospital immediately after the ship had gone down. Daisy, after a warning glance at Georgina, decided not to enlighten him about the amount of time that had passed, and asked him the name of the hospital. He put his hand to his forehead and his eyes clouded. Then, to Daisy's relief, he told them that it was in Kent.

'Near Canterbury I think,' he said.

'Did the doctor give you a letter of discharge?' Daisy asked.

'I didn't realize I needed one,' Jack replied. He looked at his sister for reassurance. 'I felt so much better. I just decided to come home.'

Georgina took his hand and kissed his cheek. 'It's all right, Jack. We're pleased to see you. But you're still not well.'

'I won't have to go back there will I?'

'No. We'll look after you here,' she told him.

Daisy got up and excused herself, going to her office where the telephone was situated. It sounded as if Jack had been in the same hospital as Dick. It didn't take long for the operator to connect her and within minutes she was speaking to the superintendent, the man she'd clashed with over her brother. After confirming that a patient had gone missing the previous day, he refused to give any details, saying that if she knew the whereabouts of his patient, he should be returned to the hospital forthwith.

'The man is not in his right mind. He needs to be kept under constant supervision,' the officious little man spluttered.

'Do you mean he might be dangerous?' Daisy asked, her heart thumping.

'Not exactly. But in a case of this kind . . .' The same words he had used about her brother, Daisy thought, anger rising in her throat.

Before she could speak her mind, the door opened and Effie came in holding Jackie by the hand. 'I'm just taking the lad down to help Dick feed the chickens,' she said, ignoring the fact that Daisy was holding the telephone. 'Oh, and Doctor Holloway's just arrived.'

Daisy spoke into the telephone. 'Could you hold the line for a moment, please?' Then turning to Effie, 'Fetch Peter quickly.'

She hoped that Peter, with his air of quiet authority, would be able to elicit more information from the reluctant superintendent. Handing the receiver over to him after a quick explanation, Daisy left him to it. When she got back to Jack's room, she found that Henry had arrived. He had his arm round Georgina and she smiled up at him as he told Jack that they'd just become engaged.

'But I thought—' Jack's eyes clouded and he looked bewildered. Then the old smile broke through. 'So you changed your mind again, eh? I knew you'd do the right thing eventually, but you like to pretend you're a rebel. Well, I'm delighted. Henry, you're a lucky chap.'

'I know,' Henry said quietly.

Daisy, watching them, felt her heart would break. It was almost as if the last few years had never happened, as if he'd just come home on one of his weekend leaves. How could he have forgotten the war, his friend Tom, and most of all, how could he have forgotten their time together in Malta? She wanted to protest, to make Georgina tell him about Tom and little Jackie. But they were smiling and going along with him, as if they too hadn't lived through these past years.

But what else could they do, she asked herself, trying to remain calm. Perhaps Peter would be able to advise them on the best way to deal with it, she thought, hoping he'd finish the telephone call and join them quickly.

Suddenly Jack leaned forward in his chair and gazed intently at Daisy, who still stood by the door. 'I know you, don't I?' he said.

Daisy's hand went to her throat but she spoke calmly. 'We met when you arrived last night. Do you remember what we told you?'

'Yes, they've gone and turned my home into a blasted hospital and you're the matron,' he replied impatiently. 'But I meant – I know you – from before.'

Daisy's heart leapt momentarily and she would have gone to him. But his voice trailed away and the uncertain look came into his eyes again. She wondered what to say and looked to Georgina for help. But her friend had turned to Henry, stifling a sob as he patted her shoulder.

Best to stick to bare facts, Daisy decided, taking a deep breath. 'I used to work here, when your family owned the house. Before the war,' she said.

'The war – yes. They told me about that.' Jack's voice was low, hesitant. Then he looked up. 'I was hit on the head, you know. There's a scar, but you can't see it. My hair's grown now, you see.' His hand went to his head, his fingers working their way over his scalp. His voice dropped lower, mumbling.

Daisy leaned forward to catch the words. 'Lucky to be alive. All my friends, dead and gone. What's your name? What's your unit? Not a spy.' He started up, eyes wild, looking from one to another, not recognizing them.

Georgina started to cry and Henry put his arms around her. Daisy ignored them. She knelt in front of Jack, grabbing his flailing hands and holding them firmly. Now he wasn't just Jack, he was another patient. Someone to be cared for, reassured.

'It's all right you're safe now. The war's over. No one's going to hurt you.' She continued to murmur until he was calm.

An alarming blankness had replaced the wild look by the time Peter entered the room and Daisy thankfully relinquished her place to him. The doctor briefly examined Jack, then recommended that he be put to bed with a sedative. 'He's still far from well, and managing to get here by himself all the way from Kent has taken it out of him. He needs plenty of rest. We can leave the questions till later.'

Daisy rang for Susan and they left her to get him back to bed, while they went back to the office. 'Any joy from the hospital?' she asked, hoping her voice sounded steady.

Peter took her hand. 'I'm afraid Lieutenant Davenport is in a very bad way. The superintendent was most insistent that we send him back there.'

Georgina wasn't able to hide her distress and turned to Henry for comfort. But Daisy was determined to keep a tight rein on her emotions. It wouldn't help Jack if she broke down too.

Peter waved them to silence. 'I persuaded him that the lieutenant was in no condition to travel and that he was in the best place to receive the treatment he needs.' He smiled at the relief on their faces, then went on to tell them what he had learned.

The scars on Jack's head had alerted the hospital to the probable cause of his amnesia, a severe blow on the head. And the fact that the wound had healed badly told them that, not only had it happened some time ago, but that he'd received no medical treatment at the time.

Jack's version of how he had arrived back in England was confused and garbled and the authorities had surmised he'd been a prisoner. Many prisoners at the end of the war had walked out of the camps when they were abandoned by the Germans and managed to find their own way home. They thought this was what Jack had done.

Because he was still confused and had no memory of who he was, or where he'd spent the war years, he'd been kept in hospital, where he had recently begun to show signs of improvement.

'Then yesterday, he just walked out. He wasn't missed for some time but by then he'd probably got quite a long way. They sent out search parties, of course, worried that he'd come to some harm,' Peter said.

'No wonder the superintendent sounded so relieved when I said he'd turned up here,' Daisy said. 'They must have been frantic.'

'Yes. But I wonder why he just upped and left?' Henry asked.

'They couldn't throw any light on that, of course. The staff were questioned but no one had any idea what was in his mind,' Peter replied.

'You don't think he was being badly treated, do you?' Georgina asked fearfully. 'You hear such dreadful stories about these places.'

'Highly unlikely, I would say,' Peter told her firmly. 'Besides, if it was that kind of institution Daisy's brother would have given some indication of it when we fetched him home.' He smiled and turned to Daisy. 'I know neither of us thought much of that horrid little man when we met him, but on the telephone he sounded quite reasonable. Falling over himself to be helpful, in fact, once I'd reminded him of our previous meeting.'

'I expect he feels guilty because he allowed Jack to simply walk out of the place,' Daisy said grimly.

'Well, he's home now. And we're going to make sure he gets well,' Georgina said, wiping her eyes and standing up. 'I'm going to pop up and make sure he's all right and then I must go and find Jackie. Poor lamb, I haven't even said hello to him this morning.'

'I'll come too, darling,' Henry said, following her out of the room.

When they were alone Daisy turned to Peter. 'Have you told us everything?' she asked. 'He is going to get well, isn't he?'

Peter looked down at his clasped hands and there was a lengthy pause before he began to speak. 'Daisy, my dear, I don't mean to paint a gloomy picture, but I think it's best if you can accept that the Jack you once knew is not the person who turned up here last night. We know so little about amnesia, it's such an unpredictable condition. He could be like this for years.' He put out a hand at Daisy's quick intake of breath. 'On the other hand, its very unpredictability means that we can always hope.'

Daisy rewarded him with a little smile and dared to voice that hope. 'His memory is coming back, though? You said he remembered nothing when he was in the hospital. But he managed to find his way back here and he remembers Georgina and Henry.'

Peter explained to her that it had been known for amnesia victims to remember selective incidents. 'Probably the blow on the head caused the first blackout. Then, as he recovered and things started coming back to him, he would have blocked out anything that caused him distress or that wasn't important.'

Daisy couldn't restrain a little sob. So she was right. That magical time in Malta had clearly not meant as much to him as it had to her. Why else expunge it from his memory? She wiped her eyes on the back of her hand and gestured to Peter to go on.

'I'm sorry to distress you, my dear. But it's better to face up to reality. You do want to help him, don't you?' he asked. Daisy nodded and he went on. 'It seems that he has wiped out the war years completely and has gone back to what he remembers as a happier time – when Ryfe Hall was his home and his family were here. He remembers his sister becoming engaged to Mr Thornton and the fuss over her breaking the engagement.'

'But he doesn't remember me though, does he?' Daisy said, beginning to cry again.

Forgetting his professional detachment, Peter put his arms round her and let her cry. When she'd regained control of herself and pushed him away, he smiled ruefully. 'I can't pretend to be pleased the fellow's turned up after all this time. Of course I'm pleased for his family – and you. I truly want you to be happy. But I can't bear to see you upset like this, and I think this is only the beginning.'

Daisy looked at him, a questioning look in her eyes. 'The beginning?'

'Yes, the beginning of a long and painful road for you.' He turned away impatiently. 'Daisy, how long will you wait? What if he never remembers?'

'I could tell him, remind him of what we once meant to each other, that we were going to get married.'

'That's not the way, Daisy – and you know it.' Peter was pacing the room now. 'Yes, you could remind him. But then what? He's in no condition to make decisions. Suppose he agrees to marry you out of some sense of obligation. And then it all goes wrong?'

'Why should it all go wrong? We loved each other once.' Daisy wasn't sure if she was trying to convince Peter or herself.

'And I love you now, Daisy.' He broke off and moved away from her, then turned and threw his hands up in a defeated gesture. 'Oh, why did he have to come back now? We were getting on so well. I had begun to think, to hope . . .'

'I'm fond of you, Peter. But I never gave you cause to think we could be more than friends. You always knew how I felt about Jack.' It was true. Even after all this time, she had dreamed that one day Jack would return. But not like this, she thought.

Peter's shoulders slumped. 'I know, Daisy, my love. But believe me, I am thinking of you, not just myself. All I ask is that you don't do anything hasty. Take one day at a time and let things take their course.'

'You know I'd never do anything that wasn't in the best interests of my patients. And Jack is a patient now.' It was hard for Daisy to adopt the brisk professional tone she usually used and she glanced at her watch, to cover the quiver in her lips. 'I ought to go and check on him – and Mick. He wasn't too well first thing. Susan will be busy with the others and Ruby will be seeing about lunch.'

'You look all in. Why not get some rest?' Peter said. 'I'll check your patients and then I'll be off. I've got a session at the hospital this afternoon.' He picked up his bag.

'Thank you, Peter, but how can I rest when I've got so much on my mind? Besides, there's so much to do.' It would be a relief to do something physical like turning out the linen cupboard. Activity always helped when her mind was in turmoil.

'Well, don't overdo it,' Peter said, pausing at the door. 'I'm sorry I let rip a few minutes ago. But it's hard to stand by and see someone you love hurting. You do know I only have your happiness at heart.'

'I know,' Daisy said softly, closing the door behind him. With a sigh, she threw herself down in the chair. It was true that she had things to do but now all she could do was think about her conversation with Peter. She hadn't meant it when she'd threatened to remind Jack of their past, although it had been tempting – especially when he'd shown that little glimmer of recognition earlier on. But it wouldn't be fair to him.

Peter was right. Who knew what such a revelation could do to his mental state? Deep down she knew it was fear that kept her from speaking out. Suppose he married her from a sense of duty and then one day remembered that for him that magic interlude in Malta had been just a wartime dalliance to take his mind off the horrors of war?

CHAPTER TWENTY-SEVEN

It was Christmas Day and Daisy was handing out presents in the large drawing room, assisted by an excited Jackie. He toddled round the room, his face flushed with importance, presenting the parcels as she called out the names. Residents and staff were gathered round the Christmas tree in the drawing room. Even Mick, who since Jack's dramatic return to Ryfe Hall had become withdrawn and anxious again, had been persuaded to join the party.

Everyone had joined in with the preparations. Dick and Joe had brought in baskets of logs early that morning, stacking them in the hall so that no one would have to brave the icy wind outside to replenish the fires. The house was filled with the rich scent of burning apple wood.

Ernest had cut a fir tree and dragged it in, even staying to help Millie decorate it. Daisy hoped the girl wouldn't end up getting hurt. It was obvious she was smitten but she knew it would be no use warning her. Still, Ernest seemed much less surly these days, although she didn't really believe he'd changed. She forced herself to smile and handed him his gaily wrapped gift.

She glanced across at Henry, who was chatting quietly with Peter. He and Georgina had originally decided to get married on Christmas Day but Jack's unexpected return had thrown their plans into disarray. Georgina was determined that Jack would give her away and had persuaded Henry to wait until her brother was fully recovered.

Remembering the night of the engagement party, Daisy's smile faded. Her joy at Jack's return, quickly followed by despair that things would never be the same between them, had settled now into a dull acceptance. Jack was home, safe. But he wasn't the Jack she'd known in happier times. And, while she still hoped, she often asked herself if he ever would be.

He was laughing now at something Georgina had said, but behind the laughter Daisy could see the bewilderment and uncertainty that clouded his eyes so often. Since his return he had shown flashes of the old Jack and gradually pieces of the past were coming back to him. But he still looked on Daisy as the servant she'd once been, or as now, treated her with the respect due to the matron in charge of the home.

The presents were all handed out and opened, amid laughter and teasing. When Roger went to the piano and started to play 'Silent Night', Daisy couldn't bear to listen. She got up and left the room quietly, going to the kitchen to prepare tea.

She hastily wiped away a tear when she heard the door open, thinking it was Mrs Harris come to help her. Peter's voice startled her. 'Brings back memories, doesn't it?' he said.

Daisy nodded. She too had been thinking of that Christmas in Malta, the simple decorations, the scrounged gifts and extra food for the patients. Since her return to England the season hadn't meant much to her. She'd still been ill and grieving for Jack the first Christmas at home, then last year they'd just opened the home and most of the residents were too sick to enjoy the celebrations.

This year had promised to be different and it would have been if only Jack would recover.

'I shouldn't be hiding out here snivelling,' she said with an attempt at a smile. 'I have so much to be thankful for.'

'I understand, Daisy. I just wish there was something I could do,' Peter replied.

'I know – I just have to be patient. I could bear it if only I knew for sure that one day Jack would get better. It's this uncertainty,' Daisy said with a sob.

'But he is getting better. Every time I see him, I notice more improvement. He's remembered a lot of what happened after the ship went down, hasn't he?'

Jack hadn't recalled everything. In fact, there had been no sudden flash of remembrance. Little things would come out in the course of conversation and they had been able to piece together his adventures after being picked up by fishermen off one of the Greek islands. They had cared for him for months and when he'd recovered physically they had taken him to the mainland where he had tried to find his way back to the allied lines. But he had been picked up by the enemy. In the prison camp he'd been beaten and starved in an attempt to make him reveal who he was and what he was doing so far behind the lines.

The beatings had confused him still further as well as weakening his already frail constitution. If the war hadn't ended when it did, Peter felt it was doubtful he would have survived. The miracle was that he'd made it back to England by his own efforts.

Daisy sniffed and blew her nose, then started stacking crockery onto a tray. 'Don't worry about me. I'll be all right. Just so long as I keep busy,' she said.

Peter put his hand on her arm. 'You don't have to drive yourself like this. It's not the answer.' He turned her to face him. 'I know how hard it is for you, seeing him every day. Perhaps you ought to get away from here – for a while at least.'

'Where would I go?' she asked. 'Not that I want to leave here,' she added hastily.

'You could marry me,' he said quietly.

Daisy was silent for a moment. 'Do you really think I would, loving Jack as I do? And what's more, do you really want me, knowing you'd always be second best?' She gasped and bit her lip. She hadn't meant to be cruel.

Peter sighed and dropped his hands to his sides. 'I love you enough for both of us. And I just hate to see you wasting your life, living in hope of something that will probably never happen.'

'But you said he would get better, that one day he might remember,' Daisy protested.

'The possibility is always there, of course. But I think if it was going to happen, it would have by now. He's been back two months, nearly three. He sees you every day, Daisy. Surely something of what he felt for you would have surfaced by now.'

He paced the kitchen floor, stopping beside the sink and pounding his fist on the wooden draining board. 'God, I wish he'd never come back,' he muttered.

Daisy was by his side in a moment, her eyes flashing. 'How could you? That's a wicked thing to say.'

His face was stricken and he held out a placating hand. 'I'm sorry. I didn't mean it. I wouldn't hurt you for the world. It's just – I thought you were beginning to accept – that maybe I stood a chance.' His shoulders slumped.

Daisy took his hand and was about to speak when the door opened. Millie came in, closely followed by Ernest.

Peter turned away and picked up the tray. 'Time for tea, I think,' he said. Daisy filled the big teapot and the jug of hot water and put them on the trolley, which was already loaded with plates of sandwiches and cake, ready for Millie to wheel into the drawing room. There was only one more tray to take through and Daisy picked it up, ignoring Ernest.

He gave a mock bow and held the door open for her. As she passed, he murmured, 'Good catch, the doc. I hope you'll both be very happy, Matron.' The insolence was back in his voice and Daisy, disdaining a reply, knew he hadn't changed.

Back in the drawing room she tried hard to enter into the spirit of the occasion. Everyone else seemed to be enjoying Christmas but she couldn't forget Peter's words, or the gleam of malice in Ernest's eye.

She watched Jack playing with his nephew and smiled, despite the ache in her heart. The frown had gone and he was laughing. Although he sometimes got confused, thinking Henry was the boy's father, he seemed more himself as he played with the boy.

When the party began to break up, Georgina and Henry took Jackie upstairs for his bath. The residents went to their rooms, tired out by the celebrations, and the servants resumed their roles and set about clearing up the debris of their late tea.

As Peter got up to leave, Daisy went with him to the front door. She'd hardly spoken to him since they'd left the kitchen and she wanted to reassure herself that they were still friends.

'I'm sorry,' they both said together as Peter hesitated at the top of the steps. Then they both gave embarrassed laughs.

'I shouldn't have spoken out,' Peter said. 'It's just – well, you know how I feel.'

'Yes. I'm sorry too – that I can't see things the way you do. I must keep hoping. There's nothing else I can do.'

He nodded and ran down the steps to his car, pausing to wave before driving off. Daisy stood looking after him until a gust of cold wind sent her inside. She went round the house checking that all was secure, then upstairs to look in on the men before going to her own room. As she prepared for bed she went over the conversation with Peter in her mind, biting her lip as she acknowledged the truth of what he'd said.

Peter was right – if Jack was going to remember, surely he'd have done so by now. Since his return, the thought that their love affair hadn't meant as much to him as it had to her would often intrude, despite her attempts to deny it. The thoughts often came during the black hours of the night when she couldn't sleep. Then she would ask herself if she was being foolish in refusing Peter. But in the cold light of day, she had only to catch a fleeting glimpse of Jack as he played with Jackie or laughed with Georgina, to know that she would always love him and that she would wait as long as necessary.

I won't give up hope. I can't, she told herself as she vigorously brushed her long dark hair before getting into bed. Jack was here, he was safe, and she should be grateful for that – even if he carried on calling her 'Matron' for ever.

The decorations had been taken down and the tree was turning brown and dusty in a corner of the yard. Peter hadn't visited since Christmas but he telephoned to say he was on duty at the hospital on New Year's Eve. Daisy was relieved that he seemed his usual self and hoped that he would never mention his feelings for her again. If only he'd meet a nice nurse and forget about me, she thought.

But there were other more pressing matters for her to attend to and she sighed as she shut herself into her office to go over the accounts and make lists of items that would need ordering. She'd rather let the paperwork lapse lately, due to the holidays and her worry about Jack. I really must get down to some work, she thought, opening the ledger and picking up her pen, only to throw it down again with a sigh as a knock came on the door.

'Come in.'

'Daisy, I wondered if you've got time for a chat,' Georgina said, smiling. 'Don't look like that. I know you're busy, but this is important.'

'I'm never too busy for you, Georgie. What's the problem?'

'I hardly know how to begin really,' her friend said, chewing her lip.

Daisy looked at her in concern. 'What is it? You're not having second thoughts again, I hope?'

'Of course not. No, it's Millie.'

'Oh dear.' Daisy's heart sank as her own fears were confirmed.

'I think she might be pregnant. But I didn't want to say anything. I thought you or Mrs Harris might have a word with her.'

'Jenkins, I suppose? The man's nothing but trouble!' Daisy exclaimed. Why had she let herself be talked into letting him stay? Still, this could be the chance to be rid of him at last.

'I don't think he forced her – they seem fond of each other,' Georgina ventured.

'Let's hope you're wrong but he'd better marry her if he's responsible,' Daisy said, getting up and poking the fire, venting her feelings on the hot coals. 'I knew I should have warned her about him.'

Georgina sat down. 'We must sort this out before she starts to show. I don't think the trustees would be happy about it if they knew.'

Daisy hadn't thought of that. 'I don't care – it's the perfect excuse to get rid of him.' She sighed. 'I'd better speak to Millie first.'

'I'll leave it to you then,' Georgina said. 'I must go and help Susan,' she said.

Daisy abandoned all thoughts of doing the accounts and hurried down the corridor towards the kitchens. Despite her satisfaction that she now had the opportunity to dismiss Ernest, her sympathies were with Millie.

Mrs Harris was rolling out pastry when Daisy entered in search of Millie. 'In there crying,' she said, jerking her shoulder in the direction of the scullery. 'We won't need any salt in the potatoes if she keeps this up.'

'Georgina told me she thinks the girl's in trouble.'

'She won't confide in me, but I guessed.' Mrs Harris turned the pastry round and thumped the rolling pin down.

Daisy found Millie sniffing and wiping her nose with the back of her hand, in between attacking the potatoes and throwing them into the pan of cold water.

'What's the matter, Millie?' Daisy asked, pretending she had no idea.

The reply was a loud wail, followed by a torrent of tears. Daisy sat her down in front of the range and took her hands. 'Tell me. I promise we'll help if we can.'

'There's nothing you can do. You'll just send me away.'

'Nobody's going to send you away. Now dry your eyes and tell me.'

Millie gave a shuddering sob and wiped her eyes. She stared into the fire, twisting her apron in her hands. After a few minutes she looked up into Daisy's face. 'I've been a bad girl, Matron. But I didn't mean no harm. I love him and I thought he loved me. I would never have let him . . .' Her voice trailed off and tears threatened again.

'You are talking about Ernest, I take it?' Daisy asked.

Millie nodded. 'When I told him we'd have to get married, he just laughed.'

Daisy let go of Millie's hands and jumped up. 'I'll give him laugh. Mrs Harris, send someone to find him. He'll get a piece of my mind, treating the poor girl like this.'

As the housekeeper wiped her floury hands on her apron, Millie grabbed at Daisy's arm. 'No, please. Don't say anything,' she begged.

'He must be made to see where his duty lies,' Daisy said and Mrs Harris nodded.

'But you don't understand. It doesn't matter now. It was a false alarm.'

'Oh Millie, why didn't you say so?' She put her arm round the girl. 'Why all the tears then? Mind, I'm not condoning it. But I think you've had a lucky escape.'

'But I love him. I thought he wanted to marry me.'

Daisy sighed. Couldn't the silly girl see Ernest Jenkins for what he was? She couldn't be angry with her though.

'Did he ever say he wanted to marry you?' she asked.

'Not in so many words. But we was walking out.' Millie began to cry again. 'I thought it'd be nice, living in his flat over the stables, a place of our own,' she snivelled.

Daisy sympathized, knowing that Millie came from a very poor background. She'd been glad to get the position at Ryfe Hall with her own room and decent food. A home of her own must have seemed a dream come true. She sighed impatiently. He'd laughed when Millie told him she was pregnant and yet the silly girl said she loved him. How could she possibly want to marry him? Still, she'd promised to help, so she would talk to him.

'Do you really want to marry him?' she asked.

Millie nodded, then shook her head. 'I don't know. He was really nasty when I told him.' She put her apron up to her face again and Daisy waited for another flood of tears. But she wiped her eyes and gave a shuddering sigh. 'I s'pose my mum was right,' she said in a small voice. 'Once you let them – you know – they don't have any respect for you.' She straightened her shoulders and stood up. 'Well, I've learnt my lesson. Now, I'd better get on with those vegetables.'

Daisy smiled. 'Good girl. Now, are you sure it really was a false alarm?'

Millie nodded and managed a tremulous smile in return. 'You were right, Matron. I've had a lucky escape.'

'I think so. You're far too good for him, Millie.'

'That's not what he thinks,' Millie retorted. 'He said he had his sights set higher than a scrawny little kitchen maid.'

Hot anger surged through Daisy's body like a forest fire, but she managed to restrain her furious retort. He just wasn't worth it, she told herself.

When the girl had returned to her chores, Daisy vented her feelings. 'Why did I let myself be talked into employing him, Mrs Harris?' she asked. 'I knew what he was like.'

'I never liked the man. But he works hard and I did hope he'd changed his ways,' Mrs Harris said. 'What will you do, Daisy?'

Daisy admitted she wasn't sure. 'I would have made him face up to it, if Millie was going to have a baby. But now, I think we should just let it lie,' she decided.

'Well, I'm not having him in my kitchen again,' the housekeeper said. 'I put up with him hanging round when I thought he and Millie were courting proper like. He can have his meals in his own quarters from now on.'

Daisy agreed and left Mrs Harris to get on with her cooking. 'I'll just go and set Georgina's mind at rest. She was rather worried about Millie,' she said. As she went into the drawing room, she pondered Millie's remark. What had Ernest meant by 'setting his sights higher'?

Georgina was talking to Mick Collins, who still hadn't completely recovered from the setback caused by Jack's unexpected return. Although they'd persuaded him to come downstairs for Christmas Day, he'd soon retreated to the sanctuary of his room. He had even lost interest in gardening, despite Joe's pleas for his help. Daisy could only hope that when the milder weather came they could tempt him outside but for now she felt it was best to leave him alone.

She beckoned Georgina out into the corridor. 'How is he today?' she asked, nodding in the direction of the room.

'A bit better, I think. At least he's talking to me. But we ought to get Peter to have a look at him next time he comes.'

Daisy agreed and she went on to reassure Georgina that her fears about Millie's condition were unfounded. 'She thought she was pregnant, but it was a false alarm.'

'Why was she looking so miserable then? I would've thought she'd be relieved.'

Daisy explained how deluded the girl had been about Ernest's intentions and what he'd said about setting his sights higher.

'Well, I knew he fancied you,' Georgina said, 'and I've seen the way he looks at you when he thinks no one's about.'

'Nonsense,' Daisy replied, colouring angrily. 'He hates me. We should never have let him stay. He's trouble.'

'It occurred to me that this trouble with Millie might be grounds for sacking him but she was a willing party. We'll just have to hope he steps out of line,' Georgina said.

'His trial period is up next week but so far he hasn't put a foot wrong with me, outwardly at least.' Daisy got up and went to the door. 'I'm going to talk to him right now. He shouldn't be allowed to get away with it.'

Georgina stood up too. 'Calm down, Daisy. It won't do the slightest good. You can't dismiss him without explaining your reasons to the trustees and you don't want to do that, do you?'

Daisy resumed her seat and put her head in her hands. 'You're right, of course.' She looked up with a determined gleam in her eye. 'But I'm going to keep an eye on him from now on. The slightest sign of trouble-making again and out he goes, disabled war veteran or no.'

211

CHAPTER TWENTY-EIGHT

'I'm worried about you, Daisy. If you go on like this you'll make yourself ill,' Georgina said. 'You never relax, always on the go. I know it's a big responsibility, keeping everything running smoothly. But at least Jack's on the mend. And you've had no more trouble from Ernest.'

Daisy knew Georgina was trying to cheer her up and she tried to respond, lifting her face to the sunshine of the mild February day. There was a tentative hint of warmth in the air and she was glad she'd joined Georgina and Jackie for their daily walk in the grounds. The paperwork could wait for once. They strolled across the lawns, smiling as Jackie ran ahead, impatient to help Dick to feed the chickens.

As they approached the gate, Georgina voiced her concern about Daisy's health.

'I can't help it. It's the only way I can cope,' she replied with a sigh.

She tried to shrug off Georgina and Peter's worried comments, but looking in the mirror this morning she'd been forced to admit that she was not her usual self. Sleepless nights worrying about Jack, and days filled with frantic activity to stop herself from monitoring his every move had combined to strip the flesh from her bones and the bloom from her skin.

'It's hard,' Georgina said. 'But making yourself ill won't bring the old Jack back.'

'I should be thankful that he's here at all. But every time he calls me Matron or, worse still, looks at me as if we were strangers, it's like a knife in my heart.'

Jack had been back for nearly five months and although there'd been occasional flashes when she'd begun to hope his memory was returning, he still hadn't really recognized her. He'd recalled much of what had happened between the sinking of his ship and his return to England but his memory of life before the war was still patchy. Daisy could only be thankful that, physically at least, his health had improved. His hair had grown over the scar on his head, the sores had healed, and his body had filled out.

His first step on the road to recovery came when he met his nephew for the first time. He'd taken to little Jack immediately, seeming to understand his baby prattle. He'd roused himself from his apathy to get dressed and join him for games in the nursery. For Jackie, no day was complete unless he spent time with 'Uncle Dack'.

From then on Jack started to regain his physical strength and although sometimes he would struggle to recall events of the past, for the most part he seemed happy and content. With the coming of milder weather he'd started to walk in the grounds, holding Jackie by the hand and pointing out the birds and plants he'd known in his own boyhood.

It was Jackie who had instigated Jack's friendship with Dick. Although he loved Uncle Dack, no one could take Dickie's place in the toddler's affections. On one of their walks he'd steered Jack towards the chicken run and introduced him to his friend. Since then, Jack often helped with the mucking out or feeding the livestock.

Now, Daisy smiled as she watched him struggling with the gate, and to take her mind off her problems she asked Georgina about the wedding. 'I know you wanted to wait until Jack was well enough to give you away. But poor Henry's being so patient.'

'He understands that I can't make any plans until Jack's better,' Georgina said, noticing Jackie's frustration with the gate and opening it for him. They watched as he ran towards the chicken houses, but Daisy wasn't going to let the subject drop.

'It's not fair to keep Henry hanging on like this. He's already waited long enough,' she said.

'I do feel awful about it.'

'But you do realize Jack's not going to get better overnight? I know that physically he's almost fit. Peter's very pleased with his progress, but . . .' Daisy let the sentence trail off. Georgie didn't need it spelled out for her.

The other girl's eyes filled with tears. 'He's not going to get well, is he, Daisy?'

Hugging her friend, Daisy tried to stop her own tears from falling, biting her lips to keep from sobbing aloud. After a moment she said, 'We must keep praying, Georgie. As Peter keeps saying, his memory could return at any time.'

'Or never. Oh, Daisy, I don't know how you can bear it – seeing him like this. It's so unfair – you deserve to be happy, after all you've gone through.' Georgina sniffed and wiped her eyes quickly as Jackie ran up and tugged at her skirts.

'Mummy, come quick. Dickie and Uncle Dack feeding chickens,' he said.

Daisy smiled at him. Whatever her personal problems, Jackie could always help her if not to forget then at least to push them to one side. His sunny smile and joy in living had the same effect on everyone.

She took the little boy's hand and they walked across the small paddock, giving the tethered goat a wide berth. Daisy opened another gate into the chicken run and Jackie toddled through, calling out to the men. Daisy and Georgina stood by the fence watching.

Since Dick had taken over the responsibility for the livestock, he'd improved out of all recognition, no longer childishly dependent on Daisy and his mother. And Daisy was sure this was partly due to his friendship with little Jackie.

I've got my big brother back, Daisy thought, smiling and giving a little wave as Dick looked up from his work. He had filled a basin from the covered bin at the side of the shed and put it into Jackie's hand, letting him throw handfuls of the grain to the squawking gaggle of birds at his feet. For a moment Daisy felt almost content as she linked her arm in Georgina's and took in the little scene. At least Jack was here and she could see him every day.

Then he appeared round the corner of the building, pushing a wheel-barrow loaded with chicken manure. He strode purposefully towards the gate, pausing only to ruffle Jackie's hair as he passed.

Georgina opened the gate for him and he smiled and kissed her cheek. Then he turned and said, 'Good morning, Matron. Lovely day, isn't it?' and walked briskly away in the direction of the vegetable garden.

Daisy turned and watched him move out of sight, a coldness in the pit of her stomach and a tightness in her chest that made it an effort to breathe. Would it always be like this, she wondered. Would he never call her his Daisy-bell again? Even just Daisy would do. With an effort she turned to Georgina and answered her comment.

'Yes, he is looking much better.' Suddenly she couldn't take any more and she turned away. 'I must get back. There's so much to do,' she said.

'Nonsense, Daisy. Everything's under control. Ruby and Millie will do the lunches. If they need another pair of hands, your mother will help.'

But she was already striding quickly across the paddock towards the workshops.

Ernest had a day off and had gone into town. It was an opportunity to inspect the work on the dairy conversion. Her dislike of the man hadn't abated, especially since the incident with Millie, and she avoided him whenever possible. But he wasn't around and she cautiously entered the building which was being converted into an apartment.

Bill Smythe and Ruby's friendship had blossomed into love and Daisy wasn't surprised when they said they wanted to get married. Her pleasure was somewhat marred by the realization that she would lose Ruby. Daisy had become very fond of her and would miss her cheerful hard-working presence. She'd miss Bill too. He was one of the home's success stories. The recent publication of his book of war poems had boosted his confidence and he'd now completely recovered and his cheerful laugh could often be heard as he entertained the other residents at the piano.

He should have left them ages ago. But where would he go? His family contributed generously to the upkeep of the home in return for keeping their embarrassing relative out of the way. And, despite his recent publishing success, they still refused to have anything to do with him. Then Daisy had thought of the old dairy. As with the stable block, the walls seemed to have been held up by the tangle of creepers which almost covered it. Much of it had now been pulled away, exposing crumbling brickwork to the side of the building.

Although they'd employed professional builders to do the work, Ernest had cleared the building of the accumulated broken furniture and antique household equipment that had been dumped there over the years. Daisy took care never to go near the outbuildings unless one of the other men was around. But she felt safe today since she had heard him telling Mrs Harris he would not be back till late.

Inside, she looked round the gloomy interior, which seemed much larger now that the rubbish had been cleared away. On the far side, the crumbling wall was supported by two baulks of timber. Once that was repaired, the dairy would be divided into three rooms with the addition of a bathroom and kitchen. It would make a snug home for Bill and Ruby, Daisy thought. Not what Bill's used to, I suppose, but he seems happy enough. It suited her too, she thought with a satisfied nod. Ruby could carry on working at the Hall and they wouldn't lose Bill's financial contribution. It had been agreed that the money his family sent would be rent for the newly named 'Dairy Cottage'.

If only all their problems could be solved so easily, Daisy thought, envying the couple their prospect of future happiness. Everyone seemed to be moving on with the onset of the new decade. People were putting the horrors of the war behind them and reaching out for a new way of life. Daisy thought of Georgie and Henry being given a fresh chance, and her mother, happy now that Dick was well and Billy engaged to be married. And Dick himself enjoying his new life as a smallholder. Even Jack seemed happy, back in his old home with his loving sister and the pleasure he was gaining from his nephew.

Was it time for her to move on too, she wondered. The young men on whom she'd lavished such care and who'd depended on her when they first came no longer needed her. Perhaps Peter was right. She should put the past behind her and look to the future. But was that future with him? Fond as she was of Peter, the Jack she had known and loved was never out of her mind.

She had a sudden mental image of him, striding confidently past her with his cheerful 'Good morning, Matron'. He didn't need her. Nobody did, she thought with a little sob, forgetting what was left of her family and the remaining patients who did depend on her.

There, alone in the ruined dairy, she wondered whether she should make a new life. Not with Peter, but somewhere far away. She was a qualified nurse, could get a job anywhere. And she'd be caring for those who *did* need her. Perhaps then she'd be able to forget the past. She'd almost convinced herself that's what she should do. Why then did this black tide of grief engulf her? She looked out of the window which faced the Downs. How she'd miss all this though, she thought, tears falling as she gave way to despair.

The sun started to sink behind the distant blue hills and a mist crept up from the valley, before she dried her tears and gave herself a mental shake. How could she leave and spend the rest of her life never knowing if Jack had truly loved her?

She shivered and turned away from the window, recoiling as a shadowy form loomed out of the dusk and she heard the voice she hated. 'So there you are, *Matron*. Inspecting the work, are we?'

Daisy kept her voice calm and said, 'You've done a good job, Ernest. All ready for the builders next week.'

He moved towards her and she sidled away.

'You've really landed on your feet, haven't you, Daisy March?' he sneered. 'I never thought I'd see the day you'd be giving me orders. But them as rides high is due for a fall.'

She suppressed a shiver and summoned up her most authoritative manner. 'I worked hard to get this position, Ernest,' she said. 'And let me remind you, it was your choice to work here. Any time you decide you no longer wish to take orders from me, please feel free to leave and look for a position elsewhere.'

He laughed and came closer and she could smell the beer on his breath. His hands reached for her and she tried to dodge away. But he pushed her against the wall.

'It's no use fighting. I've got you now, my lady.' The arms came round her, pulling her closer. The beery breath made her gag and she guessed the drink had given him the courage to attack her.

Terror gave her strength and she brought her knee up. She missed her intended target but he gasped and let go momentarily. As she tried to run, he grabbed her hair. She cried out in pain and kicked out again. But this time he held fast, spinning her round and throwing her to the ground. Then he was astride her, tearing at her clothes, swearing and muttering viciously.

Daisy hit out at his face but he grabbed her wrists, imprisoning them in one hand while with the other he pulled her up by her hair, letting it fall with a thud against the stone-flagged floor. Light burst behind her eyes, fading to blackness. She was barely conscious but she could still make out his muttered words.

'You refused me not once, but twice, you bitch. But you'll not get the chance again. I've watched you, Miss High and Mighty March, worming your way in with the gentry. Master Jack's no good to you now. So you set your sights on the doc.' He gave a short, strangled laugh and fastened his wet lips over hers. She gagged and he laughed again. 'He won't want soiled goods,' he said.

She turned her head away and tried to wriggle away but he slapped her face and fastened his hand in her hair again while with the other he tore at her clothes. 'It's no good struggling,' he hissed. 'Why don't you just give in? You might find you enjoy it.'

'Never,' she hissed through clenched teeth, renewing her struggles.

'I know your type, pretending to be so cool and haughty. Well, I can give you better than what any of the gentry can.' He laughed, ripping her dress from neck to hem, and fumbled with his belt. 'Oh yes, I've been waiting for this moment for a long time.' All his bitterness at her rejection spilled out as he viciously tore at her underclothes.

Her struggles became weaker and she closed her eyes. She turned her head to one side as pain throbbed through her split lip and she tasted salty blood. All the fight had gone out of her now. Just let it be over soon, she prayed silently.

Suddenly the weight was lifted from her and she opened her eyes in shock.

'Leave her alone, you bastard!' Jack roared, lifting Ernest up bodily and throwing him to the ground. 'How dare you!'

Daisy scrambled away and struggled to her feet, clutching the remnants of her dress around her. She stumbled to the door and swayed, catching hold of the frame to support herself. Behind her the sounds of fighting grew louder and she turned to see that Ernest was on his feet now. Despite his gammy leg, he was quick. He ducked, then took a swing at Jack, who was more than holding his own, fighting back gamely. But he was still not strong and Daisy could see he was already tiring. She went to the door. Where were Dick and the others?

She turned back as Ernest grabbed a chunk of wood, advancing menacingly on Jack, who was now backed into a corner looking dazed. The makeshift club swung towards Jack's head and Daisy snatched up a piece of broken window frame. She rushed at Ernest, screaming out her rage and hatred.

He half turned. 'Bitch!' he roared, as she lunged towards him. He parried her intended blow and she stumbled and fell. With a satisfied grin, Ernest turned back to Jack, swinging at his head again. But Daisy's intervention had given Jack a momentary respite and he ducked under Ernest's arm and they cannoned into the wall, sending up a cloud of dust.

A low rumbling that grew to a roar filled the air and the timber supports toppled. The wall slowly disintegrated, enveloping the fighting men in a cloud of dust. One of them was sprawled face down on the ground, not moving, the body covered in pieces of brick and crumbled mortar. Beyond the prone figure a pair of feet protruded from the debris of the collapsed wall.

'Jack!' Daisy cried rushing over to the still figure. She brushed away the dust and mortar fragments to reveal a strand of pale gold hair. Sobbing, she turned the body over, gasping her relief.

'Daisy, is it you?' Jack said, opening his eyes. 'What are you doing here?'

Not Matron? Had he really said her name? She hardly dared to believe it as she laid his head in her lap and bent to kiss him, washing the dust from his face with her tears as she did so. 'It's all right, darling. You're all right,' she murmured.

She held him close, whispering softly, hardly aware that Henry and Dick had rushed in to scrabble at the fallen bricks and pull Ernest's body from beneath the rubble.

There was only Jack whispering, 'I told you I'd come back, didn't I, my love, my Daisy-bell?'

Bending to kiss his lips, her hand cradled his head and she gasped in horror as she felt the stickiness of blood. The old wound in his scalp had reopened. 'Phone Peter quickly. Jack's hurt,' she called.

'I'm all right, Daisy, especially now you're here. If you kiss me again

I'll believe I'm not dreaming,' Jack said, his voice slurred.

'It's not a dream. I'm really here.' This time he returned her kiss.

When she pulled away to catch her breath, she saw that his eyes had clouded once more. That uncertain expression she so dreaded was back and her heart sank. Had he remembered her so briefly, only for the blackness of amnesia to envelop him once more? She cradled his head to her breast, murmuring his name through her tears.

'Daisy, tell me, please.' His voice was faint but urgent. 'What happened? I saw the ship go down. Some of the men got off. I don't know about Tom, though.'

Daisy gasped. It was the first time he'd mentioned his friend since his return. But could she tell him that Tom was dead? It might be too much for him to take in.

She bent her head to catch the slurred words. 'I was hit on the head. Thank God I was picked up. I always knew I'd get home to you, my Daisy-bell.' He closed his eyes and let his head fall back against her supporting arm.

He hadn't really regained his memory, she realized, beginning to sob. He thought this injury had happened when the ship was torpedoed. As she sought for the right words, he opened his eyes and this time he seemed more alert. 'Tom. What happened to him?'

Before she could reply, he struggled upright, his face creased in pain. 'I remember. He didn't make it. Georgina told me.' Conflicting thoughts chased themselves across his face.

Henry reached down to help him up but Daisy waved him away and Georgina said, 'Leave him alone a moment. I think it's gradually coming back to him.'

Jack looked at his sister standing there with Henry's arms round her and he smiled. 'I'm really home, Georgie,' he said, trying to struggle to his feet again.

Daisy helped him up and he turned to face her. For a moment she held her breath. Had that brief flash of memory been a fluke?

But he looked into her eyes and said, 'Daisy-bell. I'm home. And you're here. You waited for me.'

She looked into his eyes, then her smile turned to a look of horror as his eyes glazed over and he slumped against her. She staggered under his weight and was grateful when Henry stepped forward and relieved her of her burden.

Together, he and Dick laid Jack's unconscious body on an old door, while Georgina hurried ahead to alert the rest of the staff. Daisy, tears streaming down her face, kept hold of Jack's hand as they manoeuvred the makeshift stretcher out of the ruined building.

At the door Daisy turned back to look dispassionately at the body of her tormentor. Someone had covered Ernest's face with a jacket. He didn't even deserve that mark of respect, she thought.

She was about to say as much when a ray from the setting sun parted the clouds and she gasped as she caught sight of something glittering among the debris. Slowly she let go of Jack's hand and bent to pick up the shiny object. Even after all these years, the sapphires and diamonds still held their brilliance.

She turned to Henry, holding it up to the light. 'It's Georgina's ring. I told them I didn't steal it.'

'We never thought you did. But it doesn't matter now.' He nodded towards Jack. 'Let's get him up to the house,' he said, taking the ring and slipping it into his pocket.

Jack was still unconscious when Peter arrived an hour later. They had put him to bed in Daisy's room on the ground floor. She and Georgina sat beside him, each holding a hand and taking turns to bathe the reopened wound in his head. Once the blood was washed away Daisy was relieved to see that the cut was not deep.

Only when Peter reassured her that Jack's condition was stable did Daisy become aware of her own dishevelled state. Reluctantly she allowed Georgina to lead her away to bathe her split lip and help her out of her torn clothing.

By the time she returned, Peter had gone and Jack was sleeping. The frown that had creased his brow ever since his miraculous return had gone. He looked as young and carefree as little Jackie. Daisy watched him sleep, gazing at the loved face, while her heart soared from joy to doubt and back again.

That second blow might have momentarily restored his memory. But was it a fluke? Suppose when he woke up he'd forgotten her again? Daisy clasped his hand and bent to kiss him. She knew they might still have a long road ahead. But he had kissed her and called her his Daisy-bell and she would be content with that for now.

She smiled at Georgina, willing to relinquish her seat to her friend. But Georgina told her to stay where she was.

'I've had my brother back for months,' she said. 'Now it's your turn. I know how hard it's been for you. Maybe now you'll have a chance of happiness too.' She turned to Henry, who had just come in, and he smiled and put his arm round her waist.

'You'll be able to set a date for your wedding now, Georgie,' Daisy said. 'You were only waiting for Jack to get better.'

Georgina looked down at her sleeping brother. 'But we won't know till he wakes up. I'm frightened to hope for too much.' She turned to her friend. 'Let him sleep for now. And you could do with some rest too,' she said.

Daisy protested. She was reluctant to leave Jack, but she finally agreed to join Henry and Georgina for a late supper.

'We'll leave the door open so you can hear if he stirs,' Georgina said.

Henry took the ring from his pocket. In their concern over Jack, they had forgotten it. Now, Henry held it up to the light and tightened his lips.

'I suppose that scoundrel Jenkins was the thief all along. Though why he held on to it all these years is beyond me,' he said.

'You're right, Henry. That must be it!' Georgina exclaimed. 'I wonder why he didn't sell it?' She turned to Daisy. 'I always knew you were innocent but it's a relief that the real thief's been exposed.'

Daisy looked at the ring, a doubtful expression on her face. 'I don't think he took it,' she said. 'I know he was mean and vindictive, but I didn't think of him as a thief.'

'Then how did it suddenly appear after all these years? It must have fallen out of his pocket,' Georgina said.

Henry nodded, a slow smile dawning. 'I believe I know the answer. It was caught up in the ivy. I'd be willing to bet it was in a jackdaw or magpie's nest. They're known for being attracted to shiny objects.'

Daisy nodded. 'That must be it,' she said, remembering how she'd been doing Georgina's hair for the celebration dinner. They'd been talking about Henry and Georgina had taken off the ring and tossed it onto the window sill. Minutes later she was leaning out of the open window, waving excitedly and running downstairs to greet Jack.

Daisy too had gone to the window, hoping for a glimpse of the man she loved. She'd been just in time to see him glance upwards before he disappeared round the corner of the house. The hopelessness of her position, despite her hope that Jack returned her love, had kept her at the window lost in thought. She remembered the cawing of the rooks in the elm trees and the jackdaws flying to and from the corner of the dairy where they had nested in the ivy every year. The mystery of the ring's disappearance had plagued her ever since she'd been dismissed with no way to prove her innocence. The explanation was so simple, she wondered why it hadn't occurred to her, or anyone else, at the time.

Georgina was tugging at her arm. 'Daisy, don't look like that. It's all in the past. I've always believed in you and I'm sorry that it's all been raked up again.'

'It doesn't matter. As you say, I should be pleased the mystery's solved.' Daisy looked across at Jack, then took a step towards the bed as he stirred and mumbled.

'Daisy, where are you? Don't leave me,' he muttered.

She was at his side in a second, clasping his hand and smoothing his hair. 'I'm here, darling. I won't go away.'

His eyes opened, clear sapphire blue eyes, with no hint of the doubt or uncertainty. 'Daisy, you're really here. It wasn't a dream. Everything's so confused. I couldn't believe I was back home and that you were here too.'

Georgina crossed the room to his bedside. 'Do you remember everything now, Jack?' she asked.

'Don't badger him, Georgina,' Henry said. 'There'll be plenty of time for questions and explanations. He needs rest now.'

Jack struggled to sit up. 'Rest? I've never felt better.'

But Daisy pushed him gently back on to the pillow. 'Rest – doctor's orders.'

He grinned at her, that old carefree smile that she'd thought never to see directed at her again. 'Yes, Matron,' he said.

She laughed but it was half a sob. She looked at him earnestly. 'I know you're feeling better. But you're not completely recovered. Doctor Holloway will be here again tomorrow and I'm sure he'll let you get up. But until then you must do as you're told.'

'Yes, Matron,' he said again, meekly, but still with the twinkle in his eye. His smile faded as he looked at her closely, noticing for the first time her bruised and cut lip. 'Did he do that to you – that swine Jenkins?' He tried to get out of bed again. 'Where is he – the bastard.'

'Jack, he's dead,' Daisy said quietly, trying to restrain him.

His face paled. 'My God, what happened?'

'The wall fell. It could have killed you too.'

'And you too, Daisy. Are you hurt?' He clasped her hands and pulled her towards him. 'If anything had happened to you . . .' His lips sought hers and Daisy surrendered to his embrace, oblivious to his sister and her fiancé.

She sighed with pleasure and tried not to wince as Jack's lips became more demanding and her split lip started to throb. Soon the pain was forgotten as she realized that Jack, the Jack she had fallen in love with as an innocent young maid, had been restored to her. She returned his kisses, joy flooding her body as all her doubts were laid to rest. Jack really loved her and his murmured words told her that he always had.

ROBERTA GRIEVE